TH

LUANNE BENNETT

The Conclusion of
THE FITHEACH TRILOGY

CHAPTER ONE

The Oracle will be born of mutated lineage: a sire of black, a dam of white. Unparalleled power will be invoked, and the key will be made manifest. The vessel answers only to the true Oracle.

D id the gods know? Had they orchestrated the fate of Isla and Maeve Kelley? Was it all planned, my conception from darkness and violence? Part of me was that darkness, but a greater part of me was a Raven. I had to believe that, or this place would be my grave. I would rather die than let my dark side dominate and turn me into one of Maelcolm's Rogues.

I'd been a "guest" in this house for seven days, each torturous hour passing like an eon. My captor kept the door to my tomb of a bedroom locked, leaving me quartered like a caged animal while I waited in mind-numbing silence for his return. Maelcolm made no attempt to deny his paternity. When I confronted him with the question, he freely admitted that he was indeed my father, and then he announced with clinical directness that I would be sharing his home until a suitable partner could be arranged. I was a prisoner while the Rogues initiated their plan to build an army with me as their bloodstock.

So much for fatherly love.

On this morning, the door was wide open when I turned over on the bed to check it. It had become a daily habit, eyeing the door the moment I woke, tiptoeing across the cold floor to check the lock, waiting for a grave error from the poor fool in charge of sealing me in at night. But I knew this morning's slipup was no accident. Maelcolm was expanding my freedom to the outer territory of his house.

I quickly dressed in the same clothes I'd worn for days and headed down the stairs to check the exterior doors. The place was massive, gaudy and ostentatious with all the heavily carved wood and ormolu trim dripping from the edges of the overstated furniture. The sheer amount of it exhausted my eyes, making me dizzy from the smell of linseed oil and lemon juice embedded in the grain of all that wood.

With its bold panels and medieval iron lock, I assumed the large door in front of me marked the main entrance of the house. It was no surprise when I found it unyielding, requiring a key to open from either side. The windows weren't much help either. Even if I managed to break the thick glass, the metal bars covering them with barely a six-inch gap between the long rods was impossible for anything bigger than a cat to slip through. In a word, the house was a fortress.

I walked down the main hall, listening to the hollow echoes of the empty house as I approached a doorway. A sliver of the room came into view, and I could see the edge of a cabinet and a group of shiny copper pans suspended from a rack hanging over a butcher block the size of a farm table. It was the kitchen, silent and empty. There were no sounds of utensils hitting the edges of pans, or the smell of eggs and bacon. No Sophia on the other side of that doorway. God, what I wouldn't have given for a slice of her French toast and a cup of hot coffee.

"Are you hungry?"

I turned toward the tall figure with black skin and sharp onyx eyes standing behind me. "Who are you?" I asked, taking a step back.

"Ian." He extended his hand. "I run this house when Maelcolm is away."

Cautiously, I examined his dark eyes while I contemplated what that meant. "And when he's here?" I replied without taking his outstretched palm.

He smiled wryly but didn't respond. He was well dressed for a butler or whatever he was, his gait quiet and graceful as he passed me and continued into the kitchen. There was an air about him that suggested he was more than that, more than the hired help. Maybe he was Maelcolm's version of Sophia. Or maybe he was just another Rogue pulling house duty, spying on me while the boss was away.

I remained in my spot just outside the doorway and listened while a pan and bowl clanked against the counter, the refrigerator door opening and closing several times. A few minutes passed, and I heard the whistling of steam coming from a kettle.

"You might as well come in and help," he said as I eavesdropped on his movements.

The intoxicating smell of coffee hit my nose the moment I stepped inside. In the week I'd been there, I'd subsisted on the cold pastries and lukewarm tea Maelcolm brought me every morning. Lunch and dinner weren't any better; bagged entrees from some corner market or nearby restaurant, delivered by one of his minions. Clearly he didn't cook, and until now Ian's services hadn't been implemented.

"I can cook for myself," I said, eyeing the egg he cracked into the bowl.

"Yes, I'm sure you can. But then I wouldn't have the pleasure of your company. It *is* a pleasure to meet you, Alex."

I hated to admit it, but I liked him. There was something

honest about him, a nonthreatening vibe that I hadn't encountered since being taken. But I knew better than to trust anyone in this place past the extent of a few words and a plate of food. I had no intention of letting my guard down for any of them.

"Why haven't I seen you before? I've been locked in this house for a week."

He glanced at me, considering his words. "I believe Maelcolm wanted some time alone with you before he brought strangers into the house."

"*He's* a stranger," I replied sharply.

My comment shut him down. Not another word was said while he moved through the room in his perfectly fitted suit, whipping up a meal of scrambled eggs and toast. When he was done, he presented my breakfast on the butcher block, cleaned the pan and bowl, and left the kitchen.

"Thank you," I muttered after he'd already left the room. It was the first homemade meal I'd had in over a week, but it was also a stark reminder that I might never taste Sophia's cooking again. I might never again see her stern but wise face, or stare at Greer's over the dining room table at breakfast and dinner. Even if I made it out of here, I wasn't sure what I'd go back to. I was nothing like the girl who disappeared from Battery Park. I'd been disassembled and put back together with all new parts, reinvented with the truth of what I was. How could I go back and look Greer in the eye with all that shame?

I took a seat in one of the grandiose chairs masquerading as a stool and forced myself to take a bite of the food I'd suddenly lost my desire for. My appetite was gone, but I needed to keep my strength up for the fight that was coming, the battle that would leave me a free woman or a slave to men for the rest of my days. The eggs were thick and tasteless in my mouth as I chewed mechanically, forcing them down my throat. Each bite was worse, but the coffee was a welcome stimulant that ironically had a calming effect on my brain. For that one precious moment of a sip, I was at peace.

And then I wasn't.

The sound of footsteps came from down the hall as I took a bite of toast, growing louder until they stopped just outside the kitchen entrance. It was the heavy but controlled sound of boots that I'd learned to recognize when Maelcolm entered a room. The man who called himself my father showed up every morning with a bag of food, then disappeared for the next twenty-four hours. He was late today.

"Such a beautiful sight for these sore eyes," he boomed, rounding the corner.

It was not Maelcolm.

Familiar, terrifying, and enraging all at once, the sound of his voice flipped my panic switch. My stool gave way, sending me crashing to the floor in a pile of useless limbs. Like a wild animal, my heart pounded against my ribcage, causing me to choke on the piece of toast at the back of my throat.

"And here I foolishly thought you'd be pleased to see me." He took a long stride toward me, his expression agitated as his chest rose and sank heavily in the wake of my cold reception. "I forgive you," he hissed through a clenched grin that chilled me to the bone. "Now get up, or I'll yank you off the damn floor myself."

Every part of my body vibrated from adrenaline as I pulled myself off the floor before he could touch me. I grabbed my plate and threw it against the far wall. The distraction was only good for a few seconds, but it was enough to get me past him and out of the room. I flew down the hall and up the flight of stairs to the second floor. He was a handful of steps behind me, and I knew if he got hold of me one of us would die before the morning was over.

"Where do you think you're going?" Daemon stopped at the top of the stairs and leaned against the rail, clearly amused by my frantic pulling at a locked door. Where was I going? Where could

I go? I suffered a sickening bout of déjà vu as I realize for the second time that he had me cornered against a wall I couldn't possibly climb over. "Haven't you realized by now that there is no escaping me? I own you. Your father has seen to that. Think of it as an arranged marriage—without the wedding."

I slid to the floor as his words sank in. My own father had handed me over to my rapist, sold me for power. "Get it over with," I bit out between my tight jaws, flinching when he took a step closer.

"That's a good girl." He took his time strolling down the hall, the stalking being part of his foreplay. He reached the second door on the left and turned the knob. The hinges opened with a whine as he lowered his eyes and beckoned me with a flick of his outstretched hand. "Come on. Up."

"No," I defied, watching his frown turn into an amused sneer.

He released the knob and ran his finger along the wall as he walked toward me. "I'm going to enjoy dragging you into this room, Alex. And then I'm going to enjoy punishing you for making me look bad in front of Maelcolm. You should have kept your mouth shut." He crept closer and dropped to his haunches, gripping my chin harshly to force my face up to his. "Did you really think he would choose you over me? A female?"

With a rough yank, I was on my feet and being dragged down the hall toward the bedroom. "Get off me!" I screamed, more from rage than fear. The door slammed shut and he threw me across the room toward the bed. The reality of what was happening must have registered on my face, because his own expression heated, a predator feeding off the fear of its prey. It was when he pulled his shirt off and then worked his pants to the floor that I knew no one was coming to stop him from making me his victim for the second time. My own father had lied to me and was now handing me over to Daemon like sugar or a sack of wheat. I was nothing more than a commodity.

His determined hands grabbed at me when I climbed on top of the bed and scurried toward the other side, catching me at the edge of my collar and ripping my blouse halfway down the front. He caught the heel of my right foot when I kicked it squarely at his chest, then gripped my ankle to drag me back down the length of the bed. While I struggled to get out from under him, I drifted away for a moment as the irony of what was happening distracted me from my escalating fear. But a second later, I was right back on that bed with his full weight on top of me, the vulgar smell of smoldering cedar strangling my nose. With each breath the smell intensified, growing in conjunction with his arousal.

"Let's give it a good ride, shall we?" He leered down and forced my legs apart with his knee, dropping on top of me until I could barely breathe under his weight. I managed to turn my face away from his suffocating chest, focusing on my arm as it fell straight out to my side, palm up and limp. Every sound faded like I'd dropped to the bottom of a deep hole. But I could hear my mother's voice clear as a bell telling me not to just lie down and die. And then I heard Isla Kelley repeat the words she'd spoken in my vision, threatening to kill me herself before she let that happen. I doubt Daemon planned to kill me, but what he was about to do to me was as good as pulling the trigger of a gun.

Just a drop of blood, I thought. *That's all it would take.* If I'd been a virgin the first time he attacked me, he'd already be dead.

My outstretched hand began to move, itch with an irritation that bordered on something pleasant. Something was crawling under my skin, down the length of my arm until the mirage reached the center of my hand, intensifying into a sharp burning sensation. I focused on the lines of my palm, visualizing the bright flame I could feel under my skin. To the left of my life line and directly on top of my fate line, it flicked as clear as day. And then I was on fire. In the center of my hand was a ball of flames, alternating between blue and red as it licked at the surface of my skin.

Daemon's hands stopped grabbing at my clothes, his eyes catching the flicker as the flame grew brighter. He jumped off of me and backed away toward the other side of the room, his eyes mesmerized by the brightness of the fire, by what he must have known he was no match for. Oddly, I had no fear of it. For the first time I understood that the power was mine, and that he'd finally pay for what he'd done to me.

Without forethought or hesitation, I hurled the ball of fire across the room, striking him right between his eyes. For a moment, the flame lowered to the size of a single matchstick burning between his brows. But a second later his face lit up into a blazing torch, his shoulders convulsing as the fire spread across his torso and down his legs, sending him up into an effigy of flames. I stood silent without a drop of pity as he burned. Daemon incinerated before my eyes without making a sound. No screams or struggle. He just stood there and allowed it to consume him as if frozen or resigned to his own fate. Or penance.

When it was over and Daemon was reduced to a cloud of fine ash scattered in the air, the flame came rushing back and hit me squarely in the chest. My body absorbed it like mist sinking into parched skin. The fire was part of me, just like the birthmark on the back of my head.

I pulled my blouse together, fastening the few buttons that were still attached, and walked calmly out of the room and back down the stairs to the first floor. Maelcolm was waiting in the living room, staring out the large barred window. I stood silent when he turned and examined my damaged clothing, trying to formulate something to say to him. But I was just too damned confounded for words. When it was clear that we would stand there all day if one of us didn't break, he did what any authentic

Scot would do—he went for the cabinet against the wall and poured two glasses of whiskey.

"Drink," he ordered, shoving the glass under my nose.

Normally I would have thrown it in his face, but I was feeling a bit less aggressive now that the immediate threat was gone, and I really did need that drink. I took the glass from his hand. "I thought you said Daemon was dead."

He looked at me steadily. "I said he was being dealt with." He swallowed his drink in a single swig and went back for another. I did the same, holding my glass out for a refill. He returned with the replenished drinks and then continued to the center of the room, expelling a loud rush of air as he planted himself in one of the grand chairs. His palm slid along the length of the armrest and settled over the carved claw at the cap. "I thought you might like to finish the job," he continued. "You did want to end him yourself, yes?"

I couldn't argue with that. After Daemon raped me, I'd vowed to kill him. Maelcolm was dead-on about that. "And what if I couldn't? What if that little talent I just discovered hadn't manifested up there?" My head motioned toward the second floor as I polished off my drink. "You were watching, weren't you? What if that monster did that to me again? Would you have just stood there and let it happen?"

Maelcolm ran his massive paw over his face. His fuse was burning short, and I could tell by the way his mouth sank and his breath accelerated that he wasn't interested in discussing what-if scenarios with me. But he damn well owed me an answer.

"Answer me!" I demanded, slamming my glass down on the table next to his chair, nearly shattering it.

Instinctively, I stumbled back when he vaulted out of his chair. He'd already demonstrated his lack of parental affection, and I had no doubt he'd throttle me or lob me across the room if I pushed his temper too far. And that was if I was lucky. Maelcolm and his

Rogues were violent creatures. I kept that at the forefront of my mind at all times, regardless of my blood connection to him. He snatched my wrist, painfully squeezing the bone until I thought it might snap. Then he was dragging me down the hall, making me fight to stay upright and not trail behind him like a dangling ragdoll. He pulled me into a parlor room that seemed a little out of place for the twenty-first century, and yanked me in front of a giant mirror that must have stood seven feet tall, leaning against the wall. My refection next to his massive frame was comical.

"What are you doing?" I spat.

He looked down at me and inhaled deeply, calming himself before he spoke. "What do you see?" he asked, gripping my chin and forcing my face back to the mirror.

"Right now I see a giant bully standing next to me."

He lifted my right wrist, the one he'd dragged me by, and held it out toward the mirror. He began to squeeze it even tighter. The pain radiated down my arm until panic started to set in. I imagined the bones cracking under my skin and the muscle rupturing against the broken shards. I tried to pull away, but he had me around the waist with his other arm and held me in place effortlessly while I fought against the pain.

"Take another look," he ordered.

I looked in the mirror and saw my eyes begin to change. I was used to seeing the blue fire radiate from them when my blood flowed, but I wasn't prepared to see the emerald green staring back at me. I blinked to clear the hallucination, but now I was looking at something very different: not one face, but three. I had my mother's bright emerald eyes and the snow-white hair of Isla Kelley. The rest was mine. But in that moment, I knew I was all of them.

The pain abruptly stopped and my hand began to itch and burn, just as it had the moment before the flames appeared. I looked at Maelcolm through his reflection in the mirror and extracted my wrist from his grip without effort. It was as if he'd simply let go. But I knew he was holding on just as tight as he had been before. I was stronger than him. A smile spread across his face, but it had no joy in it—it was pure satisfaction. I stared at my hand for a few seconds, and then it occurred to me that if I was strong enough to pull away from him, maybe I was strong enough to overpower him and find the key to the door. Maybe he hadn't even locked it when he came in.

I bolted for the hall and headed for the front door, but the handle wouldn't budge. When I looked back, Maelcolm was standing at the entrance of the parlor with that smug grin on his face. I stalked down the hall, ready to beat the damn key out of him. He grabbed my fist as I aimed it at his chest, my newfound strength not so powerful anymore.

"Oh, you think—" He couldn't even finish his sentence as the laughter caught hold of him and had him practically doubled over.

"What the hell are you laughing at?"

He sobered up and pinned me with a venomous stare. "Don't get cocky. You'll never outfight me."

A standoff ensued, and we stood there glaring at each other for several seconds before I finally demanded answers. "What did I see in that mirror?" I knew what I saw, but he seemed to know more about it than I did. I was hoping he'd shed some light on that apparition and what happened in the bedroom with Daemon. Maybe my killer instincts were some hereditary trait from his side of the family. After all, half of my DNA came from him.

"Clever woman, that mother of yours," he commented, ignoring my question. "Alex. Short for Alexander. Thought a simple name could throw me off the trail." He leaned in closer. "You know what the funniest part is? It worked. Had I even suspected that Maeve gave birth to a female, I would have turned over every rock and every blade of grass across this planet to find you. And then you walked right into our little hub and filled the city with that smell of yours. After that it was like plucking an apple from the tree."

My mother told me a different story. She thought she was pregnant with a boy, and the name she gave me while I was in the womb just stuck. She was clever all right, with that small white lie.

"You are the rarest of things," he continued. "You are a Rogue —and three witches in one."

CHAPTER TWO

"Has he touched her?" Greer asked, the calm in his voice masking the murderous thoughts in his head.

Ian took his eyes from the untouched cup of coffee and leaned closer to Greer. "He hasn't hurt her. At least not physically."

Greer stood up. "What does that mean?"

Ian took a moment to choose his words, careful not to agitate his new colleague. "My intention was not to alarm you. I just got the sense that something was troubling her under all that bravado she displays." He smiled slightly at the memory of her fearless presence. "I imagine she's quite a handful."

"That about sums it up," replied Greer with a raised brow.

The front door opened and both men looked at Sophia as she walked past the library. She glanced at her employer before her eyes settled suspiciously on Ian, waiting for an introduction or something.

"Sophia," Greer nodded, "Ian."

Ian opened his mouth to speak but was cut short by her boldness. "I know who you are." Her eyes rolled indiscreetly over the dark skin of his face before rising back up to look into his determined stare. "*What* you are," she added.

"Sophia," Greer chastised. "Ian is a guest in this house. Please make him feel like one."

She gave them both a final look and headed for the kitchen, muttering something under her breath as she dropped the bag of groceries on the counter and listened to the conversation that they made no attempt to hide.

"She doesn't approve of me being in this house," Ian said.

"Sophia is very intuitive. She'll come around."

"She's more than that, Greer. I learned my lessons many times over about stepping foot on the toes of an agitated sorceress. A Strega, no less. The last time I felt that much animosity breathing down my neck, I was running from an angry white mob waving a noose." His half-formed grin lightened the seriousness of the conversation and segued back into the matter at hand. "So, the plan?"

"Yes, the plan," Greer sighed. "I guess we need one, don't we? The others will be here tonight so we can devise one."

Sophia finished putting the groceries away, then grabbed a knife and started taking her anger out on an onion. "I give you a plan," she grumbled, dropping the onions into a pan of hot oil without a clue as to what she was actually making. She just needed to cook. Cooking was her therapy for all the things that troubled her. And there were a lot of things eating away at her these days. It had been over a week since she threw up a spell around Shakespeare's Library, declaring it Monday indefinitely whenever someone walked through the front door of the shop. Monday was Alex's day off, and as long as the spell held, she'd have a job to go back to when Mr. Sinclair brought her home.

"Sophia," Greer said, standing at her back, "is it too late to make enough for seven?" She glanced at him without answering, his question a mere formality. She always knew who was coming to dinner.

· · ·

IT WAS JUST past eight p.m. when everyone started filtering in. Thomas arrived first followed by Loden and Rhom. Leda showed up fashionably late fifteen minutes later wearing a black shirt, black pants, and a pair of black combat boots more suited for fashion than war. Greer eyed her attire, a far cry from her usual couture. "Are you expecting a raid?"

She glanced down at her outfit. "What? Was I supposed to wear white?"

He shook his head and led everyone into the dining room to eat and come up with a plan for getting Alex out of Maelcolm's fortress. Thanks to Ian, they now knew exactly where she was. No longer buried under a bakery in Little Italy, they were holding her at Maelcolm's house in the Hudson Valley, two hours north of the city. Cocky of them, thought Greer. But that was to be expected from a group of outlaws with an unwavering belief that they were the true gods, that they were untouchable.

Sophia's chopped onions had turned into chicken Marsala. She placed the large platter in the center of the table and stood back with her arms folded. Her eyes traveled around the ring of guests while the men politely waited.

"Oh!" Leda exclaimed, taking her cue. She was used to Greer filling her plate, but tonight he seemed a bit preoccupied. Understandable, all things considered. The woman he'd bonded with was in the hands of a monster, and that meant part of him was missing, too.

Greer finally picked up on the bottleneck and reached for her plate. "It's okay, dear. I've got it," she said, gripping the other end. He relented and allowed her to serve herself.

Satisfied that the meal was underway, Sophia went back to the kitchen for the wine and bread. Thomas followed her and returned with a large salad bowl in his hands.

Ian carefully watched the people around the table filling their plates while they bantered back and forth, helping Sophia cart food from the kitchen, Thomas hugging her as she batted him away. They seemed more like a happy family than seasoned assassins preparing for battle.

Sophia placed a bottle of wine in the center of the table and walked around to where Ian sat. "What's the matter?" she asked with a touch of sarcasm, glancing down at the empty plate in front of him. "Not hungry?"

He flicked his eyes up to hers. "I've never been hungrier."

Greer gave her a warning look. She headed back toward the kitchen, a low grumbling sound stretching out until she disappeared through the doorway.

"Fantastic food," Leda called out to neutralize Sophia's smoldering mood. "Dear Lord," she continued, spearing a mushroom. "The tension in this room is wearing on my nerves. Can we please just get down to business? I put on these godawful boots for a reason."

"You're absolutely right, Leda." Greer sat silent until the chatter at the table came to a halt.

"We're listening," Rhom said.

The momentary reprieve of good food and light moods was a pleasant distraction from the well-hidden agony Greer had lived with for close to ten days. Some of them knew what it felt like to be irrationally consumed by a mate who had been chosen for them; the others hoped to know what that felt like someday. They also knew what the outcome would be if they didn't bring her back alive—they'd have two bodies to deal with.

"We know where they've taken her," Greer announced.

Thanks to a very strange but useful cat, they'd found the basement where the Rogues had been keeping Alex and Dr. David Oxford. But by the time they made their move, Alex and the doctor were gone. The only thing left in the room when they burst through the door was a plate of half-eaten French toast. Isabetta Falcone—Mafia princess—had agreed to house the Rogues under the bakery until Maelcolm arrived from Scotland.

"They've moved her to a mansion in the Hudson Valley. Maelcolm owns it. We don't think it's used as a headquarters, which is to our advantage since it won't be overrun with his men."

"Normally," Ian clarified, drawing all eyes from around the table, "it's his personal residence when he's in the States. His man cave, so to speak. It's also the one place where he thinks you'll never find him. I don't mean to boast, but if I hadn't offered Greer my assistance, you'd still be looking. He might as well be keeping her in a space station on Mars."

Greer looked at the man on his left. "My apologies. Ian has had the inside track on Maelcolm for years. Knows him better than most."

"And how does Mr.——" Leda glanced at Ian. "What did you say your last name was?"

"I didn't. The benefits of a last name ran its course quite some time ago, for me anyway."

Leda ran her eyes over his face and then down to where his arm rested next to his bare plate. "I see your point."

Rhom stood up abruptly and glared at Ian. "What the fuck is he doing at this table?"

"Easy, Rhom," Greer warned. "Ian has generously offered his help."

Rhom was formidable, but Ian didn't flinch from the large threat sitting across the table. "It's all right, Greer. Your man is loyal—and smart. I'd react the same way." Ian leaned into the table and gave every one of the strangers seated around him a firm look. "I can assure you all that I am no more Rogue than anyone else at this table. I admit that I used to buy into Maelcolm's promises of power and his vision of a new world order, but it didn't take very long to recognize his distorted views and see the Rogues for what they are."

"They're narcissists," Loden sneered.

"Oh no," said Ian, looking matter-of-fact. "The Rogues are much smarter than that. They know exactly what they are. That's their brilliance—their keen ability to recognize and fix their flaws, or leverage their strengths to make up for them. Take for example their inability to produce female offspring. Instead of letting that stop their proliferation, they use their power to exploit human women for that purpose. It's not much different from humans harvesting animals for food or exploiting them for medicine, yes?"

Thomas scoffed. "I'd hardly compare the two."

"Well," Ian continued, "I'm sure the cow sees it differently. It really is all about perspective."

"So, how do we get into this fortress?" Leda asked.

"I say we storm the fucking place and kill anything that gets in our way," Loden suggested, his fearless youth getting the better of him.

Thomas leaned sideways to give him a head-on glare. "Well, son, ain't you full of vim and vigor today. Why don't we just throw a few grenades through the window? That'll have about the same effect."

"More like piss and vinegar," Rhom snorted.

"Enough," Greer said, putting an end to the banter. "There's a reason for Ian's visit. He's seen Alex. Spoke to her this morning."

All eyes turned back to Ian. "She's doing surprisingly well for a woman who's been kidnapped by Rogues. Women usually don't fare well under those circumstances. She's fortunate, given the fact that—"

Greer's hand went up to silence Ian from continuing. "They don't know." He looked around the table but hesitated to speak. At a time when calm, level-headed planning and decision making was critical, he was about to reveal something that just might turn the room into a boiling pot of anarchy. Aside from Ian, there wasn't a man or woman in the room that wouldn't have murder on their mind once the truth was out.

Greer released his pent-up breath and revealed the smoking gun that would change everything, challenge the loyalty of every person at the table. "The Rogues have taken a very personal interest in Alex. She isn't just a means of getting their hands on the prophecy—she's the means for making sure they keep it."

"For God's sake, Greer, spell it out," Leda said, her patience waning. "I'm growing roots in this damn chair."

"Maelcolm is Alex's father." He saw no reason to sugarcoat the news. Just a plain statement of the facts would determine if they were still with him, or if he would now be forced to choose between his own men and the woman he would die for.

The room went unnervingly quiet as the news sank in. Greer looked around the table at the faces, watching their expressions go from anticipatory to shocked, then cold and neutral. It was Thomas who finally broke the uncomfortable silence. "Well, *fuck* me."

"How is that possible?" Rhom asked, his jaw rigid and tight around the words. "There are no female Rogues."

Greer's expression revealed the unsettling reality. Alex was an anomaly, something the Rogues would exploit as long as Alex drew breath. After she was taken at Battery Park, Ava had told him the entire sordid truth about what prompted their disappearance the night Maeve was murdered twenty-one years earlier. True, Alex was the Oracle and was at risk of being used for that reason alone. But Maeve was on the run for other reasons. Maeve was pregnant with a girl, and that meant an enormous bounty on her child's head. A boy's name was supposed to be a minor diversion until she could come up with a better way to hide her daughter. They would eventually figure it out and come for Alex, use her as breeding stock to build an army of the most powerful beings outside of the God kingdom. The male child of a Raven and a Rogue chieftain was powerful enough, but a female would make them kings, level them with the very gods they used to serve.

Leda stood up and placed her napkin on the table. Her mouth tightened as her chest began to heave. As her breathing grew louder, her eyes took on a look of pure hatred. "That... monster!" She shook as the full picture came into focus with brutal clarity. "He raped Maeve," she whispered, half declaration and half question. "I'm going to make sure he isn't capable of ever doing that to a woman again."

Greer stood up and cupped the side of her trembling arm. He lifted her chin with his other hand and looked her in the eye. "Maelcolm is mine," he said quietly, but with a firm warning.

Rhom was up next and heading for the door.

"Where are you going?" Greer asked.

"To do my job," he replied coldly. "I was supposed to protect her, and I didn't. I'm going to rectify that, and then you can deal with me any way you'd like."

"You should rethink the whole guns-blazing approach," Ian said, settling back in his chair, watching their individual reactions to the news. "You won't make it past the guard post."

Thomas leaned closer. "Pardon me if this sounds a little rude, *Ian*. You don't know jack shit about me." Then he glanced at his colleagues. "Or them."

Ian smirked. "True, but I could smell you before you walked through Greer's front door. And if I can smell you, I can assure you that Maelcolm will taste your molecules the second you get past that rather impressive gate of his. You're going to need a distraction."

"I will do it." Everyone turned toward the voice. Sophia was standing in the doorway, an empty saucepan dangling from her right hand. "I can get in there. Easy. I do a little *incanto* on the guard, you go in, you get our girl back."

Leda looked back and forth between Sophia and Greer, shaking her head. "Am I missing something here?"

"For those of you who aren't aware," Greer explained, "Sophia has come out of retirement, taken up the old ways again."

Thomas nearly dropped his fork. "Sophia? Is this true?"

"Yes, Mr. Thomas. Is true. No more lies." She noticed the disturbed look on his face and quickly put him at ease. "But I still cook for you, okay?"

His shoulders dropped from their tensed position, and the air he was holding in expelled from his lungs. Then a wide grin slowly spread across his face. "*Now* will you marry me?"

She suppressed her own grin and continued with her idea. "This Maelcolm," she began, her finger circling around the table. "He knows all the faces in this room. But he don't know this face," she said, pointing to herself with her thumb.

Greer shook his head. "Sophia, you don't know who or what you're dealing with. Maelcolm is—"

"*He* don't know who or what *I* am," she interjected before he could finish arguing his point.

SOPHIA WAS a fifth-generation hereditary witch from the depths of Italy's old country. She was the first and only one to ever break that tradition, and had it not been for tragedy, she wouldn't have wasted nineteen years living a lie that included crucifixes and the dogma of the Catholic Church. Had it not been for the death of her youngest child, she would have never abandoned a belief so powerful it was a daily fight to suppress it and leave it buried under the floorboards of her house in Brooklyn.

It was the day of Rue's thirteenth birthday. A day when all the things she'd prepared her daughter for would finally come to fruition. The circle had been cast, and the bowl burned brightly from the flames dancing around its rim. Adrianna—Sophia's eldest daughter—was there too, along with the faces of many other women who would witness Rue's initiation into the world of magic, the old ways, and the honoring of the gods and goddesses who ruled that world.

The ritual started the way it had for centuries: the circle was prepared by the elders, and the initiate was prepared to offer her service to the higher ones. Rue circled the fire, casting her offerings to each of the monoliths marking the directions and the elements. And then she spoke the words that would change everything. The gods entered the circle and took note of the young girl offering herself to them. It was meant to be an introduction and a temporary journey to test her will and her intentions. But when they took her, they refused to give her back. They'd claimed her like the sea swallowing a grain of sand to its bottom. Her limp body lay in the circle like a vessel weighed down with dark water that couldn't be bailed from her insides. When her mouth finally opened and the words spilled from it, the message was clear: *We like this one. We'll be keeping her.*

Of course, the gods didn't actually say that. But all that was left in Sophia's arms was the lifeless body of her youngest daughter and a betrayal that she felt in the deepest part of her soul. It was weeks before they learned of Rue's hidden heart condition, pushed to the point of failure by some external event. Sophia blamed herself, and so did her husband. Had she not allowed the ritual that opened the soul and exposed it to the elder gods, Rue might still be alive. But after nineteen years, Sophia was finally able to see the unfortunate accident for what it was. Her gods would never dance with such force, never harm one of their own.

Sophia had developed a soft spot in her heart for Alex. Alex had that mettle in her belly like Rue. And after losing one daughter to death and one to the grips of grief that made her less of a mother, she would not lose a third.

·   ·   ·

As ABSURD AS the notion sounded, Greer knew the idea wasn't as farfetched as it seemed. After all, Sophia had some pretty powerful roots, and he'd seen what she was capable of when cornered. But that was a long time ago, and the witch standing in front of him now was a bit rusty, less venomous than the one who dealt in short order with a drunk husband brandishing fists and threats. What would happen if Sophia went knocking on Maelcolm's door? Worst case, they'd ignore her and hope the saleswoman standing on their threshold went away without persistence. Or maybe the worst case was that they opened the door and allowed her in. Greer had enough on his plate without having to rescue two women. He wouldn't abandon Sophia in the hands of the Rogues any more than he would Alex.

"All right," Greer resigned himself, dreading all the things that could and probably would go wrong.

Thomas nearly choked on his drink while Leda, Rhom, and Loden just stared at Greer, waiting for the punch line.

Ian's eyes darted to Sophia and then back to Greer. "Are you mad?"

"Possibly," Greer responded. "But then again, you don't know Sophia."

Ian glanced back at Sophia and smirked. "Well then, let's see how good a witch you are." He focused back on Greer and began to detail Maelcolm's routine. "Maelcolm values his solitude. Unfortunately, in his position he doesn't get much of that. He sends his men out every night for an hour or two to satisfy his need for a little alone time."

"What does he do during this 'alone time'?" Thomas asked.

Still looking at Greer, Ian answered. "I suppose he does what any man does when left to the freedom of an empty house—turns up the music, runs around the mansion naked, puts on a dress and high heels." He glanced at Thomas. "Who the fuck cares? Any more useless questions? Or can we get back to the plan before our window of opportunity slips away?"

"Jesus," Thomas smirked. "You're a sensitive son of a bitch."

"My apologies, Thomas. And yes, I can be a sensitive son of a bitch. Especially when it comes to matters of life and death."

Greer interrupted. "Now that we've all kissed and made up, let's get on with it."

"I'll give you the signal when the place is clear," Ian continued. "Send her to the gate alone. If she can depose the guard and get into that house, and I'm sure a seasoned sorceress like Sophia can manage, you'll have your window."

"And the wards?" Greer asked.

"Maelcolm's wards are for keeping the likes of you out," he answered. "The Rogues could care less about anyone else. Their mistake. No offense, Greer, but the problem with warriors is that they tend to underestimate what they deem inferior." His eyes stretched around the room. "Sophia won't feel Maelcolm's wards any more than I feel the ones wrapped around this house. All she has to do is pull the plug from its power source and the wards go dead."

Sophia nodded her head. "Don't worry. I pull his plug."

CHAPTER THREE

"What do you mean by three witches in one?" I glanced down at my hand, still tingling from the flame it held hours earlier. After our standoff, Maelcolm disappeared for the rest of the afternoon and most of the evening. When he finally returned around nine p.m., I was hungry and curious. Though I hated to admit it, he had my attention with the comments he'd made just before he left.

Having just returned, he walked past me without a word and headed for the row of decanters on the bureau. He poured himself a drink without offering me one, which seemed a bit rude. He swallowed it and poured another. This one he handed to me. I gladly took it, needing to settle the anger and revulsion that was rising fast in the pit of my stomach.

"You are the trinity," he said, taking a seat in the chair next to the fireplace.

Isla Kelley had made a similar declaration the night I dreamed of her. However, I was beginning to believe less and less in dreams, and more in the manifestation of my ancestors. In fact, I knew they weren't dreams. I had too much physical proof of that. *The trinity is complete.* That's what she said the night we

met, the night she ran her fingers over the triangular birthmark at
the back of my head.

"I wish everyone would stop speaking in tongues and just get
to the point." I polished off the whiskey and sent the glass sliding
across the table. "What in the hell is this 'trinity' I keep hearing
about, and what do you want from me? Just... *tell* me so I can
plan the rest of my godforsaken life and move on with it!"

Maelcolm showed no reaction to my outburst. He just sat in
his chair and watched me pace across the room like a caged
animal—like Greer. I stood by the large barred window draped in
thick sheets of dark brocade fabric that smelled musty and old.
The house was a museum that no one bothered to visit, stale and
unappealing outside of the nineteenth century.

"Your eyes are different than hers," he commented. "But
they're the same. Of course you wouldn't know it, but there's a
brief shift in them when you're angry. It's Maeve's green stare
shining through." He was up again, walking toward me but
keeping just enough tolerable distance between us. "I suppose the
manifestation is relatively recent, brought on by our introduction. You see, your mother went to great lengths to keep you
from me. But now that I've found you she's been forced to show
herself, draw weapons."

"You raped my mother."

He ignored me and continued with his speech. "Maeve has
brought reinforcements. Isla." My grandmother's name slipped
from his mouth in an incredulous whisper. "Who would have
thought the grand matriarch herself would show up for the
battle."

"They're with me, you know," I warned.

He turned suddenly and raised his brow. "Yes. They *are* you.
And you are them. Three witches in one."

Suddenly the walls began to spin, and Maelcolm's voice
blended with all the other sounds in the room. The ticking of the
clock, the faint sound of a bird outside the window, clanking of

old pipes through the vents: it all became a single unified mutter as the truth came smashing into my mind. I held my hand out as the flame began to ignite. It burned but then subsided into a warm and pleasurable heat. My head snapped around toward Maelcolm as I forced him down on one knee with a single thought. His head lowered to his chest as a thunderous howl came from his throat, but as he rose and walked toward me, I realized he wasn't in pain. He was laughing.

"Extraordinary," he said, touching my cheek. "I couldn't be prouder."

I stumbled back against the edge of the sofa, breaking the spell of the epiphany.

"Maeve could throw a flame with the best of them. The finest fire witch I've ever seen. And Isla could bend the mind of any man, woman, or child. Animal, too. And now those gifts are yours."

There was a faint, barely detectable smoldering coming from my palm. I gazed at it in disbelief, speechless and confounded by my new gifts. But what confused me more was the powerful sense that my mother and grandmother were inside of me. I couldn't deny Maelcolm's claims because I could feel them strolling around in my head, not like visitors but like they lived there. I was the trinity: daughter, mother, and the grand matriarch of the Fitheach clan—the three Ravens chosen by the gods.

"You're wondering why your powers have no effect on me," he said, extracting the question from my mind. "I can assure you they do. But this is my domain. My wards keep those powers at a low simmer when they're aimed at me. Unfortunately for Daemon, he had no such protection. Hence that satisfying kill of yours."

"You never answered my question." I had no interest in drudging up the dirty details of my conception, but I needed to hear it from his mouth. He needed to confess his vile crime to my face so I could hate him even more.

"I didn't realize it was a question. More of an accusation, wasn't it?" He cocked his head as he read my face. "I see. You want my confession. You want to know what happened between your mother and me twenty-six years ago."

"I know what happened. I just need to hear it from you. I need to understand how a woman as powerful as my mother could end up a victim." It never occurred to me until that moment to question that. How did a witch as powerful as Maeve Kelley become victim to a Rogue? "You can start by saying the word—*rape*."

Maelcolm's calm demeanor broke. His nostrils flared as the confident smirk on his face neutralized into a flat line. The suggestion had clearly struck a nerve, and I wondered if I was about to hear something I wasn't prepared to accept.

"Maeve was so beautiful," he began. "Those bright emerald eyes could stop any man in his tracks." He was staring at the window, distracted by the memory. "I knew from the moment I first saw her that she was going to be trouble." He slowly turned back toward me, glowering, sending a cold chill racing up my spine. "And by God, I was right."

"*She* was trouble?" I smirked. "Why? Wouldn't hold still while you violated her?" A vision of the night she died came rushing back, what the wolves had done to her. I felt sick at the thought of how she suffered at the hands of men.

"We needed new blood. Blood that would produce warriors. Maeve's blood mixed with mine was the perfect solution." He turned back to the window in thought. "I tried to keep it all very professional. No emotion, no attachment, just a simple transaction. But I'd never tasted a Raven before. None of us had ever experienced the power of a Raven. I foolishly thought I could make her want me." He glanced back at me before continuing. "I would have wed her, you know. But she refused me, broke off our relationship."

His words jolted me, made my legs go weak. "You and my mother—"

"Yes. Me and your mother. Usually we don't waste our time courting, but Maeve was something worth courting. She was an enchantress. A walking pheromone. I would have given that woman my name, but she refused me." I could feel the heat from his skin as his anger built, the memory still provoking a trigger in him. "So I took what I wanted. Call it whatever you like, but it was mine to take."

He took a step closer and reached for a lock of my hair. As much as I wanted him dead, I let him take it between his fingers, baiting him with my acquiescence while I figured out a way to survive this nightmare. "Something very special came out of all this, didn't it?" His justification was just as delusional as Daemon's had been. "I have you, my lovely daughter."

Before I could pull away and end our little father-daughter moment, he dropped my hair and walked toward the bureau. "I almost forgot." He pulled a key from his pocket and unlocked one of the side cabinets, carefully removing an object from inside. "I have something for you." A black sphere the size of a large grapefruit, smooth and shiny like a crystal ball, sat in his palm. As he offered it to me, his massive hand cradled it like the foot of a ball and claw table.

"What is that?" I asked, hesitant to touch it.

"Take it and see." He held it closer to me. "It won't bite, Alex."

I'd learned my lesson about accepting things from people who wanted to control me, but for some unexplainable reason I took it from his hand. It seemed innocuous enough, just a ball of black glass. "What do I do with it?"

"Give it a good shake," he instructed.

It reminded me of a Magic 8 Ball. The black ball you asked a question to and then turned upside down to see the answer written in a triangle floating underneath. I shook it with both hands. The solid black surface began to shimmer, and a miniature snowstorm roiled up in the center. The diminutive flakes glistened bright silver as they whirled in a tornadic storm within the convex walls of their glass cage. I thought it was just a darker version of a snow globe until I saw them, the tiny robed figures in the center of the sphere, circling around a fire with their hands joined. I gasped as each one slowly turned and looked at me through the storm of snowflakes that had gone from silver to black.

"Will you be having a late dinner, sir?" A man stood at the other end of the room with his long arms pressed tightly to his rigid torso, his face a blank slate of boredom.

"Who are you?" I asked, shaking off the hallucination and dropping the ball on the cushion of the sofa.

The man glanced at Maelcolm, obviously annoyed that I'd addressed him directly. He seemed to be waiting for his instructions to speak. "Frederick keeps the house in order," Maelcolm said. "He runs the place while I'm away." He glanced at the clock and then at me. "Are you hungry?"

I examined Frederick's starchy white shirt and highly polished shoes, then his painstakingly groomed mustache. His thinning gray hair was neatly trimmed and smoothed back against his small ears. He looked the part of a dutiful servant. "What happened to Ian? I thought he ran the place."

Maelcolm's eyes flared. "What? Where did you hear that name?"

"He was here when I came down to the kitchen this morning." My eyes wandered toward the hallway where I'd first seen Ian, and then I glanced at Frederick.

Maelcolm's brow constricted, his mouth opening on a half-formed word. "That's not possible," he eventually managed to say.

"Sure it is. We didn't talk much, but he was here. The man cooked me breakfast, for God's sake."

He laughed in a sort of mocking way. "Breakfast? You spoke to him?"

"Yes."

"And what did this man look like?"

"Black man in his mid-forties, tall, attractive. He had an English accent." He continued to laugh, only now the humor was genuine. "What's so damn funny?"

"Well, you see, Ian is dead. At last count for over sixty years."

"Bullshit," I spat. "You're just trying to make me—"

Before I could continue, a deep bell sounded—the doorbell, I assumed. It echoed off the steep walls and seemed to resonate toward the high ceiling, the perfect accompaniment for the grandiose door it served.

Maelcolm's face shot in the direction of the hall. Clearly he wasn't expecting a visitor.

"Shall I get that?" Frederick asked.

It was nearly ten o'clock, but the Rogues seemed to do most of their business in the dark.

Maelcolm motioned toward the door with a flick of his head. Frederick obediently strode toward it with the silent, rigid glide of a vampire. No wonder I hadn't seen him earlier. He was probably there all along, hiding in plain sight under the guise of a floor lamp.

The door was out of view, but I could hear the key turning the lock that was meant to keep me inside, and the squeak and yawn of the hinges as it opened. Maelcolm kept his eyes on me while we waited to find out who it was, but as a commotion ensued we both looked in the direction of the hall. Frederick's voice rose from a monotone drawl to a higher pitched squabble as something ruffed his feathers on the other side of the wall.

"I'm afraid that is out of the question," I heard him say. "You will leave immediately." But the person—or thing—on the other side of the door was persistent.

"Five minutes. Maybe ten," a woman's familiar voice replied, getting louder as she obviously barreled through his line of scrimmage and entered the cavernous foyer.

My eyes flew wide and my heart began to beat wildly. I almost gasped as my mind played tricks on me and coaxed me into thinking I recognized that voice. Maelcolm shot me a suspicious glare as my adrenaline spiked. He could smell it as easily as Greer could.

Sophia came marching around the corner, and I forced myself to remember all the small ways I'd learned to conceal my thoughts and telltale physical responses from Greer. She glanced at me and quickly looked away. "You must be this man's employer," she said, motioning toward the outraged butler standing next to her.

Frederick looked mortified. "Sir, my deepest apologies. This... woman pushed right past me." He continued to whine and grumble excuses under his breath for how a mere woman made it past him and into the house. But Sophia was anything but *mere*.

My eyes darted to the hall, half expecting to see Greer come around the corner next, or an army of Rogues investigating the commotion. But no one else was there. Maelcolm looked down at Sophia, who was a good foot and a half shorter than him, and waited for her to explain her presence in his living room.

"My Bear is in your backyard," she claimed.

"Are you insane, woman?" Frederick scoffed. "There is no bear on this property."

Maelcolm's jaw tensed, silencing Frederick with a single look before turning his attention back to Sophia.

"Not *a* bear," she retorted with a quick dart up and down his face. "*My* Bear. My cat. His name is Bear. He climbed your wall and went over the top."

Maelcolm glowered at Frederick until the man finally turned and left the room.

"You don't like him very much, do you?" I asked.

He smirked and motioned us into the hallway, then led us toward the kitchen and eventually to the back entrance of the house. "Be my guest," he said to Sophia, pointing to the door. "You have five minutes to find your cat." I took a step to go with her, but his arm went up to stop me.

Those five minutes came and went. "*Fuck,*" Maelcolm spat, beginning to lose patience with the. Italian cat lady searching through his garden. "Do not move," he warned as he stepped out to find her.

It was black as pitch outside, the only light coming from an occasional firefly blinking past the window. I watched the opened door nervously as another few minutes ticked by. It was dead quiet when I stuck my head out to listen. A hand wrapped around my mouth, and I lifted off the ground and started to move backward. I was moving down the hall, away from the door that Sophia and Maelcolm had gone through. As I was dragged farther away and the back door got smaller, a man walked through it—it was Rhom.

My chest screamed with pain from the wild panic sending my heart into overdrive. It slammed against my ribcage as breathing became more difficult. I couldn't get any air. My eyes shut and I envisioned Daemon's face as he wrapped his body around mine and pushed inside of me, the lust in his eyes sickening me as he forced his tongue into my mouth. I shook off the memory and clawed at the hand wrapped around my waist, like a panicked creature in the jaws of a tiger. My eyes flew back open. I could see Rhom barreling down the hall after us, closing the distance.

"Rhom," I barely uttered before Greer's familiar scent lulled me unconscious.

GREER STEADIED the back of my neck and held something vile and awful smelling to my lips. "Drink. It'll make you feel better."

I breathed him in, and the beautiful sensation of being home again filled my heart and mind like a dream. Nothing would ever feel this good again.

"It tastes worse than it smells," I complained. "What is that?"

He put the cup on the bedside table. "It's one of Ava's concoctions. She's been here all night."

I glanced around the room, feeling a sudden need for a motherly presence. "Where is she?"

"I had Thomas drive her home to pick up some fresh clothes. She didn't like it, but she needed a break. She'll be back soon."

He leaned over my lap and braced his hand on the other side of the bed, filling me with his heat as he caged me against the pillows. "We have a lot to discuss. Alex, I don't know where to begin. I—"

I shook my head. "No. I don't want to talk about any of that right now. I can't." A thick lump knotted up in my throat as all the commotion in my head came together in a mass of thunderous noise: Maelcolm being my father, Greer wanting to claim me, Daemon. And then there was this business about the trinity, my powers increasing threefold. But all I felt was weak. I wanted to curl up and sleep for a month, ignorant to all of it. But there was no time for ignorance. We had to get back to finding the vessel, more now than ever.

And then it hit me.

"Dr. Oxford?" I asked, praying that Greer would tell me that he was safe and sound in the next room.

He hesitated, trying to spare me from one more thing to lay heavy on my heart. Then he finally leaned in and cupped the side of my face with his warm palm. "He's disappeared."

"They have him, Greer. I was in a room right next to him. I spoke to him through a vent in the wall." The memory of Dr. Oxford's whimpering sobs carrying through the vent in the basement of the bakery haunted me. I was the reason that poor man wasn't safely sequestered in his laboratory at Cornell.

He nodded. "They've either hidden him very well, or—" He stopped short of saying what we were both thinking.

"Let me up, Greer."

"Alex, you need to stay right where you are. You've been through a nightmare. Now you need some rest."

I climbed out the other side of the bed, grabbed a pair of jeans draped over the chair and headed for the door. Greer didn't try to stop me as I took the stairs two at a time and headed for the kitchen. I broke down in tears when I saw Sophia standing over the cutting board. She dropped the knife and turned around right about the time I threw my arms around her and practically squeezed the life from her chest.

"I was so scared when you walked out that back door. And when Maelcolm went out there after you… "

She took a step back when I released her. With her hand, she swept the tears roughly from my face, kind of like a mother lion grooming her cub with her tongue. "It was nothing. I made him sleep for a while on the grass. Probably woke up with a little dirt in his mouth," she snorted. "I should have fed him worms."

"You made him sleep on the grass?" I stared at Greer's Italian housekeeper and let the preposterous scene from the night before work its way back into my head. "Wait a minute. How did you know where I was? And what was Rhom doing in the backyard? What were *you* doing in that backyard? Greer let you—"

"As I said, we have a lot to talk about." Greer was standing in the doorway when I turned around. "Perhaps Sophia would like to tell you herself."

My sudden anger blocked out his words. "You let her do that? You let her knock on that door and walk into that house? Maelcolm could have killed her! What if he had a bunch of Rogues in the house?"

"We knew he'd be alone last night." He smirked and glanced at Sophia. "Maelcolm has an inflated ego. He seems to think he's out of reach up there behind his gates. I'm sure he's not very happy about being bested by a cat lady with a powerful talent for persuasion."

"Alex—" Sophia began.

My index finger went up to shush her. "Are you insane, Greer?"

A small grin spread across his face as he looked behind me. I turned around just in time to see the knife coming back down on the cutting board—on its own—quartering the onion and rendering it into a neat pile of perfectly chopped pieces.

CHAPTER FOUR

I knew Sophia was special, but I never imagined that the devout Catholic woman—who chastised me for months about everything from living in Greer's house without a wedding ring to my occasional inappropriate choice of clothing —was a witch. But we were nothing alike. She was Strega, and I was still trying to figure out what kind I was. But for the first time since finding out what I was, I was actually eager to explore my lineage. In fact, it was vital.

"What do I do now?" I asked Ava who was mixing up another batch of that foul-smelling liquid.

"You can start by drinking this." She handed me a cup and waited for me to swallow it down.

"What exactly have I been drinking?"

"Oh, a little of this and a little of that. Has a little marjoram in it."

I sipped the concoction and felt something move at the bottom of the cup. "What is that?" I blurted, nearly dropping it.

Ava winked. "It's a bloodstone. Careful not to swallow it."

I had to remind myself that Ava was a witch, too. Seems I was surrounded by them. She never called herself one, though. She simply said she was a facilitator and friend for those who did.

"You knew, didn't you?" I asked.

"Knew what?" she replied, busying herself with the task of cleaning up the empty cups.

"That's why you left me in Indiana. You faked your death for me."

Her hands went still and she took the seat next to mine. We were in the dining room eating lunch. Or rather I was, staring at my plate, pushing the sandwich from one side to the other as I picked at the bread.

"Alex, your mother and I were very close. Sometimes I think we were closer than sisters. There was just something between us that neither of us could explain." She smiled weakly and glanced at me before averting her eyes back to the polished mahogany table. "Did Maeve ever tell you how we met?"

I shook my head. Ava had always been a part of our lives. From as early as I could remember, she and my mother seemed to be joined at the hip. Although it had a different name at the time, a name I couldn't remember, Den of Oddities and Antiquities was our second home.

She looked back up at me and began to fill in some of the missing pieces. "I was involved with a man when I met your mother—a very bad man." Her eyes softened. I mistook it for melancholy but quickly recognized it as discomfort more than anything else. "He was quite wealthy. Told me he was some sort of angel investor. I didn't know it at the time, but he was involved in some pretty despicable things. A drug dealer, for one." She sighed and rubbed her exhausted eyes. "There were other things, too. Had I recognized the signs I was undoubtedly choosing not to see, I would have ended it before the second date." She went silent, lost in a memory she clearly preferred not to recount.

"Are you okay, Ava? You don't have to tell me this if it makes you uncomfortable."

"Oh yes, I do. You deserve to know everything. I want you to understand, because the thought of you thinking I could ever abandon you for selfish reasons is eating me alive."

She squeezed her fists tight and continued. "He was good to me. Never so much as raised his voice. Fancy restaurants, weekend trips to the Adirondacks. He hated leaving the city, but he took me because I loved it up there. We were together for about five months—maybe it was six." Her brows scrunched tight, trying to remember the insignificant timeline. "I stopped by his apartment unannounced one evening. He had a penthouse on the East Side. I'd struck up a friendship with his doorman over the months, gave him tinctures for his chronic headaches. I even made him a salve for his balding head. He sent me right up the elevator unannounced."

I knew how these stories ended. Woman comes home early and catches boyfriend or husband with someone else. Even a witch isn't immune to male infidelity. "Was he cheating on you?" I asked before she could continue, seeing how difficult it was for her to retell the past.

She huffed an ironic laugh. "As soon as I stepped off the elevator, I had this overwhelming feeling that I was making a huge mistake. I remember approaching his door and putting my ear to it. Someone was crying on the other side. Then I knocked, against my better judgement."

"What happened?" I asked, baited by the buildup of the story. She just sat there, fixed on the wall with a vacant stare. "Don't do this to me, Ava. You can't stop now."

"You're right," she continued. "The door opened, but another man was standing there with his shirt open. He said I was late and told me to get inside and take my clothes off. Well, all right then, I remember thinking. I walked into the living room, but Matthew—that was his name—was too preoccupied with the teenager he was fucking to notice me. I just stood there paralyzed while he rammed himself into that girl bent over the arm of the sofa. She couldn't have been more than thirteen or fourteen. I'll never forget that poor girl crying while he—"

"I get it. Your boyfriend was a real prick, but what does this have to do with you meeting my mother?"

"We're just getting started with the story," she said. "When I finally came to my senses and realized that an assault was taking place, I did what any self-respecting woman with half a wit would do—I shoved the bastard off of her. He was furious."

"*He* was furious?" I repeated.

"He turned around and looked at me with eyes I'd never seen before. Then he grabbed me by my hair and dragged me down the hall to his bedroom. I thought he was going to rape me. Instead, he grabbed a pair of pants and composed himself, smoothing his hair back with his hands, wiping his sweaty chest with a towel. I'll never forget the smirk on his face when he told me to get used to it. I naively told him we were through and headed for the door. But he made it very clear that there was no walking away. Said he owned me and would make me watch next time."

Ava was one of the strongest women I'd ever met. I could only imagine what he did to her when she went for that door, to get his point across.

"A couple of hours later he let me leave. The doorman glanced away when he saw me step off the elevator with a scarf wrapped tightly around my head and face. He'd obviously seen it before. I walked around the city all night, too scared to go home in case he sent someone for me, make good on that threat to make me watch."

As Ava's story unfolded, Sophia came into the dining room with a fresh pot of tea. She kept her eyes on Ava as she replenished our cups, a comment or a question begging to leave her lips. "You want me to make him pay?" she muttered. "I don't mean to snoop, but I hear everything in this house." She shrugged. "Is a curse." Sophia knew what it was like to be the target of a man's rage. She was a member of that very unpopular club, and the idea of a man hitting someone she cared about was enough to bring out the killer in her. She was a reborn witch after all, and after an extended hiatus from her craft, it would probably feel damn good to practice her rusty skills on an asshole like this *Matthew*.

"That's generous of you, Sophia, but it won't be necessary." She smirked just a little and continued with the story. "I got careless that night and decided to do something stupid, like curl up in the doorway of an empty building. I'd walked all the way down to the Lower East Side and found a comfy spot. You have to remember, I wasn't myself. I woke up with a man on top of me. Maeve was standing right behind him."

"*No!*" Sophia gasped, seating herself at the table. "What did you do?"

"Well, Maeve took one look at my horrified expression and knew that guy wasn't invited. The next thing I knew the man's hair was on fire. He screamed and rolled on the ground for a few seconds, and then he took off."

I glanced at my right hand. "My mother set the guy's hair on fire." For the most part the comment was rhetorical.

"Your mother was good with fire. Then she picked my sorry butt up off the ground and took me to the room she was renting. She'd just arrived in New York a few days earlier, pregnant and scared."

"What happened to Matthew?" I asked, knowing the story wasn't finished.

"Maeve's place was a dump. I felt a little bolder the next day, safety in numbers and all, and told her to pack her bags and come home with me. At the time, I lived in the back of the shop. She took one look at the hundreds of drawers lining the wall and knew she'd come to the right place." Ava hesitated, a curious expression crossing her face. "You know, your mother was the first person who ever called me a witch. She was one, obviously, but no one had ever called me one before. I didn't even know it."

"Blind fools," Sophia remarked to no one in particular. "I spotted you the first time Mr. Sinclair brought you to this house. But I mind my business."

I looked around the table at the three of us, all witches, very different but the same at the core. "So that's how it all started. That's how the two of you became inseparable."

She started to speak but hesitated, thinking carefully about what she revealed next. "Considering the skeletons in all of our closets, I think it's safe to be candid. After all, every woman at this table has had blood on her hands—for good reason. It took me a few days to tell Maeve the whole story about what happened that night with Matthew. When I finally did, she walked me to the front of the shop and handed me a list of ingredients to source from the wall. We spent four hours conjuring the spell. I won't go into the details, but when it was over Matthew was dead—by his own hand. The world was rid of one parasite, and I was safe from a monster we both knew would come for me." She glanced at Sophia. "As I said, thank you for the offer, but that little problem has been dead and buried for years."

"She saved you," I said. "That's why you two were so close."

"We saved each other," she corrected. "Now, about Indiana. Maeve was running from something too. The night we… disposed of Matthew, she finally felt comfortable enough to tell me what that was, seeing how we were bound by our crime."

"Maelcolm told me he was in a relationship with my mother. Is that true?"

Ava scoffed. "If you call *stalking* a relationship. She didn't know what he was. Well, not exactly. There was something different about him, but it wasn't until his dark side came out that she realized why he made her so uncomfortable. But your mother was not immune to that *bad boy* attraction. The way she described it to me, she was like a moth drawn to a flame. He excited her and terrified her at the same time. She cut him off when she realized what he was and the mistake she'd made letting him into her life. That's when she said it started—the relentless stalking. And then his darkness came out and took what it wanted."

Sophia's face was usually stern or neutral, rarely riled by emotion. But her expression after listening to Ava describe the circumstances around my conception had touched a rare nerve. "That man lay his hands on you? Calls himself your father?" She slowly shook her head. "I should have killed him in that backyard."

"I get to kill him first," Ava said.

Seems there was a long line waiting for the head of Maelcolm. Regardless of how much we all wanted our pound of flesh, I knew Greer would be the one to end his life. The final battle would boil down to Maelcolm and Greer. And if I told him what Daemon had done to me, it would be an unequivocal bloodbath. Daemon was one of Maelcolm's own, and that was that.

"When Maeve found out she was pregnant," Ava continued, "she knew they'd come for you. In five, maybe six years, you'd be lost. And then she had the dream. The gods had come to her and revealed a baby girl." She shook her head, unable to say the rest aloud. She looked me square in the eye for confirmation that I knew what that meant, to be the female offspring of a Rogue. I nodded once. My mother let everyone believe that she was the Oracle, to keep the spotlight off of me. Now I understood her vital need to maintain that guise, and it must have eaten away at her every moment of every day.

Sophia glanced back and forth between me and Ava. Recognizing our need for privacy, she got up and headed back to the kitchen. "You don't have to leave, Sophia," I said. "You're family."

She stopped without turning around. "Yes, I do." I could feel the subtle rage hidden beneath her skin, carefully suppressed due to her vastly experienced will. Sophia was a woman who knew what it was like to be tortured by memories, knew what loss between a mother and a daughter felt like.

"My job was to get you away from here and make sure no one ever found you." Ava's hand slipped over mine and squeezed tight. "For fulfilling that promise, I make no apologies."

I'd never really made peace with her since the night I found out she was alive and well, living her old life back here in New York. I stood up and reached for her, hugging the breath from her lungs like a clinging child suffering from playground trauma.

"Something's wrong," she whispered into the crease of my neck. "Did he hurt you?"

I was one short breath away from collapsing into a heap of uncontrollable sobs, confessing the sins that I somehow felt responsible for.

"There now," she consoled. "You need to talk to Greer."

Someone walked into the room. I pulled away from Ava and glanced over my shoulder. Greer was standing in the doorway, a tentative look on his face. Did he know? Could he smell Daemon's sweat absorbed into my bones? Was it written all over me like a brand, a simple shower too little too late to wash the deed from my skin? I'd dreaded this moment since the morning I lay in that bed, knowing Greer would never look at me the same way again. But it didn't matter if he knew or not—I knew. I swore to never become a victim. Victims were weak. I thought I had too much power to be someone's victim. But that was before I actually became one.

I opened my mouth to say something, the words drying up in my throat before my tongue could move. There was somewhere I needed to be, and it wasn't here feeling sorry for myself and wasting precious time while Dr. Oxford was still missing. I pushed past Greer and headed for the stairs. Bear was on the bottom step, following me up as I went back to the bedroom to finish getting dressed. I don't know what I thought would happen when I walked into Shakespeare's Library. Katie would sympathize, having shared absurd secrets. Apollo, on the other hand, would probably laugh me out of the place after I'd been a no show for going on two weeks.

"Where do you think you're going?" Greer called as I reached the top step, incredulous for my audacity. I ignored him, afraid to utter a single word for fear of bursting into sobs.

I reached my room and searched for my shoes. They weren't next to the closet where I'd kicked them off the night before. "Damn it!" I growled, agitated beyond belief that I was apparently capable of manifesting a ball of fire in the palm of my hand, but incapable of finding my own shoes.

Bear watched me intently as I threw objects across the room and grumbled more choice words. At one point, he actually looked amused. It unsettled me the way his eyes fixed on mine. They were different but familiar. He got up from the spot he'd been sitting in, unfazed by my outburst, and walked to the bed. Then he climbed under it and made that crackling noise cats made when they spoke to unsuspecting birds through the window.

"Bear?" I got down on my knees and peeked under the bed. The shades were drawn and the darkness of the room made it difficult to see. I spotted his orange tail next to my missing Converse sneakers. Then he turned to look at me. A set of dark blue eyes offset by brilliant white around the edges shined back at me. I nearly cracked my skull on the bed frame as I jerked back and stood up, flying through the nearest door in the room. I stood in the bathroom with my back to it. "It's just Bear," I told myself. But Bear's eyes were bright green, and there was no mistaking what I just saw looking back at me under that bed. The darkness was just playing tricks on my eyes, I reasoned. I cracked the door and looked around the room. It was empty. I quickly got out of there and went back downstairs, mindful of all the things that were after me.

"There you are," Ava said, stroking Bear's back while he

lounged on the sideboard, midnight blue eyes blazing. "Bear was concerned that he may have given you a coronary."

Sophia was standing in the doorway to the kitchen. "I tell you, *gatto*, I kill you if you jump on my counter. That means sideboard, too," she scolded, aiming a wooden spoon in his direction.

My eyes darted around the room as I listened to all the absurd conversations taking place.

"I knew there was something wrong with that cat," Greer said as he joined the circus in the dining room.

"Greer! That's no way to speak to a colleague," Ava chastised.

"Wha—" I shook my head, mystified. "What's wrong with my cat's eyes?"

Ava and Bear looked at each other for an extended moment. A short burst of laughter left her mouth as she tried to compose herself. "You mean you don't know?"

"Know what?" I asked.

Greer sighed and sat in a chair to watch the show.

"About Bear." She seemed oddly perplexed by my ignorance. "Well, he's your guide."

"My guide?"

"Yes. All witches have one."

Sophia shifted in the corner of the room, looking uneasy like she'd missed that lesson on witch basics, too.

"I'm sorry, Sophia," Ava corrected. "I mean all witches of Raven lineage. I'm sure the Strega have their own unique traditions." She turned back to me and continued. "Bear was sent to you—by the gods."

"That's funny. I thought he was sent to me by some homeless guy on Seventy-Ninth Street."

Ava cocked her head, not quite following my meaning.

"Hmph." Sophia planted a hand on her hip and walked back toward the kitchen. "I guess I cook for him too, now," she snorted, exiting the room.

Greer chimed in. "Well, he was responsible for telling us—in a roundabout way—where the Rogues were initially holding you." He glared at Bear. "Too bad he was a little late."

"So what happens now?" I asked. "Does he morph into a man and live with us?"

Ava chuckled. "No. Everything stays the same. He'll just be around to help when needed."

Bear jumped from the cabinet and wound his body around my legs, his blue eyes fixed on mine. "Fine." I bent down to rub the back of his neck and an image flashed in my mind of shapes and symbols covering his face. I pulled my hand away. "Your eyes will take some getting used to, Bear. But right now I have to go."

Before Greer could object, I cut him off and made it clear that my leaving for an hour or two was non-negotiable. "I'm just going to see Katie and Apollo. Since I'm sure I don't have a job anymore, it shouldn't take very long."

Sophia, who had been listening to the conversation from the kitchen, stepped back into the dining room with her handbag dangling off her arm. She looked particularly pleased with herself as she informed me that I indeed still had a job, detailing the day she walked into Shakespeare's Library and threw up a spell to make every day a Monday—my day off—until I returned.

"Let's go." She shooed me toward the door and looked at Greer. "I come back and cook after removing the spell."

I thought it was brilliant. "Thank you, Sophia."

"Don't thank me." She nodded to Greer. "I owed a debt. Thank Mr. Sinclair."

Greer hated me working. But he knew what that measly little bookstore job meant to me, and the gesture was no small thing. *Thank you* I mouthed to him.

A moment later, Rhom walked through the door to escort us to the shop.

CHAPTER FIVE

I walked through the front door of Shakespeare's Library, half expecting to see letters spelling out MONDAY floating through the air, only visible to Sophia and me. Or the day calendar stuck on the most dreaded day of the week, waiting to be released from its stymied job. Despite my heritage and the powers I hadn't quite figured out how to manifest and properly control yet, I knew nothing about spells.

"God, I've been worried about you," Katie whispered as she threw her arms around me and squeezed. "Are you all right?" She stepped back to get a good look at me. Her eyes were bloodshot, and the dark patches circling her usually vibrant blue orbs went alarmingly deep.

"I should be asking you the same question. You look exhausted, Katie."

She glanced at Sophia, a silent question exuding from her eyes. Sophia nodded once. "Do we need to—" She motioned toward the stacks.

Sophia shook her head, leaning in closer to whisper. "Is not necessary. Spell is much easier to take down."

Like two old friends in cahoots, I watched the two of them

converse. "Is someone going to let me in on what's going on?" I asked. But before I could inquire further, Sophia looked around the room and then held out her hand. She muttered something in Italian, and four balls of brightly colored light came rushing toward her. Each of them smashed into her outstretched hand, culminating into a single white light that diminished to a flicker in her palm. She reached inside her bag and her hand came back out empty.

"Is done," she proclaimed.

My head shook. "I'm not even going to ask."

"Apollo," Katie called out without turning around to look at him. "What day is it?"

His head popped up sharply as if he were noticing us for the first time. Out of the corner of my eye, I saw the slight movement of the calendar on the counter flipping its pages. Apollo glanced at it a moment after it stopped. "It's Friday."

Apollo looked worse than Katie, and it dawned on me that they'd both been pulling double shifts since I disappeared. "Why don't you go home, Apollo?" I suggested. "You don't look so good."

"Yeah, I know. I've been exhausted lately." He scratched his head and seemed to contemplate doing just that. "Jesus, I hope I'm not getting sick. I've got too much to do, and I don't even know why I'm here. I think I'm supposed to be off today."

Katie smirked at me. At least she knew why she was exhausted. She was here when Sophia activated the spell. She knew exactly what day it was, while poor Apollo had no idea he'd been pulling his usual Monday double shift for nearly two weeks.

"All right. I'm out of here. I'll be working from home for the next few hours, so call me on my cell if you need me." He grabbed a folder of work documents and left. At least he could pass out on his own sofa if the sleep deprivation got to him.

"I can handle the shop alone if you need to go home, too," I said to Katie.

"No way. You're telling me everything."

Sophia, who had been standing there passively watching our exchange, cleared her throat. "You told Mr. Sinclair you'd be right back. I don't think it's a good idea to leave you here."

"Rhom is right outside that door, Sophia. And you know as well as I do that Katie is a pretty good second line of defense if anything uninvited walks in. I'm her village—remember?" Sophia knew that Katie was a dragon, and anything that tried to harm me would suffer the wrath of the beast on her back.

"I don't like this," she protested, shrugging her shoulders in a dramatic gesture of concession. "But who am I? I'm just the maid."

"Oh, don't be silly, Sophia. *You* are a rock star."

"I can attest to that," Katie added. "I watched you conjure that little time spell."

"Okay," she agreed. "I tell Mr. Sinclair you're working until—"

"Until closing. Tell him I'll be home at the usual time, nine thirty or ten. And on your way out let Rhom know."

After Sophia left the shop I headed for a pile of books on the floor. We usually straightened them after we closed, but I was wired with nerves and needed busywork to take my mind off everything that had happened over the past two weeks. As I started sorting them by genre on the library table, I waited for Katie to badger me into sitting down and telling her everything. That never happened. She just went back to her book, reading intently but never turning a single page. She must have read that unfortunate page she was stuck on ten times, not a word making it past her eyes and into her brain as she patiently waited for me to break down.

"All right! You win."

Her tensed shoulders dropped. "Thank God. I was about to throw this damn book across the room."

I was a little surprised that her new boyfriend hadn't slipped up and told her the ugly truth about me. Constantine—Mr. Know-it-all—must have known. He also must have had some real integrity after all, because everyone knows how easily secrets get spilled in the bedroom. It occurred to me that maybe he'd proven me right. Maybe he'd dumped her and she was putting on a world-class act in light of my own troubles. Or maybe she was just too humiliated to admit that I was right and he'd tossed her aside as soon as he was done with her. *God!* What if he hadn't released her from his enchantment, and she was secretly suicidal?

"Everything all right with you and Constantine?" I asked.

She grinned like a Cheshire cat. "Constantine, Constantine, Constantine," she sing-songed, giddy from the mere speaking of his name.

"Oh God," I groaned. "I guess that means the two of you are still at it?"

"Yes, we're still madly happy," she sighed, her languid face firming up as the distraction faded. "We can talk about me later. Right now, I want to know where you've been for the past two weeks." She took a seat at the table and waited for me to explain, among other things, why it was necessary for Greer's housekeeper to cast an incantation over the shop to manipulate time.

"Remember when I told you about the guy who attacked me in Central Park last fall?"

Her eyes darkened as if a switch had been flipped, an involuntary reaction to knowing something unpleasant was about to follow those words. She knew I'd nearly been raped by Daemon and that he'd been stalking me ever since.

"God, Alex. Please don't tell me that." Her head shook in anticipation of the worst.

Katie was the one person I could confide in who would sit there and suppress her opinion while I let it all out. I just needed to tell someone who wouldn't demand the details until I was ready to give them. Eventually I'd tell Ava, but I had a feeling she'd already figured it out. She knew me better than anyone, and

I was sure she could still see inside my head after we'd shared our blood the morning before I was abducted, after drinking her potion and reliving that day in the forest almost twenty years ago.

"Yes," I simply said, seeing no reason to ease into the conversation. It was always better to just come out with things that were difficult to say, easier to just get it out there. "He abducted me. He held me for a few days before—"

Katie leaned closer and pinned me with her concerned eyes, waiting for me to continue the story. Daemon's assault was one thing, but how could I tell her about Maelcolm? That I was half monster, half the man who did this to me. I'd never had a friend like her, one that really got me and liked what she saw. Dragon or not, I wasn't sure she was strong enough to juggle all the landmines attached to a friend like me, or if she'd even want to.

"I met my father."

Her spine straightened as she pulled away, her curiosity turning to caution.

"I hate that look, Katie."

"Look?"

"Yeah. Like you're afraid of me."

A tepid smile crossed her face. "Don't be ridiculous, Alex. I'm just a little confused. You said you didn't have a father. I assumed you meant he was dead."

My eyes averted to the marred surface of the old table as I began to recite the rest of the bizarre story. "Turns out he's very much alive. His name is Maelcolm, and he's the leader of Daemon's people. They're called Rogues." I glanced up to see if she was still sitting there. Her mouth was slightly ajar as if something were about to come out of it, but then she closed her lips and covered my hand with hers in a consoling gesture.

"Well, damn," she said. "And here I thought you were going to tell me he was some kind of zombie, or God forbid some troll your mother was slumming it with."

The room fell silent as I processed her comment. "Troll?"

We burst into laughter simultaneously, overcome by the sheer absurdity of it all. God, I loved her. A person could spend their whole life looking for a friend like Katie Bishop, and I had the original.

I spared her the gory details, saving them for another day, knowing she had the patience of a saint and wouldn't push for more until I was ready to volunteer it. Instead, I changed the subject and told her about my new talents, knowing she'd be fascinated and even instrumental in helping me figure out how to actually use them. She was a dragon, after all. My neat little fire trick was right up her alley. We could learn together.

"Turns out I'm a walking manifestation of three witches: me, my mother, and my grandmother. In other words, I have their powers, too." I held out my hand and turned it palm up, but no matter how hard I concentrated on a flame, nothing happened. "Believe it or not I can manifest this flame in the center of my palm. Doesn't seem to be cooperating today, though. Got that little trick from my mother."

Watching her reaction closely and weighing the bonds of our mutual secrets, I got up the nerve to say the next words. "I killed him."

I detected a slight hitch in her breath as she froze and considered what I'd just confessed, her wide blue eyes eventually flicking up to meet mine with a question mark.

"Daemon. I killed him with the fire when he attacked me again. It was him or me."

The room fell silent, a few quiet seconds feeling more like minutes before she spoke. "Well, then I guess he deserved it. Men who fuck with powerful witches get burned. One less predator on the streets." A grin crept up the side of her face in conjunction with the one forming on mine. "We're fire sisters," she announced proudly. "You throw it, I breathe it. Now, if we could just figure out how to control it."

"Apparently I have some kind of mind bending powers, too. Got that from my grandmother, Isla."

"Hmm. That'll be fun to experiment with. Maybe we'll hit one of the clubs and wait for some asshole that doesn't want to take no for an answer. I can hold him down with my tail while you play around with his head." Her voice trailed off as she stared at her fingertips. "I know a few guys who could use a good lesson."

The front door chimed. We both glanced up at the empty shop. "Creepy," Katie commented as we resumed our conversation.

A whoosh of air breezed past me. This time Constantine was standing a few feet away when I looked up. Katie's face lit up like a beacon when she saw him, but then it sobered when she noticed the scowl on his face.

"How did you manage to get past Rhom?" I asked, glancing at the door. The question went unanswered, presumably because he thought it too mundane to address.

He stood between us at the edge of the table and gave Katie a long look before turning to me, lifting my chin to examine my face. His eyes rolled over mine, and I was struck by the care and concern in his. Constantine made an art form out of aloofness. He was a master of composure and neutrality. But today I saw only anger.

"Are you all right?" he asked.

What does it mean when someone asks that? Does being alive count as "all right"? Was the mere fact that I wasn't consumed in angst and self-pity a valid benchmark for my level of stability?

"Not really," I answered, feeling candid. "But I'll work through it. I always do." I played the role of victim horribly. Sometimes I wondered if I had a trace of sociopath in me, never quite following the rules of grief the way people expect. But then there was my crippling sensitivity to seeing anything suffer, which ruled out a neat diagnosis of lack of conscience.

He released my chin and then reached for Katie, smoothing his hand over her hair before resting it at the base of her neck. Then he bent down to kiss the spot where her hairline met her pale white skin. He whispered something into her ear and she stood up to leave.

"You don't have to go, Katie," I said.

She looked at Constantine and then back at me. "Are you sure? I don't mind giving you two some privacy."

I shook my head. "No secrets. I trust you as much as anyone."

"Very well," Constantine said, motioning for her to sit back down. "I want you to know, Alex. If there was anything more I could have done, I would have come riding in on that shiny white horse to take you out of that place." He grimaced and glanced at a book on the table. "Unfortunately, Maelcolm and his Rogues are powerful adversaries, protected quite heavily within their own walls."

Ironically, allowing a determined Italian witch to slip right over those walls.

"Anything *more*?" I asked. "Did you do anything?" My feelings were slightly bruised by his suggestion that he'd made any effort at all. He knew I'd been taken. The great and powerful Constantine—who knew everything—had to know the nature of my abduction. He also must have known all along that Maelcolm was my father. He'd said something to me the day I went to see him in the park, the week before Daemon abducted me. We were standing on the path when he took my hand, commenting on the softness of my skin. *You are too light to be so dark*, he'd said, obviously referring to my paternity.

"Yes, well," he muttered, averting his eyes back to that damn book on the table. "I was counting on Ian's defection and ability to move unnoticed within Maelcolm's abode. *That* is no easy task. He's working for Greer now. His intel was vital for your rescue."

"Ian? You know Ian? *Dead* Ian?"

"Quite well," he confirmed. "I've known Ian since long before his death. Used to be quite a bad character. A hunter."

Katie looked confused. "Who's Ian? You guys know dead people?"

"Do I want to know what a hunter is?" I asked, ignoring Katie's question.

"A tracker. He used to track down the children sired by Rogues. Years after the fact. A time consuming but lucrative occupation." Constantine's eyes grew darker as he pierced me with them, making me uncomfortable for so many reasons. "I suspect you would have been his prized quarry had he been alive when you were born. The bounty on you was priceless, and I doubt any amount of distance from this city would have prevented him from smelling you out." His predatory glare softened. "Good thing the legendary hunter died before you were even conceived."

I was speechless. The likable gentleman who'd cooked me breakfast was not only dead, he was as much a monster as the Rogues. He could have hunted me down on that farm in Indiana and delivered me to my father before I even knew who or what I was.

"How did he die?" I asked, suddenly curious about the refined specter who'd managed to ingratiate himself to me.

Constantine took a seat on the other side of Katie, spreading his legs to accommodate her chair as he slid it backward. He leaned forward to wrap his arms over her shoulders and around her neck, nuzzling his mouth into her jet-black hair. "Stop it." She feigned annoyance, but I could tell by the way her eyes softened that he had her hook, line, and sinker.

"Oh, don't mind me," I said, suddenly uncomfortable with his foreplay. I recalled the first time I was alone with Constantine, squirming on Arthur Richmond's floor as he played with my mind. "I know how persuasive he can be."

Katie's brow raised. "A history? Should I be jealous?"

"Absolutely not." I looked at him and waited for an answer.

"Ian had one thing working against him," Constantine continued. "He was human."

I was surprised that the Rogues would form an alliance with a human for a task that was so critical to their despicable mission. How was that even possible? Maybe they advertised in *Soldier of Fortune* for a child abductor.

"He tracked down one of Maelcolm's offspring in the Bronx." He hesitated as a thought distracted him. "Your half-sibling, I suppose."

It never occurred to me that I probably had half-brothers by the dozens, or that the chances were pretty high that I might be forced to kill one of them someday. A sickening thought crossed my mind as I remembered the men who'd tried to attack me the day after Daemon locked me in that room under the bakery.

"Ian got sloppy, retrieved the wrong child, a mere human boy with no blood connection to the Rogues." Constantine did his best to mask his contempt, but I knew he found the whole sordid history as distasteful as I found it reprehensible. "Maelcolm was not pleased, to say the least. Ian offered to return the child and bring the correct one back, but the damage had been done." He dropped his arms from around Katie's shoulders and stood back up, slipping his hands into the pockets of his pants as his eyes slowly examined the room like he was seeing it for the first time. With his back to us, he continued. "Maelcolm doesn't allow mistakes—he makes examples of them. He gave Ian a choice: kill the child or kill himself."

Maelcolm was more ruthless than I thought, if that were possible. What would he do to me for the unforgivable act of escaping his prison? Would he make an example out of me? As valuable as I was to him, I imagined my punishment would not be as kind as death.

"After all the unforgivable things he'd done over the years and all the children he'd stolen and handed over to the Rogues, you'd think the choice would have been easy. But he couldn't bring himself to cold-bloodedly kill a child."

Katie finished the thought. "So he chose death."

"What happened to the boy?" I asked. He turned back around to look at the two of us but didn't answer. The look on his face was answer enough. Ian was dead, and so was an innocent child.

Curiously, he looked at me as if he'd just remembered something. "How is it that you're here? In this room? I can't imagine Greer would let you out of the house, in light of recent events."

"That's not Greer's decision to make. Besides, Rhom is outside." I glanced at the window, now wondering if my bodyguard was still out there.

"He didn't do a very good job of keeping me out, did he?" he said dryly.

"Oh, here we go." I knew the minute I mentioned it he'd boast about how clever he was at slipping past Rhom. "Look, Constantine, you're not exactly an amateur. Rhom is good, but you're an expert at squeezing into tight places, aren't you? What did you do, transform into a rat and slip under the door?"

"Of course not," he smirked. "I referred the guise of something much more ancient and cunning—a *dragonfly*."

"Not that it's any of your business, but Greer had no idea I'd be staying here for the day."

That smirk suddenly left his face as he glanced behind me. "Well, seems he's not happy about your decision to undermine him."

I felt a hand slip over my shoulder and the heat of a furnace at my back.

"It's good to see you again, Katie." Greer was towering over me when I looked up. He gave Constantine a look that made me fear for the organized stacks of books in our little shop, and I didn't revel in the thought of having to reshelve them all if things got out of hand. "Alex, get your things. I'm taking you home."

There was something different in the way he ordered me around today. The feel of his hand against my shoulder was gentle and soothing, connected to me in a way that made me crave more of his touch. Out of habit, I opened my mouth to protest but shut it as I found myself wanting to comply.

"I think that's probably a good idea," Katie said, shooting me a commiserative look with her Elizabeth Taylor eyes.

"I can't leave Katie alone in the shop," I said. "It's too much work for one person."

Katie looked around the room. "Alex, what do you see?"

My eyes followed hers around the empty shop. "Fine. I get your point."

"Besides, Constantine will stay and keep me company, won't you?" She flashed him one of her million-dollar smiles.

His eyes lingered on hers. Then he assessed the deep—and deserted—aisles on either side of the room and recognized the opportunity. "As long as you don't expect me to sell books," he replied only half-jokingly. He turned back around and shooed me with the back of his hand. "Run along now, little Raven. You and your man have things to discuss." His light mood turned grave as he stared at Greer, and I sensed that he knew. Not just about Maelcolm, but about what Daemon did to me. I could see it in his eyes.

I couldn't hide at Shakespeare's Library forever, and the sooner I faced the hurricane of emotions spinning around in my head, the sooner I'd find some peace. Facing my fear was the price I'd have to pay for that peace.

CHAPTER SIX

The house was so quiet I could almost hear the water from the Hudson River a few blocks to the west. But it was just the blood rushing in my ears, pulsing through my veins as my heart pumped wildly. Sophia had left for the day, so there was no one in the house to interfere with the conversation we were about to have.

I could feel Greer standing somewhere behind me, waiting with the patience of a priest for my confession. Either that or he was waiting for my decision about him. He'd made his intentions quite clear, or at least his instincts. This imprinting thing wasn't going away, and it had to be dealt with one way or the other. Either I was in or I had to leave this house.

His breath was on my neck. He was standing right behind me, practically touching me as a wave of his heat snaked around me like a warm blanket. My eyes turned slightly as his right hand touched my arm, the other sliding around my waist and splaying flat across my stomach, pulling me firmly against him. But it was the feel of his mouth on my neck that turned my legs to rubber.

"Greer," I protested, shaking my head. "You don't want me. I'm different."

He turned me around to face him, his brow raised. "Oh, but I do." I felt that old familiar panic creep up from the center of my gut as his mouth came within an inch of my forehead. He kissed me just above my brow and then pulled back to take in my face. "But I can wait until this irrational fear of yours is put to rest."

There it was, that button he always managed to push. "Fear?" I hated that he could always read me so expertly. "What do you know about my fear?"

His chest expanded, closing the space between us as my back met the wall. "I know that every time we get to the point where we stop avoiding our needs, you tighten up like a vise."

"You don't need me, Greer. You don't need anyone." I pushed him back, slipping out from under his cage. "And *I* certainly don't need anyone."

He grabbed my wrist before I could walk away. "Then I suggest you stop throwing that scent."

"What scent?"

"The one that exudes from your skin every time I come within ten feet of you. You may be able to hide from most men, but don't forget what I am."

Well, didn't that leave me speechless. Did I actually have a scent? I caught myself discreetly sniffing the air, but the only thing I could smell was *his* unique scent. A muffled gasp left my mouth as it dawned on me that I'd been able to identify him by his smell since the day we met. Was it possible that I was the only one who could detect it? Was that scent just for me?

"Now you understand," he said, reading my thoughts. "You can't control attraction, Alex."

I went for the kitchen, suddenly needing a glass of water to combat the uncomfortable heat flashing through me like a napalm explosion. I grabbed a glass but held my shaking hand under the running water instead, letting the excess energy flow out of it. That flame was starting to burn in my palm, and I feared what I might do with it if it wasn't quelled quickly. How could he let this little game go on for all these months without telling me what was happening? I had the right to know that I was being set up as the gods' mail order bride.

"That choice was not ours," he said, following me into the library as I attempted to put some needed distance between us. I needed to cool down—literally—before something unpleasant happened. He caught up to me and took my face in his hands. "I regret none of it. Our path may have been chosen for us, but it is *our* future to write."

"Yeah? Well, read this." I pulled his hands away, conjuring up an image in my mind of the night Daemon cornered me and then calmly raped me in that deceptively lovely bed, the whole time telling me that I was meant for him and the consummation would nullify any claim Greer had on me. The memory turned my stomach, but Greer needed to know what he was investing in. He needed to see the damage he was taking on. That would fix it. That would clear up any misguided ideas he had about our future together. There were prettier, subservient, whole girls out there just waiting for him to beckon them into his bed. Do anything he asked, they would.

He reached for me again but stopped, reduced to stone before he could touch me. A strange look crossed his face as the images caught up to his brain and revealed in stark detail just what happened over the course of that night. It was like watching a chemical reaction, an element quickly changing from one form to another.

A mild tremor hummed under my feet, and the books wedged neatly against the library walls began to vibrate and cascade from the shelves. I stumbled back, catching the edge of the chair as the small quake intensified. I shouldn't have done that to him, but he needed to know, to see it for himself. No matter how he found out, I suspected his reaction would be the same. But it was the coward's way. I'd taken the easy way out with no regard for what it would do to him, and it was the worst thing I'd ever done.

"Why didn't you—" He cocked his head, answering his own question before it left his mouth. Then his bewildered look turned cold, his words icy and declarative. "You thought I wouldn't want you anymore. You thought I'd abandon you."

I could see the wound in his eyes. Like a sticky substance I couldn't swallow, the shame choked me and filled me with self-hatred. Saying all the wrong things was my specialty. Things that pushed most people away. That was the point, and I was damn good at it. But today I wanted to take it all back and try something different for a change. I wanted to try a little trust.

He turned toward the door. "Where are you going?" I asked, as if I had the right to ask him anything.

"To destroy him," he said matter-of-factly without looking at me.

"He's already dead. I killed him myself."

I could see by the way his shoulders stiffened and his fists contracted at his sides that I'd added insult to injury. It was the one thing that would have alleviated some of his grief, and I managed to take that, too. He started to look back at me but stopped as his eyes met his shoulder. Then he calmly walked through the library door and vanished.

I POKED around the refrigerator for leftovers. Greer had sent Sophia home early that afternoon before we got back from Shakespeare's Library, presumably to give us some privacy while we addressed the elephant in the kitchen. He'd been gone for hours, and based on his history I knew it could be days or even weeks before he showed up again.

Rhom stuck his head in the kitchen. "Jesus, Rhom! You scared the crap out of me." I should have known he was somewhere in the house. Greer always had me covered, even when he hated me.

"Sorry," he apologized, opening the refrigerator door wider to hunt for food with me. Still warm to the touch, he removed a large pan from the second shelf. "Damn, that smells good. Remind me to marry Sophia tomorrow."

"Careful. Thomas might get jealous."

"Yeah, yeah. She loves me more." He carried the pan to the kitchen island while I grabbed plates and cutlery. Inside was a layer of crusted mashed potatoes. "I don't know what it is, but it smells like something I need to be eating immediately."

I inhaled the fragrant spices and cut into the dish. "It's moussaka, I think."

"That's a new one," he said.

Sophia could cook rat stew and have us coming back for seconds.

We ate our food in an uncomfortable silence that I rarely experienced with Rhom. We weren't strangers to our quiet moments, but they were never awkward like now.

"So, where is he?" I asked.

He took a deep breath through his nose while he continued to chew. By the way he stared at his plate instead of me, I assumed Greer had opened his big mouth and spilled my secrets. I didn't mind Rhom knowing what happened. I just hated not being the one to tell him. He dropped his fork on the counter and wiped his mouth with a napkin. "You two are killing me," he said, half irritated and half concerned. "Alex, what the hell did you do to him? He's off the grid. Warned us all to stay back and give him some room."

"I don't understand it either," I said, choosing to be pleasant rather than combative. "I really don't understand why he wants anything to do with me. I mean, I can be difficult as hell sometimes."

"No argument from me."

"Thanks, Rhom. And here I thought you were my friend."

"I am your friend, Alex. That's why I'm sitting at a table and breaking bread with you, discussing things that are usually not discussed." He shook his head, resigned to whatever code he'd just broken. "A man's business is his business, but Greer isn't an ordinary man, now is he? His job is to keep this godforsaken world from cannibalizing itself for greed and power. You think he asked for this? You think any of us asked for this?"

I'd never thought about it before, how and why they ended up here. In a cryptic and roundabout way, Greer had told me months ago what their mission was. He even referred to himself as the governor of the city. I scoffed at him at the time, pointing out that cities didn't have governors. Now I wondered how much truth was in that statement. If Greer's domain was New York City, then who was keeping the peace in the rest of the world? Who was keeping the peace in London or Paris? Does every major city of the world have a team of gods watching over it? Do they all have a Constantine?

Rhom polished off his moussaka and got up. "Done?" he asked, looking at the half-eaten plate I was ignoring. I nodded, and he took it and headed for the sink to rinse the uneaten food down the garbage disposal. Rhom would make some woman a fine husband. He didn't just toss the plates into the nearest open spot in the dishwasher; he methodically placed them in an orderly row on the bottom rack, right where Sophia would have put them. And since she'd be the one emptying it tomorrow morning, that methodical positioning would not go unappreciated.

"Are you telling me none of you want to be here?" I asked. "Don't you have any say about where you're *stationed*?" Sounded like the right word to use.

He laughed. "I thought you'd say that. We are all servants, Alex. Even you." He walked back to his stool and sat. "I think we need to have a little come-to-Jesus."

A cloud seemed to form over the room as a sense of dread filled it. It wasn't the first time Rhom served as my voice of reason, but it was the first time I'd ever felt such a heaviness in his eyes. This was going to hurt. "Whenever one of you looks at me that way, it usually means I'm about to hear something I don't want to hear."

"You're too young to be such a pessimist, Alex. Why don't you just relax and listen? No one's trying to make do anything you don't want to do. But you do need to choose what it is you want." He punctuated the remark with a slight nod. "Or don't want."

"I'm listening, Rhom."

"I assume you're aware of Greer's feelings for you, and since he's gone AWOL I'm also assuming the feelings aren't reciprocated." By the way he was looking at me, I could tell he was hoping I wouldn't nod my head in confirmation that Greer wasn't the guy for me. "Just say it, Alex. Then we can get on with a plan to mitigate the damage."

"Damage? What do you mean *damage*?"

"When one of us imprints and bonds with someone, we do it head-on. None of this courting shit—no movies, no dinner, no nervous small talk before planting a kiss. We just go for it." He stopped and eyed me strangely. "I'll admit I was a little surprised that the two of you are sleeping together."

"Wait. What? We're not—"

"I think I know how this works, Alex," he snickered under his breath.

"Look, Rhom. There was this one time, but it was a mistake." I left it at that. I had no intention of going into the details about the night I threw myself at Greer under the influence of some misguided spell. "It doesn't matter anyway. I'm sure he's realized by now that I'm not the girl for him. He's probably just taking a little time to figure out the politest way of telling me that."

He looked surprised. "Alex, what are not telling me? This is important. Now swallow your pride and tell me what happened between you two."

Maybe Greer didn't tell him about Daemon. I just shook my head and continued to stare off at the wall. It was bad enough that Greer knew, but Rhom was my guard. He'd take it almost as hard as Greer. Blame himself for not doing his job. I hopped off the stool and headed out of the kitchen. The moment I walked into the foyer, a sharp pain struck me square between the eyes. I winced as the pain quickly spread down my face and into my chest.

"Alex!" Rhom came from the kitchen a second later and caught me as I hit the floor, just in time to spare my head from cracking against the hard wood. "What the hell?"

My vision started to blur and a high-pitched ring pierced my ears. I focused on a beam of light coming from somewhere in the room, pointed at the floor in front of the library door. *Where is it coming from?* I glanced at Rhom from the corner of my eye and waited for him to explain the light, but he just looked at me with as much bewilderment as I felt. The question hadn't actually been articulated, and poor Rhom was at a loss for how to help me.

"Let me go," I demanded as the pain subsided to a dull ache and I found my feet again. He pulled his arms away, still perplexed by my collapse. I turned back toward the light and followed it into the library with Rhom behind me. The beam had become a glowing ball, moving around the room like a playful ghost before coming to a slow crawl on one of the shelves at the top of the bookcase. It seemed to be scanning the books, methodically looking for something. Not surprising considering how prevalent mysterious books had become in my life. First it was the massive tome of magic at Den of Oddities and Antiquities where we found the amulet, and then the book on prophecies at Shakespeare's Library after that. I guess I was overdue for another one.

"Don't you see it?" I asked, pointing toward the light.

Rhom followed my index finger, then slowly shook his head as he looked back at me. "See what?"

I looked at the shelf and blinked several times to make sure it wasn't some sort of glare or illusion from fatigue. But that damn light just grew brighter, coming to a stop on a row of books. The light dimmed as I approached it. The closer I got, the more it faded. The light vanished as I reached for the shelf. It was a row of children's books and fairy tales. I'd never noticed them before. Greer had books on all kinds of subjects, some hard to reconcile with the man who owned them. Books on history, poetry, mathematics. He even had a section on organic gardening for which I teased him. But in all the months that I'd fingered through the spines of his bookcases, I'd never noticed the books by Hans Christian Andersen, Lewis Carroll, and the Brothers Grimm.

"What do you have there?" Rhom asked as I pulled out an old edition of *Grimm's Fairy Tales*. I flipped through the text and stopped at the story of Hansel and Gretel, remembering it vividly from when my mother used to read it to me. He came from behind me and took the book from my hands. "Talk to me, Alex."

Suddenly curious about his lineage, I looked up at his face and wondered if his mother and father were still alive, which one of them was a god and which was an ordinary human being. Did they read him these stories? Did he even know the story of Hansel and Gretel?

"You didn't see it, did you?" I asked, somehow knowing the light was meant for my eyes only. Maybe it was Maeve or Isla trying to tell me something. Or maybe there was no light, and I was on the verge of a breakdown. "I think I'm just tired." I slid the book back on the shelf and walked toward the door. It was early evening, but all I wanted to do was curl up in bed and sleep until Greer decided to come home.

CHAPTER SEVEN

My sleep was anything but restful, my mind refusing to shut down. I must have laid in bed half the night running all the scenarios of my next conversation with Greer through my head. It felt like I was running lines for a play, repeating the same phrases over and over again until I woke and shifted on the mattress, starting the rehearsal all over again with a different script.

Bear hopped on the bed and did his usual face licking routine to get me up, only this time it kind of creeped me out, knowing what he was. I sat up and pushed him away. "Maybe you should leave the room before I get dressed." He flashed a smile, causing me to do a double take when I saw the gleam of his white teeth. It quickly vanished, and he was just an ordinary orange tabby sitting next to me on the bed. "*That* is going to take some getting used to, Bear."

I climbed out of bed and grabbed some clothes before heading for the shower. "Sorry, Bear. Girls only," I said before shutting and locking the bathroom door. I showered quickly, eager to see if Greer had come home during the night, although I was pretty sure I'd already know it if he were in the house. His absence gave me more time to figure out how to live in this rabbit hole I'd been dropped down, but God I missed him. I missed his face, his smell, the annoying way he tried to control my every move. But most of all I missed the way it felt to have him near me, the heat from his skin and the intensity in his eyes when he looked at me. He was my safe house, and I could deny it from here to kingdom come, but Greer Sinclair was my rock.

Bear was sitting in the middle of the floor when I came out of the bathroom, the amulet lying on the floor at his feet. "What are you doing with that?" His tail swished back and forth in an agitated motion when I approached. A hum came from his mouth, turning into a low growl as I reached for the chain. "What's wrong with you, Bear?" I grabbed it quickly, barely avoiding his extended claws as he swung his paw at me. It was a warning. If he really wanted to keep me away from it, I'm sure he would have nailed me with those daggers. The last time Bear drew my blood, I was enchanted with the idea that Greer and I were husband and wife. If I ever figured out this whole "guide" thing and how to communicate with him, that would be our first conversation.

I stuffed the amulet under my shirt and left the room. The smell of fresh coffee mingled with bacon triggered a hefty load of endorphins in my brain. A Sophia breakfast was just what I needed before heading for work. That is, unless Greer had a change of heart and decided to cut the disappearing act short. I stopped halfway down the steps and listened for his voice, but all I heard was the occasional clank of a coffee cup meeting the marble counter and the refrigerator door opening and closing. I turned into the kitchen and stopped in my tracks. Ian was standing with his back to me, pouring a cup of coffee.

"Where's Sophia?" I inquired a little sharper than necessary, alarmed at her absence in a kitchen no one dared make themselves cozy in without her blessing.

Ian turned when he heard my voice. "Good morning, Alex."

He greeted me pleasantly and handed me the freshly made cup of coffee as if he were expecting me to walk into the room at that exact moment. "I was pleased to hear that your rescue was successful."

I glanced at his offering. "Thank you, but I can pour my own cup." I headed for the French press, surveying the room for signs that Sophia had been there.

"That one don't drink no coffee. Is a waste of a good cup," Sophia said from the doorway of the dining room, watching our exchange. "Can't eat no food either."

I bugged my eyes at her, because dead or not, she was being rude to him. "Be nice," I muttered.

"She's quite right," Ian confirmed. "Can't hold anything I put in my mouth." He took a large mouthful of coffee and mimicked swallowing. The milky brown liquid fell to the floor, trickling down around his shoes as if he'd pissed himself.

"Hey!" Sophia scolded, grabbing a kitchen towel and tossing it at him. "Clean your mess."

Ian bent down and started wiping the coffee from around his feet. "I don't know why she dislikes me so much," he said with a half-formed grin.

"Because you're dead," Sophia replied. "I know ghosts, but you're no ghost. You're just dead. You're a demon."

"Don't be so mean, Sophia. He's working for Greer now." I looked at Ian. "You are working for Greer, right?"

He stood back up and adjusted his suit. "I'm afraid she's right —again. I'm not a ghost." His eyes shot to Sophia. "But I can assure you I am no demon. I'm caught somewhere in between. It's very frustrating not knowing what you are. And I would kill to be able to taste a piece of bacon or a sip of that coffee." He gestured toward the cup in my hand. "Now that's torture."

I sat the cup on the counter, suddenly feeling self-conscious for enjoying it in front of him. "I know what you do for a living —or used to do," I said.

"Good," he replied. "Then I don't have to drudge up the past."

"You used to be a hunter. You used to hunt children like me and hand them over to monsters like Maelcolm."

He sighed heavily. "And there you go, drudging it up for me. If I could only get through one day of not remembering. But I suppose I deserve to be reminded."

"Yeah. I suppose," I agreed.

"And my penance continues. Hence the reason why I'm here." His eyes walked over my face, scrutinizing every detail, and I knew he was looking for similarities. "You look nothing like him, except for the eyes. Your eyes are identical to Maelcolm's, down to those golden rings around your irises."

That was something I'd recently discovered. I'd gone almost twenty-seven years without ever noticing those rings until the night my mother showed me my reflection in the black water of a mirror bowl. The rings, lightly feathered at the outer edges of my irises, barely detectable, only revealed themselves when my eyes flashed. That was the moment that I knew Maelcolm was my father.

I caught Sophia squinting at me to see what he was talking about.

"There's something else very different about you, Alex. You're more powerful than him, than any of us." His curious gaze turned sly. "You don't have a clue how powerful you are, do you? Had I been alive when you were being tracked I don't know that I could have found you." He seemed genuinely mystified by me. Of all the children he'd tracked down and handed over to the Rogues, I was the one that probably would have gotten away. But I wasn't one of his bounties today. I was just a stranger whom he decided to help.

"Why did you do it?" I asked, curious of his motives for entering Maelcolm's house to help Greer get me out.

He held his hands out, palms facing down with his fingers

spread. "I used to be quite proud of these hands. Kept the nails trimmed to a sensible length. Short enough to be appropriately masculine, but just long enough to function as useful tools. Men have never embraced the art of the manicure or the practice of exfoliating and conditioning the skin. But I find that women quite appreciate a man with soft hands."

I looked closer at them. The dark skin around his knuckles was thick and deeply ridged. His nails were uneven, and the edges were torn where his teeth had bitten off the excess growth. But it was the cracked skin stretched across the top, ashy and chalk-like, that must have bothered him the most. They looked almost painful, and there was nothing remotely manicured about them.

"I've been in this place far too long, and I'd like to move on." He dropped his hands back to his sides and continued. "I was a very bad man for a long time, Alex. This place—" He stopped and rolled his eyes around the room, but I knew it wasn't Greer's kitchen he was seeing. "This place is a slice of hell, my purgatory for all those bad things. I know that now. A price must be paid, and God knows I'm paying it."

"So you thought you'd start by helping me? Reparation for your former livelihood?" I'd found myself liking Ian the morning I met him in Maelcolm's house, and as he stood in front of me with his neglected hands and humbled demeanor, I still liked him. I had every reason to hate him, but I didn't.

"Enough talking," Sophia interrupted. "Food is getting cold. Sit. In the dining room."

I did as she instructed and sat at the table, waiting for the plate I knew she'd prepare for me. Ian followed and sat in the seat across from mine. It was eerie how he moved without making a sound, and now that I was aware of his material state, I noticed a slight translucent quality about him, like he was composed of very thin paper. Sophia placed a plate of eggs and bacon on the table in front of me. She glanced at Ian. "You want breakfast?"

They gave each other mutual dirty looks before she headed back to the kitchen.

"Sophia doesn't like you," I stated the obvious.

"Really. How can you tell?" He flashed me a genuine smile and nodded toward my plate. "Eat. Saving the world will require a great deal of strength."

I got over my guilt for enjoying food in front of him and stuffed a piece of bacon in my famished mouth. "So how did Greer know where to find me?" I'd been wondering about that. Did Greer know all along that Maelcolm was my father?

"He didn't. I've been hanging around Maelcolm's estate for decades, waiting for lost children to appear. He's still a bit mystified by how some of them managed to escape over the years."

"You?"

"Well, it's the least I can do. But my penance will persist for years before the gods absolve me of my crimes. You should earn me quite a few points toward that goal."

I had a feeling the comment was said in jest, but there was some truth to it. After all, he did seem genuinely concerned with making right his past wrongs. I was about to discreetly delve deeper to see how much he knew about the prophecy when he jumped out of his chair.

"Goddamned cat!" he spat.

Surprisingly, a thin line of blood ran down his hand, pooling at the outside edge of his palm. A crimson drop slipped from his skin and then disappeared into thin air before hitting the ground. My eyes darted around the dining room, looking for the offending feline—Bear. He was sitting on the other side of the room looking innocent of the deed.

Sophia came storming in from the kitchen when she heard the commotion.

"What are you planning to do with that?" I asked, pointing to the very large knife in her hand.

"I hear screaming. Where is he?" She surveyed the room, but Ian was gone. "I don't trust that corpse."

"Bear went all tiger on him." I looked back at what was once my benign little kitten. "You don't trust him either, do you?" I did. So did Greer, apparently. If he ever showed up again, I'd follow my instincts—with caution—and find out if that was a mistake.

As USUAL, Rhom escorted me to the front door of Shakespeare's Library. It was just before nine a.m. and it was already starting to get warm and humid outside.

I looked at his impeccable black suit, secured by a single button in the front. His stiff collar was held together by a constricting tie that I wanted to wiggle loose. "You're going to fry in that suit if you stand out here all day. Why don't you just go home and meet me here at five o'clock when I get off?"

"I'm touched by your concern, Alex, but it's not necessary. I don't sweat." He pulled the paper from under his arm and leaned against the wall. "If I see so much as a butterfly going through that door, I'm coming in."

"I really don't understand why you're so concerned about Constantine. He's not a threat. And by the way, he also looks out for me. You should be happy to have the backup."

He grumbled. "Harmless my ass. That satyr has his motives. Don't be fooled by his charm." He smirked and flipped his paper wide open. "Run along to work now. And keep the calamity at a minimum, Alex. I'm not in the mood for drama today."

My mouth dropped open but I didn't know how to respond to that. Every day did seem to be more dramatic than the last. But did he think I liked all the drama? I turned and walked into the shop without another word, questioning my innocence in the instigation of all the *drama* that seemed to follow me.

"What?" Katie asked as I muttered my way past her.

"Katie, am I a drama queen?"

"Yes," she replied, handing me a cup of lukewarm coffee from the deli across the street. "But I don't think you really have a choice in any of it. I think it comes with your territory, Alex."

"You should talk, Puff."

"I know, right?"

It was hard to take ribbing about being overly dramatic from a woman with a dragon on her back. Now *that* was drama.

I looked around the deserted shop and hoped it would stay that way for a few hours. Slow days were usually a drag, but today I had plans that required a little privacy.

"Katie?"

"Alex?" she mimicked, glancing at me out of the corner of her blue eyes. Her mouth twisted into a grin as she sensed something mischievous in my voice.

"Feel up to investigating my new skills?" I'd failed miserably when I tried to manifest the fire the day before, not even a spark. But yesterday was an awfully stressful day. Today was better for so many reasons: I had my job back, I still had my best friend, and I was freed from the burden of telling Greer what Daemon had done to me.

"Hell yeah." She grabbed my hand and ran her thumb across my palm. "You know, magic works best when you're not trying so hard. It's sort of like meditation. You focus so hard on trying to empty your mind and find that still spot, but all you get is your grocery list or reminders of all the things you need to do." She dropped my hand and headed for the metaphysics and occult section. "Watch the front desk. I'll be right back."

Rhom was nowhere in sight when I looked out the shop window. But I knew he was out there somewhere. I also knew that as long as Katie was with me, Constantine wasn't far away either. And then there was Greer. Rhom was usually his eyes, but I could feel him watching me. He needed distance from me right now, but that didn't include leaving the gates wide open for anyone else to waltz in. Collectively, Katie and I were probably the most well-guarded females on the planet, Shakespeare's Library being our fortress.

She returned a few minutes later with a book in her hand. "Let's see what the experts have to say." With a blazing pentagram on its flimsy soft cover, the book didn't look particularly scholarly. Katie picked up on my skepticism. "It's the best we've got, unless you want to wait and head down to Den of Oddities and Antiquities after work?"

I shook my head. "I don't think I can wait that long. Let's just do a little poking around this afternoon and I'll head down there after work. You can come with if you want."

"I invited myself before you asked," she smirked.

"Good. I need backup. Ava's going to kill me for not telling her about this sooner."

Katie cocked her head at me. "You haven't told her yet?"

"I planned to, but it got really crazy at the house yesterday morning. She started telling me about how she met my mother, and then Greer walked in the room and hijacked the conversation. I got a little overwhelmed by it all and went upstairs to find my shoes so I could head over here, and Bear—" I gasped, covering my mouth with both hands as I remembered the part about Bear. "I forgot to tell you!"

"What? Tell me what?" Her blue eyes flashed green as she read my excitement. It was a dragon thing I'd seen her eyes do before, an involuntary reaction to her own adrenaline.

"Yeah, apparently Bear—you know, that innocent little kitten Apollo *found* in some homeless guy's box on Seventy-Ninth Street —isn't a kitten after all. Well, technically he is a cat, but he's also my *guide*."

"Guide?" She seemed confused, but then her face had an aha moment as she nodded knowingly. "You mean like a *familiar*?" Her fingers curled into air quotes around the word. "I thought that was just a bunch of BS. I didn't think witches actually had familiars."

Ava didn't call Bear a familiar, but it sounded similar. "She said it's a Raven thing. Sophia doesn't have one, so I guess not all witches do."

"So, that kitten really found you?"

"Apparently."

She flipped through the pages of the book and stopped on the section that described the elements. "Let's see what we have here. Earth, air, fire, and water." She flipped a few more pages to the heading titled Fire.

ELEMENT OF FIRE:
Direction: South
Elemental: Salamander
Season: Summer
Hour: Noon
Colors: Red, orange
Rules: The will
Magical Tools: Athame, sword, wand
Animals: Lion, horse, scorpion, dragon
Magical Uses: Energy, strength, sex, protection
Goddesses: Brigit, Hestia, Pele, Vesta
Gods: Agni, Horus, Prometheus, Vulcan
Archangel: Michael

She ran her hand down the list of fire correspondences and stopped at animals. "Lion, horse, scorpion, and what's this —*dragon?*" Her face lit up like a bonfire when she pronounced yet another reason we were so compatible. "Says here that fire is used for sex magic. Could come in handy, Alex. Maybe you can bag that Adonis you live with."

"We don't need a spell for that," I muttered.

"What was that?"

I ignored the question. "What else does it say?"

"Fire is also used for protection. Let's see. What do we need for this magic?" Her finger reversed back up the list. "Magical tools include: athame, sword, and wand."

I gasped. "Athame?"

CHAPTER EIGHT

Before heading down to Den of Oddities and Antiquities
to consult with Ava on my new powers, I decided to run
back to the house to retrieve the athame. Toting it
around Manhattan in my purse probably wasn't the best idea, but
I figured if it was half as powerful as Greer described it, that blade
wouldn't let anyone but me lay a hand on it. God help the
mugger who tried to grab my bag.

I hadn't pulled it out of the box since the night it arrived on
Greer's doorstep, wrapped in black velvet inside a neat brown
package with a note from Alasdair Templeton—the high priest of
my mother's former coven—telling me to come home. Home for
the Fitheach clan was Ireland, and as much as I wanted to see my
mother's homeland, it wouldn't be on the arm of Templeton.

I headed for the door, but Rhom stepped in front of me
before I reached it. "Going somewhere?" he asked.

"Why? Am I under house arrest?"

"I've got my orders, Alex. The boss doesn't want you leaving
the house to go anywhere but the bookstore."

"Well, he's your boss, not mine." I glanced around the foyer
and living room. "And he's not here, is he?"

He shook his head and sighed. "Jesus, Alex. You just pissed off the head Rogue in the city, and you *want* to go out there with a target on your back? You think Maelcolm isn't waiting for you to do something stupid like stroll down the street and say 'Here I am. Come and get me'?"

I smiled sweetly. "That's what I have you for, Rhom. Besides, I've got my own weapons now, and he knows that better than anyone because he's the one who introduced me to them. So why don't you just come with me?"

"Come with you where?"

I opened my mouth to tell him that Katie and I were going downtown to Den of Oddities and Antiquities but stopped. The look on his face told me he had no intention of letting me leave, and I didn't have the time or patience for a confrontation.

"You're right, Rhom. It's probably a bad idea." I dropped my bag on the chair in the foyer and headed for the kitchen to see what Sophia was cooking. He followed me. Sophia was stirring a pot of soup on the stove.

"Minestrone," she announced as we hovered. "The bread is almost ready." It was a little early for dinner. She nodded to the bowls on the counter, indicating that we could fend for ourselves.

"Let's eat in the dining room," I suggested, grabbing the bowls and spoons and heading for the doorway. I held my breath as Sophia opened the oven door, hoping Rhom would wait and help with the soup pot when the bread was ready. All I needed was a minute or two.

I set the bowls on the table and continued through the other doorway into the foyer. Then I grabbed my purse and quietly opened the front door. Before I could step out and disappear, I felt Rhom's hand on my arm.

"Don't do it," he warned.

I didn't even turn around. I simply willed him back. His hand released my arm, and I could hear him stumble against the table a few feet away from the door. I glanced over my shoulder and felt a bit of guilt from the way he was looking at me. Stuck in place from a force he couldn't see or fight, he stared at me incredulously.

"I'm sorry, Rhom." That was all I could think to say as I continued to hold him back with Isla Kelley's gift. I didn't even realize I was doing it. It was so automatic and effortless that it made me uneasy.

KATIE WAS WAITING outside when I arrived back at Shakespeare's Library.

"We need to get going." I wasn't sure how long the power would last, and the last thing I needed was for Rhom to come barreling around the corner. "Did you bring the book?"

She cocked her head at me like I was a little slow in the noggin. "Really, Alex. You think Ava needs a book called *Wicca for Beginners* to help figure out your powers?"

She was so right it was embarrassing. There were probably dozens of old texts buried in the bowels of Den of Oddities and Antiquities that could clarify everything and whip me into a proper fire witch, and now a mind bender, too.

We hailed a taxi and headed down to the Village. Deadly or not, I was not carrying my mother's athame on the subway, crammed with thousands of commuters heading home with the five o'clock whistle. On the way down I recapped the night I acquired it, and told Katie more about Alasdair Templeton's plan to bring me back to Ireland. She'd met him—for lack of a better word—the day he came to the shop and tried to lure me into taking a raven pendant that could have sealed my fate. Greer used the analogy of signing a contract in blood if I had accepted the necklace. Even Constantine agreed with Greer on that one, and those two never agreed on anything. It seems the pendant came with some pretty heavy strings attached. Willingly accepting it would have made me an indentured servant to the coven from here to eternity—if not longer.

Ava was waiting at the door when we stepped out of the taxi. Since I hadn't called ahead to let her know we were coming, I assumed it was just a coincidence. But as she smiled and held the door open, I knew she was waiting for us.

"How did you know?"

"Know what?" she asked, leading us into the main room of the shop.

"That we were—" I shook my head, muttering to myself. "Why do I bother?"

The late afternoon sun was shining brightly through the tall windows of the second floor, highlighting the old finish of the hundreds of tiny drawers lining the two-story wall. Patinated from a century of use, the wall seemed to breathe with life as if each little drawer were a golden-brown wren waiting to spring into the air and fly around the tall room in a flurry of wings.

"What brings you ladies south today?" Ava asked. "Not that you need a reason to visit." She looked at Katie. "How's that dragon of yours? Behaving?"

"Well, so far I haven't burned down any buildings or made the front page of the *New York Times*."

"Excellent! You let me know if you ever need a little serpent anxiety tonic to keep her in line."

Katie looked amused, glancing at me to mouth the words *dragon Xanax*.

"I'd like to think the two of you just came for a visit, but based on what I'm feeling, there's something important on your minds. So out with it."

I held out my hand, ready to blurt the fact that I could call forth a ball of fire in the center of it. Ava sucked in a sharp lungful of air and stepped closer, fixated on it, anticipating my next words as if she didn't already know what I was about to say.

It took her a moment, but she picked up on it as soon as she saw my outstretched palm.

"You have the fire," she whispered as she slowly reached for my hand. When she made contact with my fingers, I felt a spark buried beneath the skin and muscle, deep within my bones.

"Did you feel it?" I asked.

Ava nodded. "Maeve." Her eyes travelled from my palm to my face. "She's in you."

I nodded back. "Maelcolm told me. He said Isla was in me, too. Said she was some kind of mind bender." I glanced nervously toward the front door. "I think I might have just used that one on Rhom."

"You didn't mention that on the way down," Katie said, looking at the door herself as if suddenly noticing that my constant companion was missing.

"It wasn't intentional. He tried to stop me from leaving the house and it just happened."

Ava ran her index finger over the lines of my palm. "What else did Maelcolm say?"

"He called me 'the trinity.' "

Ava's face went grave. "Tea. We all need a good cup of tea." She motioned to the sofa in the reading nook and then turned toward the back kitchen. "I'll make some."

Suddenly feeling my legs go weak, I deposited myself on the sofa while Katie poked around the room. I was used to all the strange and fascinating things that occupied the shop's walls and shelves, but it would take Katie many more visits before her senses would acclimate.

She flipped through an old cardboard box on the display case and pulled out something neatly wrapped in a clear plastic sleeve. It was an original photograph of a man with a head of hair and a beard that looked like white cotton candy, teased away from his head in all directions. He was sitting inside a circle edged with runes. *Gerald Brosseau Gardner, 1956* was written in neat, slanted script on a white sticker in the bottom corner of the sleeve. "I'm definitely buying this." The price tag on the back of the sleeve sobered her shopping spree. "Then again, maybe not."

Ava came back in the room carrying a tray with a teapot and three cups. "Chamomile with a little skullcap and lavender. Good for the nerves." She set the tray on the coffee table and poured our cups. "Tea, Katie?" Katie carefully placed the photo back in the box. "Are you a follower?" Ava asked. "Of Gardner?"

"Not really. I collect old photographs, though. This one is pretty amazing."

"Then it's yours. My gift for being such a good friend to Alex."

Katie glanced at the rare photograph. "Ava, it's too much. I wouldn't feel right about taking it."

"Nonsense. I have boxes of those things. Gardner, Doreen Valiente, Leland. I have some very interesting Aleister Crowley images. I'll have to dig them out and let you rummage through them sometime."

"Thank you, Ava." She slipped the generous gift into her bag and joined us in the reading nook.

"Now, back to this business about the trinity," Ava said. "Why didn't you tell me about this sooner? I'm surprised I haven't picked up on it already. I sat at Greer's table and told you the story about how your mother and I met, and you never once thought it important enough to mention that you had the fire in you? Even after I told you about Maeve using it on my attacker?"

"The fire. Is that what it's called?" I snorted.

My humor was not shared. "The fire, fire witch, bloody flame thrower: call it whatever you like, Alex. It's a pretty powerful gift —and damn dangerous if you don't have a clue how to use it." She stared at me for a few uncomfortable seconds and then shifted her attention to Katie, who was watching our exchange with bated breath. "Have you seen it?"

Katie shook her head. "She tried to bring it out yesterday

afternoon but nothing happened. I was kind of glad, seeing how we were in a shop full of flammables."

"Katie! You should have said something if it made you so uncomfortable. I wasn't going to burn the place down."

"As I said," Ava reiterated. "The power of fire can be dangerous—downright disastrous in the hands of a novice." I opened my mouth to protest but she put the kibosh on it. "And you, my sweet girl, are a novice. Lucky for you, I can help." She glanced at the clock hanging next to the three-eyed boar head. "Reinforcements should be walking through the door any minute now."

"Who? *Patrick?*"

"Don't be ridiculous, Alex."

"You can't be serious." Sheepish, mild-mannered Melanie Harris was the only other person I knew who was a staple at Den of Oddities and Antiquities. Surely a woman who struggled with permission to tie her own shoes wasn't whom Ava was referring to as "reinforcements." The only fire in Melanie's belly was from heartburn or too much spicy food. But then I remembered the night she and Ava knocked on Greer's door with a metal box— the one containing the coven's life force. It was the night we returned from Cornell University after paying a visit to Dr. Oxford, the night the package arrived containing my mother's athame. Melanie nearly came out of her chair that night when I asked why the coven wouldn't let my mother leave, why someone else couldn't take her place. Maybe that's the Melanie Ava was referring to.

"I've never been more serious." She frowned at me, clearly recognizing my judgement of a woman she trusted completely, and I barely knew. "There is no one who knew Maeve Kelley better than Melanie Harris. Not even me. She may come across as a little meek—well, skittish at times—but don't underestimate her. She can be quite powerful when she's in her element. She's a fire witch like your mother. They learned from the same teacher —Isla Kelley."

I knew they grew up together, but I would have never thought that Melanie was as gifted as my mother. I just couldn't quite reconcile the idea of Melanie as a mentor.

Ava took a seat next to me and put her cup on the table. "Hold out your hands." I held them out, palms down. She took them both and turned them palms up, examining them individually. "You're right dominant."

"What does that mean?"

"It means your power comes from your right hand. That's very interesting since Maeve's power came from her left."

My mother was left-handed. As a child I didn't understand why she always wrote and led with the wrong hand. I just assumed everyone was supposed to use their right. I just assumed she was doing it to entertain me. Even when I'd laugh and tell her she was doing it wrong, she'd laugh along with me and awkwardly switch to her right. I was a five-year-old. I guess it was easier to play along than to explain the left hemisphere of the brain or the presence of the C gene.

The front door chimed as Melanie walked in carrying a box. She headed for the display case and slid it on the counter. "Hello, ladies. Found this outside next to the door."

I stared nervously at the box that wasn't outside the shop when we arrived, because strange packages were usually bad news.

"Why would someone leave a package outside when we're clearly open?" Ava asked, looking at Melanie with her own suspicious eyes.

Melanie paused before turning back toward the box. "Well, let's find out."

Everyone in the room seemed to hold their breath while Melanie pulled back the top flap. She peered inside and then took a step back.

"God, don't tell me there's something alive in there," I said.

"More kittens?" Katie commented only half-jokingly.

Melanie glanced at Ava, a silent message clearly transpiring between the two of them. Ava nodded her head and Melanie reached inside. "There's a note." Melanie opened it and read it aloud. "It just says, 'You forgot your gift.' There's no signature." She reached back in and carefully pulled out the contents of the box: a shiny black ball the size of a grapefruit.

I sank deeper into the sofa, instinctively trying to put a few more inches between me and that thing. And then I gained my confidence back and jumped to my feet. "Maelcolm gave it to me the night Greer got me out of that house. It's some kind of weird snow globe. I swear I saw something alive inside of it." The pressure in the shop seemed to drop as I sensed a storm coming. "I threw it on the sofa when his *butler* walked into the room."

"No, Alex!" Ava's arm shot out to block me from approaching it.

Melanie held the ball at arm's length as it began to vibrate and grow hot in her hand. I could hear words coming from her mouth, barely discernible words in a language other than English.

I glanced at Katie. Nothing really scared her, but at that moment I could feel the adrenaline exuding from her pores. If the excess energy in the room didn't dissipate soon, I feared we would all get a good look at her dragon. By the look on Ava's face, she was thinking the same thing. She rested her hand on Katie's thigh, trying to calm the beast waking from the threat. But it was the instinct to shield me that would set Katie off. I was her village. I was the one her dragon would try to protect.

Melanie's hand began to shake from the force of the ball as the vibrations intensified into a boil of kinetic energy. She howled as the heat burned her palm, the ball dropping from her retreating hand and descending toward the floor. It shattered, sending black shards flying in all directions, shards that flew with glimmering light that turned into soft, feathered wings.

The room went up in a collective gasp as hundreds of tiny

black ravens spilled from the center of the broken ball and ascended around the room into the second story. I looked up at the birds spinning into a halo, flying faster until all I could see was a black ring filling the space above us.

"Take cover, ladies. It's about to rain," Ava said calmly, grabbing my hand and pulling me toward the back kitchen. I reached for Katie's hand but she was transfixed, frozen as her eyes turned a vibrant green—dragon green.

"For fuck's sake, Katie. Not now," I muttered.

Ava saw it, too. "Leave her, Alex! They won't bother with her. It's you they want."

"Katie!" I screamed one last time, trying to break the spell and get her to move. She took a sharp breath and jerked her face in my direction. Her eyes flashed between blue and green as the dragon fought to surface. "Come on!"

The Katie side of her won as Melanie swept her up and the four of us ran through the cloth veil that served as the only door to the back room.

"That sheet isn't going to stop them," I said.

Melanie was the last one into the kitchen. She tore the thin cloth from the rod and threw her hand up toward the doorway, palm out with her fingers splayed wide. A few seconds later she expelled a relieved breath and brushed her bangs from her eyes. Ava seemed relaxed, too. I looked back and forth between them, wondering if I was the only one who saw a problem with the exposed door.

"Calm down, Alex." Ava went for the cabinet and pulled out a handful of small containers. "Backup magic," she said. "I learned a long time ago to never rely solely on those drawers in the wall. You never know when you'll find yourself holed up in the kitchen."

"You should see what I have stashed under my bathroom sink," Melanie added. "And I always have some blessed thistle in my purse. A smart witch is a prepared witch."

I was about to reiterate our dilemma when a loud noise drew everyone's attention toward the doorway. A large black bird stopped in mid-flight, splayed against some invisible barrier like an inkblot on a clear card. Another one hit. Within seconds, the entire doorway was one big display of birds smashing into and bouncing off the invisible wall Melanie must have thrown up.

"Hurry, Ava!" Melanie pleaded. "The barrier won't hold much longer."

Ava worked faster with the herbs, pouring them into a mortar bowl and grinding them roughly with the pestle. She raised her hand to her mouth and gripped the large malachite ring with her teeth. The stone opened on a hinge and a cloud of yellow dust emptied from the ring, settling into the bowl. As she continued to grind the concoction of herbs and dust, the smell of sulfur filled the air and a blue flame licked at her fingers as they gripped the pestle. Without looking away from the bowl, she extended her hand. "Give it to me." Katie and I looked at each other, not knowing what *it* was. "The athame!"

"How did you know—"

"Now, Alex!" Ava demanded.

I pulled my mother's athame from my purse and quickly unwrapped it from the velvet cloth. My butterfingers lost hold of it as I nervously reach toward Ava's waiting hand. It hit the floor and slid to her feet. Without missing a beat, she picked it up and drew a deep breath before splaying her left hand on the maple counter. With her right, she jammed the tip of the blade into the wood surface between her pinkie and ring fingers.

"No!" I screamed as the blade came down with a neat crunch, severing her pinkie just below the top knuckle. She winced and let out a muffled moan, and then proceeded with her recipe for saving us.

A loud thump got everyone's attention as Katie hit the floor.

"She's fine," Melanie assured me. "Just fainted." She rushed to Ava's side and tended to the tipless finger while Ava kept working.

"Blood is a powerful ingredient, but bone, now that will super-charge any spell."

The invisible wall was beginning to concave toward us as more ravens flew into it. Over and over they hit and bounced back, their wings breaking but still managing to propel them back into the barrier like limping machines.

"Here." Ava handed Melanie the bowl. "You'll have to do it. I'm spent."

Melanie took the mortar bowl and stalked toward the door-way. I'd never seen such an expression on her face; anger and a vicious pleasure for what she was about to do. "Here, little birdies," she taunted. "Take this back to that old fart and tell him he's met his match." She threw the contents of the bowl head-on into the breaching barrier. It released into the air in a cloud of fine red confetti, cutting into the black feathers like tiny little knives dissecting their flesh. The sound they made was terrifying, a sea of banshees wailing into the wind.

Katie stirred on the floor just in time to see the birds recede and then disappear. I went to help her up and then looked point-edly at Melanie. "Old fart?"

Ava heaved a sigh of relief as she collapsed into one of the kitchen chairs. She unwound the cloth wrapped around her wounded hand and noted the regeneration that was already taking place at the missing tip.

"God, Ava. Your finger." I gently pulled back her intact fingers to get a look at the damage. The bleeding had stopped and the tip was almost restored.

"Don't worry, dear. I told you once I have some pretty powerful blood running through my veins. Who's afraid of a little cut?" She tossed the bloody rag in the trash can and stood back up, glancing at Melanie with a look of exhausted resolve in her eyes. "In a million years I would have never thought I'd see the day." She stopped and shook her head. "But now that I have I can't say that it's that much of a surprise."

"We'll have to pull out the big guns from now on," Melanie added. "No more dime store magic."

I looked back and forth between the two women, waiting for one of them to tell me what the hell was going on. Katie recovered, standing there with her mouth gaping open and her bright blue eyes flashing with the excitement of a child who'd just ridden her first roller coaster.

Ava did the honors. "It seems that Alasdair Templeton will work every possible angle to get to you. Arthur Richmond, Isabetta Falcone, and now he's even lowered himself to partnering with the Rogues. That black globe was his Trojan horse. Clever bastard."

"I think you need some rest, Alex," Melanie suggested.

"Yes," Ava agreed.

"I'm not resting," I argued. "What about Katie?"

"Strong willed as ever." Ava held up her hand and blew a small cloud of dust directly into my eyes. "But you will rest. I'll see Katie home myself."

Before I could bat the dust away from my eyes and argue more, the room faded away.

CHAPTER NINE

I woke in a hot sweat, an atomic bomb of heat radiating from my chest and across my arms toward the tips of my fingers. I kicked the sheet off my legs and pushed away from the damp mattress at my back. But it was skin I was pressed against, with arms pulling me back as I resisted. My airway constricted as I panicked, and a sharp pain struck my chest and shot all the way up to the center of my forehead. My arms flailed around the darkness, searching for a weapon. I kicked him and went over the edge of the bed, landing headfirst on the floor. As the pain lessened and my eyes began to adjust to the dark room, I saw him standing over me, a large form with one foot planted between my knees.

My panic flared again, the memory of the shadow in Central Park towering over my paralyzed body. Something was burning. I was on fire. I looked for the source of the heat, and a bright glow radiated from the center of my right hand.

"Don't do it," I heard him say.

The glow flared into a ball of flames, and I remembered what I was. With my left hand, I pushed myself up from the floor and hurled the fire at him. He dodged it and the room went up like a bonfire, claiming the edges of the drapes and igniting the fringe of the rug beneath me. The fire illuminated the room, and I saw Greer staring back at me as if I were a stranger to him.

"Why?" he whispered.

My head dropped back to the floor as black dots filled my peripheral vision and smoke choked my lungs.

MY HAND WAS TINGLING when my eyes reopened. The lights in the room were on and Bear was licking my right hand—my fire hand. The memory of the room on fire catapulted me to my feet, but when I looked around everything was intact. There were no burnt drapes, and the rug was unsinged.

I sat on the edge of the bed when I saw Greer sitting in the chair. "Was I hallucinating?"

"No," he answered. "You set the room on fire."

I didn't bother to ask how he'd managed to remove all traces of the fire. Even the smell of smoke was gone.

He glanced at my right hand. "I haven't seen such an impressive flame thrower since your mother, only she wouldn't have missed."

"Good thing I did." A short, nervous laugh escaped my mouth, followed by a shuddering breath.

The annoyance in his eyes softened. "You thought I was him."

I could tell by the way his eyes turned away that it disturbed him, me mistaking the feel of his skin for Daemon's. It disturbed me, too. There was nothing remotely similar about them, and regardless of how many times I rejected it, Greer's touch could never repulse me. But it terrified me, made me weak and feel like I was spinning out of control, like I'd scatter into a billion particles of dust if I allowed myself to feel it. If I let him in and he left me, I'd die. In a cruel way, I think I was as crippled by Greer as I was by the memory of Daemon.

"I would never leave you, Alex." His eyes flicked back to mine. "Never."

He was reading my thoughts again, because I let him.

He rose from the chair and came toward me in his old pair of jeans, thinning at the knees and hanging loosely at his hips. He stopped a few feet away and stood there gazing down at me, waiting for something. The silence was unbearable. I focused on the spot just above his button, where the fabric ended and his bare skin began, and it occurred to me that he was waiting for permission to touch me.

I trusted my heart for once, and nodded my head. My face pressed into his skin as he pulled me to my feet and crushed me to his chest.

"If we do this," I said, fighting back that familiar devil telling me to run, "promise me you'll break my heart kindly if you ever leave me. Do something really unattractive to make me want to leave first. Start picking your nose or stop bathing."

His chest shuddered as he quietly laughed. "How about if I grow a beer belly and knock out a few front teeth?" he offered. The laughing stopped, and he raised my chin to look at my face. "You still don't get it, do you?" His scent bloomed around me, easing me as my body reacted to it. Then he brought his mouth closer, barely touching mine. The back of my thighs met the edge of the mattress, and then I was a languid mess of a girl lying on the bed under the weight of a god. His hand wrapped around my waist and slid up the inside of my shirt, pushing the fabric over my skin until it reached the underside of my arms. Rising to his knees, he gazed down and waited for a sign, anything that said *continue*. My arms rose above my head, and with a swift motion he slid my shirt off and inhaled sharply as his eyes walked over my bare skin, stopping at the intersection of my breasts still trapped beneath the lace covering them. My breath caught as his fingers released the front clasp.

"Say it," he murmured.

At first I wasn't sure what he was asking for. But as I gazed at his soft mouth and the movement of his chest as he strained to control his breathing, I understood. There would be no question about consent tonight.

"Yes," I whispered, closing my eyes and waiting for him to strike, a mouse welcoming the hungry hawk. But instead of feeling his body ease against mine, I felt the dip of the mattress and the cold separation of him moving farther away. My heart sank at the realization that my worst fear had come true. At the last moment he'd changed his mind, seen me for what I was.

I opened my eyes and saw him standing halfway across the room, putting a good ten feet between us. His stare was just as intense, but it was more cautious than heated. I pulled the lace back over my breasts, securing the clasp with clumsy fingers. My eyes remained glued to a bright blue swirl in the rug as I swung my legs over the edge of the bed and retrieved my shirt from the floor. Then I sat quietly and waited for him to say something. He could probably still smell Daemon on me. But I had to give him credit for at least trying to get past it.

"Is that what you see?" he asked.

He came closer but stopped when my head snapped up. "I see a man who had a half-naked girl under him a minute ago, and now he's looking at me like he has no idea how to get out of this room fast enough." A wall of tears was about to explode from my eyes, and the last thing I wanted was for that to happen before he left the room. "I'm humiliated enough, Greer. Just leave. *Please.*"

He swallowed hard before answering. "Alex, you tensed up like a cornered animal, like you were afraid of me." The caution in his face eased and his voice seemed mildly wounded. "You think of him every time I touch you. Don't you?"

The room was shaking. I looked down at my fingernails digging deeply into the tough skin of my palms, and I realized it wasn't the room—it was me. I shot to my feet as a flood of adrenaline blew a hole through my main artery and flooded my chest. At least that's what it felt like. "Get out!" I screamed. The walls were moving in, sliding toward the center of the room like some torturous chamber preparing to squeeze the life out of me. I ran toward the mirror over the dresser and gazed at the girl with the crazy eyes. Then I smashed my palm into my reflection, sending a series of cracks rippling across the surface. A long, pointed shard fell on the dresser. I grabbed it and turned. "Get out!" I screamed again. "I hate you! I *fucking* hate you!"

I ran toward him, the sharp piece of mirror tearing into my skin as I clutched it and aimed it at his chest. He grabbed my hand, cutting into his own skin as he wrestled the weapon from my blood-smeared fingers.

"Stop it, Alex! I'm not him!"

After disarming me, he turned me loose on the room and stood stoically watching while I demolished it. I started with the walls, pulling the framed paintings from their anchors and throwing them to the floor, dotting the now empty spots with dents from my fists. Then I cleared the top of every surface in the room, smashing an irreplaceable porcelain vase and a few other beautiful things that I would regret destroying later. The drapes came down next. He must have come to his senses as I eyed the bare window and searched the room for something to throw through it.

"Enough." He grabbed me around the waist and pulled me against him. "Enough," he repeated in a whisper. "He's not here. But I am." He spun me around and cupped my face with his hands. "Look at me."

I looked in his eyes and felt such shame for not stopping it. I lay in Daemon's bed and let him do it. I never screamed. I never fought. I never said *no*. I just closed my eyes and thought about everything I was about to lose the moment he pushed inside of me. I thought about all the reasons why it was my fault: my carelessness for not paying attention the night Daemon grabbed me in Battery Park, my carelessness for thinking I could cross Central Park in the dark all those months ago. But the most careless act of all was coming back here, to New York.

He studied my eyes and waited for me to say something. I supposed he thought I'd finally released all my rage and everything would be better. No more secrets between us. Nothing more to hide behind. But if that were true, how could he possibly see me the same way?

"God, Greer." My temporary resilience was starting to crumble again. "I don't know how you can look at me like that. How you can stand to touch me?"

"If anyone is to blame for this, it's me," he said, letting go of my waist. "I'm the one who should have stood my ground and made you stay home that night. I'm the one who let him slip past us at Battery Park." He swallowed the lump obstructing his throat. "But you know what I'll never forgive myself for? I'll never forgive myself for not finding you first. I should have dropped everything the day Patrick called me and told me you were back in New York. But I didn't want to scare you away. We'd waited twenty-one years, and the thought of you running again —" He dropped his hands and turned away. "Maybe if Constantine had found you in the park sooner."

I could hear the loathing in his voice for admitting that Constantine had found me first. Patrick was the one who told Greer I was back in New York, the morning I went the Den of Oddities and Antiquities. But it was Constantine who found me in Central Park that night. He just dragged his feet a little too long before sharing that information with Greer. Daemon got to me first.

I cautiously touched the round of his shoulder. "The Rogues knew I was here, Greer. Just like everyone else. If it wasn't in Central Park that night, Daemon would have attacked me somewhere else."

His head snapped around. "Not if you were in my house!"

I stumbled back, his sudden rage jolting me.

He laughed in a short burst. "And now I've frightened you when all I want to do is love you."

The words made my heart leap and then terrified me a second later. I focused on the former emotion and took my own leap of faith before I lost my nerve. "I want that, too." It was a whisper so quiet I wasn't sure if he'd heard me.

His face went still, a bit of hope in his eyes. "What? Say it again, Alex." A deep baritone surfaced in his voice. "Louder."

Love is a scary thing for those who don't know what to do with it or how to graciously accept it. I steeled myself and fought the fear making its way back up my spine. "I said, I want that too."

A thousand years must have passed as I stood a couple of feet away from him and waited to see if I'd just exposed myself to complete and utter heart shatter. When he said nothing, I felt my legs go weak, and a wave of grief that threatened to knock me off my feet. I'd somehow gotten it wrong, misunderstood him.

"God," I whispered, turning away. He hooked me around my waist before I could bolt, and then began to lift my shirt an inch at a time, giving me ample opportunity to object. I let him continue. Piece by piece he stripped me, slowly and methodically until I was naked against him. Then he swept me off my feet and carried me to the bed. I was so tired. Too tired for anything more than sleep. If he wanted me, he could have me, but he'd have to fend for himself and make do with the zombie girl in the bed.

He lay me down with my back to him. I listened to his own clothes rustle and fall to the floor. Then he climbed into the bed behind me, molding his limbs around my body.

And then we slept.

CHAPTER TEN

He was still there. When I reached behind my back, he was still lying behind me. A bolt of heat shot through me at the feel of his warm palm gripping mine.

"I'm not going anywhere," he murmured against my neck. "No matter how old—or fat–you get, I'll never leave you," he teased.

I punched him playfully in his right kidney, thankful for the lightening of the mood "Me fat? Never."

The sudden reality of what he'd said began to sink in. The thought had never occurred to me before, but his joking about growing old wasn't a joke at all. I'm sure he didn't mean it, but he was right. I would grow old while he never aged a day. When I was eighty, he'd still be in his prime, craving the touch of younger women but committed to his promise to never leave me. What on earth was I thinking? How could I do that to him?

I tensed when he released my hand and wrapped it around my waist to pull me deeper into the nook of his body. He noticed it immediately and loosened his grip, rising up on the bed behind me, turning me to look at my face.

"I'm sorry," I apologized, not understanding why I felt the need to. It was this very reason intimacy made me so uncomfortable: feeling out of control and having to explain my reaction to being touched. A girl has every right to say no or pull away without having to justify it. But this was Greer. I loved him, and he was probably the most patient man I'd ever met. God knows it would have been easier to give up on me and moved on to someone less complicated.

He sat up, putting a small distance between us. "Don't ever apologize to me again. I want you freely, without fear. If you're not ready, you're not ready." He moved to climb out of the bed. "Let me know when you are. I'll wait."

"Don't leave." I grabbed his arm, meeting his intense gaze, but still a bit shaken by the revelation of his immortality and my very real inevitable death.

"Thank you," I said, selfishly suppressing the thoughts and choosing instead to live in the moment.

"For what?"

"For having the patience of a saint and not kicking me out of the bed."

He laughed and cupped the side of my face. "As if I could."

My mind shifted to the evening before, Katie and I going down to Den of Oddities and Antiquities, the black sphere filled with birds and Ava declaring that Templeton was working with the Rogues—my father.

My eyes flew wide. "Jesus, Greer. Ava thinks that Templeton—"

"It's true," he said, anticipating my words. "The coven will align with anyone or anything that will help them get their hands on you, and I suspect Maelcolm's fatherly devotion stops at the foot of greed. He and Templeton will use each other, but I'm sure only one will be left standing after they have you." He gazed at me with conviction and continued. "But that will never happen.

I'll bring the wrath of the gods down on them before that happens."

I shuddered dramatically. "I don't want to talk about it anymore. Not right now. I just want a few hours of peace before we resume saving the world." It was early and I had the late shift at the shop. "Why don't we just stay in bed all morning? I don't have to be at work until this afternoon."

He took an ominously deep breath and ran his hands through his hair, combing it away from his face. "There is nothing on this earth that I would rather do than spend the day in bed with you, but I have an appointment at the club." He hesitated before confessing. "With Isabetta Falcone."

"What?" I pulled away and sat up on my thighs. After everything that had happened at Battery Park—the ambush she'd set up, her alliance with the Rogues—what could he possibly have to discuss with her? And why was she even walking the streets? I figured Greer would have killed her after what she'd done.

"She disappeared. Right after—"

"It's okay, Greer. You can say it. After Daemon took me." I knew we'd never get past it if we couldn't even mention it. The unspoken words would control us. I took his unshaven chin in my hand and looked him squarely in the eye. "Fortunately, I've been blessed with the inability to sink into the depths of despair beyond the length of a good cry." I glanced around the wrecked room. "I've had that cry. Now tell me what's going on."

He nodded once and continued. "She contacted me yesterday. Said she has information about David Oxford. There's a chance he's still alive."

The last time I spoke to Dr. Oxford he was scared to death on the other side of a wall in the basement of the bakery where the Rogues were keeping us, suspicious of the way our captors were looking at him. He believed the vessel containing the prophecy couldn't be seen by the human eye, and he'd been working on something that could possibly locate it, a prism that could be used to reflect a new spectrum of light, rendering it visible. Simple science. Isabetta and her accomplices thought the prisms were embedded in a pair of prototype glasses, but he'd gone to the extreme and had them surgically implanted in his eyes. Lens replacement surgery at its ultimate.

It was my fault that an innocent professor from Cornell University was either dead or about to be, and that was unforgivable. No one blamed me, not Greer, not his men. I doubted the doctor himself would blame me for his unfortunate demise. But I would blame myself until the day I died, and that was something I couldn't live with. But just as important was the need to recover those lenses. Not just because it was our best chance at finding the vessel, but because it was imperative that if we didn't, no one else did either.

"Greer, we need those lenses. And if he's alive, we need to find him before they decide to kill him. We owe him that much."

"Right," he agreed.

"Where and when are you meeting her?" I asked. "I'm going with you."

He climbed off the bed. "I don't think that's wise."

"Why not? I'm in this as deep as you are, Greer. *Deeper*. And I can't hide in this house forever."

"Yes, I know how you feel about house arrest. Rhom is a little ticked off at you."

I winced. "I guess I have some groveling to do. If it makes any difference, it was unintentional. Isla Kelley just came out without warning."

He was still fishing for a reason to keep me away from Isabetta. "We can discuss it over breakfast."

"We can discuss it right now," I countered. "Are you forgetting what I am? What I'm capable of?"

He glanced at the carnage I created the night before: the

broken frames on the floor, the shards of mirror scattered everywhere. "How could I forget?" His eyes trailed down to my right hand, to the cuts that were already healing nicely and the spot where the flame lived under my skin. "I'll have this mess taken care of while we're gone."

"Good. It's settled." I jumped out of bed and headed for the closet. "I'm starving."

He grabbed his Rolex from the dresser and noted the time. "We have a little over an hour before the meeting."

"Make her wait," I sneered. "I want her to know who's in charge."

His brow arched. "Very bold of you, Ms. Kelley. I like this confidence. Just don't get too cocky."

"Oh, let me play with her, Greer. I've earned the right to have a little fun with that traitor."

He collected his clothes scattered across the floor. "I'll grab a shower and meet you downstairs. Unless you'd like to join me?"

"Baby steps, Greer."

He gave me a look that stirred my stomach and then left for his own room. I prayed that Sophia wasn't standing in the hallway. Breakfast would taste better without her glaring at the two of us, judging our morality. I supposed one day her Catholic conditioning would fade and her old pagan liberalism would resurface, but probably not today.

When he was gone, I flipped through the shirts hanging in the closet. For some reason, I wanted to look good for Isabetta. I wanted her to see that she hadn't broken me, that her little betrayal had brought out my beast. Maybe I'd give her a little taste of fire. I considered the flaming-red sheath dress Leda donated to my closet, but settled on a blue blouse and jeans instead. I still had to go to Shakespeare's Library after the meeting and didn't relish the idea of schlepping around the stacks in four-inch heels.

When I emerged from the closet Bear was sitting in front of

it, his tail swishing across the floor in an agitated motion. I glanced down at my naked body and reflexively covered it with the clothes still on the hangers. "Quit staring at me." I couldn't get past the memory of the morning he'd scratched my leg, drawing my blood and then morphing into some *guide* with tribal markings covering his face. "Boundaries, Bear. That's what we need."

His body jerked as a muffled mew came from his mouth. Then he turned and walk through the door that somehow opened on its own.

I dressed and pulled my hair into a tight ponytail. When I caught my reflection in the mirror, I saw what Isabetta would see —a young, unencumbered girl. The hairband landed on the dresser, and I combed my long auburn waves with my fingers. A youthful but bold look with a vibrant red punch. Today Isabetta Falcone would see a woman.

The usual smell of coffee and bacon hit my nose the moment I stepped into the hall. I followed it down the stairs. But as soon as I hit the midway point, a piercing sensation struck me between the eyes, making me cry out from the pain. It was the same pain I'd felt a couple of days earlier when I was having dinner with Rhom. My hand gripped the rail as my legs gave out, stopping me from tumbling down the remainder of the steps. The noise brought the whole house running. Sophia ran into the foyer with a metal spatula in her right hand and Rhom at her side. I looked up at Greer who was staring down at me from the top step.

"*Alex!*" He made it to me in a second and lifted me off the stairs.

My eyes darted around the tall space, looking for the light I'd seen before. There wasn't one. My legs started working again as the pain subsided. I wiggled out of Greer's arms and continued down the steps, heading for the library. All three of them followed me and watched while I ran my eyes across the books, searching the shelf. I found the section. At least I thought I did.

The shelf was filled with books on history: *The History of WWII*, *Collapse of the Roman Empire*, *Vikings: A Concise History*. I ran my fingers over the books, reading each title as if a closer look might render the names of Hans Christian Andersen or the Brothers Grimm.

Greer's hand came from behind me and covered mine, pulling it away from the shelf. "What are you looking for?" he asked in a steady voice as his other hand extracted one of the books I'd been touching.

I turned around, looked at the book in his hand and shook my head. "That's not the one. Where are they?"

"Where are what?"

"The children's books. The fairy tales. Hansel and Gretel and all the other stories in the *Grimm's Fairy Tales* that was sitting right there." I pointed to the spot where I'd plucked the book the other night. "There was a whole row of them. Hans Christian Anderson, Lewis Carroll, *Grimm's*."

He shook his head, a suspicious look on his face. "I don't have any children's books. Or fairy tales."

I cocked my head, irritated by the inference that I was mistaken. "Yes, you do."

"No, I don't. Look for yourself." He nodded behind me toward the expansive shelves covering the wall. "We can walk through every one of them if you'd like."

"Rhom saw them, too," I said.

Greer turned and look at his man, but Rhom just stood there looking uncomfortable. "Rhom?" he asked, waiting for corroboration.

"Christ," Rhom muttered, heading for the shelf. His hand moved across the book spines and then settled on one. I could see from his profile that his eyes were still roaming across the row before he plucked the one titled *The Jacobite Rebellion* and handed it to me. "This is the book you were holding, Alex. I remember seeing the word *Jacobite* on the cover."

He'd looked at the book I was holding that night, but I was fairly sure there was no Hansel or Gretel in the army of Charles Edward Stuart. I stared at the book in disbelief and then glared at him, wondering if this was a joke, payback for yesterday. "Still irritated with me, Rhom?"

"I forgive you, Alex, but I won't lie for you," he said. "That's the book you were holding the other night."

"Well, I'm not crazy."

"I have no doubt that you're perfectly sane." Greer took the book from my hand and placed it back on the shelf. "Now, why don't you tell me what this is all about? And what made you nearly break your neck on the stairs?"

Before I could respond to Greer's slightly condescending question, Rhom piped up and filled in the details. "We were having a perfectly nice discussion over one of Sophia's perfectly nice meals the other night when your little princess here hit the floor. Kind of like she just did on those stairs."

"Thanks, Rhom." I glared at him harder.

Sophia, still standing in the doorway, rolled her eyes. "I keep breakfast warm." She turned back toward the kitchen, shaking her head and grumbling something in Italian.

"Sorry, Sophia," I called after her. "We'll be there in a minute."

"I thought we were past this, Alex. No more secrets." Greer took my hand and squeezed.

"I'm not hiding anything. Like Rhom said, we were having dinner the other night and suddenly this horrible ringing started piercing my ears and blurring my vision. I just heard it again on the stairs, only this time there was no light."

"What light?" Greer seemed a little annoyed now. But seeing how it happened while he was in the middle of one of his notorious disappearing acts, *said* annoyance was hardly justifiable.

"There was this ball of light bouncing around the room. It led me to the library and settled right on that shelf. I was holding a copy of *Grimm's Fairy Tales* in my hand. Hans Christian Andersen, Lewis Carroll—they were all right there."

"Since I happen to know that you're dealing with a full deck," Greer said, glancing one last time at the shelf, "it sounds like someone's sending you a message."

"Or some*thing*," added Rhom, looking at me sympathetically. "I don't think you're crazy either, Alex."

"Come on." Greer took my hand and headed for the door. "We can talk about this later. Let's just have a nice breakfast before heading over to the club. As you said, Isabetta can wait." It pleased me to think of her pacing the floor of the club in one of her power suits, tapping her bejeweled fingernails against the bar, infuriated that Greer wasn't bending over backward to accommodate her.

Ian was standing in the foyer when we came out of the library. Next to him was a sour-faced Sophia, her hand welded to her hip as she held him in place with her stare. "You have a visitor," she announced wryly.

"Ian." Greer greeted his specter colleague with suspicion, nodding his head toward the dining room. "You're just in time for breakfast." His hand tightened briefly around mine. "My apologies. I keep forgetting. I hope you don't mind if we eat while you explain why you're here. We're late for a meeting."

"No rush," I said, smirking. "Isabetta can wait all morning for all I care."

Ian smirked back when he heard her name. "Then I've come at just the right time."

Sophia went back to the kitchen to retrieve breakfast while we headed into the dining room. She returned with a platter of food and snatched the plate sitting in front of Ian.

"What is it with you two?" I asked, reacting to Sophia's obvious hostility toward our guest. "God, you're acting like an old married couple."

"You're right," she conceded, heading back to the kitchen.

She returned with the French press, smiling sweetly. "Coffee, Mr. Ian?"

He smiled drolly but didn't reply, choosing instead to ignore his nemesis and get on with the reason for his visit. "A little blonde bird flew into Maelcolm's castle last night."

Greer hesitated and then proceeded with his sip of coffee. "Isabetta?"

"That's the birdie."

"And you know this how?" he asked, cutting into his waffle as if the fact that Isabetta was still working with the Rogues and was about to meet with us was business as usual.

"I was doing my scheduled sweep of his abode and got lucky."

"He can't see you?" I asked.

His sultry brown eyes shifted to mine. "I'm only detectable if I choose to be. Isn't that right, Greer?"

"Yes. That's quite a talent you have. It's also the reason you're on my payroll. Now, tell me what they said."

"Payroll?" Ian smiled mirthfully. "You mean I can expect a check for my services?"

"For crying out loud," Rhom interjected. "Just tell us what you know."

Ian exhaled an imaginary breath from his incorporeal lungs. "Unfortunately, they adjourned their conversation to Maelcolm's war room."

"What's the war room?" I asked.

"The room with the red door. The one room even I can't penetrate, and believe me it's very difficult to keep me out when I wish to enter. Whatever they do in that room must be pretty damned secretive to go to such lengths to throw up that type of a ward—the kind that can drain you to the brink of death."

"And you thought it necessary to pay me a visit versus picking up a phone to tell me basically nothing?" Greer asked. "You are capable of holding a phone, correct?"

"Yes, but that would deprive me of the pleasure of Sophia's company." His eyes swiveled to hers as she stood in the doorway listening to his spiel. "And I wouldn't call it *nothing*, Greer. You're about to walk into a meeting with the enemy, and now you know who she was in bed with last night, so to speak."

CHAPTER ELEVEN

W hen we walked into Crusades, I could hear Isabetta's heels clacking impatiently against the terrazzo floor. I doubt she was used to being kept waiting, and since we were thirty-five minutes late and she was still there, whatever she wanted to talk to Greer about must have been damned important. I glanced around the room for her hench-man, Demitri, but she'd come alone.

"Where the fuck have you been, Sinclair?" she snarled as Greer approached her.

He glanced at his watch. "Are we late?"

At the word *we* her eyes darted around the room, stopping when she saw me standing at the end of the bar. A smile slid up one side of her face. Apparently I had a knack for diverting her attention. One of these days I'd use that little skill to make her walk right into oncoming traffic. Payback for selling me out and practically handing me over to the Rogues—to Daemon. But right now we needed her. If she could lead us to Dr. Oxford, she had value. All bets were off after that.

"What's the matter, Isabetta? Surprised to see me?" I almost added that she must have known that I was back with Greer, seeing how she was with Maelcolm the night before. I bit my tongue for the sake of the doctor.

Her eyes softened with heat as she perused my breasts and then dropped them below my waist.

Really, Isabetta.

The woman had absolutely no discretion when it came to what she wanted. I guess what the Rogues had offered her was more tempting than what I could give her. But I'm sure she thought she could have both in the end. I doubt she knew Maelcolm was my father, and I'm sure in her twisted mind she thought they'd discard me once they had the vessel, right into her waiting hands.

I glanced at Greer. He seemed less blasé about the innuendo she was throwing at me now than he was the night she propositioned me with her knee under a table in Little Italy. Of course, that was before he'd staked his claim on me. I smiled faintly, reassuring him that I was well aware of her motives and not the least bit threatened.

"*Now* can I get you a drink?" Thomas offered Isabetta, apparently for the second time. She rebuked him with a sniff. "Alex? Would you like a drink?"

"Thank you, Thomas, but I think it's a little early for alcohol."

He leaned into the bar and nodded toward Isabetta. "That one could use a few shots. Give the floor a break from those icepicks on the bottom of her shoes."

"Stick it up your ass, Romeo," she shot back at him.

"Now, now Isabetta. This is my castle," Greer warned. "I was a gentleman in yours, and I expect you to be a lady in mine."

Her pupils flashed wide as her manicured nails curled into her palms. She caught herself and managed a fake smile. "Fine. But next time we meet I'd appreciate a little promptness."

"Fair enough," he conceded before getting to the point. "Why are we here?"

Isabetta took a measured step toward him, straightening her cropped jacket with one hand and smoothing her pale blonde hair at the temple with the other. "We're here because I have something you need." Her cocky grin would have been irritating if it wasn't so pathetic, as if we didn't already know exactly what her angle was. "I know where Dr. Oxford is." Her head jiggled back and forth as her jaw cocked to the left. "Play your cards right and I'll lead you straight to him."

"Is he alive?" I blurted out. I don't know why. If he were dead, she'd lie about it.

"Of course he's alive." She eyed me like I was an idiot. "And by the way, those ridiculous glasses he was carrying at Battery Park were cheap fakes."

Yeah, no shit.

"Really?" I said, glancing at Greer. "I guess he fooled us."

She just stood there looking mean and accusatory. My guess was she was wondering if we already knew that the glasses were a ruse. I displayed my best poker face while Greer and Thomas cocked their brows in mock surprise.

I approached the next question as delicately as possible, careful not to mention his eyes. I wasn't about to give her or the Rogues any help in figuring out that the real lenses he'd developed were implanted in his irises. If they had figured it out, David Oxford would be blind—at the least—or dead.

"Has he been hurt?" I asked. "Is he intact?" A more appropriate word escaped me.

Greer discreetly shifted his eyes to mine. *Intact? Really?*

The question seemed to confuse Isabetta. "You mean did they torture him? Like cut off his..." She waved her hand around her crotch area.

"Oh, *God* no!" I blurted.

"Don't worry, your little pussy doctor is just fine." Her mean expression returned. "But if he doesn't talk soon, there's no guarantee."

"What's it going to cost us?" Greer asked, interrupting the line of questioning.

Her eyes wandered around the room, taking in the elaborate bar and the expanse of the club. "Fancy place you got here, Greer. I could take you for a lot of money. But I don't need money." Her expression hardened, a bitterness constricting her lips into a scowl. "I need power. Cut me in on the prophecy."

What was she thinking? Did she think the power of the prophecy was some tangible thing we could divide up and hand over to her?

"Jesus, Isabetta," Greer began. "It must be uncomfortable."

"What the fuck are you talking about?"

"That neck of yours. The way it whips back and forth between angles. If you're not careful, one day it's going to snap."

Isabetta had the worst temper I'd ever seen in a human being. I could almost see the steam coming out of her ears as she took a lunging step toward Greer, foolishly thinking she could strike him. I almost laughed out loud at the thought, but that impulse was stymied by the sudden images jarring my mind. I'm not sure how I knew it, but I was getting the images straight from Isabetta's conniving little head.

"How—"

Greer looked at me when he heard me start to speak, sensing my strange discomfort. I gazed back at him intently. *Of all the times not to read my mind, Greer.* Any other time he'd be in my head, siphoning my thoughts. Something was keeping him out, and it wasn't me.

A panoramic picture kept flashing in front of me: a green wall covered with maps and photographs of children; a long table with a chair at the head, ornately carved with the claws of a lion; a cage with iron bars; a red door.

My head whipped toward Greer and then back to Isabetta. It was Maelcolm's war room, the one Ian mentioned that morning.

Back off, you traitorous bitch, I sent back to her.

Isabetta flew backward as if a rope around her waist had yanked her off her feet, hitting the floor in an unattractive heap of flailing limbs, her carefully swept hair losing its pins and flopping around her shoulders. Stunned and confused, she regained her bearings and climbed back to her feet.

"Who the fuck pushed me?" she spat, twirling around to see if someone was behind her.

I did.

Her eyes darted to mine as the unspoken words were sent straight into her head. She actually heard it. I could tell by the way she was looking at me, trying to figure out how I'd spoken without moving my lips.

I decided to try it again, only this time I'd have a little fun with her. *Dance!*

Her hips began to swivel and gyrate to some imaginary music, a horrified scowl stretching across her face. I almost lost it, catching my laugh before it blew up into a full-fledged roar. Greer slowly turned to look at me and then back at Isabetta who was dancing her way around the room, tears streaming down her face, wailing from the humiliation and the fear of not knowing what was happening. For a second I felt sorry for her, but then I remembered what she was, what she'd done to me.

"Alex?" Greer whispered.

I nodded my head with my eyes still trained on Isabetta. *Stop.* She fell to the floor and just laid there, still and comatose.

"What the fuck just happened?" Thomas asked, staring at Isabetta's limp form in the middle of the dance floor.

Greer's eyes were glued to mine. "I think Alex is getting the hang of her new skills."

"Jesus, Greer." The thought of what I'd just done to Isabetta gave me a rush and terrified me at the same time. Stopping Rhom in his tracks was one thing, but manipulating Isabetta

Falcone into a dancing bear was far more impressive. It was easy as pie. A little too easy for my comfort. What if I got pissed off at a stranger on the street or a rude customer who came into the bookstore? My mind went back to Rolph Milford, a nasty customer I nearly got myself fired over a few months back. "You have to teach me how to control this. What if I kill someone for bumping into me on the street? Sidewalk road rage. God, Greer. I don't want this."

"Easy, Alex." He glanced cautiously over my shoulder at Thomas. "Calm down before someone else gets hurt." The two of them locked eyes for a moment and then began to snicker. Before I knew it, they were both wheezing with laughter.

I was horrified. "You think this is funny? You think this is *funny*?"

Greer composed himself and pulled me into his chest. "No, Alex. There is nothing funny about it."

"It's just the image of Isabetta—" Thomas started laughing again, unable to finish his sentence.

Greer released me and stepped back to size up his new project. "I guess that means another trip to the CTC. Right, Thomas?"

The CTC—Central Training Center—was their version of a gym. It was the one place I dreaded because every time I ended up there, I got cut.

"You're not getting me anywhere near that place," I declared.

"Fine," Greer agreed, glancing at Isabetta's still form. "But don't come crying to me when you do something impulsive."

"Greer," I began, squashing the humor with a darker subject, "I think I know where Dr. Oxford is."

"How do we know this isn't a trap and Ian hasn't been working for Maelcolm all along?" Thomas asked.

It was midafternoon and I had two choices: get ready for

work, or beg Katie to cover for me while we went off to save Dr. Oxford from my father's infamous war room. Sophia came into the library with a tray of gorgeous sandwiches, her ears perking up to catch fragments of our conversation.

"Thank you, Sophia." Greer picked up half a pastrami and took a bite, chewing slowly while contemplating the lead.

"Why would Ian lie?" I asked, choosing a colorful tomato and mozzarella panini from the tray. "I saw that door and that cage plain as day in Isabetta's head. I'd bet my life that the doctor is in that cage."

"Maybe they're all in bed together," Thomas speculated. "Maelcolm, Isabetta, Ian."

Having suppressed her opinion long enough, Sophia offered her own take on the situation. "Ian is a spook, and spooks don't lie. He's dead. Why would he lie?" She shrugged and leaned in, crooking her mouth to the side. "In the old country, we work with a lot of spooks. I never see one lie. Maybe do stupid things. But lie?" She shook her head. "Never."

"Sophia's right," Greer agreed. "Ian has something to gain by working with us—redemption. What does he get out of helping Maelcolm? Another hundred years in that limbo he's stuck in?"

Sophia picked up the empty tray and headed for the door. She stopped at the threshold and looked back at us. "I will do it. I'll go back into that godforsaken place and find the doctor."

Greer nearly choked on his bread. "No, you won't, Sophia."

Her hand found her hip. "You think I can't handle that bastard?" She glanced at me and then turned her eyes back to Greer. "I know how to handle bad men. After what he did to Alex, I could kill him."

"I'll do it," I announced before the argument could escalate. Every face in the room turned to me, like I'd just announced my intent to commit hara-kiri. "I'm the only person in this room who has an open invitation to enter that place."

Greer stared at me in disbelief, like I had six heads. "You're not going anywhere near that house." He waited for me to come to my senses and agree. When I didn't, he stood up, the sandwich slipping from his hand and landing on the rug. "You know what will happen if you walk through his door. Maelcolm is smart and ruthless. I can assure you he won't make the mistake of losing you a second time. And neither will I."

I was used to Greer's possessive caveman mentality, but the look in his eyes was different now. Losing me was different now, but there were many surefire ways to do that. Boxing me in and trying to control me, for one. Denying me the chance to make this right, another. I was his equal and he knew it. But I was also his heart.

"Think about it, Greer. He needs me, so he certainly won't hurt me. If I can make him an offer that checks all his boxes, he'd be a fool to turn it down."

"Now, let's be reasonable here," Thomas chimed in. "Alex, I know you think you're invincible with all your new powers, but you're still wearing your training wheels."

Greer didn't hear a word. He just kept staring at me like I'd eventually come to my senses and back down. We stood still in our own private bubble, having a silent conversation as Thomas and Sophia babbled away in the background. If this had happened even a few weeks earlier, he would have thrown me every curveball he could muster. But things had changed. I had changed.

The spell between us was interrupted as a harsh sting spread across my cheek. Sophia was standing next to me with her hand readied to slap me again if I didn't snap out of it and listen.

"Stop this nonsense right now," she ordered with her finger wagging under my nose. "You selfish, stupid girl!" She covered her face with her hands and ran for the door. In all the months I'd shared the same space with her and all the tragedy she'd confided, I'd never seen a single tear come from her eyes. She wiped at her face, embarrassed for showing the emotions she worked so hard to conceal.

"Wait!" Greer ordered before she could disappear through the door. He took a few long strides toward Sophia and took her by the arms, pulling her hands from her wet face. He snapped his eyes to mine. "Are you happy now?"

Shame on you! I glared at him for pulling that card, playing on my emotions by parading Sophia's pain. He was desperate.

Sophia stood taller as she pulled her arms free and cleared her face with a swipe of her fingers. "I lose my girls. Now I lose you, too."

"I can't believe you made Sophia cry," Thomas chastised, joining in on Greer's conspiracy to guilt me into doing nothing.

I shook my head at all the fuss they were making over me. "I'm sorry, Sophia. I didn't think you liked me *that* much."

The room went silent. She looked at me like I'd committed a cardinal sin and then began to wail, her arms flying up in the air as she spouted off in Italian and marched out of the room. I'd really done it. I'd managed to totally offend the woman who I'd worked so hard to win over for the past half a year.

"What the hell just happened?" I asked, staring at Thomas and Greer as they shook their heads.

Greer was the first to set me straight. "Sophia loves you, Alex. Do you think I made her walk into Maelcolm's house that night? She did that for you, and you just dismissed her."

God, I felt like an awful shit. The thought of starting over at ground zero with Sophia made me feel sick. She'd opened up to me and trusted me with her secrets, and I intended to make it right between us again.

"I had no idea. I didn't know she cared about me like that." I headed for the door to find her.

"Sophia's a prideful woman," he said, stopping me before I could leave. "Give her some time to cool down."

Thomas was eyeing me from the door, silently agreeing with

Greer. That was that. I'd wait a while and then grovel for forgiveness.

We got back to business. Shamed or not, I was going into that house, past that red door to get David Oxford out. "We need those lenses, Greer. If Maelcolm figures out what he has, we're all screwed. This is bigger than us. Besides, I'm the reason the doctor is in there. If they kill him, it's on me."

CHAPTER TWELVE

Sophia was standing near the stove when I walked into the kitchen. She hunched over the marble surface and gripped something in her hand as I walked up behind her to make amends.

"Sophia?"

She tensed, and the object disappeared inside her sturdy hand. "You hungry?" she asked.

"No. I didn't come in here for food. I—" I was at a loss for words—that's what I was. As Greer said, Sophia was a woman of pride. She wasn't going to simply open herself up to me and spill her feelings all over the floor. "I was an ass earlier. Honestly, Sophia, I had no idea it would bother you so much, me going in there."

She turned around slowly and looked at me incredulously. "You need to love yourself, Alex. You got no idea how much the rest of us do." Her eyes furrowed, and I thought she was about to spout tears again. Instead, she sighed and shook her head, her broad shoulders sagging as her breath rushed from her nose.

I heard a faint sound and looked down at her hand. A gold chain dangled from it, the locket at the end bouncing against the

cabinet door as it fell free and swung back and forth. She slipped
her hand behind her back as my eyes reached back up to hers.

"What is that?"

She hesitated, but knowing that I'd seen it, she held it up and
grasped it with both hands to open the tiny hinges. "It's all I have
left."

Inside was a picture of a girl and a small lock of hair, brown
and dulled from age. There was an inscription, a date just a few
days away.

"My baby was taken away twenty years ago. I try to sleep
through that day. Mr. Sinclair pays me every year to sleep on that
day. I wake up the next day, and I have three hundred and sixty-
four more to prepare for it again. Hmph." She snapped it shut
and slipped it in her pocket. "Now you're going to walk out that
door tomorrow and disappear, too."

We were coming up on the twentieth anniversary of Rue's
death, and here I was making that horrible day even worse
for her.

"Sophia, I'm coming back. I have a plan to get Dr. Oxford
out of there and bring myself home, too. You just make sure to
have a good dinner waiting for me because I'm going to be
hungry when I walk through that door."

"Yeah?"

"Yeah. And I'm sorry for being so damn insensitive."

She surprised me with a hug. And then she turned back to
her kitchen and got busy. "Now get out of here," she ordered,
"before you make me all mushy again."

GREER and I argued for hours, but in the end, I convinced him
I'd do it with or without his blessing. And as much as he hated to
let me walk out that door to face my father alone, he did so
because he knew he had no choice, and because the plan had
merit.

The plan was to offer Maelcolm the perfect bargain. A total sham as far as Greer was concerned. My father, on the other hand, would be convinced that the offer was legitimate. Now I just needed to decide which one of them was right.

The guard opened the gate after hanging up the phone. I walked the distance from the road to the house with my adrenaline pumping wildly through my veins. Second guessing my plan was par for the course when confronting someone like Maelcolm—the monster who called himself my father but did little more than plant his seed in my mother against her will. He would have no problem keeping me there unless I convinced him that it was in his best interest not to. If I didn't, we'd have World War III on our hands.

The front door was a massive slab of carved oak, garish and overdone just like the interior of the house. I wasn't sure if I should knock with my knuckles or the large brass contraption hanging from the top. Maybe I should just walk in. It was my father's house, after all. The door opened before I could do either.

"Ms. Kelley." Frederick stood behind it and invited me in, examining me out of the corner of his eye.

"Frederick," I replied with just as much pretense.

He led the way down the hall and motioned to the sofa in the living room. "Maelcolm will be with you shortly." He stopped halfway out of the room. "Would you like something to drink?" he asked without looking at me, a forced gesture of civility.

"No. Just your boss, please."

My heart pounded as I sat on the sofa and waited for Maelcolm, sweat exuding from my palms as the feel of the place seeped into my skin. I rubbed them across my jeans, trying to hide my fear so he wouldn't smell it the moment he walked in the room. Confidence, that's what I needed. That's what he would respect.

"I never thought I'd see the day when you knocked on my door," Maelcolm said from the entrance of the room. He stood at the threshold, examining me with suspicion while I nervously tried to hide my fear. I just stared back at him, waiting for him to enter the room or tell me to follow him to another. The awkward standoff finally ended with me caving under the uncomfortable pressure.

I cleared my throat. "I have a proposition for you." No need to beat around the bush.

"Really." His brow cocked as his interest piqued.

"But first I need to see that Dr. Oxford is safe—and sound."

He smirked, finally striding into the room and heading straight for the bureau to grab a glass and a bottle of whiskey. "Would you like one?"

"This isn't a social visit."

"I'm aware of that. You've come for the doctor, and you think you can bargain with me." He tsked as he poured the amber liquid into the glass. "That was unwise. But since I know damn well you're smarter than that, I assume you've come here to make me an offer I can't refuse. A proposition, you say?" The rim of the glass hesitated at his lips as his suspicions grew.

"Don't worry, Maelcolm," I baited. "Greer's housekeeper isn't standing outside the front door." His nostrils flared slightly as I hit the nerve. The great Maelcolm outwitted by a cook. It was probably a bad idea to piss him off so early in our negotiations, but I couldn't resist. "By the way, do you have a last name?"

"Just Maelcolm," he answered. "You can call me Father, if you'd like."

I didn't like. I would never call him Father. "Maelcolm, then."

"As you wish. Now, tell me about this proposition of yours."

I stood up to even out the playing field—and to stop my knees from trembling. "I'm here to take Dr. Oxford home."

His head dropped back as he laughed. "And what makes you think you can do that?" The laughter stopped and his expression grew agitated, probably from my audacity.

"Because I'm here to offer myself in exchange for his freedom."

Maelcolm drew a steady breath through his nose. "But you're here, and so is he. Since I need you both, I'd say neither of you will be leaving." He planted his glass on the fireplace mantel so hard it cracked. "Stop wasting my time with your ridiculous notion that you can walk into my house and offer *bullshit*." He stalked up to me, his chest almost touching mine. "You played me well the other night, *daughter*. Now I'm going to administer some fatherly discipline." He wrapped his massive hand around my wrist as if it were a twig and started dragging me across the living room floor.

"Let go of me!" I gritted out between clenched teeth. Unfortunately for him, he grabbed the wrong wrist—the left one. I raised my right hand and felt the heat begin to build in my palm. It was almost kinetic the way it grew as I waved my hand in the air. He turned just in time to see the ball of flames burn through his shirt and sear the skin of his forearm, the worst I could do to him under the protective wards of the house.

"*Fucking hell!*" He dropped my arm reflexively from the pain. Then he glared at me and bared his teeth. He took a single step toward me, but I stood my ground, terrified but prepared to have my say.

"If you ever want to see the prophecy, you'll hear me out." My chest expanded as I postured and pressed my arms firmly to my sides, concealing the trembling in my limbs.

His face sobered as he glanced at my chest, obviously wondering if I was wearing the amulet.

"You didn't think I'd be stupid enough to wear it here, did you?" I asked. "Now you're going to listen to me."

Frederick ran around the corner, a strand of gray hair licking his forehead as he came to a clumsy stop. "Is everything all right, sir? Shall I alert the men?"

"Idiot," Maelcolm muttered under his breath without taking

his eyes off me. "No. I think I can handle my own daughter." Frederick tensed. I wasn't sure if it was from the angry tone of Maelcolm's voice or the mention of the word *daughter*. He slicked back the wayward strand of hair and bowed slightly. "She'll be staying for lunch. We'll have it now." He composed himself and turned toward the mouse of a man. "Please."

"Yes. Right away, sir."

Maelcolm escorted me into the dining room, his manners improving as he realized I had something worth listening to. I agreed to eat his food if it earned me his attention. A few minutes later, a short woman with a white apron hustled into the room with a tray. It was topped with a tureen of soup and a bowl of fried balls. She placed two of them on each of our plates and then ladled the creamy tan soup into our bowls.

"Thank you," I said as she lifted the empty tray and left the room. I whiffed the soup and my face went sour. "What in God's name is that?"

He looked at me peculiarly. "Cullen skink. What did you think it was?"

All I heard was *skunk*, and that's what it smelled like. "I'm not eating that." The soup was chunky and fishy, something I wasn't a fan of on a good day.

"God, woman! You're half Scottish and you have to ask what Cullen skink is? Smoked haddock, potatoes, and cream." He watched me push the soup away and then eye the strange fried balls on the plate.

"Scotch eggs," he clarified before I could ask.

That I could eat. I took a bite, and despite myself, I groaned from the delicious flavor of sausage wrapped around a hard-boiled egg. The deep frying was icing on the cake.

"This proposition of yours," he began. "What is it?"

"I'm taking David Oxford out of this house today." I waited for his reaction, but he just kept eating his soup and listening with a poker face. "In exchange, I'll surrender myself to you once the vessel has been found. That is the most important objective right now, isn't it? Securing the prophecy?"

He swallowed his mouthful of food and pointed his fork at me. "What do I get out of this little arrangement? Besides you, which I already have."

"My cooperation. When this is all over and the vessel is found, I'll walk through that door and do whatever you ask me to."

He pushed his bowl away and sat deeper in his chair. He was considering it. I could tell by the way he was studying me and taking his time with a response. "You've bonded with him, haven't you?" He leaned forward again and pointed at me, wiggling his fingers in my direction. "You've got that thing going on in your eyes."

I considered denying it, because that information might complicate our accord. But he would spot the lie a mile away. "Well, technically he bonded with me."

"Even a half-breed is capable of bonding," he said. "You just didn't recognize it."

Half-breed. I'd never thought about myself like that. But he was right. Maelcolm and Greer came from the same kind, and that made me half of what they were. It might also explain my powerful attraction for Greer since the moment we met, despite our rocky start.

"You do know," he continued, "a bonded male as powerful as Greer Sinclair will never let you surrender yourself to me."

"Then you also know he'll come for me again if you don't let me walk out of this house today—and he'll win. If I come back to you later of my own free will, he can't stop me. But I will stay with him until the vessel is found." That brought up another important bargaining point. "And don't think for a second that our agreement includes handing it over. You're on your own with that."

The prophecy was only half the reason the Rogues wanted

me. They needed my blood for a new race of unstoppable warriors. If he agreed to my terms, they would have their blood and a fifty-fifty chance at getting their hands on the vessel only in Maelcolm's egotistical mind those chances were more like one hundred percent.

He looked at me with disdain, obviously irritated that his own offspring had the gall to bargain with him in his own house. "You're a foolish girl. What makes you think you could ever have an eternity with him anyway? You'll grow old and he won't. Do you want that for someone you love?" He leaned in closer and smirked. "The older you get, the more you'll have to get used to the smell of younger women on him."

I maintained my blank expression. It was a lie, of course. All of it. I had no intention of handing myself over to my father. I generally didn't consider myself a liar, but the stakes were too high to worry about my integrity with a man who had none of his own. But his words did strike a chord deep inside of me. Was I that selfish that I could obligate a man like Greer Sinclair to a life of watching me slowly die? Could I handle the smell of younger women on him, or at least have the decency to condone it? I shook off the distracted thoughts and refocused on the job of convincing Maelcolm of my sincerity, planning to use his own words as leverage.

"I should just take my chances and keep you here while you're young and fertile," he sneered. "A lot of good you'll do me if that damn vessel isn't found soon. And you will find it, whether you cooperate or not. That mission is written in your DNA. You can thank the gods for that." He glanced at my bare neck. "I'll get my hands on that amulet, one way or another."

I leaned over the table and looked him dead in the eye. One shot was all I had to convince him, or the entire plan would come crashing down and I'd find myself in another locked room. "I will never help you find the vessel. *Never.* I'll slit my own throat first. So it would be in your best interest to take the offer."

His face turned bitter, infuriated by my lack of subservience. "If you break our agreement, I will come for you. And you don't want me to come for you. Is that understood?"

"Completely."

He stared at me strangely as the bargain was struck. "Why are you looking at me like that?" I asked.

"I'm still trying to figure out why you're doing this. Why would a smart woman put herself on the line and come here to rescue a man she hardly knows? It may take you a little longer, but you'll find the vessel with or without the doctor."

A man like Maelcolm would ask that question because there wasn't a drop of integrity in his bones. "Because I'm the reason he's here." I left out the part about the doctor's research being in his eyes. I needed to convince him that it was all about nobility and my human flaw of conscience. "If he dies, I might as well have pulled the trigger myself. I'll be able to sleep at night once he's safe. And like you said, it will take longer to find the vessel without his research."

"And of course you'd prefer to take that advantage out of my hands," he added.

"Well, why dilute everyone's odds when it would be so much easier to work together?" Then I added mortar to the guise by feigning concession to his insights about Greer's fate if stuck with me. "And I happen to agree with you about the ethics of binding Greer to a life with a mortal woman. He deserves more than that."

"Hmph. Compassion. Isn't that interesting? You must have gotten that trait from your mother."

"Do we have a deal?" I asked.

"Frederick!" he bellowed. The man came rushing into the dining room and Maelcolm tossed him a key. "Get the doctor." Frederick caught it and disappeared through the doorway.

"Why do you treat him like that?" I asked.

"Like what?"

"Like a dog."

Maelcolm watched his servant scurry away and then looked back at me. "A man is treated exactly the way he allows himself to be treated."

I supposed he was right.

We sat in silence for the next few minutes while we waited for Frederick to retrieve Dr. Oxford, me with trembling knees and Maelcolm with a superior smirk on his face. It wasn't over yet. It wasn't over until he let us walk out that door, and despite his agreeable demeanor I knew he could pull the rug out from under me at any moment and throw me in that cage alongside the doctor.

A shuffling sound came from the hall. I looked up at Frederick and the man standing next to him. It had only been a couple of weeks since our abduction, but David Oxford was barely recognizable. His frame appeared wasted as if he'd lost a significant amount of weight, and his head had been shaved clean. Even the hair jutting from his ears was gone. His eyes were bloodshot but intact, which meant they hadn't figured it out. Thank God for that. And then I noticed the manacle around his neck and the heavy chain leading to Frederick's hand.

"Doctor?" I stood up and stared at him, then turned my furious eyes on Maelcolm. "Why? Why would you do this to him?"

"The art of psychological warfare is not for the weak minds of women," Maelcolm replied. I don't think he even realized how insulting his comment was. It was just his character, a chauvinistic prick.

"Take it off," I demanded. "And get him some clothes." He'd been stripped to his underwear. I gave Oxford a slight nod and a smile, reassuring him that I was here to make things right.

Maelcolm stood up forcefully, shoving his chair against the wall in the process. "Careful with that mouth of yours. You'll be remembering whose house you're in."

The look on his face chilled me to the bone, reminding me of what he was capable if pushed too far. But I didn't back down or grovel, because in the end I was the one with the real power. I was the smartest guy in the room.

GREER WAS WAITING at the road when I walked down the driveway with Dr. Oxford at my side. Rhom and Thomas were in the car, and I suspected Greer had spent his time pacing a hole in the asphalt in front of Maelcolm's gate. He said nothing as we walked through the opened iron bars and headed for the car. But as I walked past him, he reached for me and looked me steadily in the eye. I glanced at his hand, grasping my arm almost painfully, and met his eyes with a question mark.

"I will never let you surrender to him," he stated with unfaltering conviction.

"Of course not," I replied, smiling faintly, allowing him the illusion that the topic was completely settled and true. But I knew there were still decisions to make. When this was all over and the smoke cleared from all the fires we'd undoubtedly set in our quest to secure the prophecy, I would weigh which war would be least catastrophic—the one waged by my father when I reneged on our bargain, or the one waged by Greer if I walked back through those gates.

CHAPTER THIRTEEN

The smell of food hit our noses as soon as we walked off the elevator. The ride from upstate had been long and uncomfortable. Greer staring at me silently the entire time, Dr. Oxford sinking into the back seat in a POW-like state, me trying to swallow my secrets and keep them buried and hidden from everyone in the car.

"Well, it's about time." Leda came into the foyer, visibly relieved as the right number of heads exited the elevator. "I was beginning to think I had to figure out how to drive a car and come up there myself." She took one look at Dr. Oxford who was still slightly catatonic, and her relief turned to anger. "What on earth did they do to you?" She took him by the hand and led him toward the stairs. "Come on, sugar. Let's get you to bed."

For the first time since Frederick led him down the hall with that cuff around his neck, he looked up and acknowledged the voice speaking to him. He nodded and followed Leda up the steps.

Sophia was standing in the doorway when I refocused on the incredible smell coming from the kitchen. She motioned toward the dining room and we headed in for dinner. Scotch eggs and fish soup had nothing on Sophia's lasagna Bolognese and home-made bread, but before I could put a bite in my mouth, I fixed a plate for the doctor and headed upstairs. By the looks of him, he hadn't had a decent meal in weeks, or the appetite to eat one if they'd shoved it right under his nose.

I found them in one of the guest rooms. Leda was coming out of the bathroom with a damp washcloth when I walked in the room. She glanced at me and continued toward the bed where Dr. Oxford was lying down, corpse-like in a staged pose. Even his usually bright, prismatic eyes had dulled and were unresponsive.

"Those bastards did a real number on the poor man," Leda hissed.

"Has he said anything?" I placed the plate of food on the table next to the bed and then gently rested the back of my fingers against his forehead. He felt warm but not feverish, which was a small blessing considering all the other damage that was obvious but invisible.

She glanced at the tray of food and shook her head. "I'm afraid he won't be eating tonight. Maybe his appetite will be back by morning when the shock begins to wear off."

"God, Leda. What did they do to him?"

"I don't know." She wiped his face with the cool cloth and tucked the comforter around his shrunken frame. It was a side of Leda rarely seen, but I'd experienced her nurturing powers first-hand after Arthur Richmond attacked me months ago and left me in a three-week catatonic state even worse than the one Oxford was in right now.

"You'd make a good mother, Leda."

"Yeah, right," she laughed.

I wondered if the thought ever occurred to her to have kids. I wasn't even sure if it was possible. And what about me? If I was a half-breed like Maelcolm said, was I barren?

"David," she whispered, reassuring him with his given name.

"Alex and I are leaving for a few minutes, but we'll be right downstairs." I thought I detected a slight tensing of his limbs and a flash in his eyes as Leda raised off the edge of the bed. The doctor was in there somewhere. He just needed a little time to figure out how to resurface. I understood that, having experienced it myself. I also knew Dr. Oxford would find his way back when he was good and ready.

We walked back down to the kitchen and I set the tray on the counter, shaking my head as Sophia looked at it disappointedly. "We'll try again at breakfast."

Loden was sitting at the table with the others when we walked in the dining room. I greeted him with a smile but knew by the look on his face that he wasn't here just for one of Sophia's spectacular meals.

"How's the doctor?" Greer asked as we took our seats.

"Just grand," Leda replied, adding, "if you're a rock or in a coma."

"I take it he didn't expound on the details of his stay in that room."

She reached for her wine glass and held it out. Thomas took his cue and poured. "Not a word. He needs a good night of sleep without worrying that he'll be blind when he wakes up."

I watched Loden *not* be his usual playful self, suspecting he was waiting for his own cue to speak. Greer picked up on my focus and nodded to him.

"We found another one," Loden announced.

I'd become accustomed to what "another one" meant. It was code for *marker*—and the ever-increasing presence of the wolves in the city. "Go on, Loden," I encouraged. "Tell us all the gory details. I won't break." They were here for me. My last encounter with wolves had resulted in the death of two of them, but replacements had arrived and were hiding in the shadows, leaving their calling cards all over the city in plain view for Greer and his men to find. It was all part of their psychological game: hide and seek with subtle intimidation to sink under my skin. Fortunately for me, Greer was immune to that intimidation and buffered me from it. Maybe a little bit too much.

"East Sixty-Third Street. On the roof of a condo for seniors." This seemed to amuse Loden. "Caused a lot of excitement. Apparently the gentlemen residents were taking up arms to defend the women folk."

"That's not funny, Loden." I had to admit, the thought of it made me grin even though it wasn't funny at all. Neither is someone falling flat on their face, but we still manage to laugh at things that are quite tragic. I supposed we weren't actually laughing at them. It was just so damn absurd. Why not just leave the dead animal heads on Greer's doorstep? That would guarantee our attention.

"They're up to something," Greer said.

"Well, of course they are," Leda sniped. "Those rotten dogs are after Alex."

Greer shook his head slowly as he stared straight ahead at the wall, half away in thought. "No. They're up to something much worse. Something very unpleasant is coming. I'd stake all of our lives on it."

"I'll stake my own life on it if you don't mind, Boss." Thomas turned to look at me. "But I will. Don't you worry, sugar. This time they won't get anywhere near you."

Thank you, I mouthed back.

Rhom hadn't said a word. He just sat stoically and listened to the conversation traveling around the table. When the room finally went quiet, he reached for my plate and filled it with a generous helping of lasagna. Always the gentleman, he served Leda next and then filled his own plate. Something was obviously bothering him, though.

"Say what's on your mind, Rhom," Greer probed. "We don't keep secrets at this table."

Ha! Wasn't that the pot calling the kettle black.

Rhom's fork halted halfway to his mouth and settled back down on his plate. I could tell by the way he exhaled and sat deeper into his chair that whatever was bothering him was more of an annoyance than an actual grievance. "Look, Alex." He turned to me and shook his head. "You need to get out of my head."

"I'm flattered that I'm on your mind, Rhom, but I have no idea what you're talking about."

"Every time I come near you I get this ringing in my head. A pressure. *Damn it*, Alex." His hands gripped an imaginary object in front of him as he shook it. "It makes me want to—"

Greer almost came out of his chair, an involuntary reaction to Rhom's sudden agitation that seemed to be directed at me. He gave a silent warning.

"Wow, Boss." Rhom glanced at me and then back at Greer. "You don't think I'd actually hurt her?" He looked a little pissed off and incredulous. "Do you?"

"All right, boys," Leda scolded. "Jesus. The testosterone level in here is beginning to stink."

"My apologies, Alex. I'll clarify." Rhom squeezed his eyes shut for a second as if a sharp pain were traveling through his head. "It started the night you had that spell. The night you saw that light and followed it into the library."

"Oh," I began sarcastically. "You mean when I saw those books that don't exist?"

"It was mildly irritating at first, but it's getting pretty bad, Alex. Like a toothache in my brain."

Leda looked around the table. "Anyone else repelled by Alex?"

My mouth dropped.

"All right, everyone calm down," Greer said. "Rhom. Take the night off—and a couple of aspirin. I'm sure it's just another side effect of Alex's new talents." He glanced at me for confirmation. I just shook my head in ignorance. "We'll pay Ava a visit in the morning. Sort it all out."

. . .

A WREATH of ribbons studded with bright flowers hung from the door of Den of Oddities and Antiquities. An even brighter bouquet sat on the display case when we walked inside the shop.

"Someone has spring fever," I commented as Ava greeted us.

"Beltane," she chimed. "It's just around the corner." Her brow arched as she mused about the seasons. "Then it will be Midsummer, and before we know it, the new year."

By "new year", Ava was referring to Samhain—Halloween for the rest of New York. It was my mother's favorite day of the year. When all the other kids in the building were dressing up as witches and ghosts for trick-or-treating, I was here with my mother and Ava, feeding the spirits as they passed through an invisible veil. At the time, I had a limited idea of what it all meant, but my mother made sure I knew the importance of the ritual and always rewarded me with cupcakes and chocolate after the last spirit slipped through that invisible doorway.

"So what brings you two downtown this morning?"

Ava wasn't stupid. Greer and me showing up together this early in the morning meant we needed her help. "Well, it appears I've developed some kind of repellent toward people that used to like me."

She frowned and glanced at Greer, sniffing as if *said* repellent were detectable in the air.

"Not that kind of repellent," Greer clarified. "Apparently Rhom picks up some sort of high-pitched sound when he's near Alex. A very painful ringing in his head."

Initially, she seemed perplexed by what Greer described. But then a lightbulb seemed to go off in her head. "Hmm... based on your mother's stories, it sounded like Isla was pretty damn good at spotting them."

"Them? Who is *them*?" I asked, beginning to put two and

two together when she mentioned my grandmother, the mind bender in the family.

She ignored my question, pursing her lips as her eyes squinted in my direction. Greer was watching me, too, as if he were on the same wavelength as Ava. They held each other's gaze for a moment, then Ava continued probing. "I'm going to ask you a question, Alex. Don't think about it. I want you to just tell me the first thing that comes to mind. Okay?"

I nodded and waited for the question.

"When you look at Rhom, what do you see?"

My mouth opened, but I hesitated as I did exactly what she told me not to do—I started thinking about the question.

"Uh-uh!" Her hands clapped loudly, distracting my pondering.

"Darkness," I blurted, surprised by my answer.

Ava smirked and slowly nodded her head. "Now we're getting to the heart of it. Maeve used to say that Isla could spot a bad seed from a mile away. Your newly inherited powers are detecting those bad seeds and 'repelling' them, as you called it."

"Rhom?" The first time I laid eyes on Rhom sitting at Greer's dining room table last fall, he reminded me of a mob hitman, a human Rottweiler. But that was before he spoke and displayed his intelligence and kindness. He'd never once been anything less than respectful and loyal. "I don't believe it." My eyes darted to Greer for backup. He just stood there, saying nothing in Rhom's defense. Ava glanced at him, too. Their eyes locked, and I knew they were having another silent conversation.

Greer eventually turned back to me. "Rhom wasn't always such an upstanding citizen," he said. "A couple of decades ago, I would have never let him near you."

I laughed nervously, waiting for the punch line. "You're fucking with me, right?"

"I'm afraid not," he said. "Rhom has a rather checkered past. He's the quintessential example of the power of redemption."

"What did he do? Kill the wrong person? Piss off the gods?" Not that it would impact my trust in Rhom, but I had the right to know who my personal bodyguard really was.

"Let's just say he was heading down the road to Rogue status when he did a complete turnaround," Greer said. "He decided that a life on this side of the fence was more appealing."

"But—"

"A man's past is just that—the past." Greer interrupted. "If you want to know Rhom's history, you can ask him yourself."

I was curious, though. If I was so good at spotting and repelling the bad guys, then why hadn't it worked on the darkest one of all—Maelcolm?

"If I'm so good at this, why is Maelcolm still so intent on keeping me under his roof? Shouldn't he be running in the opposite direction?"

"He's your father," Ava said. "Your powers will naturally be diluted or completely ineffective against your own blood."

I remembered what Maelcolm said to me the morning he forced me to look in the mirror and see what I'd become, as he halted my attempt to hurl a ball of flames at him: *Don't get cocky. You'll never outfight me.* I guess he knew my powers were weakened against him. I believe he said they were reduced to a low simmer, hence the annoying burn I gave him the day before that would have taken off any other man's arm.

"Well, that's just great. I've got all this *stuff* inside of me, and I can't even use it on enemy number one."

Ava patted my arm. "Don't worry, darling. There are plenty of bad seeds out there that aren't immune to your powers. Alasdair Templeton, for one." Her eyes narrowed, a smirk stretching up her right cheek. "I'd like to see that one burn."

"Does this mean Rhom and I can't be around each other?" The thought sickened me.

Ava pondered the question. "Not necessarily. Now that you're aware of what's happening, you should be able to apply it at will. It's all part of the gift, darling. Practice, practice, practice."

I was relieved that I didn't have to avoid Rhom permanently, especially since he was my daily escort to work. Speaking of which, it was getting late. "I have to get ready for work, Greer. We need to head home."

I hugged Ava goodbye and headed for the door. Rhom was leaning against Greer's car when we walked outside. He cringed a bit less when I approached him. But he still cringed.

I GOT to the shop fifteen minutes early. Apollo and Katie stared at me as I walked right past them without saying a word and headed for the back room. I sat in the small space where we parked our coats and bags, staring at the mini fridge, debating whether to get on my knees and stick my head inside. My adrenaline was through the roof, an unpleasant side effect from all the powers competing for space underneath my skin. Something cold would help.

Katie peeked her head past the door as I was grabbing an ice cube from the tiny freezer. "You okay?"

I deflated as a puff of air rushed from my mouth. "This must be what hot flashes feel like."

"Menopause? And here I thought you were just a moody shit." She shut the door behind her and took me by the wrist, leading me to the bathroom sink where she turned on the faucet. "Hold your hands under the water. It'll get rid of some of the excess energy."

God, was it written all over me? Katie could read me like a book. Either that or she could feel the heat and electricity filling the room, her dragon sensing it.

The water cooled me down and my hands stopped shaking. I watched her closely while she held them under the faucet like my mother used to do when I got them dirty or caked with food.

"Thank you, Mommy." She didn't reply, and I wondered what had her so distracted. "Something's wrong with you," I said, a statement, not a question.

Her forehead scrunched. "I'm fine."

"No, you're not," I insisted, waiting for her to come clean and admit that something had her sharp blue eyes restless.

"Come on," she said. "Apollo's going to walk in any second now if we don't get out there. He's anxious to leave today."

I let it go—for now. We had all afternoon and evening to play this game. Apollo was indeed watching the door when we finally emerged, with a rare look of annoyance on his face.

"About time. I have to get out of here at two o'clock sharp." He glanced at the clock, which read three minutes before the hour.

"Oh, live dangerously," Katie said, jokingly. "A whole three minutes early. We promise not to tell."

His face colored. "Right. I'm being ridiculous. It's just that I have an appointment I can't be late for."

"Then *go*," I said, handing him his backpack and pointing toward the door.

Katie headed for the library table and started shuffling stray books around the top, randomly stacking them with no rhyme or reason. She formed neat stacks of romance mixed with thrillers, and fantasy with gardening. Then she scattered the books again and started over.

"Okay, that's enough housekeeping," I said, grabbing her arm to stop the madness. "Let's have a little chat."

She dropped into one of the chairs, motioning me into the one next to hers. The shop had a single customer browsing the self-help aisle, so I sat where I could keep an eye on the front register just in case he decided to buy something. Knowing Katie's moods, I thought it best not to probe, allowing her to unfold the discussion at her own pace.

"I can't take it anymore," she eventually said, leaning back in her chair and covering her eyes with a dramatic wave of her hands.

"Take what?"

"He's suffocating me!"

"Who's suffocating you?" As soon as I said it, I knew who *he* was. "Constantine?" I'd dreaded this moment from the second I saw him standing half-naked in the doorway of her apartment, only I'd predicted it would be him pulling away like a caged Lothario needing space.

"I say I'm going downstairs to check the mail, he has to go with me. I went to get my nails done the other day and he sat in the waiting room. He shows up here every afternoon just to check in. For God's sake, Alex! I'm sneaking out an hour early for lunch just to have a few minutes alone!"

She started to tear up just as the customer emerged from the aisle. He took one look at the crying woman sitting next to me and slid his book back on the closest shelf before heading for the exit.

"Sorry," I called out as he vanished through the front door, Katie completely oblivious to his presence.

I shook my head. "See. I warned you about getting involved with him. But I have to admit, I'm a little surprised that it's *you* who can't stand being with *him* anymore."

She looked shocked by my words, like I'd just said something absurd. "I love being with him, but I'm not *in* love with him." Now she seemed more frustrated and angry than distraught. "It was so perfect in the beginning, and then he had to go and ruin it. He's obsessed with me, Alex. And you know I'm not the touchy-feely type. God, I can't breathe with all his smothering. What am I going to do?"

CHAPTER FOURTEEN

By the time Katie and I finished our shift the night before, I'd gotten an earful for seven hours straight. I had a feeling Constantine wasn't going to be democratic about Katie's decision to end it. By the way she described his behavior, he'd gone over the edge, and that was a dangerous thing for a satyr as powerful as Constantine. I decided the best thing to do was get to him and try to reason with him before he went to see her at the shop.

Central Park was bustling with activity when I arrived. Unfortunately, Constantine wasn't waiting for me as he usually was, always seeming to sense me the second I stepped foot over the park's threshold. I entered at Seventy-Second Street, which was where he'd appeared the last time I went to see him. Today he was MIA, so I started walking across the park. I figured at some point he'd have to show up. I'd about given up by the time I reached the boat pond near Fifth Avenue when I spotted him. He looked ridiculous sitting on the bench of the *Hans Christian Andersen* statue looking out over the water, the tip of his shoe resting on the bronze duck in front of the monument.

"Hans Christian Andersen," I muttered, conjuring an image

of the children's books and fairy tales on Greer's shelf that apparently didn't exist. He crooked his finger at me, making no attempt to lift away from the bronze figure. "That's just great," I sighed and walked up to the statue.

He patted the spot on the bronze bench next to him. I sat obediently, debating the benefits of a full-on browbeating or a much gentler begging session to see if he'd have the decency to let Katie go in peace.

"What have we here?" he mused. "I sense an unpleasant exchange is about to take place between us."

"Why did you make me walk all the way across the park? You must have known I was here the moment I entered your *domain*."

He made an uncharacteristic sound in the back of his throat as he expelled his breath through his nose, but still no answer. "Do you see that?" he eventually asked, motioning to the large paved area directly in front of the statue. "Saturday afternoon there will be a mob sitting out there, listening to tales written by this fellow." He touched the giant bronze hand resting on the bench between us. "Your kind is fascinated with tales of other worlds. Always running away from their mundane lives in search of fantasy." He turned slowly to look at me. "Most people would envy you, Alex. You're living exactly what they come here for—only they don't know the dark side of that fantasy, do they?"

I slumped deeper into the hard bench and groaned. "Not now, Constantine. *Please.*"

"What?" He pulled back and turned so he could look me directly in my eyes, lifting my chin to study my face. "Ah, I see. You have serious business to encumber me with on this lovely day. What a shame."

"What's going on with you and Katie?" There. I asked the question, hoping he wouldn't just leave out of annoyance from me butting into his business. Like he'd never done that to me. Like he didn't butt into my private life every time we crossed paths. But for him it was an entitlement; for me it was an imposition of his privacy.

He stood up and turned away from me. Now we were getting to the truth. I watched his massive shoulders expand even larger as he readied himself to confess to me that someone had finally hooked him by the beating threads of his heart. Leda had owned that designation for many years until Katie Bishop, a dragon with the bluest eyes, knocked her off that pedestal.

He turned back to me with a slow twist of his torso and came clean. "That woman is driving me insane!"

My mouth gaped as I struggled for words, my mind catching up to what he'd just said. But the more I tried to figure out what the hell was going on between them, the more I thought it wise to let him speak freely before imposing my own opinions on their apparently confused relationship.

He began pacing in that same way Greer always did when he was agitated or flustered. Constantine was the cockiest male I'd ever met. Nothing flustered him—until now.

"I—" I began, but he continued with his rant before I could get a word in.

"The woman is needy. Always wanting and demanding my attention." He stopped pacing and looked at me, astounded. "Do you know she insists on lunching with me every day? Do you have any idea how difficult it is to walk through the door of that shop every afternoon with a toothy grin on my face? Jesus, Alex! She can't even check the mail without an escort."

I suppressed the grin that was fighting to surface on my face. Here I was thinking the wrath of an obsessed satyr was about to explode in front of me, and the truth was they both anguishing over the same dilemma. Two like-minded tigers trying to escape the same cage without damaging the other.

"Imagine me, henpecked and led around by my cock! Tell me you cannot imagine that, Alex," he beseeched, his voice dropping two full octaves.

Actually, I couldn't.

"What about Leda?" I asked. "Didn't the two of you play a similar game?"

"That was different. I was in complete control."

He was in control all right, pursuing a goddess like Leda, the most unattainable female in the city. I wondered if he'd be crying foul right now if Leda had taken him up on his relentless attempts to make her his devoted lover. Maybe it was all about the chase. Typical male posturing.

"Never in all my days have I felt the need to hide from a woman. I usually just say goodbye and hand them something shiny and expensive to ease the pain. A memento."

"God, you're arrogant," I murmured, stating fact, not insult.

"Yes, I know. A world class prick when it serves me."

I shook my head and flicked my eyes up to his. I thought about telling him that Katie had the same grievances as he'd just spouted off to me, and that I was here as arbiter to break it to him gently and plead for his decency to let her go. But that might reignite his competitive flame to conquer—reignite the ever-intoxicating chase. Then we'd be right back where we started, an endless loop of push and pull.

"Why didn't you just walk away the second it became uncomfortable?" I asked.

His face went lax as his eyes softened, almost perplexed by my question. "I could never do that to her, destroy her. I love her. My Katie is extraordinary."

"I think the two of you are seeing the same thing in very different ways. You say she insists on meeting for lunch every day? Has she actually asked you to pick her up for lunch every day?"

He smiled with a slight smirk. "No. But some things do not need to be spoken. I don't mean to sound vain, Alex, but what woman wouldn't desire such attention from me?"

There was that arrogance again. How was I going to put this? "I'm here to tell you that Katie loves you, too."

If it wasn't for the involuntary twitch at the corner of his mouth and the sudden flicker in his eyes, I'd swear he was a heartless stone, which would have made the next sentence much easier. "She just isn't *in* love with you. In fact, she thinks the two of you need just a little bit of time off." I squinted my eyes and demonstrated with a half inch between my index finger and thumb.

He snorted before sobering up. "Surely you're not suggesting that the feeling is mutual?"

"Well, I kind of am. She loves you, Constantine, but she feels smothered."

"*Smothered*," he scoffed, suddenly smirking at the absurdity that they'd apparently both been reading the same book in two completely different languages. "Well, I'm sure my uncanny ability to project my moods has had a profound influence over her perception of things. She must be sensing my discomfort with our situation, allowed herself to be projected upon."

"Yeah, Constantine. That must be it."

I don't think he knew the meaning of rejection. He was far too vain and self-absorbed to see a single flaw or think himself anything less than irresistible to both sexes. Stab him with a knife, and he'd treat the wound and forgive your clumsiness.

"Perhaps one day I'll show you who I am and what I've seen," he promised, plucking the assumptions right out of my head.

I felt my face turn hot with the shame of being caught yet again trying to have a mind of my own. When would I learn that wasn't always so easy in the company I kept these days?

"Just talk to Katie, please."

"*That* I will do," he agreed.

He moved a piece of broken stone with the point of his shiny black shoe. "You know," he began, taking a panoramic glance around his domain, "this wasn't always America's great municipal park. There was life here before they took it. There were families here, a community of those who took care of each other, all living in the center of unspeakable wealth that wanted nothing more than to eradicate them."

"Yeah?" I said, having no idea what he was talking about, but my interest piqued.

"Central Park," he clarified, seeing my confusion. He nodded toward the north end of the park. "It was called Seneca Village. A settlement a few blocks from here. Mostly African-Americans and a sprinkling of Irish. They were good people. I liked them. Some of their graves are still here, buried under all this concrete and sod." His chest expanded as he shifted back to me. He looked around the boat pond and all the green grass bordering it. "Some say this very spot is a doorway, a portal."

"Portal? What kind of portal?" I asked, wondering if he was fucking with me again.

"Well, I don't know, Alex. Maybe the vessel is right here under our feet, balancing atop this mysterious portal."

I gasped before I could catch myself. It was always best to restrain your emotions in his presence, hold a few cards back.

Charmed I'm sure by my gullibility, he let loose a robust laugh before straightening back up and gazing at me thought-fully. "It is always such a joy to spend time with you, Alex." He looked at his Cartier. "But now I have a lunch date that apparently isn't a date at all, is it?"

I was about to head back toward Central Park West when I caught a final glimpse of the statue behind him, again stirring images of those mysterious books. "You haven't by any chance been trying to get in touch with me, have you?"

Constantine laughed at my question, then left me standing in the park while he disappeared to have that overdue conversation with his dragon. If the two of them managed to have an adult discussion and come to a mutual understanding about their brief love affair, I expected to find a relieved and happy Katie at the shop when I arrived for my shift.

I took my time walking back across the park to the west side. It was the first time since the night Daemon attacked me that I'd been in the park on my own, without Constantine watching me from wherever it was he usually perched. I was beginning to feel grounded. Alasdair Templeton was keeping his distance, and my growing powers were giving me a needed boost in confidence. In other words, the target on my back was getting smaller, if for no other reason than my ability to match my opponents. The sitting duck was growing into a fierce swan.

"There you are." Rhom was leaning against the wall at the Seventy-Second Street entrance of the park, his usual copy of the *New York Post* tucked under his arm.

"Why do you read that rag?" I asked.

He tossed it on the bench for the next person to consume. "It entertains me." Central Park was off limits to Greer and his men unless Constantine lifted the wards. Today they must have been strong, stopping Rhom from following me in. He planted his legs in front of me and clasped his hands together. "Talk to me, Alex."

I walked past him and headed north on Central Park West. "About what?"

He sighed in frustration and followed, expanding his protective sphere around me. "You've been looking at me funny for the past couple of days. Have I done something to offend you?"

"No, Rhom. I'm just a little afraid you'll go running for the hills every time you come near me, seeing how I *repel* you these days."

"I'm not running from you now." He thumped his right ear with his finger. "No ringing today."

"That's because I'm aware of it now and have a little more control over who gets the brush off. It appears I have a talent for repelling very bad things. 'Bad seeds' Ava calls them." I turned to face him. "Greer told me about your past. Well, the gist of it anyway. I guess I can turn it off once you're redeemed in my mind. And believe me, Rhom, *you* are redeemed."

He looked displeased about having his dirty laundry dumped on the floor. "I wish he would have let me tell you."

"He didn't give me any details. Just said you used to do some pretty bad things." I watched him, waiting, fishing for him to volunteer those details. It didn't matter, though. Rhom would have to commit some pretty despicable acts to change my opinion of him. Abuse children or torture animals; either of those would do the trick.

He pinched the bridge of his nose, squinting his eyes tight. "Well, then. Let me fill in the details. Then I guess we'll see how you feel about me."

We began to walk again as I listened to him confess his deeds, hooked on every word for the next nine or ten blocks. The whole time he had a look on his face that revealed the hatred he still held for the sins of his past. The kind of look you get for revealing things you've never forgiven yourself for. But if Greer trusted who he was today, so did I.

"My mother was the daughter of a drug lord."

I waited for him to go on, but he just stared straight ahead as we walked, waiting I assumed for my reaction to hearing the revelation. When I didn't shrink away, he continued.

"She was also an addict. There were benefits—or drawbacks, depending on your view—to having access to an unlimited supply of product. My grandfather put an end to it. A little too late, though. He knew about it for a long time before finally acknowledging it." He glanced at me and smirked. "Never under-estimate the power of denial, especially when it involves one of your kids."

"So your father was a…" The word seemed odd on the tip of my tongue.

"Yes, my father was a god. I didn't know for a long time. My mother married one of my grandfather's chief officers in the operation. When she got pregnant with me, she let her husband believe I was his. But he knew. Men can be pretty fucking stupid about things like that, but he knew I wasn't his kid." His mouth tightened, and I swear I could hear the tension in his grinding jaw. "Don't think he didn't make me pay for that."

The light filtering through the trees highlighted his face, accentuating the loathing he was carrying for himself, or maybe his father. Either way it startled me. It was the first and hopefully the last time I would see the chink in his very heavy armor. Rhom was one of the most formidable beings I'd ever known, and it shamed me to be selfish and want his demons to just go away and not taint the safety and comfort he provided. But I needed Rhom to be Rhom.

"You are not your parents," I told him. "I know it sounds like some corny affirmation, but you're the sum of your own deeds."

My psychobabble seemed to annoy him, like he'd heard it all before by those more qualified to spew it. But still he nodded in agreement. "Exactly."

I listened to him explain those deeds, my heart sinking as he described a life no child should ever live, and the subsequent adulthood riddled with unthinkable acts of violence.

"Procuring my mother's drugs right under my grandfather's nose was like playing Russian roulette. I used to wonder which one of us he'd kill first. I was seven years old when she started sending me out for it. By the time I was sixteen, dear old 'dad' had me working for him under the table."

"He was stealing from your grandfather's operation?" Even though I knew there were evil people in the world who considered their own children a commodity, I still found it unbearable to fathom what he said next. "Did he make you run the drugs?"

"No. He made me kill anyone who found out." He stopped walking when I did but wouldn't turn around to look at me. "I've killed a lot of people, Alex. I may not do that anymore, but I'm still the same monster who took lives for nothing more than an order from a man who hated me. I won't blame you if you ask Greer for someone else. You can trust Loden. He'd be a good replacement."

I took his hand while he still refused to look at me. "You were a child, Rhom."

Now he turned around, dropping my hand as if it stung. "You don't understand, Alex. I liked it. For the first time in my miserable life, I had power."

That, I wasn't prepared for. Nor did I have a convenient response. My mouth opened but all I could do was breathe and look at his eyes, which had turned nearly black. He must have sensed my discomfort, because his expression softened and he reached for my rejected hand.

"I would never hurt you," he vowed. "I no longer take pleasure from death."

Feeling unsteady and lost for the right words, I changed the subject. "How did you end up with Greer?"

"That's when my life began." The darkness in his eyes brightened just enough to be noticed. "As addicts usually do, my mother overdosed when I was eighteen. She was hospitalized. During those last days before she died, she told me a fantastic story about a man and a boat. Not a man at all, was he?" He laughed quietly. "Her family lived by the sea. She was high on heroin one night and fell off the dock. When she woke up she was on a boat. I guess it was a yacht, the way she described it. She woke up in a strange bed with a man sitting in the corner watching her. For twenty-seven days he took care of her while she puked all the poison out of her system. Cleaned her up good."

He went quiet, like the story had ended. "There's more?" I asked, prompting him to finish.

"She wanted to stay on that boat, with him." He shook his head. "Maybe if she had she would have found a little peace in her life. But he made her go back. Said she belonged to the land. Said he'd given her something he'd be coming back for."

"That's a strange thing to say." I guess it wasn't that strange when I started to predict how the story would end.

"Yeah, isn't it?"

"And then nine months later, there you were?"

He nodded. "She liked to call me her gift from the gods. A real miracle," he mocked. "But even I wasn't enough to keep her straight."

"You were telling me how you ended up with Greer," I nudged.

"I was at the hospital the night she died. Everyone else went home, but I wouldn't leave her. I remember looking up at the clock on the wall at the exact time she took her last breath—8:14 p.m. Before I could even look back at her on the bed, I felt a hand on my shoulder. I thought it was the nurse coming to turn off the machines and tell me what I already knew. But it wasn't the nurse. It was the man from the boat."

He smiled for the first time since we set off up Central Park West. It was like a dark veil had been lifted from him as the memory went from a bleak crime to a bright and shiny redemption.

"They forgave me," he said. "Every last one of them forgave me."

I left it at that, understanding who *they* were, feeling the brightness from the new light radiating from my guard and friend.

CHAPTER FIFTEEN

The house was dead quiet when we walked through the front door, me with a whole new perspective on my companion, and Rhom with a lighter load on his shoulders for confessing his sins.

"Sophia?" She didn't answer. I looked at Rhom, cautiously considering whether to be concerned with an empty house. "Where is everyone?"

The door to the laundry room opened and Sophia came through it with a basket full of freshly folded sheets and towels. "You two hungry?" she asked before heading for the stairs. Rhom snatched the heavy basket from her hands and nodded for her to lead the way. "Just put it at the top of the stairs. I make lunch."

"Where is everyone?" I asked again. Greer would be at Crusades by now, but when I left that morning Leda was in charge of babysitting Dr. Oxford. The poor man hadn't said a word since being rescued from behind the red door of Maelcolm's prison. But he was intact, and that was a blessing.

"Mr. Sinclair is at the club."

"Is the doctor okay?" I asked, growing more alarmed by the second. "Where's Leda?"

"She left an hour ago. Errands." Her hand waved dismissively as she headed for the kitchen. "Something like that."

"Errands?" I repeated, not able to picture Leda paying the power bill or dropping by the grocery store.

Rhom came back down the stairs as I said it, the look on his face setting off more alarms. He glanced back up the steps and then took them two at a time. I followed, growing warier as we approach the bedroom where the doctor lay catatonic just a couple of hours earlier. Rhom barreled through the door without a knock, but the room was empty.

"Where is he?" I asked, checking the bathroom. It was empty. I ran for the hall and started searching every room on the floor. "Dr. Oxford!" I called, but he was gone.

Rhom went downstairs and searched the main floor. By the time I made it back down to the kitchen, he was standing next to the stove with Sophia.

"Sophia, where the hell is he?"

"Calm down, Alex." Rhom turned back to Sophia who was panning back and forth between the two of us, absently fondling a loaf of bread. She slapped it back down on the counter and positioned her freed hands on her hips.

"Sophia, did Leda take the doctor with her?" Rhom calmly asked.

She stood silent, lips pursed with her eyes level and blank. "What do you think?" she replied. "The man can't even hold a cup, and you think he just gets up and runs errands with Leda?"

"I *swear* I will never take a cab in this city again." Leda waltzed into the kitchen and dropped her purse on the counter with the grace of a bull. "The driver refused to take directions." She looked at the three of us as we stared accusingly at her. "What?"

I glanced behind her. "Is Dr. Oxford with you?"

"Well, of course not. He's upstairs in bed." She straightened the edge of her ivory cashmere sweater and headed for the refrigerator. "I had to get out of here for a while before I blew my brains out from boredom."

"Leda." The sharpness of my tone stopped her as she reached for the handle. "He's gone."

"What do you mean *gone*? The man is comatose."

"Apparently not," Rhom chimed in. "We've searched the house. He's not here."

Her expression went grave as she turned around and gave us her full attention. "You don't think Maelcolm—"

"Not in this house," Sophia said with venom. Her index finger wiggled in the air. "*I* know if someone comes in this house."

"But you were down in the laundry room," I gently replied, trying not to point fingers.

She looked a little offended by the suggestion that she'd dropped the ball while guarding the castle. "So it's my fault that the doctor is missing?"

"I'm not blaming you, Sophia."

"Would everyone please calm down," Rhom mediated. "No one's blaming anyone." He pulled out his phone and dialed. "We got a problem, Boss."

DR. OXFORD HAD SIMPLY VANISHED. Not a single trace of him was found in the house other than the sheets he'd slept on for the past couple of days.

Greer stepped off the elevator and headed straight for the library. The three of us followed and watched as he removed a laptop from the top drawer of the desk and fired it up. He motioned for us to gather around and then pulled up a screen with four different views of the house.

"A surveillance system?" Rhom asked. "When did you install that?"

"It's been up for a while."

Sophia seemed unaffected, while I was horrified by the fact that our every move was being recorded. "I don't know what to say, Greer. I feel a little violated. Have you been watching everyone in this house?" I glanced around the room for cameras but saw none.

He saw the mistrust on my face and shook his head. "This is the first time I've looked at the footage. I have no intention of invading anyone's privacy."

"Then why have it?" I asked accusingly.

"For this very reason." He motioned to the screen. The video clearly showed the doctor leaving his bedroom and walking down the stairs, past the kitchen and out the front door, the whole time looking straight ahead as if completely oblivious to the fact that he might be seen.

"Looks like the doctor left by his own volition." Greer said. "No foul here."

"But why would he leave?" I asked, perplexed as to why the doctor would walk away from the safely of Greer's house, especially after we'd rescued him from a cage in Maelcolm's war room.

Greer shook his head. "That's the million-dollar question."

I looked closer at the naïve scientist walking out the front door and into the lion's den and wondered what was going through his head. He seemed to make no effort to conceal his exit, as if it had never occurred to him that someone might try to stop him. "Am I the only one who thinks he looks a little dazed?"

Everyone in the room muttered their own suspicions.

"My guess is he's heading for home," Greer speculated. "Binghamton."

The night Isabetta Falcone met us in Little Italy and told us about Dr. Oxford's work, she gave us his home address. But we found him in his office at Cornell University before having to pay a visit to his house.

"Or he's back at Cornell," Leda guessed.

"I'll send someone up there to check." Greer shut the laptop and gave me a sympathetic look. "I'm sorry you went through all that for nothing," he said, referring to my risky meeting with Maelcolm to negotiate the doctor's release.

"Yeah," Rhom added. "Oxford could have been a little more appreciative. Ungrateful bastard."

"I appreciate that, Rhom, but he sure didn't look right. I wonder if he even knew what he was doing when he walked out that door."

"Anyone hungry?" Sophia broke the long silence as we all stood around the desk silently formulating our individual hypotheses as to why Dr. Oxford snapped out of his coma and just walked away.

With a sigh, I turned to leave. "I have to be at work in a half hour. Call me as soon as you know anything, Greer."

"Alex," he called after me as I headed for the door. "Be careful. The air is a little thick today, and I don't like it."

"I'm always careful these days, Greer." I glanced at Rhom who I knew wouldn't be far behind me.

I grabbed a banana from the kitchen counter on my way out and headed toward Columbus Avenue. Greer was right about the air feeling stagnant and dense. I passed a few leering faces as I headed for the end of the block. A few months ago, they would have been all over me. But my growing arsenal of powers seemed to announce themselves wherever I went these days, blocking all but the most formidable opponents from doing anything stupid. Besides, I was probably repelling the worst ones, just like I'd done to poor Rhom.

I rounded the corner and headed south just as one particularly stupid opponent reached for me. Without much thought, I took his arm with my fire hand and let him know in no uncertain terms why that was a very bad idea. He screamed and stumbled backward as I kept moving, my poker face displayed prominently. I was getting good at this.

Shakespeare's Library came into view. Even from a block away

I could see that the place was unusually busy; people coming in and out of the door, a few more peeking in through the front window. "What's going on?" I muttered to myself as I approached.

Apollo greeted me as I stepped inside. "Thank God you're here. The place is mobbed."

I looked around the room to see what all the excitement was about. Sitting at the library table—the center of all the commotion—was a man with sandy blond hair and an attractive face. He had a pen in one hand and a book in the other.

"Who is that?" I asked, standing on my tiptoes to get a better view over all the heads. "And why is everyone in Manhattan hovering around him like he's Christ himself?"

"*That*," Apollo said, tilting his head curiously at me like I'd asked a naïve question, "is Elliot Fleming."

"Elliot who?" As soon as the name left my lips, I recognized it. Who wouldn't? It was plastered on the cover of practically every magazine in the world. Well, at least every magazine that counted. You couldn't pass a bookstore without seeing that name in the front window, spread across the spines and covers of a massive book display. Elliot Fleming's latest novel was a publishing phenomenon. The rights had been optioned for film, Ryan Reynolds rumored to play the lead. But it wasn't in our window because our humble establishment dealt in used books, not current bestsellers.

Katie waved to me from across the room, all smiles and bright-eyed as she motioned me over. I pushed through the crowd to get to her and realized the people were standing in a line. They all had his book in their hands, waiting for an autograph.

"Isn't this insane?" she said, glancing at the handsome celebrity sitting at the table. "He's doing a signing for his latest book."

"We don't carry his latest book, Katie." But there he was.

Elliot Fleming in the flesh. He was attractive in an unconventional way, emitting splinters of charm without even opening his mouth. It was in his eyes, the way he communicated with a slight glance and a quirk of his mouth. Either Mr. Fleming worked very hard at fabricating charisma, or he was dangerous and lethal to anyone he set his sights on. It made me uncomfortable that I could see all that by simply watching him for a minute or two, testament to his charm.

Handsome Mr. Fleming glanced up at Katie and smiled. I'd seen that look a thousand times. It was the same look most men gave her, only this one was famous.

"Some woman bought a copy across the street and came in here next. She recognized him, and of course asked for his autograph. Another customer saw what was happening and ran across the street to get his own copy. He must have announced it to everyone over there, because it spread like wildfire. The place has been a zoo for the past hour." She snickered. "I don't think they're too happy over there. They're getting the sales, but we're getting all the attention. I'm sure it's killing them that they couldn't get him to sign at their store."

"What was he doing in here in the first place?" I asked.

She shrugged. "I asked him the same question. Said he likes books. Who'd think, a writer liking books. I guess he thought no one would bother him over here."

I went to put my purse in the back room. When I came out a few minutes later, the crowd was beginning to disperse. Elliot Fleming was standing up, chatting with Katie with that telltale look in his eyes.

Katie motioned me over. He was even more good-looking up close, with his waves of blond hair and grayish-blue eyes. "Alex, this is Elliot Fleming."

"A pleasure," he said, taking my hand. "It seems I've created a bit of a mess here." I glanced around the room, noting the discarded trash from people's hand-held lunches as they waited in the makeshift signing line. There were random books scattered on the floor and table, too.

"Not a problem. We usually have a lot of downtime around here. Not today, though."

"Elliot was just telling me about a reading he has scheduled tonight at Columbia."

How convenient. Katie could attend class and then hop over for a listen. I wondered if she'd had that talk with Constantine yet. Seemed quick, seeing how I'd just left him a couple of hours earlier. Then again, I was reading an awful lot into the look on her face.

"Has Constantine been by this afternoon?" I asked.

Her smiled faded slightly. "It was really nice to meet you, Elliot. Maybe I'll see you tonight."

He said his goodbyes and headed for the door, looking back at Katie as he reached for the handle.

"Speak of the devil," I muttered. Constantine walked in as Elliot was walking out, clearly catching the glimpses his girlfriend was receiving.

"Shit," she groaned.

"Don't worry, Katie. I have a feeling everyone will be walking away happy today."

"Apollo," Constantine acknowledged as he stepped past our manager and made a beeline for us. He gave me an inquisitive look as if wondering if Katie knew we'd spoken. I shook my head discreetly, and he turned his eyes back to Katie. "Lunch?"

It was D-day. Constantine and Katie were about to end their whirlwind romance and part ways amicably—I prayed. After all, they both felt the same way but were blind to that fact. Unfortunately for Katie, I hadn't had time to let her in on that little fact, putting her at a disadvantage.

"Sure," she said with a bright, forced smile. "I'll just get my bag."

As soon as she was out of earshot, I gave him a primer. "I

haven't had time to talk to her yet, so please go easy on her, Constantine."

He smiled down his nose at me. "Of course. I have no intention of hurting the woman I love."

God, they were confusing. He loves her; she loves him. But neither of them could stand to be in the same room together for more than five minutes.

Katie returned with her purse, and they left hand in hand for what would be an interesting lunch date. She had the day shift, which would leave us a few hours to discuss that date before she left for her next one—with Mr. Elliot Fleming.

"Something strange about that new boyfriend of hers," Apollo said as they left the shop. "I can't put my finger on it, but he seems dangerous."

"Yes," I agreed. "You have no idea."

He caught himself. "Oh, I'm sorry, Alex. He's a friend of yours, isn't he? She met him through you, right?"

"Something like that," I sighed.

We both looked back at the mess around the shop, the pain part of pleasure. I grabbed the trash can from behind the front counter and started collecting the dropped napkins and empty paper bags rolled up into loose balls. "Our customers are pigs," I said. "I would never drop my trash on someone's floor."

"They weren't our customers, Alex. I think we sold a grand total of six books so far today. But we did get a little publicity. I'm sure Mr. Fleming's impromptu signing will make some of the papers."

"Oh yeah? How do you figure?"

"Because I saw a least five people with their phones out recording it. And you know where that kind of stuff ends up—on Facebook or Twitter. We might even make YouTube. 'Bestselling author crashes bookstore dive.' People love that kind of stuff."

We spent the next thirty minutes cleaning up and putting back the scattered books callously tossed around by some other bookstore's customers. Katie came blowing through the door with a big smile on her face.

"That was fast," I said. "Based on that grin I'm assuming your little talk went well?"

"Better than well." She headed for the back to put her purse away. When she returned, her bright face had turned somber.

"I thought you said it went well? You look like you're about to have a meltdown." If that bright smile was nothing but a front to hide a less than amicable breakup, I'd murder Constantine.

"Goddamn him, Alex. He was just so agreeable."

"And that's a bad thing?"

Her breath shuddered. "Done. Finito."

She looked up when the front door chimed and a woman walked inside. "Perfect timing." Her wide smile resurrected as she zoomed across the floor to engage the customer, a distraction from the post-breakup thoughts that must have been on a constant loop inside her head.

My phone rang a moment later. It was Greer. "Please tell me you've found him alive," I said without a greeting.

I listened as Greer informed me that Dr. Oxford's home was empty and looked like no one had been there in weeks. No wife, no kids, no cat or dog; just a pile of mail shoved through the slot on the front door creating a slippery hazard for anyone walking into the dark foyer of his house.

"Maybe he's hiding out in his office at Cornell," I suggested. But whoever Greer sent up there had already made the same assumption. There was no sign of the doctor at the university either. Dr. David Oxford had walked out of Greer's house with his own two feet and left no trace. He'd simply vanished.

CHAPTER SIXTEEN

ophia should have been long gone by the time I got home from work, but the smell of cooking food made me wonder if she was still in the kitchen. It certainly wasn't Greer or Leda, and since I'd swear on my life that Rhom had trailed me to and from work, it wasn't him cooking up a late-night meal either.

"Sophia?"

Greer stepped from the library. "She left an hour ago."

"A little late to be keeping her here, don't you think?"

"She offered, and I accepted."

"Offered what?" My eyes panned around the living room and foyer and then back toward the kitchen. The light in the dining room was on. "What smells so good?"

"Dinner." I peeked into the dining room but the table was bare. "I thought we'd be a little less formal." He took my hand and led me into the kitchen. The large island was set with plates and wine glasses. On the stove was Sophia's signature cherry-red pot, its lid set slightly off center with steam escaping through the gap. Good and hot.

"Did you do all this for me?"

He nodded. "Well, Sophia made the sauce, but I cooked the pasta. Made the wine, too—in the bathtub."

"Hmm. Crushed the grapes yourself?" I got a visual of Lucille Ball standing in a barrel of red grapes, squishing the pulp through her toes. "So what's on the menu?"

He went to the stove and removed the lid from the pot. "Spaghetti."

I couldn't help but laugh. In all the months I'd eaten under his roof, this was the first time his Italian cook had made the classic. "That's exactly what I'm in the mood for."

We served ourselves straight from the stove, dropping heaps of pasta on our plates and topping it with Sophia's beautiful Bolognese sauce. A bottle of Barolo polished it off nicely, the smell making me heady before it even reached my lips.

"I'm impressed," I complimented, sampling the perfectly cooked al dente pasta. "You didn't actually make this from scratch, did you?" Now that would warrant a whole new dimension of respect for the man sitting next to me.

"No. But I did drop it into the water and set the timer."

I took a bite of food and thought about the gesture. "Thank you for this. It was thoughtful."

He smiled and continued eating, splaying his hand at the center of my back. His palm was warm through the fabric of my shirt, sending a spike of heat from my knees to my chest. "It's been a difficult few days, and I know you're upset about Dr. Oxford. I wanted to give you a little pleasure. Even if it's just a good meal and a glass of wine."

Didn't that raise the temperature in the room? Again, Greer Sinclair was trying to please me, and I was too tangled up in my own head to just relax and let him. I knew where this was all heading. The ball was in my court. I loved him, but our union would happen at my pace, if at all. I couldn't get past the image of his beautiful face and perfectly sculpted form walking next to an old woman who could barely keep up. I could get used to people complimenting me on my handsome grandson, but I doubted he'd find it as amusing. He would be miserable but loyal to the end. But who was I to make that decision for him? And then there was the matter of whose war would leave the most wreckage. If I snubbed my father and ignored our bargain, he'd come for me and start a war with Greer's people to get me back. But if I surrendered myself to him, Greer would start his own with just as much carnage, if not more. The dilemma curbed my appetite.

Greer put his fork down and looked at me, his eyes peering right into my heart. I quickly closed off my thoughts to keep him from reading them. Who was I kidding? I was his–mind, body, and soul. There had to be a solution for this conundrum.

"Done?" I asked nervously, lowering my own fork to my plate.

He nodded.

I cleared the lump forming in the back of my throat. "Dessert?"

His head slowly shook.

I felt the heat of his palm against mine as he took my hand and stood up from his seat. With his other, he took the napkin I had twisted in a death grip and placed it on the counter. Then he led me out of the kitchen and up the stairs, into his bedroom where there was nothing to hide behind; no bite of food, no small talk, just the space between us and that godforsaken wall I kept throwing up.

"Greer, I don't know—"

He ran the back of his fingers over my cheek, cupping the side of my face before kissing me lightly. "I'll take whatever you have to give."

A second kiss deepened, and before I could think clearly or reason rationally as to why I shouldn't allow it, I was lying naked in his bed with my back pressed against his chest. It was such a familiar place, with his arm wrapped around my waist and his leg possessively covering my thighs. I knew every contour of his body, every dip and groove of his muscles. My tensed limbs softened with each rise and fall of his chest, and even though I could feel him firm and ready against me, I knew nothing would happen unless I made it happen.

His breath rushed over my cheek as I turned my face toward my shoulder and moved his hand between my breasts. It was anything but salacious as I kept it locked firmly at my sternum, cupping it in place with my palm.

Without a word, he pulled his hand away and sat up on the edge of the bed, a shudder vibrating from his body along the surface of the mattress. "You're killing me, Alex." His hands combed through his hair, reaching to the back of his neck as his elbows rested on his knees. "I want you so bad I can't breathe."

I knelt behind him and ran my hands over the curves of his shoulders, kissing the left one before resting my cheek against his skin. "I know. I just have these things in my head."

I never imagined that even if I buried the wreckage left by Daemon, I'd be confronted with another reason for holding Greer at bay. How could I lead him on, deepen a relationship that might end the moment we found the vessel? The worst part was not being able to tell him why.

"Don't go," I whispered, easing him back against the mattress, running my hand over the curve of his waist. His breath hitched from my touch, and without thinking I made a bold move and led his hand between my thighs.

"Jesus, Alex," he moaned, exploring me and kissing me, but never once presuming it was an invitation for anything more than that.

I FELT like an empress when I woke the next morning. Like a pampered, deeply satisfied queen lying next to her king. His shoulder rolled lazily as I shifted to look at him, the soft waves of his hair folding into the creases of the sheet, lying on his stomach with his arms buried under the pillow with his face turned away. Greer rarely slept deeply, a unique characteristic of the children of the gods. Today was a rare exception, seeing him curled under the sheet, peaceful.

"Mr. Sinclair," I whispered to myself, falling back against the mattress with my eyes sealed shut. "I think I need more of you, please."

The words weren't meant to be heard, but I could feel him stir under the thin sheet. I smiled euphorically, opening my eyes and turning my head to look at his beautiful face. But he hadn't moved, still had his head against the pillow with his face turned away. The stir came again, only this time I could see the sheet rolling like a ripple of water over his back, a concealed snake sliding over his skin.

"Jesus!" I scrambled over the edge of the bed and nearly fell to the floor. "Greer!"

He sprang off the pillow and flipped over, staring at me wild-eyed. I must have scared the hell out of him, because I swear I could see his heart beating against his chest wall.

"What's wrong?" he asked, his eyes darting around the room.

I pointed to the mattress. "Get off the bed. There's something under the sheet."

He looked confused and followed the direction of my pointed finger. As he lifted the sheet and peered under it, his shoulders tensed briefly and then relaxed, a humorous smile spreading across his face.

"What's so amusing?" I asked, looking at his hand, which was reaching over his shoulder toward his back.

"I believe you've just met my soul."

"You'll have to explain that," I said, clueless about what he meant.

He climbed from the bed, displaying his generously cut limbs, and turned his back to me. The geometric lines of his tattoo were moving, undulating in a three-dimensional dance that waved a few inches off his skin and then settled back down to meet his flesh. I'd seen the tattoo many times but never asked what the symbols meant. I certainly would have if they'd done that before.

"Am I the only one around here who doesn't have one of those?" I asked, visualizing the inked lines of Katie's dragon. I followed the symbols down to where they terminated at the small of his back, a faded scar still marking the place where he'd cut out a piece of his own bone to give to me some twenty or so years earlier.

"Probably," he replied.

"I've never seen one on Rhom or Thomas," I said. "Or any of the others."

He turned to face me, his brow arched. "Have you seen the others naked?"

"Well, no."

"It's a very personal thing, Alex. We all carry it differently. I believe Thomas carries his on the soles of his feet. No pun intended."

He walked around to my side of the bed and pulled me into his arms. I could feel the movement of the lines, softly undulating, electric, as I reached around to his backside.

"You are the first woman to see it," he whispered against my cheek. "And you are the last."

I was thankful to be buried against his skin, because even though I'd gotten good at keeping him out of my head, the look on my face from hearing those words would have blown my secret wide open.

I might have to leave you, Greer. Just as soon as we find that damn vessel.

Recovered from the painful thought, I pushed away from him and forced a smile. I'd gotten so good at deceiving him, I questioned my own morality. But whatever I decided, it would be for him.

We found our clothes and headed downstairs toward the smell of freshly brewed coffee.

I circled my arms around Sophia's waist and squeezed, and Greer kissed her lightly on the cheek. She turned around with a spatula in her hand, eyeing us suspiciously, glancing from me to Greer. I hadn't looked in a mirror or bothered to run my fingers through my hair, and Greer's usual smart appearance was lacking. I'm sure Sophia could smell the impropriety from a mile away.

We grabbed a couple of plates and served ourselves straight from the stove, choosing to eat standing at the island instead of the dining room table. We chewed our food, watching each other thoughtfully until Sophia interrupted our gaze with a French press full of coffee in her hand.

"You want coffee?" she asked, setting the press down between us.

"Thank you, Sophia." Greer filled my cup and then his own. "I have a few meetings at the club today, but I can be home by late afternoon."

"Late shift," I shrugged.

His chest deflated. There was my pesky job again, always getting in the way. "Then I guess I'll see you late tonight."

He took a last bite of bacon and kissed me on the forehead before heading back up the stairs to change into a suit. On his way back down, he stopped at the kitchen doorway and just stood there for a minute, gazing at me with an unspoken message. I felt a flicker of heat flash around the walls of my stomach as his eyes burrowed into mine. And then he was gone. I stood up on weak knees as I listened to the elevator door shut, replaying the night over and over in my mind until I realized Sophia was staring at me and shaking her head.

"What?" I asked.

"*What?*" she mocked. She turned back to the stove and

dumped the uneaten bacon into a plastic container. "Is not my business," she shrugged.

I reached around her and grabbed one last piece before she sealed the lid. "You know I love you, Sophia, but you have got to get over this judgement. For God's sake, we're all adults in this house. And you're not even Catholic anymore." I don't know why I felt so uncomfortable with her disapproval. After all, she was the one living in the Dark Ages, not me. "Not that I owe any explanation, but we didn't do anything *scathing* last night."

"Oh mio Dio." Her left hand met that old familiar spot on her hip while she showed me one finger with her right. "Lie number one." That finger was suddenly pointed at me. "You need to go look in the mirror." She cocked her head toward the living room, and I cringed at the thought of what I'd see looking back at me. It was becoming a real nuisance, worse than the annoying pink flush that cursed a redhead every time she felt the sting of embarrassment.

I walked up to the mirror and looked at my face. The whites of my eyes where tinted a soft but jarring blue, my own personal brand that usually manifested by the onset of my powers—and apparently my pleasure, too.

I SPENT the rest of the morning reading in the library, avoiding Sophia's judgmental stare. Around noon, I finally couldn't take it anymore and left the house with two hours to spare before my shift began. Instead of the usual sandwich from the deli, I decided to kill the time by treating myself to lunch at a real restaurant.

The restaurant I chose was packed. I followed the hostess to a table against the back wall, tucked in the corner.

"Is this okay?" she asked.

"It's fine, thank you." I actually preferred the isolation, even if it did come with the noise from the kitchen.

I saw the chair across from mine slide out while my eyes were buried in the menu.

"There's something very wrong about putting you in a dark corner," Constantine said, seating himself at my table. "Excuse me," he called, raising his hand to get the attention of a passing waitress.

She looked annoyed but stopped as his hand reached out to block her path. There was a plate in her left hand and two glasses balanced in the palm of her right. "I'm sorry sir, but this isn't my table. I'll be happy to get your waitress just as soon as I—"

"That's very kind of you," he looked at her name tag, "Chloe. But I think my friend and I would like *you* to get us two glasses of red wine. House will be fine."

Her expression suddenly morphed from irritation to joy as he burrowed his eyes into hers. "My pleasure." She smiled broadly and walked off, still carrying the plate and glasses, which she promptly set back on the kitchen window ledge to order our drinks.

"Well, that was bold," I said. "Someone else is now waiting patiently for their lunch."

"Ah yes, the art of patience." He crossed his long legs and eased back in the chair. "Unfortunately, I have none."

The waitress returned with two glasses of wine and a basket of warm bread. "I thought you might like some bread while you wait."

"Thank you, Chloe," he said with exaggerated charm.

She kept her eyes on his for a moment longer than she should have, and then she went to retrieve her previous order from the window ledge, now probably lukewarm or cold.

"Shameless!" I chastised, struggling to keep from falling for that same charm. Though I had to admit it was nice to move to the front of the line. I looked at the wine and considered if it was worth needing a nap halfway through my shift. "Oh, fuck it."

"Is there a problem?" he asked.

I shook my head, "What are you doing here, Constantine? Following me again?" I sipped the wine and picked up the menu, avoiding eye contact because he could read me almost as well as Greer. I had a pretty good idea why he was here. "If you plan to ask me anything about Katie, you've ventured out of Constantine land for nothing." My eyes grazed over the menu, comprehending none of it as I waited for his next move.

"I already know everything I need to know about Katie," he replied. "Including who she spent her evening with."

I presumed he was referring to Elliot Fleming, author extraordinaire. She said she was meeting him after his reading at Columbia the night before. Who else could it be? "Then what do you need from me?"

"Nothing." He examined the cufflink at his wrist. "I suppose I asked for this. I suppose I should be happy for her. Nothing worse than a scorned woman lapping at your heels the moment you set her free."

"Set her free? Is that what you did? Because as I remember it, you set each other free." I gave him a withering look. "*Really*, Constantine."

"Right. Well, if she's moved on."

"I'm sure they're not engaged yet. Give her some credit." I suppressed a smirk, feeling a bit sorry for him. Though their affair was brief, Katie had obviously left her mark on him. A difficult thing to do, especially for a mere mortal.

"There is nothing mortal about a dragon," he corrected, mining my thoughts. "But you're right. As much as I hate to admit it, Katie Bishop has left her mark on my heart." He leaned over the table. "I just prefer to do the leading, and that woman will not be led."

Our real waitress arrived to take our order. I decided on the grilled chicken sandwich and Constantine ordered a steak—extra rare.

"You still haven't told me why you're here," I said.

His haughty expression turned dire. "I'm here to stop you from making not only the worst decision of your life, but the stupidest."

"Huh?" I feigned surprise. "And I thought the grilled chicken was a pretty safe bet."

"Under better circumstances, I'd find your humor delightful." He gave me a look that sent a shudder through me. He had a real gift for doing that to me, and it usually meant I was about to hear something unpleasant. "A little bird flew through my window this morning and told me something incredulous. In fact, I found it hard to believe. Especially after you failed to mention it during our visit yesterday." He grabbed a piece of the warm bread and then tossed it back in the basket. "Really, Alex. Did you think you could do something so stupid and I wouldn't find out about it?"

My brain raced, trying to figure out what I'd done to incite him. Not that anything I did was his business. "I have no idea what you're talking about."

"I'm referring to your bargain with the devil. Do you really think that handing yourself over to Maelcolm will result in anything but a life of misery and self-hatred—not to mention slavery?" He stopped lecturing and stared at me blankly. "You do know what he intends to do with you?"

I fell silent, finding it difficult to say the words aloud. Instead, I nodded once and dropped my eyes to the table.

"Then you have no qualms with serving as a broodmare for Maelcolm's army? You chose to surrender any shred of a life in exchange for what? For Greer's comfort? What about yours? What do you think his existence will be like when he learns the truth? That you actually went through with it. For *his* sake!"

How did he know? How did Constantine know anything? He just did.

"We had to get the doctor out of there, and you know why."

Constantine knew all about the lenses in Dr. Oxford's eyes. "I had to offer myself in exchange for Oxford."

"Yes," he laughed with a mock. "But you don't have to go through with it, woman! You're worried about lying to a monster like Maelcolm, so you justify going through with it by telling yourself that it's all for the sake of Greer?"

"Either way we have a war," I said. "I'm just weighing which one will be less catastrophic. The lesser of two evils."

"Well, that is noble of you," he said. "Just bear in mind that while you're sparing the one you love a life of sacrifice, you might be killing him, too. With kindness."

For a moment his words made me second guess all of it. "I haven't decided what I'm going to do yet, but whatever choice I make, it will be for Greer. And you can't stop me."

"You're right. It is not my place to interfere with matters of destiny."

Blah, blah, blah. I was quite familiar with that mantra of his.

"If you've made your decision, then there is nothing I can do to stop you." He leaned into the table, the baritone of his voice dropping for dramatic effect. "But if Greer Sinclair finds out that you're planning to make good on that little bluff, he'll put you in chains to stop you." He straightened back up as the waitress delivered our lunch, never taking his eyes off me as she reached over the table to set the plates down.

"Can I get you anything else?" she asked.

"No. Thank you," he replied, continuing once she was out of earshot. "Greer and I may not agree on many things, but this is one of those rare exceptions we are in complete agreement on. The status of your liberty, that is."

"But you won't tell him, will you?" I said. "You can't."

CHAPTER SEVENTEEN

I'd almost managed to have a pleasant lunch until Constantine had to come along and ruin it. His knowing about my agreement with Maelcolm and the decision to possibly go through with it made me nervous. Normally I'd have some peace in knowing he'd keep his mouth shut, but this was different. This little secret was something worth violating his "code" for.

I walked into the bookstore just as Elliot Fleming was leaving.

"Good to see you again. It's Alex, right?" He extended his hand.

"Yes, Alex." Instead of shaking, he gripped my hand and squeezed it gently. "Katie and I just had lunch. She tells me you're a good friend."

I glanced at her from across the room. "You could say that. We know all of each other's secrets."

"You'll have to join us for lunch next time and fill me in," he offered.

I agreed to a future threesome and sent him out the door. Katie was nervously fiddling with an armful of stray books when

I came out of the back room. "Lunch with the famous Elliot Fleming? I guess it didn't take you long to move on."

She smiled weakly. "He's just—"

"A distraction?" I said.

Her chest hollowed from a rush of air that left her limp as she sat in one of the chairs around the library table. "Elliot's great. Really great. But I can't stop thinking about *him*."

"Hey, you're the one who said he was suffocating you," I reminded her.

"And he was. I mean, I'm glad we 'gracefully' ended it," she said with air quotes. "But I still miss him. Jesus, Alex. You have no idea what Constantine can do to a girl."

Oh, I had a pretty good idea.

"Speaking of Constantine, *we* just had lunch."

Her eyes flashed and then cooled. "Oh yeah?"

I could see the concern on her face, her overactive imagination reading something into it that wasn't there. "Seriously, Katie? You think I'd do that to you?"

She shook her head to dismiss the thought. "Of course not."

"Besides," I assured her. "I'm already spoken for."

We both relaxed and started going through a box of "new" used books that needed to be put on the shelves. It was an effective distraction for her, but if it took me all evening I was going to get the details about this new thing with Fleming. I'd seen how hard she'd fallen for Constantine, and there was no way she was already on to someone new.

She dropped the book she was holding back into the box when she noticed me glancing at her every two seconds. "Okay! Just say it."

"Say what, Katie?"

"That I'm a soulless slut with no feelings."

"Really, Katie? You? Soulless?"

She tossed one of the books at me. "So I'm a slut with a soul, then?"

"Stop saying that word." I hated the word *slut*, the most obscene double standard on the planet.

"Look, if I don't focus on someone else, I'm going to cave and start stalking him." She bit the edge of her painted lip. "It's not like I can just go running back to him and beg forgiveness. He wanted out just as much as I did."

True. And God help her if she slipped back under that satyr's spell. Then the original nightmare I'd dreaded all along would culminate into a storm, with me stuck in the middle.

We both glanced up when the chimes on the front door sounded. I didn't see anyone, but as soon as I saw the color of Katie's face deepen to a bright flush of red, I knew who had just entered and promptly disappeared into the stacks. Her hand began to shake as it dropped away from the box, her knuckles grazing the tabletop. I could almost smell the adrenaline leaching from her skin. Cool, calm, and collected Katie Bishop had just been reduced to a cliché.

"You look well," Constantine said to her as he stepped out of the aisle adjacent to where we were standing.

"Well, you just saw her yesterday," I muttered.

"What was that, Alex?" he asked without taking his eyes off Katie.

Katie took a step toward him. I don't think she even realized she did it. "You too, Constantine."

"Oh, for crying out loud." I scooted the box of books a few feet away and plunged my hands inside, pretending to sort through it while I listened to every word.

"I see you've been busy with this *scribe*." His lips curled with disdain.

"Actually, he's an author," Katie countered.

"A bestselling author," I added.

He turned his head to look at me, a silent *butt out* in his expression.

Katie finally seemed to come to her senses. "What are you doing here, Constantine?"

His chest inflated as he stood taller. "I just thought I'd stop by to make sure you're all right. After yesterday."

"You mean to make sure I haven't fallen off the deep end of despair?" She held her arms out, wrists up. "See, everything's just fine."

They both shot me a wicked glare as I snickered quietly under my breath.

He glanced down at her pale, slender arms and took them gently in his hands. "That is good to know. I would hate to see such beauty marred by violence."

I could see her visibly shrink as he raised them up and pressed his lips to each pulse point.

Hold it together, Katie, I prayed, sensing the rapid beat of her heart as her breathing accelerated. I could actually see it pounding against her ribcage. How was that possible? My senses were on fire, flooding my brain with a constant stream of emotions. I looked around the room, half aware of voices floating past my ears, trying to make sense of all the sharp sounds distracting me. My head snapped toward the window as a woman walked past, the chatter in her head bleeding into mine.

Suddenly the room went dark, and all I could hear was the blood rushing back and forth to my own heart. My eyes struggled to focus, and when my vision finally began to clear and the sounds bombarding my head calmed to a low whisper, I could see everything as clear as a glass of sparkling water. I was in a space with nothing but the stars above my head and a sea of lush blue-green grass beneath my feet. My mother hadn't come to me for weeks, and now I was home again, in her circle—my circle.

I looked toward the north where my mother's athame lay perched with its carved steel hanging over the edge of the stone altar, just as it had the night I found a thin silver chain wrapped around my ankle, the night I discovered my shiny black wings. As the moon and stars reflected off its surface, it started to vibrate, trembling as it inched closer to the edge, precariously teetering just to the brink of falling over. It stopped, and a gust of violent wind sent it flying into the air, straight toward me. The sharp tip met the skin over my heart, pushing inward like the tufting of an upholstered chair. I looked down at my naked body and dared to breathe for fear that the slightest movement would send the blade point straight through the thin layer of skin. The circle fell silent. My eyes left the blade and traveled around the space, desperate to see my mother walk through the ring of candles circling at the edge of the grass. Even Isla Kelley—my precarious grandmother—would do.

The wind picked back up as my eyes circled back to the altar. "No," I whispered to anyone who was listening. They were all there, hidden by the veil, those who called themselves *my people*. That I knew without a doubt. My hair twisted into a cyclone above my head, in the whirl of wind wrapping around the circle space with lightning speed, and the blade pierced my skin, plunging past the muscle and bone until it found my heart.

I fell to my knees, the pain milder than I expected, leaving me curious as I looked down at the thick stream of blood seeping around the edges of the athame. I could feel my heart continue to beat around it, pumping the blood through the wound, over the steel and onto the carpet of grass beneath me. The killer inside of me remained silent. It was my own kin who'd done this to me.

"Why?" I wondered aloud.

My head fell sideways, and my eyes shut from the delayed pain that was now filling my chest. The grass undulated under my knees and I knew someone had stepped into the circle. Before I could open my eyes, a hand gripped the back of my head, wrapping around my hair and jerking my face up. Isla's long white mane fell over my forehead as she looked me in the eye. And then she nodded once and pointed toward the west.

The ground began to shake, splitting the circle as something pushed through the earth. A single stick emerged, followed by a plume of large lobbed leaves. A bush of some kind. But then it burst through the surface with the roar of an earthquake, throwing me backward as it lifted the soil beneath me to make way for it—a massive, towering tree that took up half the circle, its roots expanding far beyond the edge of the candles, stretching as far as I could see. A light glowed around it, and on its thickly scored bark was a series of lines.

I climbed back to my feet and looked down at the wound in my chest. It was still open but the blood had stopped, leaving a trail of caked crimson covering my breasts and stomach. The athame was in my right hand where it belonged. I slowly approached, reaching for the bark tentatively, glancing around for Isla Kelley. She was gone, but I could feel her behind the veil with the rest of them.

"Show yourselves!" I demanded, moving closer to the tree. "Cowards," I whispered, my fingers an inch away from the random marks covering the ancient trunk. The tips of my fingers grazed the surface and something hard knocked me to the ground.

"Alex!"

Katie's bright blue eyes came into focus, the feel of her slap still stinging my cheek. "Why did you hit me?" I asked, both incredulous and agitated that she'd stopped whatever it was I was about to see. "Jesus! Now I'll never know."

"Know what?" she asked.

"What it meant."

Constantine was staring at me, gauging my epiphany.

"You know exactly what I just saw, don't you?" I accused. But he'd never admit it. Always spouting off about things that weren't his to tell.

Katie looked completely confused, glancing back and forth between the two of us as I accused Constantine visually of something inappropriate. He just stared back at me, knowing and defiant, caught between what was right for me and what was right for the damned universe.

"Would someone please tell me what the hell just happened?" Katie demanded, shooting Constantine a look.

His chin dropped as his gaze on me intensified. Then his expression turned consolatory as he turned and walked out the door without a word to either of us.

Katie stared at the door as it closed, its chimes still ringing. I was on my feet, adjusting my shirt and tousled hair when she turned to look back at me. I could tell by the look on her face that she was as much disappointed at seeing him leave as she was to see me dazed and disheveled from some sort of trance or spell. Before she could speak, I threw my hands up in surrender. "I was back in the circle."

"Where?" A lightbulb must have gone off in her head. "Oh! The *circle*?"

I'd told her about my visions before, the ones with my mother. But there was no Maeve Kelley in that circle space today —it was all Isla. "I have a mean grandmother," I began. "It's hard to believe my mother—who was very kind, by the way—came from her."

Katie sat down to listen, literally on the edge of her seat, as I gave her the condensed version of what I saw.

"That shit is fucked up, Alex. What do you think it meant?"

I shook my head. "I have no idea, but I know who might." If anyone could read the tea leaves of that vision, it was Ava or Melanie, my perennial advisors. After all, Melanie was a student of Isla Kelley's magic, right alongside my mother. "What are you doing tomorrow afternoon?"

"Well, I was thinking about calling Elliot. It's my day off."

"Yeah, that's why I asked. Aren't you spending a lot of time with this guy? God, Katie, you just met him." I bobbed my head at her, knowingly. "I saw the way you were just looking at Constantine." I extended my wrists. "Oh look," I mocked. "I haven't tried to slit my wrists today. I thought I was going to throw up when he kissed them."

She grinned, no shame at all for being such a cliché. "Yeah, he was kind of sweet."

"Blah! Make up your mind, Katie."

"I already have. Why do you think I'm all over Elliot?" She shrugged. "I just need a buffer to get me over the hump."

"So, you want to go down to see Ava with me tomorrow?"

RHOM WASN'T WAITING at the door when I left the shop, which was unusual, and frankly made me nervous. Not that I needed him to walk me home anymore, but it was easier with a second line of defense and just plain comforting to have such a formidable creature guarding my back. I was also a little skeptical that Greer would agree to call off the guard duty, in light of Maelcolm's paternal interest in me.

Speaking of Greer, he was waiting in the living room when I walked through the front door, a book in his hand with the light of a dim lamp illuminating him. The scene reminded me of a cozy commercial peddling some peace-of-mind product.

"Finally," he said, snapping the book shut and placing it on the small table next to his chair. "I was beginning to worry."

It was barely ten thirty, a little later than usual but only by a few minutes.

"Where was Rhom tonight?"

"I thought I'd give you some of that space you seem to need. I don't think you need a man hovering over you every second of the day. Besides, you're strong enough." He cocked his brow. "*I* would not want to go up against you right now."

By "a man" I knew he was talking about himself as much as Rhom. He could sense my unease from all the smothering.

"I'm hungry." I headed for the kitchen to scrounge up whatever leftovers I could find. When I walked through the doorway,

I was immediately assaulted—in a good way—by a familiar smell.

"Pizza." He followed me in and grabbed a plate from the cabinet. "I sent Sophia home early and had it delivered."

We sat at the kitchen island while I inhaled several slices. One day I was going to regret all the rich food, but for now I seemed to be losing weight no matter how many calories I consumed. Nerves, I assumed. An overactive metabolism from all the adrenaline.

I finished my last slice and decided to hand wash the plate in the sink, taking my time drying it before placing it back in the cabinet. This was the part where we went upstairs and tried to act normal again. This was the part that made my stomach do flip-flops.

"Alex." Greer ran his hands over the rounds of my shoulders. "Come upstairs. We'll just sleep."

I turned to look at him. He deserved that much from me. He was so close it made me weak, lightheaded from the smell of his skin. "I think I'll sleep in my own bed tonight." My eyes flicked up to his for a second, and then lowered back to his chest. "I'm sorry for being so… frigid."

He took a step back, still cupping the sides of my arms. "Don't ever use that word again. It's insulting."

With his hand wrapped around mine, he led me up the stairs. When we reached the top step, he kissed me on the forehead and headed for his room. I watched him disappear behind the door, knowing he would do that every night until I said otherwise, patiently waiting for me to open up and let him in completely, something that would hinge on the decision I had to make. And then I went to my own room to sleep alone.

. . .

SOMETHING KEPT HITTING me in the face, like a large bug using me as a landing and launching pad. I swatted at it and then grabbed it, a familiar smell hitting my nose.

"What?"

I sat up in bed and looked at the collection of orange peels scattered around the comforter.

"Gawd, you sleep like a rock," someone drawled.

I nearly fell over the edge of the mattress when I saw a man sitting in the chair on the other side of the room, poised to throw another piece of peel in my direction. A scream was queued at the back of my throat, but then I saw the lines fading in and out like a mirage over his face. One second they were barely there, and the next they were as black as newly inked tattoos. His dark blue eyes wandered back to the orange in his hand as if I weren't even in the room.

"Wait. It's you, isn't it?" I asked. "*Bear*?"

"Well, I hope it's me." he replied, bemused. "If it isn't me, then I've been a fool all these years." His nose crinkled in a tight knot when he popped a wedge of the fruit in his mouth, as if the act of chewing it was forced.

"I wouldn't think cats liked oranges," I said as he took another bite.

"Honey, this one does."

My robe was several feet away, tossed over the chair on the other side of the room. Considering he'd already seen me naked about a hundred times, and he was a cat, traipsing across the room in underwear and a T-shirt wasn't such a big deal. I went for it, his eyes sweeping over me as I threw the robe on.

"I see you're sleeping alone again. Too bad. You have such a beautiful man on the other side of that wall." He nodded in the direction of Greer's bedroom.

"That's my business." He was beginning to annoy me with his chewing and his flat stare. There was something judgmental in the way he looked at me, an insufferable child standing in front of him.

"Greer is not Daemon, you know." The black symbols circling his jaw constricted and tightened. "Nor is he that thing that chased you through the woods when you were too small to defend yourself."

His expression at the mention of the unmentionable was toxic, like he had murder in his eyes. Maybe if he'd been sent to me twenty years earlier things would have been different on that farm. I wouldn't have spent all that time hiding from an old man with a hard-on for little girls.

"My dear, sweet little witch," he said, shaking his head. "That man loves you deeper than you'll ever know. That kind of love can never be fully felt. It just takes up too much space to see or feel all at once. So explore it, and bite off pieces of it until your hunger goes away." His shoulders sagged as he released his breath and tossed the last piece of orange peel at me. "*What* are you waiting for?"

"I don't know. I'm trying."

"Well, I can only push you into his arms so many times before it's up to you, my dear."

I gasped, remembering the first time I'd seen a fleeting glimpse of his real face—his markings. It was the morning I woke up and thought Greer was my husband, the day Sophia and I took a trip to Bergdorf Goodman. "You? It was you?" His tiny claws had drawn blood on my leg, transforming me into a lovestruck newlywed.

He grinned, the tattoos on his face going from black to orange as his fur began to emerge. "I *hate* this part," he muttered as his body shrank and a tail snaked out from behind him. By the time I blinked, he was nothing more than an orange tabby sitting in a chair with a few citrus peels scattered around him.

CHAPTER EIGHTEEN

Apollo had found the resources to hire Erica *part* part-time to fill in on the days when two of us needed to be out. Since it was Katie's day off and Apollo had tickets for some morning seminar at NYU, it was just the two of us for the afternoon.

She came shuffling into the shop at two o'clock for the late shift, wearing a boxy blue dress with small yellow circles printed around the neckline. I looked closer and realized they were little smiley faces forming a wide grin along the curve of her neck.

"What do you want to do today?" she asked, following behind me like a persistent puppy, nipping at the back of my heels as I traced the edge of the library table trying in vain to put some distance between us.

"Work, Erica. We're here to work. Just keep your eyes on the door for any customers while I shelve these." I took the box of books in my arm and headed for the section on suspense and thrillers. If it were Katie or Apollo, we'd find a home for the new inventory together, but Erica was odd. Too needy in the way she glued herself to people. A psychic vampire. She drained me when she walked in a room. It wasn't her fault. Some people just did that—drained the energy right out of you.

I finished organizing the books on the shelf but stalled at the back of the dark aisle, dreading having to go back out there and make chatty conversation with her.

"God," I sighed, looking at the time on my phone. It was barely two thirty, which meant I had two and a half more hours before Apollo came in to relieve me of my shift with the girl from Mars. An hour with Erica felt like six.

Erica was waiting obediently when I finally emerged. The book in her hand slipped from her grasp as I approached and put the empty box on the table. I glanced at it as it hit the floor.

She retrieved it with a flush of embarrassment. "Sorry."

"It's okay, Erica. It's a book. It won't break."

For the first time since she walked into the shop she was speechless, transfixed in some sort of suspended state while I continued with the chore of refilling the empty box with another load of inventory. I reached for a book on the table and felt an odd sensation of having under reached for it, like the table had shrunk several inches shorter or I'd grown taller. By now, Erica's face had changed. Her brows peaked at the inside corners, swooping up into question marks as they curved into little humps at the intersection of her forehead. There was a distinct pallor to her skin.

"What?" I asked, more annoyed by her sudden perplexity than her previous inability to give me an inch of breathing room.

She shrank farther back and glanced quickly at the floor near my feet. "T-that," she stuttered out, pointing with her eyes.

I nearly tumbled backward as I looked down at the gap between my shoes and the floor. There must have been six inches of clearance between me and the worn industrial carpet under my feet. A loud gasp left my mouth as my eyes darted back to Erica's. She was mouthing something unintelligible and moving backward until her rear end met the edge of one of the shelves.

"It's okay, Erica." I reached my arm out toward her, trying to stop her from bolting out of the shop. "I can explain this."

Actually, I couldn't. I was hovering half a foot off the floor and had no idea how or why. Maybe it was another power emerging. But what kind of power made you hover above the floor like a ghost?

"I—" Erica's words seemed to clog in her throat. "I have to leave now," she managed to choke out.

"No!" I barked. As soon as the word left my mouth, she stopped, frozen and unable to move. "Erica?" There was no response, and it dawned on me that I'd just halted her in her tracks. I waved my hand in front of her face, but her eyes seemed to focus straight ahead in a trance-like state, fixated on the same spot from a few seconds earlier. The clock was ticking, and I knew any second now she would snap back into animation and run for the hills unless I figured out how to plant my feet back on the ground. The last thing I needed was to be stuck here until closing because Erica had flown the coop, or to have Apollo or a customer walk in while I hovered around the room.

Levitating even higher as I made my way to the back room, praying the chimes on the front door wouldn't sound, I grabbed my phone from my purse and dialed. Ava picked up on the third ring.

"Thank God!"

"Alex? Are you all right?" she asked, clearly startled by my wail.

I took a heaving breath to stifle the sob brimming my lips. "I am so screwed, Ava!"

"Calm down, darling. Tell me what's happening."

I glanced at Erica's frozen form. "I was just putting books on the shelf and—I'm floating!"

There was a moment of silence on the other end of the line. "Floating?" Ava repeated.

"Yes. I'm literally hovering a foot off the ground. God, Ava. I froze my co-worker when she saw it."

"Katie?"

"No. Erica!"

"All right. Calm down, Alex. I need you to tell me exactly what you were doing just before it happened. Can you do that?"

I gathered my wits and calmly described my afternoon with Erica, including the part about her sucking the energy out of me.

"Hmm," Ava said. "You may be overcompensating."

"Overcompensating for what?"

"For your loss of energy. You're simply recharging, darling. A little too much, perhaps."

I spend the next five minutes listening to Ava's voice, calming me enough so that my feet could lower back down to the floor.

"Now," Ava continued. "Go back in there and tell that girl to breathe. It's all in your attitude, Alex. You just need a little training. That's all." She insisted I come down to Den of Oddities and Antiquities when I got off so she could assess my latest talent for defying gravity and stunning people in their tracks. "Believe me, Alex, you don't want this new power going unchecked. We'll whip it into shape in no time."

"Actually, Katie and I already had plans to come down this afternoon. There's something else I need to talk to you about."

I hung up the phone and walked back to Erica, still standing like a Madame Tussauds' wax effigy next to the library table. With a box of books in my hand, I did as Ava instructed and simply told her to *breathe*. Her breath rushed from her lungs as if she'd been holding it for an extended length of time—which I guess she had.

"What were you saying?" I asked, figuring it might help to distract her with a question.

She looked shaken, glancing at my feet as the memory of seeing them off the ground registered. "I—"

"Come on, Erica. Grab that other box and get to work." My

words were a little harsh, but it was all I could do to keep her at bay until Apollo showed up to relieve me. The last thing I needed was another energy drain until I learned how to recharge properly. For now, I just needed to get through another two hours.

It was a good thing Apollo showed up an hour early, because my hands and feet were beginning to tingle every time Erica came near me. Poor girl had no idea how depleting she was. Katie had called earlier from home to confirm she'd meet me at the shop at five o'clock, but when Apollo offered to relieve me early, I wasted no time getting out of there.

A weight lifted off me the moment I stepped out of the shop and dialed Katie's number to tell her I'd meet her at her apartment. She wasn't answering. I gambled and took the subway to 103rd Street and walked the short distance to her building, praying she hadn't decided to leave early and shop for an hour or so before meeting me. Worst case, we'd have to meet somewhere in between.

I stepped through the unlocked entrance, into the area housing the mailboxes with their tiny little intercom buttons reaching up to their tiny little apartments. The last time I pushed the button to apartment 6B, Constantine met me at the door, disheveled and half-naked, smelling like Katie and sex. The intercom crackled. Katie answered quickly and buzzed me through the door leading to the stairs. I hiked the six flights and caught my breath before knocking on the door. When it opened, it was like déjà vu smacking me in the head.

"Dear Lord!" I nearly turned and headed back down the stairs.

"Now who would have thought I'd be the worst thing you'd find here," Constantine said as I rolled my eyes at his bare chest.

Katie stepped from behind him. "Oh, come on, Alex. You're not really shocked that I'm sleeping with my boyfriend, are you?"

"Oh, well." I threw my hands in the air at the absurdity. "I guess that answers my next question."

Constantine interrupted. "You mean *friend*."

A coy grin formed on her face "That's right. *Friend*."

"What in God's name are you two doing?"

"That would be my cue to leave." He retrieved his missing shirt and gave Katie a peck on the cheek. "Alex," he nodded and then disappeared down the hall.

When I turned back to the door, Katie was inside collecting herself. "You can come in while I put on my shoes, you know."

"No way," I replied. "Not interested in seeing the crime scene."

She came back out a minute later and locked the door. "Shall we?"

We headed downstairs and out of the building, neither of us speaking about the atrocity that I'd just witnessed. What the hell was she doing with Constantine? What happened to *he's smothering me*? She turned left on the sidewalk.

"Where are you going?" I asked. "The subway is this way."

"Riverside Drive." She kept walking without waiting for me to catch up. "I need some air."

We turned down Riverside and walked for several blocks in silence. It was a nice day, and I had to admit I liked the walk along the park, even if the tension was thick enough to slice it with a knife.

"We're not back together," she eventually said. "We're just sleeping together."

"Friends with benefits?" I asked.

"Something like that." No matter how hard she tried to appear sullen, a sly grin kept forcing its way through. "It's better this way. Now it's just fun without all the strings."

"What about Mr. Fleming?" I asked with mock seriousness.

"Please. Elliot Fleming is a wanted man. You ought to see all the women crawling over him after a reading. I have no delusions about our relationship." She cocked her head and squinted. "I think I'll keep my love life a little less committed for now."

I wrapped my arm around her shoulders and pulled her into me. "I'm proud of you, Ms. Bishop. You're officially a loose woman. Now, can we catch the train? I don't think my feet will make it down to Washington Square Park."

We walked a few more blocks while I replayed my afternoon with Erica and the neat little gravity defying trick I'd mastered. We were about to turn down Eighty-Sixth Street toward the subway station when I saw it out of the corner of my eye. We'd curved along Riverside Park, closer to the river, when I noticed the water in the distance seemed to be flowing higher. I shouldn't have been able to see it at all, but it was clearly visible, moving past the river wall and over the green grass of the park, hypnotic in the way it rolled at a steady clip. The wall of water was heading straight for the city like a tsunami, quietly consuming the park until it would be too late.

"Katie," I whispered, terrified but fascinated by the rolling wave heading toward us in the distance. My eyes landed on the people walking along the greenway. The water would swallow them and pull them back into the Hudson. But then I noticed that the pedestrians and the cars on the parkway that ran parallel with the river weren't in the water's path, they were under it, moving unaffected as if it were invisible and formed a bridge right over them. The water was avoiding them entirely as it snaked its way straight for us.

I turned back to Katie, but all I could see was a giant wing fan out in front of my eyes, golden with glints of emerald green shimmering against the late afternoon sun. Katie's dragon let loose a scream that deafened my ears. I'd never seen her like this, a raptor framed by the sky, with wings that spanned half the river, the one that was raging toward us.

She dove and hovered a few feet above Riverside Drive, stopping traffic and inciting panic in the street. I froze and stared into her bright blue eyes. Then her tail snaked around and lifted me onto her back, at the intersection of her wings. I held on for dear life as we lifted off the ground and soared toward the glaring sun. Then we dipped back down toward Central Park and glided over the trees and past the reservoir. I shut my eyes as we veered toward the Chrysler Building, passing so close I could see our reflection in the steel eagles jutting out from the sixty-first floor. We took a sharp turn west, back out over the water, following the Hudson River past Lower Manhattan and back up toward the Village.

We finally touched down in Washington Square Park in a crowd of several hundred people who here gawking at the spectacle. Katie's dragon quickly retreated under her shirt.

"How do you do that *thing* with your clothes?" I asked, curious about how she always managed to spare her clothes when she changed into the beast.

Her eyes rolled. "I don't know, Alex. They're just *there.*"

We casually walked past the growing crowed. Those who were *in the know* smirked at our audacity for displaying our secrets in such a public place.

"Hypocrites," Katie whispered. "Half of them have worse secrets."

She was right. Half of them were freaks who hid behind their own masks during the day.

"What was that back at the river?" she asked.

My shoulders sagged as the breath I'd been holding rushed from of my lungs. "Who knows?" Nervously staring in the direction of the Hudson, I picked up the pace. "Let's just get to the shop before it heads downriver and finds us again."

Melanie was escorting a customer out when we walked up the steps to the shop. "Hello, ladies." She eyed us curiously, holding the door open while we entered.

I always felt safe when I walked through that door. Aside from Templeton's Trojan horse that had been inadvertently invited in, nothing would dare bother me in here. Not with the power and magic that had lived within these walls for decades. And who knew what was here before Ava set up shop. As far as I was concerned, this place was hallowed ground.

Toward the back end of the shop, where the room reached two stories, was a tall wooden pole made from the trunk of a tree. At the top was a ring of flowers suspended by colorful ribbons that made it appear to float like a halo. Another set of ribbons continued all the way down to the floor.

"Is that what I think it is?" I asked.

"A maypole," Melanie and Katie both said in unison.

Katie grinned like a mischievous child, running her hand up and down the bark of the pole in a suggestive way. "You don't see *this* in the middle of Manhattan every day."

"That's right." Ava walked through the cloth veil from the back room carrying a pair of stag antlers in her hands. "You do in here, though. Beltane without a maypole would be like Yule without a tree." She walked to the front door. "Melanie, would you please?" Melanie rushed over and grabbed the antlers while Ava climbed a stepladder. She adjusted several large hooks deeper into the wall above the door and then reached down for one of the antlers. "We don't want a repeat of what happened last year." With the set of antlers secured to the wall, she climbed back down and took a step back to get a better view of her handiwork.

"Nearly skewered a customer last year," Melanie explained, her eyes wide.

"Going for a little Montana lodge décor?" I asked, wondering what the elaborate display was all about.

"Some witch you are," Katie said as all three women looked at me oddly. "The King is back, baby. Make way for all that testosterone and male energy."

"Very good, Katie," Ava said, praising her knowledge of the pagan wheel of the year. "Don't you remember, Alex?"

I did remember. It just took a moment for my witch roots to

resurface. "Well, I did spend twenty-one years in the Bible Belt," I reminded her.

"Tea?" Ava asked, diverting her eyes from mine and ignoring the comment. I didn't mean for it to be a reminder that she was the reason for all those displaced years. It was just a thoughtless statement of fact that happened to make her feel like shit.

Katie and I headed for the reading nook while Ava went to the kitchen for the tea. Melanie gave me that odd look one more time before going about her business of running the shop. I caught my reflection in a mirror against the nook wall and almost laughed out loud at the image staring back. Apparently the finger comb I'd given my hair didn't quite do the job.

"Why didn't you tell me I look like I stuck my finger in an electrical socket," I hissed at Katie.

"You just look a little windblown." She forced her fingers through the tangles. "That's better."

"Here we are." Ava set the tray on the coffee table and sat on the sofa next to me. "Now, tell me all about this latest drama."

I sipped my tea and debated which was more pressing: my latest vision, or my ability to levitate involuntarily. "How do I prevent myself from floating off the ground next time someone stresses me out?"

Katie nearly spit out her tea. "And I thought I had physical problems."

"It's really very simple, Alex. When someone drains you like this… what was her name?"

"Erica," I replied. "You said I'm overcompensating?"

"Yes. You're subconsciously reaching for the closest energy source to regenerate." She must have noticed the confusion on my face. "Well, it's a witch thing, darling. Most of us don't even know we're doing it. After you get the hang of it, it'll become almost effortless. An efficient energy pipeline."

"I still don't understand how levitating off the floor equates to looking for an energy source."

She laughed softly, leaning in to place her hand on my knee. "The sun, Alex. You were simply reaching for the sun."

"Ah." Katie seemed to get it, and then her eyes popped. "The water."

I read her expression and the thought stunned me. I turned back to Ava. "And water is another source of energy." Was it possible I'd attracted the Hudson River and nearly gotten us killed because I needed a little energy boost? All because I was drained from Erica or stressed about seeing Katie and Constantine together?

"Water is a very powerful source," Ava replied suspiciously. "Why?"

I recounted our little catastrophe on the way down, and her face went grave. "You're more powerful than I thought—than any of us thought."

Melanie, who had been standing quietly behind the counter polishing the glass top, added her own two cents. "Well, what do you expect from a fire witch who can bend minds? The girl is Fitheach."

"Good point," Ava conceded.

Who would have thought that the easier problem I opened the conversation with would be worse than the vision of an athame plunging into my heart?

I looked back and forth between the two women and revealed problem number two. "There's something else I need to tell you. I think Isla Kelley sent me a message."

CHAPTER NINETEEN

Ava asked Patrick to come in for a few hours to tend shop so she and Melanie could escort me home. They'd listened carefully to my recollection of the vision and determined it was a matter that needed a wider audience than just them. Those weren't just random symbols carved into a tree, and the knife that plunged into my heart was a powerful message that I had unfinished business—business that the Fitheach demanded I finish sooner than later.

I heard sounds coming from the kitchen. A long, wooden spoon was submerged in Sophia's signature red pot cooking on the stove—stirring itself—when I peeked through the doorway. I approached the animated utensil and moved my hand through the air where you'd expect to find a person holding on to it, but there was nothing there.

"What are you doing?"

I turned around when Sophia spoke. "Oh, just wondering who's stirring the pot." I glanced back at the stove. "Ian?"

Her expression soured. "Don't be stupid. I don't let no spook cook in my kitchen." She met me at the stove and nudged me out of the way with her broad hip. "You hungry?"

"When am I not?"

"Good. I cook a lot of food tonight."

"Is company coming?" I asked, knowing a pot that size would feed a small army.

Greer stepped through the doorway. "We'll have a full table for dinner."

"Dr. Oxford? Did you find him?" Despite the bad feeling in my gut, I held on to hope that the doctor would be found, hiding somewhere safe were neither Isabetta Falcone nor the Rogues could sniff him out.

"I'm afraid not," he answered.

My eyes dropped to the floor along with my deflated spirit. I knew the odds. The longer the doctor was missing, the greater the chances of a heartbreaking outcome. David Oxford just wasn't built for this sort of game. He was too timid, a frozen rabbit crippled by fear.

Leda strolled into the kitchen. "Alex, I hate when you pull these little surprises on us." She made a beeline for me and lifted my chin. "But in this case I think you've struck the ancestral mother lode."

I glanced at Greer. "What is she talking about?"

"Come. Everyone's waiting." He took my hand and headed for the dining room.

The room was full when we walked in. Rhom, Thomas, Loden, Ava, Melanie: they were all sitting around the table. We sat as Sophia came through the doorway with a large tureen of soup, a simple dinner without the big crusty loaf of bread that usually accompanied it. No salad or wine either. Just the bare minimum.

Leda perused the sparse offering. "Are we all on a diet?"

Rhom, who was sitting next to her, cleared his throat and muttered something quietly into her ear.

Melanie seemed nervous. Her hands were concealed, but I could tell by the way her arms moved that she was wringing her fingers under the table. Even Ava wasn't her usual rock solid self.

"What's going on?" I demanded, scanning the faces at the table. They all glanced from me to Greer, waiting for their cue to speak. "Greer?"

He offered the floor to Melanie, of all people.

"Well," she began, taking the bowl Thomas handed her, "it appears that Alex has been summoned."

"Summoned?" I repeated. "What do you mean *summoned?*" My mind raced around everything I'd told Ava and Melanie, trying to reconcile how it all equated to a summons.

"The tree," she continued. "The one from your vision. The symbols carved in that tree are not just some random marks. Those marks are from the *ogham.*"

A quiet gasp, followed by whispers, traveled around the table. Everyone but me seemed to know what *ogham* meant. Even Sophia stopped in her tracks in the middle of the doorway when she heard the word.

"Would someone please explain to me what this *ogham* is?"

Melanie continued. "It's an ancient Irish alphabet. Isla Kelley just gave you a direct order."

"Can she do that?" I asked.

"Oh yes, she can," Ava said.

Something rolled across the table. "Show us what the symbols looked like." Greer motioned to the piece of chalk coming to a stop next to my plate.

It took me a moment to understand. "You want me to write it on the wall?" The wall wasn't much darker than the chalk.

"On the table," he clarified, nodding toward the dark mahogany surface.

"But—"

"It's just a table, Alex." He urged me again to draw the symbols I'd seen in the bark of the tree. At first my memory could only recall a random bunch of lines, all connected to a longer vertical line through the center of the marks. But to my surprise, the memory started to sharpen. Like an image being brought into focus through the lens of a camera, I could see every line like it was a picture right in front of me.

"Go on, darling," Ava coaxed. "Let's see what that old witch has to say."

I cleared the table in front of me, pushing my plate aside but hesitating to mar the beautiful antique finish, worn and soft and ready to drink in the chalk. Then I put the stick to the wood and drew the image I saw so clearly in my head. I started with a vertical line and then drew a series of lines along each side of it: some slanted, some straight, some single lines, and some grouped. When the image in my head was displayed for all the eyes around the table to see, I felt a sharp surge of relief wash over me. It was as if a poison had been purged, sweated out of my skin by the act of claiming the message. Now I just needed to know what the message meant.

Melanie stepped around the table and looked at the drawing from a horizontal angle. Her expression went dark, and I could feel the fear accompanied by excitement emanating from every pore of her skin.

"What does it say?" Greer asked.

She held his gaze for a moment before looking back at the table. "It says *Banríon*."

All eyes lifted from the chalk lines and looked at me, as if I knew what it meant. "Don't ask me."

"It means queen," Melanie announced, still staring at the lines on the table.

There was a lot of rumbling around the room as everyone shared their theories. Through it all, Melanie stood as still as a statue with that strange look still masking her face. Ava was the first to rein the conversation back in. "Melanie? What are you *not* telling us?"

The meeker version of Melanie reemerged, the one that made

her shrink and almost disappear into the background. It was almost painful to watch the rabbit return. I thought we were about the lose her, but then she swallowed hard and spoke. "I know where this tree lives." She glanced at Greer and then turned her eyes on Ava as if asking for permission to speak freely in a room filled with listening ears.

"There are no secrets here," Greer assured her. "You can trust everyone in this room." He followed her eyes as they landed on Sophia who was still standing in the doorway, listening unabashedly to every word. "Everyone," he repeated.

A nervous laugh slipped from her mouth as she announced the location of the giant oak tree. "Lough Gur."

Ava stood up, her chair sliding out from under her with a loud scrape as it slid past the rug and continued across the wood floor. "What? Are you sure?"

Melanie nodded and shrank further into herself. "I've seen it with my own eyes," she confirmed before retreating a few steps back from all the ruckus around the table.

Now I was standing. "Would someone *please* tell me what the hell is going on?"

Ava collected herself and took a steadying breath. "I believe we're taking a trip, Alex. You're going home." She glanced at Greer who was uncharacteristically quiet considering the conversation. "Isn't that right, Greer?"

I was more confused than ever. Wasn't this home? Surely she didn't mean Indiana. The only other "home" I could think of wasn't an option for me.

"We're going to Ireland." Ava came around the table and took my hand as I sank back into my seat. "You'll have the protection of an army. We won't let Alasdair Templeton anywhere near you."

Leda got up and went for the bottle of scotch in the cabinet. "Dear Lord. Tell me we won't have to wear those horrible black frocks when we get there."

"Not without an invitation, you won't," replied Melanie, her rabbit receding back into its hole.

"Well, thanks for that." She handed Greer a drink. "We are all going, right?"

"Aye," Thomas chimed before Greer could answer. "Right, Boss?"

Rhom was even more subdued than Greer. Strange, considering it was his job to keep me alive. He kept glancing at Greer, and I wondered what silent conversation was taking place between them.

And then Rhom spoke. "They'll smell her out the second she touches Irish soil."

"I know that." A wicked smile broke across Greer's austere face. "But if we're going where I think we are, we've got the power on our side—the gods."

"Where might that be?" Loden asked, finally breaking his brooding silence.

"The tree is in the circle of the gods," Melanie interjected with a boost of confidence before Greer could continue. Then she swung her eyes to Ava. "What day is it?"

Ava considered the date—the wheel of the year—and grinned like a Cheshire cat. "Why, it's May Day Eve."

Melanie glanced around the table with her own mischievous grin. "Looks like we're going to a fire festival. Tomorrow is Beltane, a timeless day when magic rules and the veil between the worlds will be paper thin, a doorway for the gods." She pulled out her phone and glanced at the time. "It's already Beltane in Ireland. Templeton and his coven won't get anywhere near her in that circle if the gods have anything to say about it."

"But I thought the coven was working for the gods?" I said.

"Yes, but the gods don't really need the coven if you come to their circle of your own free will, now do they?" Melanie asked with a glint of confidence in her eyes. "That would be like hiring a headhunter when the perfect candidate is already knocking at your door. The coven is nothing but a middleman."

How convenient of Isla Kelley to summon me to the land of the Fitheach on a day when she knew I'd be untouchable. Even the coven answered to the power of the gods, and tomorrow those gods would be present in full force. Tomorrow the coven would be powerless to touch me.

"One hour," Greer instructed everyone in the room. "There's no time for error. If you're not back here, we leave without you."

The room emptied except for the two of us. Sophia retreated to the kitchen to settle the dishes and the leftover food.

"How long will we be gone?" I asked, wondering if I was finally going to lose my job at the bookstore after all we'd done to save it.

"We have a one-day window," he replied. "Less than that, actually."

I did the math. "Dublin is at least a six-hour flight from New York. And God knows how far this *Lough Gur* is from there. How do you figure?"

He glanced over his shoulder. "Who said anything about a flight?" I must have looked as defeated as I felt, because he turned and pulled me into his arms. "We'll be travelling a faster way. We'll be back before anyone knows we're gone."

By "faster way," I assumed he meant the old-fashioned way—for his kind. The last time I traveled internationally via transfer of atoms, Constantine had whisked me from the top of the Brooklyn Bridge all the way to Paris. I wondered what it would be like to travel that way with an entire entourage.

"I guess we'll be packing light?"

"Only the clothes on our backs and whatever we can stuff in our pockets." He took my face in his hands and assured me with a look. "We won't be there any longer than necessary. But this *is* necessary."

"That's what I'm afraid of—the necessary part."

. . .

DESPITE GREER's confidence that we'd be back before my next shift, I called Katie to let her know what was happening. At least I'd know that if we got held up longer than expected, she'd cover for me at the bookstore. Her disappointment in not being able to come with us was obvious.

Greer and I were waiting in the living room when everyone started showing back up at the house. Ava and Melanie arrived together, Melanie wearing a black robe and Ava wearing a white one with a garment bag draped over her arm. Thomas, Rhom, and Loden looked the same as when they left. And then there was Leda, dressed to the nines in her own version of ritual gear: a beautiful champagne dress that draped to the floor and left nothing to the imagination, seeing how it barely existed. The bodice was see-through with lace bird appliqués sewn over her nipples and crotch. The woman was practically naked, a courtesan to a king.

"Don't you dare look at me like that," she scolded with a pointed finger dancing across each set of roaming eyes. "It's Beltane. And we all know what Beltane is about."

"Growth and fertility," Melanie stated with a touch of offense.

"And sex," Leda added. "It's all about the maiden tomorrow."

I looked down at my jeans and T-shirt and suddenly felt very underdressed. But my closet wasn't exactly stuffed with ritual attire.

"Don't worry, darling." Ava handed me the garment bag. "I thought you might like to wear this. It'll make you feel more comfortable."

"And fit in better at the festival," Melanie added.

I went upstairs and hung the garment bag on the door to unzip it. Inside was a white dress, simple but beautiful. Embossed at the center of the square neckline was a small circle with a cres-

cent moon on either side of it. The bell sleeves were trimmed
with silver embroidery and reached halfway down the floor-
length skirt.

"It was Maeve's," Ava said as she entered the room. "It's fitted,
but you're about the same size as she was."

Tears began to rim my eyes as I shed my clothes and stepped
into the dress that my mother once wore. Ava was right about the
size. Fitted indeed, making me feel more than a little self-
conscious. I preferred to blend into the background, but this little
dress was about to put me front and center. The chain holding
the amulet was just long enough to hang below the neckline. I
straightened it and tucked it into my cleavage under the fabric,
barely.

"Be careful with that. You don't want to flash it around," Ava
warned, zipping me in and pulling my hair back in a loose braid.
"Now you look the part. We don't want to look like party
crashers when we get there, do we? Now we just need to work on
those men downstairs."

We went back down to the living room. As I expected, Loden
and Thomas managed to tear their eyes away from Leda long
enough to share their approval of my conservative yet tightly-
fitted frock. Always sensing what I needed, Rhom nodded his
own approval and then glared at the other two men to temper
their enthusiasm. I looked across the room at Greer. He just
stood there, silent and introspective. But I could feel the heat
rising from his skin and the intensity of his blue eyes magnify as
they walked all over me. It would be difficult to put him off
much longer.

He walked toward me and kissed me on the temple, splaying
his fingers at the small of my back, directing his heat into my
sacral chakra where it licked through my entire body. "You look
lovely," he murmured against my flushed skin.

"All right," Ava said. "Time is ticking."

"I need to say goodbye to Sophia." She was standing over the sink when I walked into the kitchen, practically spit shining the plates before placing them into the dishwasher. "Sophia?"

"Yes," she grumbled without turning around.

I met her at the sink and wrapped my arms loosely around her waist, resting my chin on her shoulder. "I'll be fine." I looked down and spotted Bear sitting in the foyer outside the kitchen door. His tail was thrashing back and forth as his large cat eyes zeroed in on me. I knew what he was thinking: *That man loves you deeper than you'll ever know. What are you waiting for?*

"Take care of Bear for me, okay?"

She glanced at Bear through the doorway. "That *gatto* can take care of himself." Then she turned around and held me at arm's length. "You be careful with them Irish." With that, she nodded firmly and swatted me away with her dish rag. "Go!"

I walked back into the living room where everyone was waiting impatiently to leave, and prepared to travel some three thousand miles in a matter of seconds.

CHAPTER TWENTY

I thought it would be greener. I mean, it *was* green, but I had visions of bright emerald green, not the normal green you see everywhere else. I also expected it to be dark, but it looked more like afternoon, the sky an amazing collage of blue hues. I imagined the most vibrant colors were just starting to burst forth as the deciduous trees were not fully foliated yet, and a nearby meadow of bluebells was just beginning to flower. It was beautiful.

We'd touched down in a field in the middle of nowhere, fully intact. Memories of the night Constantine whisked me off to Paris, with me standing in a strange apartment not knowing if my parts had reassembled correctly, still haunted me.

"Where are we?" asked Thomas, his skeptical eyes surveying the expanse of open field.

"Home," Melanie whispered. Her eyes went soft, and her faint smile flattened a second after it appeared. She looked conflicted. Ava took her hand, and I could see Melanie's bones telegraph through her fair skin as she gripped down on Ava's fingers.

"County Limerick," Greer clarified. "That," he nodded toward a lake in the distance, "is Lough Gur."

"I think I've heard of this place. There's a stone circle here." I'd read about it years ago when looking up information on Stonehenge, Newgrange, and other ancient sites in the UK. I'd always had a fascination for these places, never suspecting the reason for that being my own heritage.

"Yes," Ava said. "But we're not looking for that circle. The circle we're heading for is a little more discreet. Entrance is by invitation only."

"But we haven't been invited, have we?" Was I the only one in the dark about what was really going on?

Melanie looked confused. "What do you mean? A Fitheach witch doesn't need an invitation—she extends one."

I glared at her. "You said the coven wouldn't be there."

A sickening thought stirred in the pit of my stomach. If the Fitheach had carte blanche at the festival, wouldn't the coven be there, too? Didn't she just tell me a couple of hours earlier that the coven wouldn't be there? It made no sense, and for the briefest moment I feared the people I trusted the most had tricked me. For one fleeting second, I actually considered the possibility that my entire existence in Greer's house had been a guise to get me to this exact place. A carefully orchestrated ruse.

Greer must have read my mind, because his face suddenly looked stricken. I'd cut him deeply with a single thought.

"No," I shook my head. "I could never mistrust you."

He swallowed hard and looked away from me. Now it was my turn to read *his* thoughts. Ava watched the exchange taking place between us and intervened before Greer had a chance to dissolve before my very eyes. Rhom seemed to notice it, too, intercepting Greer as he started to walk away.

"All right, you two. Enough of this!" Ava spat. She rarely lost her cool, but her voice delivered a precise message that she had no patience for our quarrel. "We have enough to deal with tonight, so whatever is going on between the two of you needs to wait until we get out of here. Are we clear?"

Greer nodded in concession as I apologized with my eyes.

Ava settled down, too. "Alex, you're confusing the clan with the coven. Every member of the coven is Fitheach, but not every Fitheach witch is a member of the coven."

"On the contrary," Melanie added. "There's a lot of bad blood between the coven and the clan. Something you'll see for yourself tonight."

"So where is this other circle?" I asked, getting back to business.

Melanie turned and looked north. Without a word she began walking toward the steep hill on the other side of the field. Blindly we followed, never questioning where we were going, because the only person who knew was ten steps ahead of us and gaining speed. She hiked her robe up to her knees and drudged up the rocky hillside with the stealth of a goat traversing familiar terrain.

Thomas was the first to catch up to her. He stared blankly at what was on the other side, watching her run into the wide clearing. He just stood there, glancing back and forth between the small woman running like a fleeing child into the open field, and us as we approached the top.

"There's nothing here," he said. "There's nothing *fucking* here!"

Greer practically leapt the last few yards and scanned the meadow where Melanie's outline was getting smaller as she disappeared farther into the open expanse. Ava rounded the top next, gasping with the same look of surprise as she watched Melanie's robe flutter in the distance, a small black butterfly diminishing in the wind. By the time the rest of us reached the top of the hill, Melanie had all but disappeared.

"We've found it." Ava ran in the same direction, motioning for us to follow.

I just stared at the empty horizon and shook my head, unable to reconcile what I couldn't see, praying that it would all make sense if I just trusted the people who brought me here. We followed without question, and as my feet pounded the hard earth of the deserted field, I could feel it. Something lived under the grass, cushioning my stride, sending a spark through my entire body as I ran deeper into the distance.

Melanie stood at the foot of a monolithic stone at the edge of the clearing. "Can you hear that?" she asked, staring keenly at its surface. The seven of us listened for sounds.

"All I hear is the sound of my patience running out," Leda grumbled, fiddling with the shifted lace on her bodice. "I'm all for teamwork, but—"

"Shhhh." Melanie raised her index finger, closing her eyes to focus her sense of hearing. "He's coming."

Thomas's eyes darted around the field, his head cocked as they circled back around to Melanie. "Who's coming?"

"The gatekeeper."

A barely discernible sound tweaked my ears, a chorus of voices or a note from an instrument. It grew louder, like a parade far in the distance marching closer. "I can hear it," I said.

Melanie turned sharply, staring at me with a look of pride. "Of course you can. They're your people."

The music and voices grew louder. I could tell by the blank look of the other faces that they couldn't hear it. How could they not hear it? I closed my eyes as a set of footsteps approached. And then a door opened and my breath caught as the sound spilled into my head like a flood, filling my heart with an overwhelming sense of peace and comfort. I knew this place, but I didn't.

My eyes flew open. The daylight was gone, replaced by the blackness of night and thousands of stars dotting the sky. Greer was watching me closely from a few yards away. "You can see it?" I asked, looking around in wonder. His smile warmed as he nodded his head.

The gatekeeper stepped aside and beckoned us in. There were people everywhere. Some dressed in black robes like the one Melanie wore, while others made Leda's scant dress look marmish. Some even forwent fabric altogether and wore layers of paint, delicately applied to their skin like a canvas. Even the night air seemed to light up in varying plumes of fuchsia, chartreuse, and blue, a billion particles of color exploding from some invisible cannon.

"Now this is a party," Leda proclaimed, slipping into the crowd, gyrating to the trance-like music playing over the field.

Loden and Thomas were already in the thick of it, each flanked by figures—male and female—hypnotically moving against them. Even Rhom was feeling it, his shoulders rolling while his feet remained firmly planted on the ground, careful not to lose sight of me.

"We need to find it." Greer's hand slipped around my waist from behind me. He nodded to Melanie. "The tree. Where is it?"

Melanie's eyes misted, a sadness washing over her as the business at hand brought her back to the here and now. This was her home, and no matter the urgency, the thought of leaving before she'd had a proper reunion with the land was clearly a conflict she had to swallow down deep. It was a bittersweet reminder of how things had gone so wrong for the sake of power.

"Melanie," Ava coaxed, careful not to upset the delicate balance of her emotions. "Show us."

Melanie turned to look at the cauldron of revelers circling an enormous balefire that must have been thirty feet wide. The flames reached toward the sky, licking at the stars and sending sparks all the way to the edges of the field.

I pulled away when she reached for my hand, uncomfortable with being led into the unknown. "It's okay, Alex," she smiled faintly, still holding out her hand. "The gods are on your side. No one can touch you here."

Without pushing my trust any further, she dropped her hand

and turned into the sea of figures. I took a step to follow but looked back at Ava. She shook her head and motioned for me to go alone. Even Rhom, who was hardwired to protect me, seemed stuck in place like a tree rooted to the earth. Greer's hand touched my shoulder as he took a step with me, but I knew that whatever was waiting for me beyond the crowd at the foot of that mammoth tree was too personal. Even Greer would eventually fall back and leave me to continue on my own.

I took a deep breath and stepped into line with Melanie. The faces in the crowd turned to gaze at me as I walked toward the blazing fire, stepping aside to part the sea and giving me slight nods as I passed. They were bowing, whispering quietly while I moved along the parted path toward a dark void obstructing the sky.

"What's happening?" I asked Greer, turning to see him already stopped and watching me from several yards back. "Melanie?"

She stepped off the path and into the wall of spectators. "Welcome home, Alex," she said, beckoning me on.

My foot struck something in the dirt. It was a root from the massive tree hidden by the darkness. But the tree was the darkness, its long branches swaying over the entire field, blocking out large portions of the starred sky. I followed the root back to the gnarled trunk that appeared to breathe. There was a small hole in the center, a tiny spot that glowed. I reached out to touch it, and a beam of light shot straight from the hole and pierced my stomach, just below my navel. I nearly ran from the base of the tree, but then I saw the marks deeply etched into the surface of its bark, illuminated by the light that was now filling me.

A hollow sound came from somewhere in the canopy overhead, the wind rustling through the leaves. *Banríon*, I thought I heard.

"No," I whispered, shaking my head.

The tree or the wind echoed back, only this time the word was clear as day. "*Banríon.*"

Something compelled me to stay put and reach for the tree again. I could feel the eyes of the crowd behind me, whispering as my fingers approached the bark but stopped a few inches away. But the life of the tree drew me closer, like a magnet. And then I pressed my palm into the center of the marks. The light beneath the ancient bark festered and glowed straight through my fair skin. In the veins of my hand it crawled, seeping into my blood and racing up my arm, through my entire body until I became a torch of light. I fell to my knees and the crowd burst into a loud cheer. All the sounds of the festival faded as I closed my eyes and let it flow through me: the crackle of the blazing fire, the beat of the music, the mingled voices of the crowd. It was just me and the light, swirling in an orange and red kaleidoscope of images, and a warm glow of golden rain all around me. And then a small hand extended from the hole, the heart of the tree, and offered itself to me.

I took it, and the world exploded.

It was as if I were holding the hand of the universe, every particle of the world fusing with mine, rendering me to atoms. I was nothing, and I was everything.

And then as quickly as it consumed me, it let me go, the hard knots of the tree roots bruising my ordinary knees. The separation was jarring as I stood up and looked back at all the faces that were focused on the spectacle—on me. They were waiting for something. As I stood under the tree, trying to comprehend what had just happened and what they all wanted, a man stepped forward into the path and untied the sash around his waist. His robe opened at the front and slipped to the ground, leaving him naked in the glow of the balefire. A healthy dose of fear hit me as I anticipated what they were asking me to do with the naked man standing in front of me. But before I could panic and react to the awkward situation, a

woman on the other side of the path stepped next to him and
disrobed, too. They hesitated, looking at me with a question in
their eyes. Not understanding what was happening or why
everyone was hanging on my next move, I nodded ignorantly.
That seemed to do the trick. The couple joined hands and
walked toward the line of trees at the edge of the field, apparently now permitted to carry on with the old traditions of
Beltane, the rites of fertility.

As the hypnotic music resumed, the crowd watched the
couple disappear and then began to dance around the circle while
the sky lit up in a wave of gold-tinged midnight blue. Suddenly
they all seemed unaware of me as I walked back the way I came,
glancing at the same faces that were now too preoccupied with
their own revelry to pay me any mind.

I spotted Leda in the distance, straddling a man clearly ten
years her junior. Her dress pooled on the grass around her legs as
her palms pressed against the ground on either side of his shoulders, her barely concealed breasts swaying over his face.

"*Leda,*" I admonished, knowing she couldn't hear me. She
looked up and spied me from across the field, grinning, and then
resumed her assault on the younger man.

I glanced over the sea of heads in search of the others. As
you'd expect from a pup in his prime, Loden had his hands full
with several women flanked at his sides while Thomas cavorted
with a beautiful brunette. Then I spotted Rhom, a sentinel
perched at the top of the hill, watching me from the distance.

As I stood there looking out over the field, I could still feel
the electricity of the tree pulsing through me. I glanced down at
the source of all that energy—a gnarled stretch of roots jutting a
good twenty feet from the base of the tree. I stepped off the root
and over the boundary of the circle, and once again I was the
center of attention. My breath hitched in the back of my throat
the moment I realized where I was. The altar was the same, and
in the blink of an eye the stone raven was seated on its surface,

presiding over its people with its shiny black eyes trained down on me.

The circle quickly filled to capacity while they all waited for me to assume my place at the altar. The gap where I'd entered the circle closed, and I found it difficult to breathe with the growing mob forming around me. I swallowed the fear and felt the mettle in my belly strengthen. I knew this circle. It was my mother's and my grandmother's, and it was mine, too.

"Stay back," I ordered, praying they might actually listen to the woman at the helm of the altar. I threw my right hand up, surprised to see them all scurry back in submission. When I looked up at my tingling raised fingers, I nearly stumbled from the sight of the bright blue light radiating from it. I steadied my other shaking hand on the cold stone and closed my eyes, trying to understand what was happening to me, what I was supposed to do. Then I heard it, the flap of giant wings followed by a rush of wind at my back. I slowly turned toward the altar where the stone raven had just stood. In its place was a trio of golden rings suspended in the center, circling in continuous orbit, just as they had the night Ava brought the box with the life force to Greer's house. I walked around the stone edge and leaned in to get a closer look. The crystal clear singing I'd once heard coming from the motion of the rings was now silent. The alternating blue and white light in the center was also missing. Now the rings appeared faded and less tangible than when I'd first seen them in Greer's living room.

"They're waiting for you to bring it home," Melanie said as she stepped forward from the crowd. "It's just a memory, Alex. Those rings are their memory." I glanced at the robed figures that were now standing out from the crowd as Melanie was, circling me. These were my people, the ones from my dreams, my visions.

I looked back at the rings, still moving silently around an empty sphere. Without thinking, I waved my hand through it, watching the rings vanish behind my flesh, a projected image interrupted by the corporeal.

Melanie smiled sympathetically as the truth bled into my expression. "You see, Alex, the rings are nothing without the light. It's the life force that gives everything meaning. *You* are the life force."

My heart began to race as my eyes fixed on the grass under my feet. It had turned a deep emerald green and waved against my skin like a living carpet of tiny fingers grabbing at my ankles.

Every blade is connected to a million others. What happens to you happens to all of us. You're being torn from your roots.

My mother's last words to me repeated through my mind in a constant loop until I finally understood. Alasdair Templeton wasn't their leader—I was.

At the thought of Templeton, I spun around frantically looking for him. If the coven was here, so was he.

Melanie must have recognized the panic on my face. "You won't find Templeton in this place," she assured me. "That abomination will never set foot in this circle. Invitation only."

"But I thought—"

"You thought what?" she asked. "That he was the almighty leader of our people? That his coven was the only one?" A low grumble spread through the crowd. "Well, he was. Until he exposed his own greed and took up with the Rogues. Took a few puppets with him. Good riddance to them, I say." The rumbling of the crowd amplified in agreement.

"Lumen?" I asked, referring to the pesky coven messenger who'd found me the moment I stepped foot back on New York soil.

Melanie looked around the circle. "Do you see her standing here?"

I guess that meant all the bad seeds had decided to splinter off with Templeton. That was the coven he'd tried to bind me to, not the one that was surrounding me tonight. Maybe now he'd move on from his fixation and look for a new source of power. But I knew he wouldn't stop. As long as I had the amulet and the prophecy was still up for grabs, he'd never stop coming for me.

"Melanie, why didn't you just tell me?" I asked.

"I wasn't sure you'd come if I told you the coven would be here, even after I explained everything. No one would have blamed you for refusing to come. Besides," she motioned to the coven members circling around the altar, "they wanted to show you themselves."

I smiled awkwardly at each of them, their reluctant and inexperienced messiah. "I guess this means we can't use the life force as leverage against Templeton." I was a bit frightened by the prospect of losing our primary trump card. Alasdair Templeton may have been run off by the coven standing around me, but he was greedy enough to try and take it back. Especially with me now in it.

"That's not true," Melanie replied. "He may be a traitor to his people, but the source of his power is still rooted in the Fitheach clan. He's a vampire, sucking the life force without permission."

"But if we destroy the life force, we destroyed ourselves, Templeton and the people standing in this circle." I looked at their faces. "I won't do that, Melanie. Not even to bring Templeton down."

She smiled slyly, the new Melanie that would take some getting used to. "Take another look at those rings."

At first I saw only the faded apparition of the same three rings I'd seen before. But as I looked closer, I noticed a fourth ring. This one was silver. "I didn't notice that silver one before."

"That's because it wasn't there until Templeton and his traitors decided to break away and steal part of the power. That fourth ring—the silver one—is a siphon. It's Templeton's power source. All we need to do is isolate that one ring and destroy it, and his link is broken."

I shook my head, confused. "Then why haven't you done that?"

"I never said it would be easy, especially with the life force hidden a continent away. And frankly, Alex, no one in this circle is powerful or skilled enough to do it." She pointed her index finger to the spot just below my navel where the tree had penetrated me with the light. "Until now."

"Me?" I shook my head, terrified at the prospect of taking their future in my unsteady hands.

"We'll figure it out," she said. "And when we do, we'll sever the bastards!" She came back down from her exuberant peak and looked at the moon. "It's getting late, Alex. Why don't you go and enjoy the festival while we still have a little time."

We'd be leaving soon, back to our lives in New York. There'd be plenty of time to worry about managing kingdoms and finding prophecies once we returned, and then the matter of my bargain with Maelcolm. In light of these new developments, I wasn't so sure that bargain would hold much water. All I knew was that tonight I didn't care about any of it. It was Beltane, after all—a day and night of celebrating life, the fullness of the earth and the union of the God and Goddess. For one night I would have peace, and maybe a little pleasure.

My thoughts were distracted by something under my feet, the slow and steady beat of a distant drum that seemed to be coming from deep inside the core of the earth. The vibrations traveled up my legs and into the base of my spine, a primal rhythm altering me in a strange way. Maybe it was all the magic in the air, the gods having their fun. I couldn't quite catch my breath or steady myself from the sensation it created inside my stomach. The beat propelled me, guiding me as if it had become the force of my legs. I worked my way through the crowd of people and the spectacles taking place all around me: the suggestive dancing, the very public displays of affection, and the unabashed voyeurs who took their own pleasure in the act of watching.

Ava stood just beyond the circle, watching me with a knowing grin as I headed straight for the one thing I suddenly knew I had to have. Tonight there was no bargain with the devil, just a moment in time when all that mattered was the man standing a few yards in front of me.

Greer reached for my outstretched hand and pulled it to the side of his face, cupping it against his bristled shadow before taking my wrist and kissing the palm of my power hand. His tongue grazed my skin and I thought it would burst into flames.

What are you waiting for? The words kept repeating in my mind, forcing out all the distractions that could so easily change the course of the night if I let them. But there were other influencers in my head. Something older and wiser was at the wheel, steering me toward my destiny.

The drumbeat grew heavier, the vibrations filling my chest, igniting my thirst like a seed needing water. I took him by the hand and led him through the mass of people. Now they stopped, watching us as we walked back toward the massive tree and into the stand of oak and alder behind it. I led him through the thick tangles of the forest until the beat stopped guiding me, letting my own will take over and give in to what I'd known all along was meant to be.

I turned around and he kissed me, speaking those strange but beautiful phrases that I'd heard before but never understood until now. The meaning of every word sang in my heart as I reached around his back and felt the stir of his tattoo, the lines rising and undulating the same way they had the morning I finally knew with utter certainty that he was mine.

He stepped back and removed his shirt with careful consideration of my face before discarding the rest. I nodded my consent and turned so he could reach the zipper of my dress. His breath grew ragged as it slipped off my shoulders and pooled to the forest floor, leaving me exposed under the thin sliver of moonlight reaching down through the umbrella of thick trees.

"Come here." He pulled me down to the soft layer of moss, atop him with the drumbeat still vibrating steadily up from the earth, through his body and into mine. I nearly lost my ability to breathe when he met my thighs with his hips, rocking into me with just enough force to dull the beat and fill me with nothing but him.

CHAPTER TWENTY-ONE

G reer's arm was wrapped around my waist when I woke. The day-old stubble on his cheek rubbed against my neck, abrading my sensitive skin in the most glorious way. I pulled his arm around me tighter and turned my face to my shoulder to get a good whiff of his perfect scent, to remember this moment for as long as possible on our first morning back at home in bed. No fear. No reservation. No pondering of the what-ifs. This morning we were just a couple waking up from a perfect night.

I turned back into my pillow as the reality of what would come of us sank in. That selfless act of sparing him a life that would only end in misery was slowing eroding away as my selfish side grew stronger. We'd crossed a line in that forest, and I knew he would never let me go. He would wage that inevitable war before letting Maelcolm get his hands on me. And the more I obsessed over the thought, the more I wanted to fight that war with him and selfishly reap the rewards of a limited lifetime in his arms.

Careful not to wake him, I sat up and found my flip-flops on the floor. Bear was lounging on the chair when I looked toward the window to gauge the light, and the approximate time. "Voyeur," I hissed quietly. I'd never make it downstairs if Greer woke up and caught me slipping out of bed.

It was almost ten thirty. Late for breakfast, but considering we'd journeyed all the way to Ireland and back the night before, a little extra shut-eye was reasonable.

Sophia sized me up when I walked into the kitchen. "I guess Ireland decided not to keep you."

"Ireland didn't have a choice," I replied, reaching around her waist for a slice of bacon. "Are those pancakes I smell?"

"Pancakes, eggs, bacon. I make a little of everything." She shrugged.

My eyes went wide. "Are you *trying* to pork me up?"

I filled a plate with a stack of pancakes, a pile of eggs, and four more pieces of bacon. On top of that, I poured a generous amount of maple syrup. With a cup of coffee in my other hand, I took my plate and sat at the kitchen island to eat.

Pursing her lips, Sophia examined my mammoth breakfast. "You sure you got enough?"

"Said the enabler," I countered, shoving a spoonful of eggs in my mouth.

She turned back to the stove and dropped another batch of pancakes on the griddle. I must have sat there for another twenty minutes, stuffing my face and perusing the *New York Times* before she finally asked.

"You find your tree?"

My chewing slowed as I thought about everything that happened the night before. One minute we were looking for the mysterious tree in the center of an even more mysterious festival, and the next I was standing before an altar with an army of acolytes waiting for their messiah to restore their kingdom. No matter how much I tried to put myself in that role, I still felt like an imposter, waiting for them to realize their mistake and look elsewhere for salvation. How could a girl who stepped off a plane from corn country six months earlier be the one? I could barely keep my own life moving along, let alone be anyone else's life force.

"Oh, we found it all right. Apparently I'm some kind of princess," I mocked with a pompous smirk.

"You're a queen," Greer corrected, walking through the doorway freshly showered and suited up.

"That was fast," I said. "How do men do that, Sophia?"

She glanced at Greer over her shoulder. "They don't wash properly."

He chuckled quietly and then turned his eyes back to mine. "Did you think you could slip out of bed without me knowing it?"

Sophia dropped a fork on the floor, muttering something under her breath as she bent down to pick it up. She seemed to rethink her judgement, though. "Coffee, Mr. Sinclair?" she asked through a saccharin smile.

"Thank you, Sophia." He took the cup and joined me at the kitchen island. His lips brushed mine, and the smell of him brought me right back to that moss-covered spot in the woods.

It seemed as if we were in Ireland for days, when in fact we'd returned shortly after we left. The minute arm of the clock had barely moved a full turn around its face when we touched back down in the living room, a testament to the idiosyncrasies of teleportation. Still, a lot had transpired in that brief visit to the Emerald Isle, and I was glad to be home.

"Are you leaving?" I asked, unhappy to see him go but remembering I had to be at the shop by one o'clock.

He kissed me a second time and moved a strand of hair from my forehead, his eyes speaking volumes, rendering actual words inadequate. "I have meetings today. The world keeps turning, doesn't it?"

I supposed it did. Most of Manhattan didn't care about my little revelation, or the fact that we needed to tune out all the extraneous noise of mundane life and focus on what had become a cold case for weeks—finding the vessel. Then there was the other side of Manhattan, the side that very much cared about who I was and the status of that mission.

"The late shift?"

"Yes," I sighed.

Sophia was reading our encounter meticulously, a warm yet sly grin appearing on her face. This made her happy even if we were living in sin. I suspected her old ways were finally overtaking the Catholic dogma that had consumed her for so many years. Old habits are hard to break, but her Strega ways had seniority. Maybe now I'd feel less self-conscious about the walk of shame down to the kitchen I was destined to take every morning.

"All right, then." He stood and finished his coffee, regarding me for a moment. "You *will* pick up your phone if anything unusual happens today, right?"

I nodded. "Of course."

"Mmm-hmm," Sophia muttered, taking the empty cup from his hand and placing it next to the sink.

I walked him to the elevator and watched the door close, feeling just a tad vulnerable. Three, maybe five minutes passed while I stood there, wondering if they'd reopen, Greer standing there declaring that his meetings could wait another day. But that was just a romantic notion, compounded by the fact that I could hear the faint sound of the car engine in the garage below the house. After last night, it seemed silly to bother with a car, with Manhattan's notorious traffic. If I ever developed his talent for manipulating matter—and with my evolving pedigree, there was a good chance I would—I'd never lay hands on a steering wheel again.

As I turned to go back to the kitchen to finish my breakfast, the doorbell rang. I froze, feeling that vulnerability creep back up my throat. I could count on one hand the number of times I'd heard that bell ring.

Sophia came into the foyer. "You going to get that?" When I just stood there like a stone, she wiped her hands on the dish towel she was carrying and headed for the door. She opened it and conversed through the narrow crack, then looked back at me. "For you."

I stepped tentatively toward the door, wondering who on earth would be calling on me. Anyone I was expecting usually just showed up in the living room. Ava or Katie were the only people I could think of who actually knocked. The woman on the other side of the threshold was a stranger.

"Can I help you?" I asked, sizing up her tall frame. She had dark hair pulled tightly into a ponytail at the base of her neck, shiny and slick with that lacquered look. Her eyes glared unnaturally green with a set of eyelashes that stretched for miles and immediately demanded your gaze. False, I assumed. Not once did they blink, sending a very uncomfortable sensation spiraling up from my stomach to my chest. My attention dropped to her mouth, painted fuchsia and slightly elevated on one side like a cat with a secret. Something told me to slam the door, but I had my manners, even if they were about to get me in trouble.

She assessed my face, vetting me before continuing. "Are you Alex Kelley?"

"Who's asking?" I replied.

Those thick lashes settled half-mast as she released the air in her lungs dramatically. "Just answer the question. Either you are, or you aren't."

"I am. Now, who are you?"

She reached into her bag and pulled out an envelope. "Alex Kelley, you've been served."

Without thinking, I reached out and took the envelope. As soon as it landed in my hand, I knew it was a mistake. But the deed was done. I'd taken it, and now I had to open it.

Without another word, she turned back down the steps and headed toward Central Park West. I half expected her to look back and smirk, but she just continued down the sidewalk as I closed the front door.

"What is that?" Sophia asked, looking a bit suspicious herself. "You know that woman?"

"No more than you do," I replied.

She followed me into the library where I placed the envelope on the desk. It was one of those padded mailing envelopes, the kind that contained things other than paper. Envelopes were usually ominous for me. Some were good—some not so good.

"Open it," she nudged.

My hand shook as I reached for it. "Maybe I should call Greer. Let him open it."

She deadpanned me. "Is just an envelope. Maybe I open it."

I blocked her hand as she reached for it. "Have a little patience, Sophia." She had a point, though. It was just an envelope. And there were two witches in the room waiting to take on whatever was inside. "I'll do it."

I steeled myself and picked it up. It felt light, like it was empty. I opened the top drawer of the desk and took out the letter opener, tearing quickly along the sealed edge. At first, I saw nothing when I peeked inside. But when I flipped it upside down and shook it, the small silver raven dropped to the desktop and bounced a few inches away. The chain pooled around it, and I swear it was still moving a moment later.

Sophia's eyes went wide as I stumbled backward and dropped the envelope, gasping for the much needed air that eluded me. "No," I whispered, finally catching my breath and shaking my head at the blood contract resting on top of the desk. It was the necklace Alasdair Templeton had shoved in my face at the bookstore. The one Greer and Constantine both warned me not to take. And here I was, looking at it again, only this time I'd just accepted it.

The library began to spin. The walls seemed to move in and out like heavily paneled lungs hogging all the oxygen in the room. Everything went quiet as a buzzing sound drowned out the other sounds around me. I could see Sophia looking at me in horror, speaking words I couldn't hear. Then my vision began to blur and disappear just like all the sound, rendering me senseless except for the buzzing in my ears. After all I'd done to escape his trickery, I'd walked right into his trap like a stupid little bird lured by a piece of stale bread.

It was the sharp smell of something toxic that kept me from passing out. Sophia was on the floor next to me with a small bowl, shoving a soaked rag under my nose until I choked and stirred back to life.

"I'm going to throw up," I warned, pushing her hand away. "God! What is that?"

"Ammonia. Works like a charm."

She helped me off the floor and sat me in the desk chair, in front of the lifeless necklace that had once tried to fly off its chain at me. Now, it looked innocuous and dead. I didn't care how innocent it looked. I knew what it was and what it meant—the equivalent of signing my life away. I believe that's how Greer likened my accepting it.

"What's the matter with you?" she scolded, exaggerating the hike of her shoulders. "*Pazza!*"

"I'm not crazy, Sophia. That necklace is from Alasdair Templeton. And it's alive!"

She glanced at the inanimate piece of jewelry lying on the leather panel of the desk. "Hmph. I don't see no life in that thing."

"I'm telling you, Sophia, that thing is dangerous. It belongs to Templeton's coven. Accepting it means I'm bound to them, and I just took it. Of my own free will!" My voice grew shrill as panic started filling my chest. "God, I am so screwed!"

Clearly convinced I was losing it, Sophia reached into her apron and pulled out her cell phone.

"Who are you calling?" I demanded.

"Who do you think?"

"No!" I grabbed the phone away from her. "You are not calling Greer. Period!"

She glared at me in disbelief, more from my audacity to manhandle the phone from her hand than anything else. "What's the matter with you?"

"Why do you keep asking me that? Don't you get it? I might as well just get on a plane and fly to Dublin." I plopped back down in the chair, a shudder rushing from me.

"Mr. Sinclair can fix this. Simple."

"I wish it were that simple." My face dropped to my hands as my head shook. "*I'll* fix this."

I could almost feel her foot tapping away on the rug. And if I looked up, she'd be smirking down at me with that skeptical *mmm-hmm* expression.

The sound of paper crinkling brought my head back up. "What are you doing?" I asked, horrified to see her stuffing the necklace back in the envelope.

She walked to the shelf and shoved it between two books. "I don't want that damn thing looking at me. If you want, I can burn it. Maybe a little *incanto*?" she offered, twiddling her fingers over the envelope.

"Best not to mix magic, Sophia. Just leave it there for now. And don't tell Greer. He's got enough on his mind." I couldn't bear the thought of seeing the disappointment in his eyes when he found out I'd accepted an envelope from a complete stranger's hand. For most people, that was normal. But I wasn't normal. Neither was this game we were all caught up in.

"How you going to fix this?" she asked, dropping her judgmental tone and looking genuinely concerned for the first time since walking in the room.

"That's a very good question, Sophia. I guess I'll have to pay another visit to the experts. I might as well move in with them since I'm down there practically every day." Ava and

Melanie were becoming a daily staple. But they *were* the experts.

"Can't you just call them?"

I looked at her like she'd just suggested I forgo fine wine for grape juice. "I could, but *no*! I think something this important warrants a visit."

I'd run down to Den of Oddities and Antiquities during my dinner break. Now I just had to avoid the enemy for the next few hours.

CHAPTER TWENTY-TWO

My heart sank when Apollo stepped from the sci-fi aisle. I was hoping to see Katie when I walked into the shop, needing a sympathetic ear and knowing my trip downtown would probably take more than an hour. That phone call was looking like my only option.

There was a long table halfway between the checkout counter and the old library table, right where the shop's heaviest traffic ran. It was empty. Clean and sturdy, but looked like it had seen better days.

"Oh, good," he said, handing me a slip of paper. "Can you look for these books?"

I glanced at the list. "What's this for?"

"We're trying something new. Now that Elliot Fleming has put Shakespeare's Library on the map, we're going to try to stay on it for a while, let the momentum of temporary fame carry us over the summer." He pointed to the new table. "We'll stack them there."

The list contained books by bestselling authors, some on Fleming's backlist before he rose to fame with his latest release. I'd seen a few of the titles on our shelves, so it wasn't a complete waste of time, but it did kind of spoil the charm of the shop. After all, we were that *other* bookstore, the one where you could find cheap reads and obscure titles currently out of print. Our bestsellers were from previous seasons, if not decades.

I was about to slip down the romance aisle when Katie walked through the front door, the infamous Elliot Fleming at her side.

"Thank you for lunch, Elliot." The batting of her eyes was disgusting. My Katie didn't lower herself to such feminine clichés. The men usually took care of that, falling all over themselves to get another date with the beautiful and mesmerizing Katie Bishop. I wondered what happened to *no strings* and *no delusions* about their relationship? And where did Constantine fit in to all this?

Elliot waved at me from across the room before leaving. By the way she lingered on him through the window, she looked pretty deluded to me. She turned around and eyed the table pretty much the way I had.

Apollo handed her a list, too. "Alex can fill you in. I'm already late for a meeting."

"What's all this?" she asked as Apollo disappeared through the front door.

"Apparently the shop is trying to fit in. Your new boyfriend has given Apollo a new idea for making Shakespeare's Library more 'relevant.' "

She frowned. "He's not my boyfriend, and I don't want to be more relevant."

"Apollo seems to think that displaying our diverse inventory of past bestsellers will keep us in business. Now, let's just find these books and stack them on the table." I was unnecessarily short with her, irritated by all the commotion of the day.

"Okay, okay," she surrendered. "Aren't we in a shitty mood today?"

I ignored the remark and headed back toward the romance

section. "And by the way," I said, turning around, "I thought you were seeing Constantine again?"

"And I told you, we're keeping it casual."

"Does he know that?" I asked, knowing what he was capable of if he had other ideas and got wind of her flourishing relationship with Fleming. "No strings?"

"This ought to be a fun afternoon," she grumbled, heading for the back room to deposit her purse.

Katie and I never argued. At least not seriously. And here I was being a total shrew because I'd had a rough morning.

"Look," I began when she came back out, "I'm sorry. I had a bad morning and I'm taking it out on you. Can we just start over?"

She walked up to me and pulled the list from my hand, dropping them both on the library table as she sat down and patted the chair next to hers. "Now sit down and tell me all about your trip." Her eyes flashed a brilliant blue. "I can't believe you've been to Ireland and back in less than twenty-four hours."

I was about to dive in and tell her everything, including the part about the necklace. It was in this very room that Templeton tried to get me to take it the first time. Katie witnessed it all, and if it wasn't for her dragon, I might not be here today.

"Well, Ireland was enlightening, to say the least. We found the tree, and it appears I'm some kind of—"

The front door chimed. A woman walked in, holding the door wide open for her young son. She screamed and began batting at her head as something zoomed past her into the shop and around the room. The bird kept hitting the ceiling and bouncing off the bookcases, trying frantically to find an exit.

Katie gasped. "Poor thing. It's going to die of a heart attack if it doesn't calm down."

I just stood there, paralyzed with fear as the small brown sparrow circled the tallest shelf at the front of the shop, like a moth compelled to a lamplight, striking it repeatedly. In my eyes a bird was a bird, and birds meant trouble.

"Get out!" I screamed, my heart beating wildly as visions of that necklace swooped around in my mind.

The woman grabbed her boy's arm, causing a scene as she ran back out the entrance. Rhom heard the commotion and barreled through the door a few seconds later.

"There." I pointed to the sparrow now sitting motionless on the table meant for relevance.

Maybe I was acting crazy. Even Rhom was looking at me like I'd consumed psychotropic drugs. He approached the bird, which was frozen in fear. "Let's just get you back outside, little man," he said, gently cupping it in his large hands. I calmed down as he walked to the door and released the bird to the sky. Then he came back inside and took me by the shoulders. "You all right, Alex? You're acting a little nuts."

"I'm fine, Rhom. You know how I feel about birds these days."

"Okay." He bobbed his head, acknowledging my irrational fear. "I'll be right out there." He pointed to the window. "You need me, I'm right there." He walked back to the door but stopped before pushing it open. "You want me to stay in here? I can help put books back on the shelves or something. Or I can just sit over there and read." He motioned to the library table.

Rhom would lose his mind sitting in the shop all day. So would I, having him babysit me so closely. "That's okay, Rhom. Go. Be free." I shooed him out the door, knowing he'd plant himself out there for the next seven hours until I closed and was ready to head home.

Through it all, Katie kept her distance, letting Rhom work his magic. "He really loves you, you know. That big guy would take a bullet for you."

I nodded. "Yeah. He would."

We sat back down to resume our conversation. I heard a sound coming from the front counter. Barely noticeable, it reminded me of the sound an umbrella made as it retracted, a whoosh of air expelling from the collapsed canopy. I looked up in the direction of the sound, and the moving shadow creeping into the corner of my eye. Perched on top of the cash register was another bird. Rhom was leaning against a parked car, reading his copy of the *New York Post*, when I looked past the large raven and out the window.

Put down that rag and look at me, Rhom.

No matter how hard I willed it, he kept reading that damn paper, distracted by the sensational stories. I slowly turned to Katie who'd also noticed the intruder. We both looked back at it when we heard the wings fan out in a dramatic display of blueish-black feathers, shiny and bold as they opened and reached a good three feet in either direction. I barely blinked before the black feathers receded, leaving Alasdair Templeton standing in their place.

"I do hate diversions. But that pit bull out there—" He motioned to Rhom's distracted form, still buried in the gossip section of the tabloid. "You really should fire him." He stepped a few feet closer. "Now, about that little trip of yours, Alex. It was rude of you not to look me up while you were in Ireland."

Katie took a step forward. "We have a policy about trouble-makers in this store." Then she boldly pointed her finger at him. "*You* are not welcome here."

Templeton regarded her fiercely directed index finger. "You should be careful with that. People have a tendency to underestimate the power of the wand, and that my dear, is a wand." The amused look slipped from his face, sending a cold chill through both of us. "If you retract it now, I'll let you keep it."

She instinctively dropped her hand and buried it in the folds of her shirt hem, twisting her finger underneath the fabric as if it would be safer there. As quickly as she'd approached him, she moved back, guarded and wary of his cold eyes. He was good at bullying.

He continued, drawing a thoughtful breath. "You didn't really think you could come home and I wouldn't find out about it, did you? I must admit my feelings were slightly bruised by the snub, but all's well that ends well."

There was a moment when I thought I could actually see inside his black heart, beating with blood as dark as a tank of old crude. But that was assuming he had a heart. I had a feeling if I cut him open I'd unleash the smell of rotting meat beneath the living skin he hid behind.

"Maybe I need to remind you that New York is my home. Always has been and always will be. I was just visiting my people for the evening. And by the way, I understand that you're not one of them anymore." I detected a slight tensing in his jaw and the tightening of his fists. "I guess a deal with the devil is more important than family."

"Well," he replied, flashing a snide grin, "that *devil* is your father. So I guess either way you look at it, it's all in the family."

The thought suddenly struck me that when this was all over and if I found myself back under Maelcolm's roof, I could very well be thrown back under the control of Templeton, too. That just escalated my desperation to find a way out of the bargain. Becoming a slave to my father was bad enough, but I would never surrender to Templeton. I'd rather pierce my own heart with my mother's athame.

We stood silent like two stones in a road, neither willing to roll out of the way for the other.

"I believe we have an agreement," he eventually declared, glancing at my neck. I supposed he was looking for it, foolishly thinking I'd simply resign myself to my fate and wear the damn raven necklace right alongside the amulet. My mind raced, searching for options while I waited for my guard to get his nose out of his paper and come rushing in.

The life force.

"I'll tell you what," I reasoned. "You rescind that necklace of yours, and Greer won't destroy that fragile life force he has neatly tucked away in that little metal box."

He looked mildly surprised by the mention of it. "I don't think he'd be stupid enough to do that, Alex." That cocky grin on his face was getting on my nerves, reason enough not to spend the rest of my days with him. "You see, if he destroys the life force of the coven, he destroys you." He opened his mouth to continue but stopped and cocked his head in thought. "You do understand what you are, and your ties to that spinning ball of rings?"

I put on my best poker face while I considered my response. The bastard was right, after all. Until we figured out how to cut off the siphon, destroying it would be catastrophic to the mother coven—my coven. "You're right," I agreed, playing my bluff card. "Greer will never destroy those rings." I took a step closer and met his eyes. "But I will."

His nostrils flared in conjunction with the expansion of his chest. I could tell his patience was wearing thin. "I'll allow you a few hours to collect your things before we leave," he offered.

A few hours. He'd called my bluff, but somehow his words seemed almost comical as I repeated them back in my head. Then I found myself actually considering his instructions, but the thought was immediately followed by a sense of complete ridiculousness. I wasn't going anywhere with him. I shook my head, not in response to his ludicrous statement, but in an attempt to clear my mind and make way for my own lucid thoughts. He had no power over me. It was so simple that I nearly laughed. That necklace shoved in an envelope on Greer's bookcase didn't hold an ounce of power over me anymore. Maybe it never did. All I knew in my gut was that today it was null and void, overruled by the fortification of three very strong generations of Fitheach witches, and the fact that I was the Queen.

My attention was brought back to the very pressing matter at hand by a steady rumble snaking through the room—a menacing growl, a dog protecting its bone. A warm rush hit my back, growing hotter as the sound escalated into a deep and steady snarl. My left hand went up, halting the beast that was now at my side. "No, Katie. It's all right. I've got this."

Templeton was retreating, his face pale but defiant as his back met the new table we had yet to finish stacking with the books from Apollo's list. "Get that lizard away from me," he demanded, clearly misjudging his position to demand anything—and his tone.

My brow arched. "Such a big mouth for such a small man."

The fear that was always present whenever Alasdair Templeton pulled out his bullying card dissolved and washed away like a stain on a sheet. "You're in my house, now," I warned.

Before I could use my fire skills on him, he winced and nearly dropped to his knees. "Isla," he hissed. I could see a sparkle in his eyes, a momentary lusting for the power he thought he could harness by controlling me.

I'd like to see that one burn.

Ava's words flashed through my mind, reminding me of my ability to spot the bad seeds and repel them. That little talent coupled with a good fire hand made me realize how insignificant he was. There was nothing he could do to me.

"Would you like to see Maeve next?" I asked, raising my right hand.

The room shook. My eyes darted to the walls as the pictures fell, glass shattering from the frames hitting the floor. A bookcase on the far side of the room began to tap dance several feet and veer sideways.

"Alex!" Katie screamed. "Focus!"

She was right. I was a raging bull, my powers ricocheting dangerously out of control. I closed my eyes for a mere second to rein it in. When they reopened, Rhom was coming through the front door, swatting at the large bird swooping past him into the New York sky.

"*Jesus*, Alex. What the fuck!" He stormed into the shop, staring at the books heaped on the floor and the broken glass scattered everywhere. At least the shelves had remained upright.

"Okay," I said, leaning over with my hands pressed against my stomach. "I think I'm going to be sick."

IT DIDN'T MATTER that Templeton was gone. Rhom insisted on escorting me down to Den of Oddities and Antiquities during my break. I welcomed the extra layer of security, regardless of my apparent immunity to Templeton's little contract.

"What on earth is that smell?" Ava asked as we walked through the door.

I sniffed the air and frowned. "I don't smell anything." Hoping it wasn't me, I discreetly whiffed myself.

Melanie came from the back room, her face puckering as if she'd just eaten a lemon. Then her eyes went wide. "Alasdair," she hissed.

"How did you know?" I asked.

"Are you kidding me?" she said. "The man smells like a dead rat."

"I didn't notice."

"Give it time, dear," Ava said, heading for the window to check the sidewalk. "Your sense of smell will become keener as you learn to detect them."

Rhom grumbled in agreement.

"Them?" I asked.

"Traitors. He didn't follow you, did he?" She came back from the window and gave me a good once over.

I shook my head. "Not likely."

"Good. Now what the hell did he want?" Ava asked.

"That's why I'm here." I glanced at Rhom, who I suspected

would divulge everything to Greer before I made it back to the bookstore to finish my shift. But since I'd discovered at least a temporary flaw in Templeton's binding birdie necklace, our trip downtown was more for confirmation that I was indeed in the clear. "Remember that necklace he tried to trick me into accepting a while back? He finally did it."

Melanie concealed her concern only slightly. "The raven necklace? We don't use them anymore to bind our members. They're much too unpredictable, not to mention unethical. You didn't touch it, did you?"

Rhom, who had been leaning against the glass counter, straightened and eyed me admonishingly. "Alex?"

"Well, yes." I thought Melanie and Rhom were going to implode. "But here's the thing. He showed up at the bookstore to collect on this *contract*, but it didn't work."

"Didn't work?" Melanie repeated.

"Well, of course it didn't work," Ava snorted. "She isn't bound by the rules of the coven—she makes them. And let me remind you that Templeton no longer has the authority to enforce them, now does he?"

Melanie seemed to find some clarity. "Of course. What was I thinking?" She looked like a child witnessing a magic trick for the first time as a wide grin spread across her face. "You're his superior, Alex. The man answers to you now."

"Well, someone needs to tell him that, because he certainly did his best to intimidate me."

Ava waved her hand dismissively. "He's an old dog who needs to be retrained. Just keep in mind, Alex, he won't go away easily. You see, he's banking on your ignorance."

Rhom brought his hand down on the glass countertop, nearly smashing through it. "If he does come back around, he better pray I'm not there."

CHAPTER TWENTY-THREE

With a brutal whack, the feathery top flew across the kitchen and landed near the edge of the island. Sophia decapitated the next carrot, and then moved on to the onion waiting in line on the chopping board. There was a time for methodical execution, lining up and systematically dicing in a more efficient way, but today seemed more like a free-form day.

She nearly took her finger off, absently gazing at the ceramic plate mounted on the far wall. It was a good thing, really, her newly revived ability to sense things that were coming. But the onslaught of visions was overwhelming, even for an old Strega like her.

With the vegetables dumped into the hot oil in the pan, she set the spoon in motion and took a small glass from the cabinet, filling it halfway with sambuca. The strong anise-flavored alcohol slid down her throat, creating a warm flush throughout her head and chest. The diversion would only last for a moment, though. As soon as the sensation passed it would require another shot, and then another to suppress what was eating away at her. But she knew a bottle of booze was nothing more than a compounding effect for misery, something her belated husband had never learned.

"Damn it." She looked at the spoon that had stopped moving and stood motionless, buried in the vegetables that were now burning on the stove. With a quick stir, she saved the heavily caramelized soffritto from disaster, added a bowl of chopped tomatoes and herbs and lowered the heat to a simmer.

Leaving the empty glass on the counter, she moved to the living room and sat in front of the window to gaze out into the late afternoon sun of a perfect spring day. May had always been the worst month for her, commemoration of all the loss in her life. Her mother had died on a May evening, and so had Rue. And in keeping with morbid tradition, it was also the anniversary month of her husband's death.

Sophia's shoulders rose and fell as her breath shuddered from her heavy chest, the memories seizing her mind as the date of their deaths approached; Rue taken by the gods, *him* by the hands of a woman with nothing to lose.

It was cooler than usual on that day. She remembered this because she still wore the old blue sweater that served as her reminder, her scarlet letter hanging in the back of her closet with its invisible stains and memories knit deeply into its wool fibers. Mr. Healy's dry cleaning service had worked its magic on the soiled garment, returning it to her fresh and like new. She could have just thrown it away with the rest of the evidence, but that sweater was her penance.

The sound of the elevator pulled her back from the memory. Greer stepped through the door and glanced in the living room where she sat, careful to gauge her expression before choosing his words. He thought about going directly upstairs but changed his mind. Glancing at the blue sweater before trailing his eyes up to hers, he walked into the living room and joined her at the window. "Are you all right?" he asked, knowing the answer but showing her the courtesy of asking.

She averted her eyes back to the window. "Is just another day in May," she shrugged. "Just another day."

He placed his hand on the cuff of her shoulder. She patted it gently but didn't look at him. Then he went upstairs to leave her to it, that ritual of grieving that always managed to result in an exemplary meal and a more stoic version of his housekeeper.

THE WEATHER HAD BEEN PARTICULARLY violent that day, sheets of rain pounding the widows, thunder cracking the black sky. At one point, she feared the glass would actually break. Maybe if it had, things would have turned out different.

Salvadore was sitting in their small kitchen, a bottle of red wine standing next to the liter of vodka. He was in an unusually good mood for a change, never once mentioning the date or reminding Sophia of what she'd done to deserve her red, tearful eyes.

It was the third anniversary of Rue's death. Usually she tiptoed around him on this day, doing her best to avoid a collision, because when Sal struck he struck hard, and she wasn't up for a late-night trip to the emergency room requiring her usual lie involving a flight of stairs and too much to drink.

Sophia realized her mistake the moment she opened her mouth. "You want food?" she asked, noting the twitch at the corner of his lips. She made it worse by continuing. "I can heat up some oxtail stew?"

His melancholy eyes turned bitter. As she reached for the refrigerator door, he stood up and yanked her back by her hair, practically lifting her off the floor. "You fucking whore!" The smell of wine and sour breath hit her nose when he twisted her face around to his, gripping the bottle of vodka in his other hand. As bad as it usually got, she'd never seen this particular look in his eyes before—wild and vacant, vengeful.

The bottle reared back, poised at Sophia's face, gripped tightly in his dirty hand. Adrianna, now nearly nineteen, ran into the kitchen screaming for her father to stop. He turned and aimed the bottle at his daughter. With a single blow, she went down to the floor, her front tooth cracking as her nose shattered at the bridge.

Her fear replaced by anger, Sophia grabbed the bottle and shoved him against the table, nearly bringing the walls down with her pent-up rage. The bottle shot from her hand and levitated above his head. But she refused to resort to magic. Her faith had shifted too deeply for that. Instead, she gave him a warning look as she bent down to tend to her injured daughter, a look he knew all too well.

"No," he muttered, eyes wide, shaking his head as he realized his mistake.

She squeezed her fist until her nails dug into the toughened skin of her palm, a stream of blood seeping through the creases of her tightly clenched fingers. "It is done, Salvadore."

She lifted her broken child off the floor and led her out of the room. That was the last time he would see Adrianna. Sophia knew in her heart that he still loved his eldest daughter. But he was broken beyond repair, a wounded animal kicked one too many times, conditioned to strike before being struck. There would be no saving him.

SOPHIA SAT CALMLY in her living room, the one that used to be filled with family, friends, and love. She glanced at the table adjacent to the fireplace where they used to play cards on Friday nights. There were the neighborhood gatherings that started inside this room and spilled outside to the front porch when the weather was warm. Those were the memories she chose to keep. Now it was just a dark room.

The front door opened without a knock. Greer stepped inside but left the lights off, knowing the brightness would irritate her swollen eyes and expose the shame she felt. Neither had discussed the problem aloud, but both knew what needed to be done.

Sophia stood up, nodding toward the kitchen where Salvadore lay drunk and unconscious on the old laminate floor, a pool of piss circling his still form.

"Where is she?" he asked.

Sophia glanced at the floor and rubbed her hands together, igniting the pain where the deep cuts were still tender on her palm. "Hospital. She has a concussion. And a broken nose." Looking out the window at the night sky, she briefly considered her decision. "He is broken. Dead inside." It wasn't the first time her husband had laid his hands on her. It was like an annual purging of his demons. But the hours, days, and months in between had become a living hell, one which she could endure. But there was the safety of her daughter to consider. Salvadore was a drunk; a drunk who'd recently acquired a gun and a nasty habit of threatening to use it on her and Adrianna if they ever tried to leave. It was only a matter of time before he made good on that threat. The attack on Adrianna was the turning point.

"Are you sure?" Greer asked.

Sophia considered his question thoughtfully. Something bad was about to happen. She'd felt it for a while now, and that was a guilt she had to live with. Maybe if she'd acted on the feeling earlier, Adrianna wouldn't be lying in a hospital bed with her last memory of her father as the man who'd put her there.

Sophia stood straighter, steeling herself against the conflict inside of her. "Do it."

Greer nodded and headed for the kitchen.

"Mr. Sinclair," she called after him, unable to refer to him by his given name after all these years out of habit and respect. "I'm making the right choice?"

He looked back at her with a neutral stare. "I don't think you have one."

. . .

SOPHIA SHOOK OFF THE MEMORY, the smell of the cooking sauce reminding her that life continued. Whatever she felt that day, she felt again, here in Greer's house all these years later. Only this time it wasn't Adrianna who needed protection. But she couldn't just ship Alex away to a different continent or get rid of the threat, because she didn't know what it was. All she knew was that something was coming. Something very bad was coming.

Greer came back downstairs and found her in the kitchen, mixing flour and eggs into a well on the marble counter. "You didn't have to cook tonight, Sophia." But it was no secret that cooking was her therapy. Sitting back idly and sulking in her memories was the worst possible place for her on this day, but he would offer the reprieve every year, if for nothing more than to reinforce his love and devotion. There was nothing he wouldn't do for her, and the feeling was mutual.

"Go." She swatted him with the back of her hand without turning away from her mound of dough. "I call you when dinner is ready."

"I'll be in the library," he said, leaving the kitchen.

She resumed her task of making the farfalle, cutting out small rectangles with a ravioli cutter and crimping them into neat little bow ties at the center. As she manipulated the delicate pasta, something black came into view in the corner of her eye, her peripheral vision. She dropped the small piece of dough and turned sharply, but it was just her standing in the kitchen. She resumed her task, cognizant that she was sharing the room with something. Again, a flash of black filled the corners of her mind, only this time there was no mistaking what she saw.

She cleaned her flour-dusted hands with a dish towel before taking a seat at the kitchen island to let the vision fully unfold in her mind. She'd been a witch long enough to know when to fight those exterior interlopers who knocked on the door of her psyche, and when to listen. Today was a day to listen.

The vision started with the night sky filling her eyes. A stand of trees rustled in the foreground with their billowing fronds silhouetted against the sky; hemlocks waving back and forth as if a storm were bursting through their branches.

Her eyes sprang back open from the warning, shifting around the empty kitchen for signs of unwanted visitors. It was just her in the room. She considered ignoring it, but the warning was too strong, too insistent that she shut her eyes again and listen.

Sophia sank deeper into the vision, focusing to see what was concealed in the center of the trees. The limbs swayed back and forth, the heavy fronds reaching all the way to the ground and then shifting into shiny feathers. The bird began to bloom like a giant black rose, expanding its wings but keeping the tips loosely folded over its breast, fanning them just enough for a glimpse inside. Its head lifted from its resting position under the shoulder of its wing, revealing the three faces Sophia prayed she'd never meet. With her fear swallowed deep, she approached cautiously, careful not to touch the feathers as she looked through a sliver in the left wing. At the center where the crow's heart beat wildly, a woman was standing, an army of talons swooping down to carry her up into the belly of the beast.

The stool nearly fell sideways as Sophia's eyes snapped open. Her heart raced, leaving her faint and stricken with the worst sense of dread she'd felt since the day she lost Rue. Something was coming. Something powerful was coming for Alex.

CHAPTER TWENTY-FOUR

Greer was already up and gone when I woke. Usually he lingered next to me, waiting until I made the first move to rise. I swear we'd never get out of bed if it were up to him.

I sat up and listened for the telltale sounds of Sophia clanking pans in the kitchen, or the smell of food wandering up to the second floor. But it was Bear jumping in my lap and telling me to *get up and go downstairs* that finally motivated me to climb off the mattress.

"That's a little creepy, Bear." He just flicked his tail and stared at me intently. "Stay out of my head."

Then get up. They're all downstairs. The flicking stopped, and he leapt from the bed and squeezed through the crack in the bedroom door.

After a quick shower, I went downstairs and listened for sounds of the "they" Bear was referring to. A conversation was coming from the library. Sophia was at her usual spot next to the stove when I peeked into the kitchen. She glanced at me over her shoulder and then back at the stove, folding the eggs in the skillet.

The conversation in the library got louder. It was early for visitors, so I assumed something had happened that couldn't wait until after breakfast. And for Greer to leave me sleeping in order to tend to that business piqued my suspicion that it may involve me. It usually did.

"What's going on?" I asked, opening the cracked library door. Rhom and Thomas were sitting in the leather chairs while Greer stood at the window, staring at the morning traffic on the street below.

He did a half turn to greet me, but the heavy sigh coming from his chest was a giveaway that he wasn't as happy to see me as he should have been. "You're up," he said.

"So are you," I countered. "What's so important that the three of you are gathered in the library at," I glanced at the clock on the bookcase, "7:13 a.m.?"

Rhom got up and offered me his seat. "I'll stand for this, Rhom," I said without taking my eyes from Greer. "I thought we didn't keep secrets anymore?"

"You're absolutely right," he agreed, nodding to Thomas.

Thomas rose and walked over to the large map that was pinned to the paneling of the wall. It was a large map of Manhattan, maybe five feet long. He placed his finger on a spot in the lower left corner, a few blocks north of Tribeca and east of the Holland Tunnel. "We've found another marker."

The wolves had been lying low, but the frequency of finding markers was increasing. The last one was found the day we rescued the doctor. But no matter how many severed animal heads we found bearing the bloody mark of the Vargr, I'd never get used to hearing those words: *We've found another marker.*

"I guess that means we need to step up our guard," I said, speaking to no one in particular.

"You could say that," Thomas replied with a little sarcasm in his voice.

With a solemn look on his face, Greer stepped to the map,

knocking his index knuckle against the spot where Thomas's finger had just been. "They left it in the usual spot, on the rooftop of a building." He hesitated, clearly uncomfortable with what he was *not* telling me.

I looked around the room at the three sets of eyes fixed on me, anticipating bad news. Even Rhom did his usual blocking of the exit points by inching closer to the door. "Okay. Now you're scaring me." I turned back to Greer. "Tell me."

With a cool, neutral expression, he did as I asked. "Dr. Oxford is dead. The marker—"

"Don't," I said, suddenly wishing he'd lied to me. "I don't want to hear this."

I knew he was about to tell me—with clinical detail—that the marker was not the usual head of a stag or a boar, or some other wild animal. The head atop that pedestal with the mark of the Vargr traced in blood across its forehead was that of David Oxford, a scientist and innocent man who'd been nothing but kind and instrumental in helping solve the mystery of the missing vessel.

Greer steadied me as I reached for the wall, a vision of the doctor's head with his eyes fixed in horror as he was decapitated, materializing morosely in my mind. I could still hear his whimpering voice from that day when a thin wall separated us under a bakery in Little Italy. The terror had rendered him despondent as he confessed his fear through a small air vent near the floor, that they'd come for him and blind him for the pair of lenses in his eyes.

My face darted to Greer's. "His eyes! Did they take his eyes?"

"Vicious sons of bitches," Thomas sneered. "Butchered them. Looked like they used a bottle opener to pry them out."

"Dude," Rhom warned.

Thomas frowned, realizing his insensitivity. "*Shit.* I'm sorry, sugar. I shouldn't have said that."

"No, you shouldn't have," Greer agreed, pulling me closer.

I absently pushed him away, confused and repulsed by what I'd just heard. "Why bother with the marker? Why would they announce to the world that they had the lenses?" If the wolves were anything, they were smart and efficient. Wasting precious energy on something that served no purpose was out of character.

"Because they give a shit about you," Greer said. "They knew damn well this would hurt you. In fact, they're banking on it. They want you to come for them."

"Then I guess they played their cards right." I lingered on each of their faces, stopping at Greer's. "I will come for them. I'll make each one of them look me in the eye as I kill them. For my mother and the doctor."

He nodded, acknowledging the need for vengeance that must have been swimming in my eyes like a shark circling its target.

Finally, I thought, relieved that he wasn't trying to defuse my need for revenge. He was finally conceding that while I appreciated all the manpower, I no longer needed it.

Thomas walked over to the map on the wall, following the series of red, blue, and green thumbtacks indicating the location where each of the markers was found, five in total since I'd arrived back in New York the previous fall. He listed off the general location of each: "Lower East Side, Harlem, Upper East Side, Upper West Side. And now—" His finger zeroed in on the latest location, sighing with a confounded shake of his head.

The four of us stood back to examine the map. The island of Manhattan is long and narrow, like a ballerina's toe pointed slightly toward the west. But the map on the wall was more like a ballerina on pointe, the length of the island straight up and down. The markers were scattered randomly across the city with no obvious pattern glaring back at us.

"What are you fuckers up to?" Thomas muttered.

Sophia distracted us as she came through the doorway carrying a large tray. "You don't come to food, food come to you," she declared, turning around to face the room. The tray was loaded with food, orange juice, and a pot of coffee.

"We were just finishing up here," Greer said, stepping forward to help her with the overloaded tray. She bypassed him and slid the tray on top of the desk.

"We eating with our fingers?" Thomas teased, noticing the lack of china and utensils. "Come on, Mama. Daddy will help." He followed her back to the kitchen to fetch the cups and plates, while we resumed our stumped scrutiny of the map.

"There must be some significance to these spots." I took a step closer and pointed at the pin stuck through 128th Street. "The building where this one was found, what was it used for?"

Greer unfolded his arms, pushing off the edge of the desk to join me at the wall. "Just an old apartment building."

"And this one?" I pointed to the one found on East Sixty-Third Street.

"Senior citizen condos."

I thought about it. "Residential buildings. Maybe we should do a little research on who lives in these buildings."

He shook his head, reminding me where the other three had been found. The second marker was found on top of an abandoned building on the Lower East Side, the third one on top of the Revson Fountain in the middle of the Lincoln Center Plaza, and the latest one on top of an office building. "There's no pattern here."

Sophia and Thomas returned with the plates, cups, and utensils. "Soup's on," Thomas announced. "Let's eat before I rip that goddamn map off the wall."

Sophia gave him an admonishing look and then turned toward the map. She stared at it, seemingly drawn to something that wasn't quite clear but wouldn't allow her to pull her eyes away.

"You see something, Sophia?" Rhom asked, noticing her fixed gaze.

She stood silent looking at the map, clearly distracted by something none of us were seeing.

"What is it?" Greer stepped next to her to try and capture with his own eyes what hers were seeing.

She glanced at me when I moved closer. "Do you see it?" she whispered.

I turned to her, confused and uncomfortable with the look in her Strega eyes, and the sound of her hushed voice. "I don't see anything but streets and thumbtacks," I answered, turning back to the map.

"You're a young witch," she replied. "But you will learn to see it."

"What's going on over there?" Thomas was preoccupied with a mouthful of bacon when he finally noticed the apparent epiphany taking place a few feet away. With a plate of eggs in hand, he joined the line of faces staring at the map. "Oh yeah," he said, bobbing his head. "Wait. See what?" His brow scrunched as he looked harder to see what everyone else was apparently seeing.

Greer shook his head. "I don't see a damn thing, Sophia." He glanced at me. I confirmed with my own shake of the head that I was just as much in the dark as he was.

Sophia snapped out of it and took a step back. She knew about the wolves and the markers. "Are these the places where you found them?" She pointed to the five large tacks scattered around the map.

"Yes," answered Greer.

"Where did you find the first one?" she asked.

Greer pointed to the bright red tack pushed into 128th Street, in the upper middle section of the map.

"And the next one?"

He pointed out the blue tack on the Lower East Side. Without waiting for her instruction, he proceeded to point out the location of each marker in the order that it was found.

Sophia grabbed a black magic marker from the desktop and handed it to him. "Connect the dots."

Greer took the magic marker and started at the highest point, where the first marker was found in Harlem. Then he drew a line down to the Lower East Side and back up to Lincoln Center. He finished connecting the lines by moving to the Upper East Side and back down to where the latest marker was found near the waterfront district of the Lower West Side.

Sophia's face went grave. She approached the wall, taking the marker from Greer's hand and drawing a line from the spot where the last marker was found, all the way back up to where the first one was found, completing the circuit.

The sound of a breaking plate jolted the room. "Well, *fuck* me." Thomas swore as his breakfast ricocheted off the carpet. "That's a goddamn pentagram, isn't it?"

"Mmm-hmm." Sophia looked at me, standing as still as a stone, staring at the map. "You see it now, don't you." she said.

"It's like a halo telegraphing off the paper." I walked up to the map and ran my finger over one of the invisible lines hovering an inch above it. Then I began to trace each of the lines, starting at 128th Street and continuing down to the Lower East Side.

"Stop!" Sophia warned in a voice I'd never heard come out of her mouth before.

I yanked my finger back, startled by her harsh tone. "Jesus, Sophia!"

"You got too much power in that finger of yours." She pointed to the map where a pentagram was clearly outlined from the connected lines identifying the location of each marker. "It is *invoking*. The whole house will come down."

"Invoking?" Rhom repeated. "What exactly does that mean?"

"That's what I said." She pursed her lips and cocked her brow. "Is bad. Those dogs are calling something in. Invoking something bad."

. . .

SOPHIA STOOD in the middle of the room as all eyes zeroed in on her, waiting for an explanation of what the symbol drawn on the map meant. Her mind went back to the night before when the vision struck her in the kitchen. She'd seen it as clear as day, and even though she'd tried to reconcile those faces as something else, she knew it was just wishful thinking, a way to mitigate the threat that Alex had little chance of defeating. As powerful as Alex was becoming, it could take months or even years before she learned how to effectively use all that power, especially against a foe like the Morrigan, the Phantom Queen—the triple threat of war, prophecy, and death.

She almost blurted it out but knew it would do more harm than good. Greer would lose his mind before the full name of the threat left her lips, and then he would do something any male would do to protect his soulmate; he would ask a favor of the gods and end up in some other realm, working off the debt for another hundred years. A lot of good that would do Alex.

After consideration, she determined it was best to concoct her own magic to stave it off. But the truth was she was no match for it either. The best she could do was throw up a few roadblocks and pray that the wolves weren't strong enough to successfully summon the Morrigan. Few were.

"SOPHIA?" Greer eyed her suspiciously, pulling her back from her distracted thoughts. "What are you not telling us?"

"Like I said, it is invoking." She pointed out the downward direction of the first line, the one from the first marker to the second, indicating the invoking pattern of the symbol. "See this?" She poked the spot where the line terminated at the Lower East Side. "This point on the pentagram represents the element of fire. It is fire invoking. The wolves are calling the fire."

"But what does that mean?" he pushed, her simple lesson on the correspondences of the pentagram not satisfactory.

"Something bad, Mr. Sinclair. I don't know what it is. I can't see it."

The lie was less than convincing to any of us. Greer pressed for the truth with his stare, but Sophia wouldn't budge.

"All right," I said, interrupting the silent conversation between them. "I have to get ready for work. I have to be at the shop by nine."

He seemed surprised by my lack of mourning for Dr. Oxford, but I supposed his real concern was for my safety now that a new threat had been introduced.

"Don't you think it might be wise to stay home today?" he asked, astonishment in his tone. "I'll take the day off, too. Thomas can handle the club."

"Yes sir," Thomas agreed.

I shot him a don't-even-think-about-it look. "We're not doing this again, Greer. It's a damn shame what they did to the doctor, but it's just another day in this fucked up world, isn't it? Sitting still and dwelling on it won't fix a damn thing."

He knew better than to push the point. But I knew it was killing him every time I walked out that door without an army of backup. "I have Rhom. Besides, I'm the Queen. Remember?"

A slight smile crossed his face. "The Queen, indeed." That smile vanished as a more Greer-like seriousness replaced it. He held Rhom's attention for a moment before turning back to me. "You be careful out there."

With the flame extinguished before the pot had a chance to boil, I headed out of the library and up the steps to get ready for work. *I'm the Queen*, I thought, trying to understand exactly what that entailed, and doing my damnedest to feel like one.

CHAPTER TWENTY-FIVE

Most of the morning was spent trying to get the image of Dr. Oxford's severed head out of my mind. All I could envision was his face, fixed and lifeless with two holes where his eyes used to be. He was just an ordinary man who happened to stumble into a very unordinary game of hide and seek that everyone was willing to kill for. David Oxford was its latest victim, and the first order of business I would attend to once the vessel was found was to rid the city of the wolves forever, and every other city, for that matter. But the stakes had just been upped, and the wolves had the lenses that increased their odds of finding the vessel first.

When I got to the bookstore, I was looking forward to the company of like minds. I got Erica instead.

He let you open the store? I had to admit, I was a little wounded that she'd been entrusted with a key so early in her tenure at Shakespeare's Library—barely part-time. But then Apollo came walking out of the back room and my jealous little demons retreated. Shame on me.

"Apollo, why don't you tell us why you're so shiny and happy this morning," I said. In general, my manager was a pleasant and amiable person. But his demeanor this morning was downright jolly, and his reckless hair was corralled into something other than a bird's nest. Even his clothes were uncharacteristically fancy for a shift at the bookstore.

"Well, it looks like my hard work just might be paying off." He shot me an exuberant grin of pearly white teeth, unrestrained and spontaneous like it had been pent-up behind his lips for years just waiting to explode. "I'm afraid you might be getting a new manager in the near future."

The book I was carrying dropped to my side, along with my arm. "What?" I asked in a small voice. "Are you quitting? You can't quit. We have the perfect team." I glanced at Erica from the corner of my eye. She looked nervous, like she was about to cry because her recently negotiated *part* part-time position was in jeopardy.

"Remember my long-term plan?" He walked toward the front counter with a document in his hand. "This," he continued, waving the clipped stack of papers in the air, "is my opportunity. I hold in my hand a business plan. A very good one, at that."

"What kind of business plan?" Erica asked, her eyes shifting from nervous to curious.

I remembered my first day at Shakespeare's Library. Katie was giving me the grand tour and telling me all about Apollo and his big designs of starting his own publishing company, his disownment from his wealthy family the price for that little dream. At the time, I had no doubt he'd do it, but I guess the thought got lost in the daily grind of work and trying to figure out my own plan.

"Since you ask," he said, clearly excited to share. He dropped the plan on the counter and took an exaggerated breath before speaking. "This, Erica, is a business plan for Greenwich Press, the next great publishing empire."

A wide grin spread across my face. "So, you're actually doing it? Did your father—"

"No," he interjected soberly. Then he brightened back up as quickly as the light faded. "I have a partner. Well, a few investors. But they've agreed to remain silent while Anna and I head the business."

"Anna?" I asked.

"We met at one of my conferences. Turns out she's been looking for a partner as long as I have. I'll tell you, Alex, I couldn't have asked for a better fit. Her vision is so clear."

He looked off into the space in front of him, a soft glow falling over his eyes. I could see that there was more to this *Anna* than a partner on paper, and I wanted to caution him about treading lightly in the area of love and work. But that would be hypocritical of me, wouldn't it?

"When are you leaving?" I asked, the reality of the upset we were about to experience at the bookstore sinking in.

"A few weeks. Maybe at month's end." He cocked his eyes at me. "Would *you* be interested in taking my place? I'd be happy to put in a good word for you."

I shook my head. "Oh no. Nothing personal, Apollo, but I'd rather stick needles under my fingernails than manage anything." I had no desire to spend my days doing paperwork and telling people what to do. Besides, despite our stagnant progress in finding the vessel, I suspected my days at Shakespeare's Library were numbered, too. I was some sort of queen, after all. My future held one of two outcomes: serving the Fitheach as some kind of figurehead, or serving my father as something much worse.

"Just thought I'd ask. I know Katie would rather die." He glanced at Erica who quickly diverted her eyes to the floor, but wisely chose not to go there. It would take more than a little time and training to make the meek girl with the Japanese anime panda sweater into management material. Maybe in another ten years. "Anyway, I just popped in to finish up a little paperwork." He glanced at his phone. "I'm running late for a meeting with

Anna. I'm sure the two of you can hold down the fort until Katie gets here around one o'clock."

I was about to answer when the front door opened. In walked Constantine with a bag in his hand.

"That's my cue to leave," Apollo muttered, grabbing his business plan and nodding as he walked out the door. It was no secret, his opinion of Constantine. The satyr made him uncomfortable. If he only knew why.

"Constantine," I acknowledged.

"I brought you this." He handed me the bag. There were two sandwiches and two bags of chips inside. It was barely ten a.m. "Brunch," he clarified. "I thought Katie might be here."

I didn't like the look on his face. He was full of shit if he thought I'd fall for his casual visit excuse. "She won't be here for a few more hours. What's going on? You look a little jumpy."

He glanced to my right, at Erica. She shyly wandered forward. "I'm Erica." She extended her hand which had been clasped behind her back. He took it and raised it to his lips, gently kissing her skin without taking his eyes from hers. An audible breath escaped her mouth.

I shot him a warning look as he did that brazen seduction thing he was so adept at.

He just couldn't resist. "It's a pleasure to meet you, Erica." Her name rolled off his tongue like warm honey, panda bear sweater or not. "Would it be a terrible imposition to ask for a few minutes of privacy with Alex?"

Her intoxicated expression turned serious as she considered her options.

"It's okay, Erica. You can take off for a few minutes." I opened the register and borrowed a ten. "Here. Why don't you go and get us some coffee? The good stuff, not the sludge from across the street."

She took the bill and nervously left. *Go*, I mouthed as she lingered at the window.

"A bit of a project, isn't she?" Constantine commented as she finally walked out of view.

I ignored the comment and got right to the point. "What's wrong? You look nervous. And you're never nervous, Constantine."

"That's because I've never felt the pressure of eminent domain before."

I cocked my head, wondering if I'd heard him right. "Meaning?"

"Meaning," his face twisted with anger, "what have you done!"

My legs seemed to work autonomously, moving in a backward motion without waiting for my brain to provide instructions. In all the time I'd known him, from New York to Paris and all the mind trips in between, Constantine had never raised his voice to me. The sound of it was terrifying.

"Why are you so angry? I haven't done anything!" I yelled back at him, scared but a little angry myself from his unclarified accusation. My mind worked frantically, trying to figure out what I'd done to set him off.

Visibly, I could see him reining in the anger, pushing back a stray lock of hair dangling over his forehead. His chest settled back into a steady breathing pattern as he calmed down but continued to penetrate me with his black eyes. "My home is under siege."

"Central Park? By what?" I asked, wondering what could possibly overrule him in his own territory. I'd seen him handle intruders, both insiders and outsiders, and I found it hard to believe that anything could have the upper hand under the umbrella of Central Park, his domain.

His eyes cooled and shifted to a deep gray. I think he knew I was afraid of him. "I'm sorry. I shouldn't have spoken to you like that." His tone was clipped, but the remorse was genuine. Constantine was all about balance. We'd always maintained a unique relationship, a mutual respect, even though he usually had the upper hand. Something had clearly upset that balance.

"They're coming," he continued, pacing in a small circle. "The walls around the park are stretching, getting taller. The squirrels have left. Even the damn elves have taken to the underground." He stopped and turned. "Do you have any idea what a park is like without squirrels? And the birds," he scoffed, continuing with his repetitive movement.

"What are you saying, Constantine? What's coming? And why is it my fault?"

He ignored my questions and continued with his distracted rant. "There isn't a pigeon or sparrow in sight. Even the peregrine falcons have stopped flying overhead. They've all been replaced by black, menacing ravens. It's just a matter of time before the crows arrive."

At the mention of the ravens I was starting to get the connection, although still in the dark about what was happening and why it was my fault. I looked at him blankly as he met my eyes, waiting for him to drop the bomb and introduce yet another variable of complexity into the mix. "Go on," I said.

He walked toward me and cupped the side of my face, examining my features closely. "Always such a magnet for drama. I don't really blame you for any of this, but I was hoping for a less theatrical ending."

"Ending for what?" I pulled away from his hand, the creep factor inching up my spine with each word coming from his mouth. "What, Constantine?"

Erica came through the door with a tray of cups in her hand. "I got cappuccinos. I hope that's okay."

He looked at the cardboard contraption in her hand and then helped himself to one of the cups. "Thank you, Erica." She swooned from the sound of his velvet voice, a neat little trick he liked to use on unsuspecting women, making them feel as if each word was personally crafted for their ears only. Erica was not immune to his charm. "I hate to accept your hospitality and leave, but I must run." His face went dark. "There are intruders in my house."

Erica looked startled. "Intruders?"

"Don't worry, love," he purred in response to her concerned reaction. "They're not here for me." There was something final in the way he looked back at me before he left, like he was leaving on a long trip—or I was.

RHOM and I walked through the front door just before six. Greer was in the library when I peeked inside.

"You're home early," I said. He greeted me at the door and pulled me to him, kissing me before my cheek met the warmth of his chest. "What's this all about?" I asked, leaning back to look up at his face.

"Can't I just be happy that you're home?" His body went rigid as the smell hit his nose. "I see the beast has paid you a visit."

"I don't know why you always call him that." I pulled away and glanced at Leda, who was sitting in the chair.

"I think you know why," he went on. "You just haven't seen enough of his true form yet. Constantine shows you what he wants you to see."

The first time I met Constantine, he showed himself to me, his fur-covered flanks and cloven hooves, and a set of horns on the top of his head. But I'd never noticed a foul odor on him.

Leda rolled her eyes. "Here comes the pissing part. Honestly, Greer, the girl has made her choice. And you should be thankful that Constantine likes her. He's a formidable ally, and Alex needs all the help she can get right now."

"So what brings you by, Leda?" I sat in the chair next to hers. "Not that you need a reason."

She puckered her perfectly painted lips and looked at the wall, the one with the giant map of Manhattan still pinned to it.

"We're just trying to figure out what those damn dogs are up to." She stood up and walked over to it. "What do you mongrels have planned?" she murmured to no one in particular.

I heard voices outside the door. Thomas and Loden came into the library, one holding a fresh bottle of scotch and the other with a bag of opened potato chips. Loden dropped into Leda's vacated chair and held the bag out to me. I took a handful and chomped on the greasy comfort food while I glanced around the room at all the forced smiles gleaming back at me.

"Okay. I know what's going on here, and I want everyone in this room to cut the bullshit and drop the façade." Greer had called in the team to surround me while they addressed the threat on the wall. "God!" I stuffed another chip in my mouth and got up, the nervous energy propelling me around the room like a live wire.

"Honey," Leda began, "you're just going to have to get used to it. I don't care if your mother is Danu herself. Everyone in this room will go to the ends of the universe for you. Like it or not, you're just that special." Her gaze was sympathetic but uncompromising. "We all know you can take care of yourself." And then her eyes went as black as Constantine's. "But there isn't a chance in hell that you're getting rid of any of us until those wolves are dead. Got that?"

"Okay," I agreed, a little wary of the she-devil in the room. "Smother away."

Greer the instigator watched Leda's sermon quietly from across the room, and I nodded to him in acquiescence.

For the second time in twelve hours, Sophia came into the library with a tray of food: an assortment of cheese, crackers, and olives. "A little snack. I roast a chicken for dinner, okay?"

A mumbling of affirmatives sounded around the room.

"What did he want?" Greer asked.

"Constantine? At first I thought he wanted to kill me," I

joked wryly. "He seems to think I'm responsible for something invading his 'domain.' "

Sophia marched toward the desk, listening intently to the conversation.

"You mean Central Park?" Leda asked.

"Mmm-hmm. Kept rambling about the walls getting taller and the squirrels disappearing. He said all the birds have been replaced by ravens." I looked at Greer, pointedly. "Ravens? Coincidence?"

I could hear the china rattle as Sophia clumsily placed the platter on the desk.

"Then he said something about crows arriving next."

The platter slipped to the floor and shattered. Sophia stood there gawking at me, completely distracted from the mess at her feet.

"What's wrong, Sophia?" Greer asked. "And don't even consider lying to me."

She pulled her eyes from mine and looked at his, her fearless face not so fearless anymore. "We got a big problem, Mr. Sinclair."

I heard a faint sound coming from the foyer—my phone. It rarely rang. When it did it was usually important. I retrieved my purse from the hall table and pulled the phone out a few seconds too late to answer. There was a message.

CHAPTER TWENTY-SIX

Sophia stared out the window of the car as it rolled down the streets of Bensonhurst, Brooklyn. It was another one of those hour-long rides that flew by in what felt like a minute, tempting her to tell her driver to circle back around to Manhattan and start the journey home all over again.

Through the glass, she could see a light in the sky, a sliver reaching the end of its cycle, barely a crescent as it waned into the dark moon. It was the perfect time for letting go, banishing things that were no longer wanted or needed.

She hesitated when the car stopped in front of her little green house at the end of the block, resisting the logical urge to grab the door handle and climb out.

"You okay, Sophia?" her driver asked, looking back at her through the rearview mirror.

"No," she replied back to the man who had driven her home every night for the past few years. "But I will be, soon," she added, meeting his alarmed eyes.

Eventually, she got out of the car and took the steps up to her front door. Without bothering to flick on the lights, she walked into the kitchen and relied on the illumination from the night sky to find a small glass. She filled it with a shot of liquor, not knowing which bottle she'd grabbed until the sweet smell and taste of almonds hit her nose and tongue. The amaretto went down smoothly, diluting the sick feeling in her stomach, if only for a few seconds. But that was the limit of her distraction as she headed back out toward the hallway.

Her feet felt like two lead weights as she climbed the stairs and headed down the hall, past her bedroom, past Adrianna's, to the second door on the right. She turned the knob and entered Rue's room, the one with the green floral bedspread and the pink sheets. She absently thought about stripping the bed to wash them, but then she refocused on why she was there. Musty old sheets wouldn't matter after tonight. Nor would the closed door to the room, or the faded memory of who used to occupy it.

Sophia had tried to think of another way to appease the gods and lessen the claim they would stake when the Morrigan arrived, but there was really only one thing she could offer them that would give Alex a fighting chance at freedom. She would offer her daughter, her memories of Rue, a witch for a witch. It wasn't actually Rue, she kept repeating over and over in her mind. It was the sacrifice of her memories that would be the offering, because nothing was more powerful than a mother's love, or a glimpse into the egregore built around the daughter of a blooded clan of Aradia.

Dust scattered into the air as she opened the chest at the foot of the bed, igniting a cough as it settled in her nose and throat. She'd neglected the room for months, finding it harder to enter as the pain seemed to get worse over time, a contradiction to what she'd always been told. She pulled a small walnut box from the bottom of the chest and removed an object wrapped in black fabric from inside. The gift would have been consecrated on Rue's fifteenth birthday, but she never made it that far. Now it was just an object covered in cloth at the bottom of a wooden box, meaningless and dull. It was time to let go.

Despite the waning moon, the night sky was bright when she stepped outside into her small backyard. The patch of herbs was still neglected, as it had been for the entire spring season. She just couldn't find the time, or the inclination, to work the garden in a way it deserved. Maybe after tonight she'd finally get it done. She glanced around the space and spotted what she was looking for— rosemary. The black fabric wrapped around the spirit blade fell to the ground, and she clumsily cut a stalk of the potent herb with the dull edge. She grabbed a rusted shovel off the ground and headed for the north side of the yard, the side nearest the darkening moon. Then she dug. The dry, neglected soil resisted the metal, requiring every ounce of strength she had to drive it deeper into the earth. Magic of this sort would require a deep hole, not some shallow indentation for the planting of a small shrub.

"Aradia," she whispered, calling out to the Holy Strega. "Give me strength."

It took some time, but eventually the earth relinquished. She dug down a good two feet and speared the tip of the blade into the bottom of the narrow hole. Then she dropped the rosemary on top of it. Rosemary for remembrance, but today she would forget. Tomorrow she would take that same shovel and uproot the rosemary bush that had grown in her garden for nearly twenty years.

With her aching knees resting on the unforgiving ground and the light from the sky illuminating a shadow of the trees over the hole, she bent over it and lowered her face to the opening. Without a sound, she screamed. A plume of black clouds left her mouth and rushed into the hole, thick as smoke before trailing off into a fine white mist sinking into the curved walls dug into the earth, filling it until the blade disappeared from view. Before the mist could escape, she feverishly pulled the dirt back into the hole, covering the mound with her body and using her stout arms and chest to drive it back into place.

When the hole was sealed and the only evidence of the ritual was a bare spot of earth at the edge of her knees, she pushed herself up and sat on her heels and ignored the searing pain in her thighs, overwhelmed by the more dominant pain of loss and grief that soared from her gut to her chest. The pain grew until her eyes burst with cold, salty tears, dropping onto her exposed legs and rolling off into the softened soil were the blade lay buried. And then as quickly as the pain came, it rushed up her neck and out the top of her head.

CHAPTER TWENTY-SEVEN

I listened to Hazel's voice on the message, a distinct wariness in her tone. I'd found my old neighbor shortly after returning to New York when I was still staying in the room above Crusades. The old building where I'd spent the first five years of my life had changed significantly, but the one thing that remained there was the woman who'd lived next door.

Alex, this is Hazel Foster. You came to see me last fall in your old apartment building, the message reminded me. As if I could forget. I could live to be a hundred and I would never forget the woman who gave me the letter written by my mother that eventually led me to the missing amulet. At the time, she'd mentioned a name my mother had screamed while chasing away a cat that had taken an unhealthy interest in me at the sidewalk café below our apartment. It happened just before my mother died. Thinking it important, Hazel had written the name down but couldn't recall where she's put the piece of paper, or even if she'd kept it. I'd given her my number and asked her to call me if she ever found it. It didn't matter, though. I already knew the name that would be written on that piece of paper—Alasdair Templeton.

When Greer asked who the call was from, I lied. I told him it was Katie asking me to meet her for lunch the next day, my day off. But it was Hazel I would be going to see. Her message was cryptic. *There's something else,* she'd said. She'd found that missing scrap of paper, but she wouldn't discuss it over the phone. I was to stop by so she could deliver it in person.

Sophia had come clean the evening before and told everyone in the room about her vision, further elaborating on Constantine's reference to the crows. The Morrigan was coming: the three sisters, the Phantom Queen, the Battle Crow. I thought Thomas was going to choke when he heard the name.

Greer practically ordered me to stay home that morning, but I reminded him that I didn't take orders from him or anyone else. He was furious with me, but in lieu of his lack of influence, his eyes settled on Rhom. I wasn't going anywhere without Rhom, which was fine with me since I rarely did anyway.

Sophia walked into the kitchen around noon. For the first time since I stepped foot in Greer's house the previous fall, she was late, which meant we fended for ourselves at breakfast.

"You okay, Sophia? You look exhausted." I took the bag of groceries from her arm.

She looked at me, her eyes weary. "I'm fine."

"Okay." I was unconvinced but knew better than to try and get water from a dry creek. Her troubles would flow on her own time, when she was ready to share. "I'll be back in a few hours." I grabbed a banana from the counter and headed out of the kitchen.

"Wait!" she cried. "Where are you going?"

"I'm meeting a friend for lunch." I guess the intel she shared the previous evening had her as worried as the rest, because she looked frantic. I glanced at Rhom who was leaning against the wall with that rag of a paper in his hand. "Rhom's going with me."

Her expression softened a little, but it was clear everyone

wanted to put me under glass. Her mouth flattened as she muttered and looked away, lifting the groceries out of the bag.

RHOM NEVER QUESTIONED where we were going. He just stood next to me as we jerked back and forth on the train headed down to the Village, his face buried in gossip the entire time. He'd suggested a cab, but the train ride was oddly calming, allowing me a little more time to prepare for whatever Hazel had to tell me. Based on her tone, I assumed it wasn't going to be pleasant.

"You don't believe everything you read in that paper, do you?" I asked.

"The Kardashians are fascinating folks," he smirked, folding the paper under his arm. "Seriously, Alex. Don't you think we've got enough shit to deal with every second of the day? A little mindless diversion does fucking wonders to lighten the mood."

"Language, Rhom."

"Sorry, Alex. I just—"

"I'm kidding. Jeez, Rhom. I'm buying you a *National Enquirer* when we get off the train."

"You're not meeting Katie, are you?" he asked.

"No," I replied, staring at him blankly.

He got the message and resumed reading his paper. "I don't suppose you want to tell me where we're going?"

I thought about it but figured it was a better idea to keep him in the dark, at least until after I met with Hazel. Rhom would be on the phone with Greer in a heartbeat if I told him why we were heading downtown, and the last thing I wanted was for Greer to knock on Hazel's door in the middle of our conversation. It was wiser to wait until I knew what "there's something else" meant.

We got off the train at Washington Square and headed west a few blocks. When we got to the building, Rhom looked at me suspiciously. "And just who are we visiting here?"

"*I'm* visiting an old friend, while *you* wait down here." I pointed to the steps. "You don't mind, do you?"

"You know, Greer's going to kill me if you do anything stupid, Alex."

"There's nothing stupid or dangerous up there, Rhom. And I promise I will tell you everything you need to know on the way home."

He conceded with a labored sigh and planted himself on the steps with his paper. "Thirty minutes."

I entered the first door of the building where the mailboxes were lined up against the wall in a neat little display that reminded me of a miniature row of school lockers. To my left was the locked main entrance that had been conveniently unlocked the last time I was here.

Hazel's cracked voice came over the intercom a moment after I pushed the button. "Come in," she said. I glanced around the small space for a camera because I hadn't announced myself. She just buzzed me in without confirming it was me. When I reached the top of the stairs, she was waiting at the door, smiling at me sympathetically as if the news were grave.

"You really shouldn't just let strangers through the door," I said, entering her apartment and instantly feeling that same déjà vu, an awkward but humbling sense of my alienated home. I would never get used to the displaced walls and the subsequent offset of the front doors from the building's renovations, but you can't modify or erase the mind's imprint. I spent the first five years of my life in this very place and that was permanently stamped on my brain.

"I knew it was you." She glanced at the window. "Who's that man you're with, the one parked on the steps?" Her brow went up in curiosity. "Handsome. Is he your boyfriend?"

She'd seen us coming down the sidewalk from the window. "Just a friend. I thought it best to ask him to wait downstairs."

She nodded in agreement and headed toward the kitchen. "Tea?"

"Yes, please."

I surveyed the room, taking in all the details as I had the last time I visited. Once again, I could visualize myself sitting on a sofa at the far end of the space where our living room used to be. I knew that by the orientation of the view, the surrounding buildings framed outside of the windows that hadn't changed, the same view as twenty years ago.

"Here we are." She set the tray on the table and poured us both a cup of black tea.

I got right to the point. "I think I already know the name written on that piece of paper. But you didn't summon me all the way down here to read me that name, did you?"

She sipped her tea, scrutinizing me over the rim of the cup. "Was your mother interested in things that were…" She glanced at the surface of her drink, considering her words carefully. "Dark?"

"What?" I let out a short laugh. "Define *dark*."

A nervous smile skimmed her face and then disappeared. "Are you Christian?"

"Hazel?" I didn't like where this was going. No, I wasn't Christian. I'd never really tried to put a label on my beliefs, but I knew as a witch I wasn't a card-carrying member of a standardized religion. Certainly not the Catholic Church, although their rituals were not unlike ours in many ways, seeing how so many of them were bastardized from the old ways. "No," I finally said, leaving it at that.

"I'm not judging you, Alex. It's just that I've found another note. Now, it may be nothing, but what's written on it is rather stigmatic." She put her cup on the table and stood up. "I'd been looking for that damned piece of paper for months. Obsessed with finding it, I guess." At the bookcase, she pulled the same folder from between two books, the folder where she'd kept my mother's letter. I remembered her pulling it from the same spot six months earlier.

"You said it's another note?"

"Oh yes. From your mother."

I shook my head. "Why didn't you give it to me when you gave me the first one?"

"I didn't notice it until a few days ago. I'd finally given up on finding that paper, but then I spotted the edge of the folder sticking out of the bookcase."

My curiosity wouldn't wait another second. I met her at the bookcase and eyed the folder in her hand. "So?"

She opened it and pulled out the missing piece of paper with the name of the cat my mother had so vehemently tried to scare off. "I found it in the top drawer, stuck to the underside of the desk." The edge of the small yellow paper was stuck to her finger. "See? It's written on a Post-it note."

Alasdair was scribbled in a shaky hand. Hazel's hand.

"Is that the name you were expecting?" she asked.

"Yes." I looked back at the folder. "What else is in there?"

"It was in the original envelope your mother sent, the one containing the separate letter addressed to you." She held out a smaller white envelope with nothing written on the front. "At first I thought it was just an empty envelope," she explained, her expression sobering. "Until I looked inside. My guess is Maeve shoved it in there with the other one as a last-minute thought. Otherwise, she probably would have put it in the same envelope with the letter. Good thing I was looking for that scrap of paper or I might not have discovered it."

Her brow pulled together as I took the envelope from her hand, her finger nervously scratching the back of her ear as I flipped the top open. Inside was a single piece of paper with a bold set of underlined numbers written in the center.

666.

The longer I stared at the paper, the larger the numbers

seemed to grow before my eyes. I'd seen my share of demonic films, and I knew the connotations associated with that number. I also knew what my mother was not.

"You can see why I didn't feel comfortable telling you this over the phone," she explained.

"Now, Hazel—"

She shook her head and waved her hands, halting my defensive response. "I'm not here to accuse. I know a good person when I meet one, and Maeve Kelley was a good person. But damn it, Alex, that number means something. Clearly she debated including it in that envelope."

"You're right, Hazel. My mother was a good person. I think I know who can shed some light on what this number means."

I quickly finished my tea and hugged her goodbye before heading back down the stairs. Rhom took one look at my concerned face and tossed his paper in the trash can on the sidewalk.

"I guess your lunch date didn't go so well?"

"Let's just say I'm learning things about my family that might not be so desirable." I hit the sidewalk and headed east.

"Okay, this time I insist on knowing where we're going," he said, folding his arms and not budging from his spot in front of the apartment building.

"To find out what the hell is going on."

PATRICK WAS TINKERING with a weird mechanical box when we walked through the front door of Den of Oddities and Antiquities.

"Patrick," I greeted, approaching him at the counter.

"Alex," he acknowledged, barely glancing up from his project.

Rhom took a seat in the reading nook, while I waited for the boy wonder to give me his full attention.

"Is Ava or Melanie here?"

"Yes ma'am," he drawled, still buried in his work.

"Can you get them, please?"

"Ava!" he bellowed across the room.

"Well, I could have done that," I said, glancing at the contraption he was so enthralled in. I strolled over to the window and pulled the envelope from my purse, tapping its edge against my palm.

"Alex." Ava came from the back room, glancing at Rhom on her way over to me. "Is everything all right?"

"No. Everything is not all right." I stepped to the glass display case and practically slapped the envelope down on the top. "*That*," I said, pointing to it with my eyes, "is my mother's latest riddle."

She looked at the plain white envelope and then back at me. "When you're finished with your mild tantrum, you can tell me what *that* is. Shall we count to ten?"

"I'm sorry, Ava," I apologized, closing my eyes for a moment. "I'm just a little frustrated."

"I think we all have our moments. Now, what's in that envelope that has you so worked up?"

Rhom was up now, wondering himself what I hadn't bothered to mention on the way over. He leaned into the counter at the far end, waiting for the big reveal.

"You remember my old neighbor? The woman who gave me the letter from my mother last year?"

Ava nodded. "Yes, Hazel."

I'd forgotten that Ava knew of Hazel through my mother.

"It seems there was a second smaller envelope in the original package my mother left me." I glanced at the envelope on the counter. "Hazel thought it was just an empty envelope all this time, until she ran across it again and looked inside."

"But it isn't?" Ava picked it up. "May I?"

"Maybe you or Melanie can tell me if there's something else about my family that I need to know about."

Ava removed the piece of paper and stared at the number. When she did finally look up at me, she seemed as confused as I was. Her head cocked slightly to the side as a pained expression dominated her face, her brows tightly drawn together in thought. "Alex, I have no idea why Maeve would send you a note with the number of the beast written across it. *Where* did this come from?"

Rhom stepped forward and took the paper from Ava's hand, gently. "I think I should call Greer."

"No!" I insisted. "Let's just figure out what's going on before we set off the alarms. It's just a number written on a plain piece of paper." The thought that my mother and our family could be part of some kind of dark cult astounded me, because that meant *I* was something dark. My mind was flooding with wild thoughts. Maybe it had all been a smokescreen to hide the real motive for finding the prophecy. Maybe Alasdair Templeton wasn't the Lord of Darkness; maybe *I* was the *Queen* of Darkness.

Rhom held my shoulders and shook me back to the present. I just stood there gawking at him in disbelief. "I'm not dark!" I kept repeating.

I glanced at Ava, who was now staring at the two-story wall of drawers. She walked over to it and stood at the base, planting her hands on her hips as a sly smile appeared on her face. "What are you up to, Maeve Kelley?" she said, following the drawers with her eyes all the way up to where they nearly reached the ceiling.

"Ava? What are you doing?" I joined her at the base of the library ladder that rolled along the length of the sky-high wall.

"You see that?" She pointed toward the top of the wall. "That wall has exactly 666 drawers in it." She grinned and shook her head. "Your mother and I had a good laugh when we counted them. Twice, actually. Seemed ironic for the good witches of Greenwich Village to have exactly 666 magical drawers in this shop. Don't you agree? The one on the top right is the last one we counted, and I'd bet the shop that that's the one she wanted you to find." Her face grew somber, the memory of laughter and better times filling her eyes. "She must have known I'd figure it out the minute you showed me that note. Good thing Hazel found it."

"I guess we need to find out what's in it." I reached for the ladder, but Rhom grabbed me around the waist and pulled me off.

"Boss will end my life if you fall off that ladder," he said, reaching for it himself. "I'm going up."

Ava pushed past him. "This is my shop and my liability, so I'll be the one going up that ladder."

He blocked her with his outstretched arm. "Greer will kill me if *you* fall, too."

"Nonsense. I've been climbing that ladder longer than Alex has been alive. The drawers past the first floor have been empty for years, but I can still reach them." She hiked her skirt and quickly ascended the first half of the wall. "See," she said, looking down at us. "Still agile as a cat."

She wasted no time scaling the ladder, like I remembered her doing when I was a child. When she made it to the top, she looked back down at us and then reached for the old patinated knob of drawer number 666.

"Now or never," she said before pulling it open and peeking inside.

CHAPTER TWENTY-EIGHT

I hadn't expected to be handed something so ordinary and innocuous. Something stuffed in a drawer designated as 666, hidden at the top of the magical wall in Den of Oddities and Antiquities, should have had qualities that left you speechless or at least made you catch your breath from the sight of it. But the book wrapped in a faded old map of Central Park was not what I expected to find.

With Ava safely back down on the ground, she laid it on the display case and asked me to do the honors. I peeled back the map from around a copy of Lewis Carroll's *Alice's Adventures in Wonderland*. It was an early edition, with a red cloth cover and a gold stamp of Alice on the front and the Cheshire Cat on the back.

"Why would she lead you to this?" Ava asked, picking up the map and examining the area circled in red ink.

"Children's books," I whispered.

"Yes, it's definitely that," Ava agreed.

"It's more than that." My eyes shot to Rhom, who was finally getting the connection, too.

Ava looked back and forth between the two of us. "Well, will one of you please fill me in? And what about this map?" She picked it up again and pointed to the red circle around Conservatory Water—the boat pond in Central Park.

My mind began to race, every memory and nuance of a hint rushing back to me like a freight train.

Some say this very spot is a doorway, a portal. Maybe the vessel is right here under our feet, balancing atop this mysterious portal. Constantine had been planting those seeds in my head all along. *Dig deep and find that door.*

"I think we just dug to China," I muttered.

Still holding the map, Ava cocked her head. "What did you say?"

I just smiled back at her. "I may be wrong about this. God knows I've been wrong a thousand times before, but I think my mother just told me where to find the vessel."

SOPHIA'S EYES lingered on me longer than usual when I walked through the front door with Ava and Rhom. She had a sixth sense about certain things, and lately I was the target of that foreboding sense. I ignored the scrutiny and walked straight past her toward the library.

The three of them watched as I marched up to the bookcase, determined to prove to all of them that I wasn't losing my mind. I scanned the shelf and reached for one of the books on Jacobite history, examining the front and back cover. "Yep. It's a history book." I pulled several others from the section and declared them all history books, stacking each one sideways on the desk as I reached for the next. Staring at the spot on the shelf, fingers tapping away at my hip bones, I waited for some sort to glow or that horrible ringing in my ears again. Anything that would prove what I'd seen.

"Alex," Rhom sighed. "You don't have to convince me. I believe you saw them."

"Right." I started putting the books back in place on the shelf. When I reached for the last one, the front edge caught my eye. The color seemed off, stained or spotted like something had been spilled or dribbled down the right edge, the side opposite the spine. I picked it up and fanned the pages, looking for further signs of damage. There were none. When I laid it back on the desk, my fingers moved the cover, shifting the stack of pages slightly sideways toward the spine. The "stains" on the edge of the book took shape and began to form a picture, similar to the way a kaleidoscope shifts from one reflection into another with a slight adjustment.

I kept my eyes on the edge of the book while I spoke to the audience standing behind me. "Do any of you see this?"

Ava stepped closer to get a better look at the rare work of art. "It's a painting. The edge of the book is the canvas." She reached for the book but stopped short of touching it. "It's called a fore-edge painting. I've only seen one before. An old one from the seventeenth or eighteenth century is quite rare, although there are a lot of reproductions out there."

While I adjusted the angle of the pages to bring the painting into focus, I bent down closer. It was beautifully done with as much detail as the finest paintings hanging on Greer's walls. The subject was a young girl wearing a dress with puffed sleeves and a pinafore, sitting on top of something round and smooth with a kitten in her lap. Her arms were extended to her sides, one toward a tall rabbit, and the other toward a little man with a ridiculously large hat. The collection of stories by Hans Christian Andersen and *Alice's Adventures in Wonderland*, they'd been there all along, invisible to everyone else, but throwing themselves at me and waiting for me to figure it out.

I released the pressure on the cover, and the painting disappeared back into the squared edge of the book. Between the disappearing collection of books on Greer's shelf, the painting under my fingers, and the clear-as-day instructions found in drawer number 666, I knew where it would all end.

"Rhom," I said, feeling oddly serene considering what we were about to do, knowing my time was up and my father would be expecting fulfillment of our bargain. "You can call Greer now."

I SAT at the kitchen island with a glass of scotch in my hand, staring through the doorway at the elevator. It was early afternoon, but I figured if there was ever a good time to drink, it was now. With each sip of the liquid courage sliding down the back of my throat, my balls got bigger and my nerves steelier. Maybe if I had a few more I'd lose the fear completely, but then I'd also lose my ability to make sharp decisions, and this was not the time to dull the senses.

With a swift chug, I finished off the glass and sent it sliding across the marble counter. Sophia's eyes tracked it as it came to rest an inch from the edge. Then she snapped it up and put it in the sink before I could change my mind and pour another.

The familiar sound of the pulley lifting the elevator sobered me. I had about five seconds to decide whether to tell Greer that my days with him were numbered, or blow off the agreement and walk into that park confident that Maelcolm would never steal my destiny. Fate of the world or not, if I told Greer I was even considering fulfilling that bargain, he would never let me near the vessel.

He was so quiet when he walked into the kitchen that I didn't notice him standing a few feet away, observing me as I stared blankly at the floor.

"Tell me," he said when I looked up at him.

Sophia stopped wiping the pristine marble counter and listened for my response. In so many ways, this was her home. What happened over the course of the next twenty-four hours would affect her life, too.

Get on with it, Alex.

"I know where it is," I whispered. "The vessel." The exact location wasn't clear, but I had faith that those small details would work themselves out once we got to the park.

Stepping closer, he reached for my chin and lifted my distracted eyes back up to his. "Now I want you to tell me the rest."

Sometimes I wondered if he knew me better than I knew myself, wiser and better equipped to make my decisions for me. But not this decision. A lie is only dangerous if it hurts, and sometimes the kindest thing to do is spare the people you love from the truth. Bullshit. Who was I kidding? There was no kind way around any of this. I had to tell him, and I *would* tell him —something.

I stood up from the stool and took his hand, pressing my palm into the warmth of it. Then I led him out of the kitchen and up the stairs, toward the bedroom where I would confess after making what might possibly be our last union memorable.

CHAPTER TWENTY-NINE

I'm no saint, but sometimes we have to do unpleasant things for the greater good. Not because it's the noble thing to do, but because it's the right thing to do. The art of true love is something few of us practice—selflessness.

I meant to tell him everything. I had every intention of confessing what I'd planned to do, and how I'd come to my senses and realized I could never walk away from him. But as I lay there studying his blue eyes, with his powerful hand cupped around the smooth, youthful skin of my hip, I couldn't shake the image of a very different woman lying beneath him someday.

That was the turning point when the decision that still wrestled with my heart no longer wrestled with my mind. When the prophecy was safely locked away, I would quietly disappear and surrender to Maelcolm, my father. There was no out clause. And when Greer came for me—and he would—I'd avoid a war by making it painfully clear that the decision was mine. Then I'd throw in a little lie about how my leaving was best for everyone, and then I'd add mortar to it by pointing out that Maelcolm was my real family. Eventually the truth would surface, but by then the deed would be done, and Greer would have learned to hate me. By then he'd have a more suitable woman to lick his wounds. Someone like Leda.

Maybe Constantine was right—there's a darkness inside of me.

Greer, Rhom, and I entered from Central Park West, while Thomas and Loden came in from the east side. Leda stayed behind, pointing out the theory of *designated survivor*. Never put all your executives on the same plane.

It was two a.m. and the park was officially closed. That didn't stop the few who were there for less savory reasons, but they were of no consequence to us. If they were smart, they'd stay out of our way.

We'd barely crossed the boundaries of the park, expecting the wards to keep us out, when Constantine made his dramatic entrance. He descended from a tall tree, floating like a bat against the dark blue sky, landing directly in our path as he brushed a leaf from his shirt.

"Well, of course," I said, eyeing him disdainfully. I admit, I was a little more than pissed off at him and his "code of ethics," disguising his lack of disclosure as a noble attempt at universal discretion. In other words, he knew all the answers but never volunteered anything. I often wondered why no one ever tried to strangle it out of him, but I'm sure there were rules in this world about such acts. A hierarchy. "I wondered when you'd show up, Constantine."

Disheveled from his descent, he brushed his jet-black hair from his face and gave me an amused look. "You've come for your prize," he said, glancing at Greer and Rhom. "And you've brought reinforcements." Greer took a step closer and placed his hand on my hip. Constantine's eyes wandered down to it and then back up to Greer's face. "I get it, big man. Save your piss. No need to mark your territory."

"You knew all along, didn't you?" I asked. But it was more of a statement. Of course he knew. He'd never actually lied to me about it; he just expertly avoided the truth.

His cheeks never so much as twitched as he smiled back at me. "Bravo for your tenacity and determination, Alex. Not to mention your keen detective skills." He leaned closer and his bare smile flattened. "But I assume you had a little help."

"That's enough," Greer said. "Either lead the way, or get *out* of the way."

"My, aren't we temperamental tonight." Constantine stepped aside and motioned us into the park. "*Mi casa es su casa.*"

Rhom gave him a warning look as we walked past him and headed for the boat pond on the other side of the park. The actual whereabouts of the vessel was still a mystery, but every clue hurled at me by my mother—or the universe—indicated that it was hidden in the vicinity of the *Alice in Wonderland* statue near the pond. I'd expected to find it buried under some impenetrable fortress, or suspended out of reach at the tip of the Empire State Building's antenna, not hidden in a statue that children and tourists assaulted daily. The possibilities were frightening.

I took note of the stars as we walked through the park, capturing the deep night sky in my memory for fear of never seeing it like this again, dark from the absence of the moon yet beautifully lit against the silhouette of trees from the lights that never seemed to turn off in Manhattan. Where I grew up, the sky would be much dimmer in the hours halfway between dusk and dawn, but in New York it was never really dark. The cliché was true—New York never slept. It just slowed down a bit during the earliest hours of the morning.

Thomas signaled from the other side of the pond and Greer went to speak with him, to discuss strategy I assumed for something that couldn't possibly be predicted. As he walked away, I glanced around the perimeter of the water and spotted our target.

Alice was perched on a giant mushroom with the White Rabbit on one side and the Mad Hatter on the other, exactly as she was in the fore-edge painting on the side of the book in Greer's library. When I turned around, Constantine was standing a few feet back, calmly watching me as I tried to figure out what he must have known all along.

"I don't own the words," he began. "They are not mine to tell."

I'd heard it all before, that night we sat in a Paris apartment discussing my mother's murder. But the smug superiority that seemed to live in his eyes was gone. All I could read was empathy, a rare emotion for him.

"Can you at least tell me if I'm warm?" I asked.

"I think you know the answer to that question." The calm left his face as his eyes darted to the moonless sky. "You might want to escalate the hunt, though."

"Why?" My eyes followed his.

He turned back to me but didn't answer, his expression suddenly nervous. "Just do it!"

I took a step back, the dreadful look in his eyes making me just as uneasy.

"Now!" he blurted, his voice just low enough to escape the attention of the others on the opposite side of the pond.

Startled by the aggression in his tone, I instinctively pulled the amulet out from under my shirt and wrapped my fingers around it tightly. With my other hand, I reached into my pocket and extracted the prism my mother had given me on the way to Cornell University to meet Dr. Oxford for the first time. For a moment, I was overcome with his memory, the innocent pawn the wolves so easily murdered.

In a matter of seconds the park went even darker, as if a giant hand had passed over the moon. But the dark moon was already absent from the sky. In general, Constantine was fearless, but the look in his eyes told me something worth fearing was heading straight for us.

"Is it the Morrigan?" I asked.

His eyes flicked up to the sky as the shadow expanded and swallowed the stars. The wind picked up, and I turned to see Greer running in my direction. Like dust under the descending wings of a helicopter, I lifted into the air and hurled backward. The gust threw my arms wide, snapping the chain I was gripping and sending the amulet flying toward the pond. The prism in my other hand flew in the opposite direction.

Through the tornado of dirt and debris spinning around the park, Greer managed to reach me and pulled me off the ground as the massive wings flew directly overhead. The black feathers glided through the sky with the grace of a heron, its wings reaching beyond my view. But as graceful as those wings seemed, I could feel their power and the ominous sense that we were all about to meet our match.

The mother ship.

"Jesus H. Christ," Thomas muttered as he followed Greer and witnessed the spectacle in the sky. "Is that what I think it is?"

"*Fuck*," Constantine hissed. "*Now* do you understand the urgency? They've arrived, and they aren't accustomed to not being paid."

"They?" I asked.

"The Morrigan," Greer clarified. "The three sisters. Sophia's vision was right."

Constantine's face turned bitter. "I knew it. They've been summoned. By the wolves, no doubt."

"You don't *tell* the Morrigan to do anything," Thomas pointed out. "They're after the vessel."

"The vessel!" I gasped, looking frantically around the ground for the amulet. I spotted it near the edge of the water, the silver reflecting the light from one of the tall lampposts bordering the pond. The prism was lying in the grass a few yards away from it.

Greer followed my gaze. "Leave it," he warned, reading my mind and motioning up toward the threat above us.

Still moving silently across the sky, the wings seemed to grow until the only light illuminating the park came from the lampposts. Then they stalled in place and just hovered over us. I got an image of a thick stream of light beaming down from a UFO, sucking up anything in its path.

I focused on the beast overhead and tried to manifest my powers to do something—send a beam of fire blazing toward its underbelly, cripple it with my thoughts, will it to touch down and surrender. Imagine my surprise when it suddenly lifted its wings in a single stroke and reengaged in flight. It moved swiftly toward the north end of the park, eclipsing the tall buildings and revealing a bright full moon over our heads where there shouldn't have been one.

Every head turned toward the light as the strange moon beamed down on the grass around us, the intensity of it sending my hands up to shield my eyes. The brightness dimmed, and the light focused into a thin beam no wider than the diameter of a dime, aiming at the prism buried in the blades of grass a few yards away. The light hit the glass, and the prism sparked like a diamond. Out of the other side came a beam of colored light, aimed across the green grass until it met its target—the amulet.

The amulet was flat with a single straight line carved down its length. I used to wonder why it was so plain, why such a simple piece of jewelry had so much power. But as I watched the moonlight hit that groove and travel across that plain surface, the reason became clear.

"Where do you think you're going?" Greer asked, grabbing my arm as I started toward the amulet.

I pointed toward the light.

He gripped me tighter. "I'll go."

"No," I said, peeling his hand away from my arm. "I'm the one it's calling."

He didn't argue, gazing at me as if seeing me differently. I suspected because he knew I was right. It was time to let go, let me be what I had become.

I walked to the edge of the pond and looked down at the plain silver pendant. My eyes followed the trajectory of light running down the length of the groove and out the other end, terminating at the statue with laser precision in the center of Alice's forehead. Their eyes were all watching me as I approached the statue and stood at the edge of the smallest mushroom. Then I climbed on top of it and stepped onto the bigger one where Alice sat, poised with her puffed sleeves and pinafore skirt, smiling down at the bronze kitten in her lap. I stood eye to eye with the statue.

Greer had moved closer by the time I glanced back at him, a regretful expression on his face as if he knew what I was about to do would steer the course of our destiny, not just mine. We were almost there, and that brought me one step closer to my father's doorstep.

I smiled thoughtfully. Then I raised my left hand and reached for the spot where the light hit her forehead, just above her brow at the third eye. My palm stopped as it came in contact with the bronze surface. The shock of the cold metal lowered the heat radiating from the powerful light beam illuminating the skin of my hand. Something wasn't right. A wave of panic welled up in my stomach as I pulled my hand away and then reached for it again. Still nothing. And then a familiar voice settled in my ear, guiding me to the obvious.

A low growl distracted me. I turned toward it and spotted them, standing under the trees a dozen or so yards to the north of the statue. The wolves. Six of them this time. A full pack. Who else could look like that: cold, icy blue eyes, snow-white hair, bright red lips, the illusion of frost emitting from their faces.

One of them tossed something to the ground. "I guess we won't be needing these after all," he sneered.

I couldn't see what it was, but I had a pretty good idea that they'd just discarded what remained of Dr. Oxford's eyes. The doctor's research had been misguided. The lenses in his eyes were no better than an ordinary prism, useless without the amulet. The poor man had died for nothing.

"Bloody savages," Loden hissed.

For a moment I couldn't think straight, the memory of the doctor's face clouding my mind. "You," I accused as the reality hit home. "How did you do it? How did you get the doctor to walk out of Greer's house?" I guess it was just throwing salt on the wound, but I needed to know how they'd so easily manipulated the doctor into walking away from the people who'd saved him.

The one who'd so callously discarded the doctor's eyes sneered. "Rule number one: know your target. The doctor had a wife. Died from cancer years ago."

The word *cancer* spilled from his mouth with mock sympathy, a sickening smile lifting to his cheeks before the last letter left his lips.

"You didn't know that, did you?" he continued, shaking his head admonishingly. "Imagine how surprised the doctor was to hear her voice again after all these years, calling him from just beyond Greer's front door. A whisper from a ghost. Amazing how the mind can be tricked so easily, isn't it?"

"I suggest you get moving," Constantine prompted, interrupting the exchange.

For once Greer was in agreement with him. The two looked at each other as if a plan were formulating between them. I stalled to let that plan solidify, knowing the wolves wouldn't make their move until I had the vessel in my hands. After allowing an appropriate amount of time, I turned back to Greer. He nodded once. I nodded back and then switched hands, thrusting my right hand—my power hand—into the light, the portal. My eyes closed as my palm passed straight through the bronze as if the metal were water, a sensation of liquid heat traveling past my wrist and up my arm, continuing to my shoulder before flooding me with the most spectacular energy. The light from the moon exploded as all sound vanished. All my senses dissolved and culminated at the same time, leaving me suspended in a warm bath of both black and white, darkness and light.

My eyes slowly opened as I came back down to earth, feeling the blood course through my veins again and my heart beat with less of a wild flutter. I looked down at my hands and nearly stumbled off the statue from the brightness of the light crawling over my skin. My feet and legs were just as bright, and when I looked back at Greer and the others, their mouths were gaping. The light wasn't just flowing over me, it was emitting from within me.

The amulet wasn't the key; I was the key—and now I was the vessel, too.

It's a rare gift to feel true peace, and the gentle power that comes with that peace. It washed over me like rain.

The shock of it made me do a full turn to face them, leaving the wolves dangerously close at my backside. "Am I immortal?" The question seemed silly as it slipped from my lips, but what else could I be with all the knowledge burning at the center of my core.

The knowledge!

I nearly panicked from the epiphany of what was in my head. I could see it all: the future, the past, and every event that would ever happen in between. I could turn it off just as easily, thank God. What made my knees feel like rubber bands was my ability to put it all on hold, suspend everything at will, turn back the clock. I don't know how I knew all this, but I did. And I didn't dare test it. It was staggering, all the traffic racing around my head. How could I, a girl who stepped off a plane half a year earlier, be the vessel for all the world's secrets?

Constantine smirked. "Immortal doesn't come close."

"And you *knew*?" I asked in disbelief.

Awkwardly, he answered. "To a degree. The part about you being the actual vessel is a bit of a surprise."

"I'll be damned," said Thomas with an astonished grin.

Greer stood stone-faced, gazing at me like I was some sort of enigma. I'd seen that look before, the night I showed him the small white charm I'd carried all my life, the bone fragment from his own back. And then it occurred to me that he wasn't breathing. For the second time since we'd met, he couldn't breathe. I'd taken Mr. Sinclair's breath away.

"Greer?" My hand reached out instinctively toward him. "Breathe, honey."

I was about to go to him when the wind rushed through the trees again. The wolves, who had been waiting patiently like good dogs, were now excited beyond their ability to sit still.

"I think we have a problem." Loden motioned to the sky as the Morrigan circled back around the park, slowing as the wings cruised over our heads. The wolves had invoked the worst possible adversary, one of the few that could stand up to Greer, Constantine, or anything else that got in the way. The Morrigan wasn't just another player in the game. The Phantom Queen was a god capable of annihilating us all.

The icy pack smiled at me when they saw the fear arouse on my face, anticipating what my heart would taste like in their mouths. But then again, the rules had changed and they couldn't just kill me like they did my mother, now that they knew I was the vessel. They'd have to keep me alive, use me like a tool just like my own father planned to.

Maelcolm.

I hadn't thought about Maelcolm for at least an hour. With more pressing problems flying overhead, I had a welcome reprieve from thinking about the bargain. I'd made that agreement when I thought Greer and I had no future together. But things were different now, weren't they? I was immortal, and I was pretty sure Maelcolm couldn't touch me. In fact, I was pretty sure I outranked him.

I looked back up at the impending threat overhead and thought about the irony of it all. Here I was, finally getting everything I wanted, everything money couldn't buy, and it might all be gone before daybreak.

Assessing my options, it felt silly to be standing atop a giant bronze mushroom. I jumped down and ran toward Greer, but the wind picked up again and pulled me back. When I looked up at the sky, the Morrigan was descending.

Greer was staring at me intently when I turned back to him, frozen in place as if his feet were fused to the ground. Thomas, Loden, Constantine—they were all frozen in place. Greer's gaze deepened, but ironically I couldn't read his thoughts. I apparently knew everything except for what was in Greer's head. He read the confusion on my face and said one word—"*Run.*"

Mesmerized by the sheer power of the Morrigan, I found my own feet fused in place. The sight was terrifying and beautiful, black as night with a glimmer of blue that shimmered against the moon. It touched down directly behind the wolves, under the trees, its wings folding like fans over its heart. A moment passed, and the wings reopened. The Phantom Queen emerged, her back attached to the belly of the crow.

She glanced at the wolves. One by one they turned and nodded to her, receiving their silent orders before turning back to me. I feared the worst—the glossy black talons that served as her feet, or the bright glimmering teeth protruding from the jaws of the wolves.

The wolves started to move closer. But before they could take another step, the Morrigan flew back into the air and landed down in front of them, barring their advance. I don't think they expected that, because their faces drained even whiter than they already were. Even their lips faded from bright red to a paler shade of flesh.

"Ha," I laughed, abruptly stopping when her head snapped back around to me.

"Take her!" one of the wolves ordered.

I almost felt sorry for the one who'd just barked an order at the Morrigan.

Her expression remained neutral as she bit off his head. It rolled a few feet and settled in front of his pack mates. The remaining wolves closed their mouths and inched back, the fear manifesting in their eyes, the icy blue replaced by black holes. Their adrenaline was palpable.

She turned back to me and sneered. But the look wasn't malicious; it was collusive. Then my heart skipped a beat when she came closer, stopping a few yards away before bending slightly—to bow—to *me*.

"What?" I whispered, shaking my head and glancing back at Greer and the others, waiting for the Morrigan to realize her mistake and bite my head off for being the recipient of that mistake. "I don't think—"

She held her right hand up to silence me, now with a very malicious look in her eyes. "You thought we were here to do your bidding," she said. "Steal what was never yours."

I pressed my palms to my chest and shook my head. "Me? I —I didn't think anything."

"Not you." She turned and gazed thoughtfully at the wolves who were now retreating toward the trees, a feather from her left wing pointed at their collective faces. "*Them.*"

"We made an offering," one of them boldly claimed. "The mother."

My heart sank. Was that the real reason they killed her? Was my mother just a sacrifice for a plan twenty years in the making?

"And you thought it wise to kill the mother of a queen?" Her deceptive smile seemed to confuse them, temporarily lessen their fear. And then she turned the heat back up with a roar. "The mother of a *QUEEN*!"

There was little we could do other than stand back and watch as she dispatched the dogs expeditiously, their plan for world domination thwarted by their own stupidity. But I had a feeling *we* were going to be okay.

I looked back at Greer's consoling face and smiled nervously.

CHAPTER THIRTY

I t was good to be alive, curled naked against the heat of his skin. How could I even imagine walking away from him? Greer sensed my movement and rolled on top of me to bar my exit from the bed.

"Not yet," he ordered.

I kissed him fully on the mouth and squirmed out from under his weight, and the growing length of him that simply refused to be sated. Although I had to admit, my newly discovered destiny had emboldened me, and for a change I was the one testing our stamina.

The night before, the Morrigan had left us in Central Park, intact with a pledge of loyalty to me—the Queen. Apparently I'd been in the making for generations, and in time I'd grow into my role as such. But for now, my biggest mission was to relax and learn to accept it, take some time to digest what the next say… thousand years would entail.

Just before the Morrigan left, she gave me another gift—a message. She'd finished the gruesome task of consuming the wolves and was standing there before us. Her feathers spread wide, and I could see the glimmer of a face tucked high up under her right wing. A young girl—twelve or thirteen—was staring back at me with a wide smile across her face. Her eyes settled on mine. *A witch for a witch,* she silently mouthed to me, laughing playfully as a young girl should. The Morrigan kissed the girl's apparition on the top of her head and then gently folded her wings. Then she lifted back into the sky and disappeared behind the moon.

"I need food. And then I have to stop by Shakespeare's Library," I said, rising from the comfort of soft sheets and the smell of love. Royalty or not, I still had my mundane life to attend to, loose ends to tie up.

Greer looked puzzled. "You're not thinking about keeping that job, are you?"

"No. But I can't just not show up. I have to give some kind of notice."

Apollo was on his way out, finally realizing his dream of starting his own publishing empire. Katie would be gone soon, too. She still had another year at Columbia, but I knew without us she wouldn't stay. That only left Erica, and as much as the poor girl repelled me, it wasn't her fault that she didn't fit into my idea of pleasant company. We just had bad chemistry.

I took a quick shower and headed downstairs to the kitchen. Sophia was flipping French toast on the griddle.

"I make your favorite," she said without turning around. "French toast with bacon."

How many years had she stood at that stove, shoving all her grief away just to make it through the daily task of cooking and cleaning for someone else's family. It wasn't the money. I had no doubt Greer would take exceptional care of her until she drew her last breath, even if she never stepped foot in this house again. But I knew the reason she kept coming back. This was her family. That house in Bensonhurst, Brooklyn was just a box of old memories.

"Sophia," I said, quietly approaching her from behind.

She turned off the flame under the pan of bacon. "Yes," she answered, staring at the wall in front of the stove.

"I think she's all right," I whispered tentatively. "Rue, I mean."

Her shoulders rose and then sagged back down with the weight of a thousand pounds of guilt. But as much as I willed her to turn around and look at me, she just kept her eyes focused toward the tiles on the wall.

"The Morrigan?" she asked in a timid whisper, for fear of knowing the fate of her youngest child.

I rested my hand on her shoulder. "Yes. She looked really happy."

Sophia finally turned around, dropping the fork in her hand on the floor. "You saw her? My baby?"

I nodded and then felt the crush of her broad chest against me. For a moment, I thought I felt the wetness of tears dampen my face as her cheek brushed past mine. But Sophia rarely cried. For as long as I'd known her, practically lived under the same roof, I'd only seen her cry once.

She pulled back and quickly turned away, discreetly wiping her face with the dish towel on the counter. Then she nodded briskly and shooed me toward the dining room.

My nerves were working overtime when I walked into Shakespeare's Library. It wasn't the first time I'd quit a job, but it would be the first time I quit a job I actually liked. I suspected it was more about the people, letting them down and seeing the disappointment on their faces. Apollo was on his way out, but I was leaving Katie with Erica, and I knew she wasn't going to like it.

"Good morning," Katie chimed brightly when I walked through the front door, a forced smile hiding my apprehension. "Or not," she added when she read my mood.

"Morning." I headed for the back room to deposit my purse and calm my escalating heart rate. I couldn't believe how nervous I was. Like I had stage fright.

When I walked back to the front of the shop, Katie was heading down the romance aisle with a customer.

"Apollo," I said, seizing the opportunity to speak to him while Katie was distracted. I thought it best to get the two weeks' notice out of the way first and then talk to Katie. "Got a minute?"

He looked around the empty room and shrugged. "What's up?"

I just put it out there. "I'm giving my notice."

He bobbed his head and waited for me to continue with the details of my exit. No disappointment or heavy sigh accompanied by an attempt to change my mind, we just stood there staring at each other.

"I'm really sorry to do this," I continued, falling into that trap of always apologizing for things that needed no apology. "It's just that I've been offered another position that I can't refuse." That part wasn't a lie. My job was Oracle, Queen, keeper of all secrets. The sooner I got busy figuring out what that entailed, the sooner I could fulfill my destiny.

He shook his head. "I understand, Alex." He glanced around the room and then settled his eyes back on mine. "This place isn't a career. It's a waystation while we figure it out."

I suspected he was reflecting on his own path. He was leaving at the end of the month, too, having finally found a partner and gained the courage to take that leap of faith.

"I just hate doing this to Katie." I glanced in the direction of the aisle where she'd gone, but she was standing right behind me.

She circled the counter and rang up her customer's purchase. As soon as he was out the front door, she looked at me. "Hate doing what?"

"I was going to call you first, but things kind of escalated last night. I just gave Apollo my notice. Two weeks?" I asked, looking at Apollo for confirmation that two weeks was enough time to hire and train someone new.

Her face was frozen, caught in some kind of suspended shock. Then a bare grin spread across her mouth. "He didn't tell you, did he?"

"Tell me what?" I asked, looking at Apollo.

The poor guy had been unhappy for so many months that I'd forgotten how warm and youthful his face was when I first met him, when he was in the euphoria of his big dreams. That look was back now. "It looks like Erica will be the lone survivor," he said.

Katie's grin widened. "Well, I was going to tell you today. I've decided to start my own business."

Business? She had another year of undergrad work at Columbia.

"What kind of business?" I asked, trying not to sound too skeptical.

"Now, hear me out before you tell me I'm crazy." She prepared herself, straightening her posture and squishing her face up as she said the words. "A tattoo parlor."

Did she just say she was throwing away three years at Columbia studying environmental engineering to become a tattoo artist?

A very judgmental sigh escaped me. "Katie—"

"Don't!" she said. "You're the one person I didn't expect to get that look from."

She was right. Who was I to judge, especially when I was about to tell her my big career switch? Never once had she questioned my choices, and here I was throwing her under the bus without even hearing her out. "You're absolutely right," I said. "I'm a horrible friend."

"No, you're not. You just love me and want me to come to my senses."

A more practical argument was in order. "Other than getting one, do you even know *how* to tattoo?" I asked. "I'm sure there's some kind of license required."

She bit the inside of her cheek and did that twisting thing with her hands when she was about to confess something. "I actually used to be a tattooist. Before I started at Columbia. Well, I was an apprentice." She looked down at the creature crawling up her thigh. "For the guy who gave me this one. My father did *not* approve. He told me to get an education or start paying my own rent."

"And you chose education," I finished. "I get it, Katie. I just hate to see you throw all that hard work away."

"I'm not throwing my education away. My father agreed to keep helping me as long as I stay enrolled part-time and finish at night. I'll be running a business, you know."

"I guess the degree will come in handy," I said.

"It's just that I've been having these dreams. All I can think about are these tattoos I keep seeing. It's a sign, Alex. I'm telling you."

"Maybe it's just a sign that you should get another tattoo," I muttered. "Like you don't have enough of them." I lightened the joke with a smile. "You know I'll support any decision you make. You're the best friend I have, Katie."

"Elliot thinks I should follow my instincts and give it a shot. I mean, if I don't do this now, I'll end up regretting it. I'll be forty and sitting in a cubicle, in a well-paying job I despise."

"Elliot?" I thought they were casual. I thought Elliot was on his way out, and here he was giving her career advice?

Apollo cleared his throat. "On that note, I'm leaving for a few hours. I have a business to plan." He grabbed his phone and backpack and headed for the door. "I'll be back by two. Call me if you need me."

Katie waited for the door to shut and then looked at me pointedly. "Well?"

"Well what?" I asked.

"You're quitting? You have 'another offer' you can't refuse?"

"It's a long story. I'll tell you everything, but you first. Elliot? I thought you two were fizzling out? What about your *friendship* with Constantine?"

Her eyes rolled as she marched over to the new table of bestsellers and absently straightened a stack of perfectly aligned books. "We've been seeing a lot of each other lately. Elliot," she clarified. "The thing with Constantine is what fizzled. We're still friends, but I think he's way too obsessed with Leda."

"Leda?" It was news to me. "Why do you say that?"

"Because I've seen them together. They were at the same restaurant as Elliot and me the other night, and they looked pretty cozy together." She saw the look in my eyes and squashed any pity I had. "Look, I'm happy for him. We had a fantastic few weeks together, but it was never going to turn into anything other than what it was—best sex of my life. His, too," she smirked.

"So it's official? No more Constantine and lots of Elliot?"

She nodded. "Now, back to you."

I opened my mouth to tell her everything when the chimes sounded. A very large and imposing man was standing near the door. I'd gotten good at recognizing a Rogue when I saw one, and my bet was that Maelcolm had sent him to collect on that bargain of ours.

"Can I help you?" Katie asked, looking him up and down with a suspicious glare, sensing his less than amiable aura.

He looked at her and then focused back on me. "Her. My business is with that one." He pointed a finger at me and advanced toward us. "Maelcolm is expecting you."

Katie instinctively stepped in front of me, blocking the big guy's path.

"Ah, I wouldn't do that if I were you," I warned. "She's got a mean bite." The truth was I didn't need Katie's dragon for protection anymore. I was a queen, and with that came certain perks. But I let her continue—to a point. "Don't hurt him," I muttered. "I need him to deliver a message to my father."

He kept coming, smirking at the pretty girl standing in his way. That's when her eyes flashed and her mouth opened.

"You better shut that pretty little mouth, baby," he sneered. "Unless you plan to use it on me."

"As you wish," she replied. The dragon stayed on her back this time, but a stream of fire shot out of her mouth and nearly scorched his chest.

"Well, shit," I said. "When did you learn to do that?"

He stumbled backward but came forward again. I stepped from behind Katie, feeling a need to address the issue personally. I wanted to make sure my position was clear as a bell when he reported back to his boss. He stopped a few feet in front of me, nearly collapsing to the floor from the pain I was inflicting in his head.

"I want you to tell Maelcolm—my father—that I won't be keeping our bargain." I'd learned something very important the night before, in the park in front of the Morrigan. I was a servant to my people, and as such, I had no authority to bargain my destiny away. The agreement with my father was, for all intents and purposes, null and void.

I walked away from his crumbling form. "Now get out!"

He rose and hobbled toward the door. I stopped him as he pushed it open. "One more thing. Tell Maelcolm that his daughter, the Queen, will not be seeing him again."

I HAD visitors when I got home from the bookstore. The four of us sat around the coffee table in the living room, staring at the silver box that looked bigger than the last time I'd seen it. It seemed downright formidable, maybe because things were different now. As soon as the walls of that box fell, there would be no turning back. I was its keeper now—its power source.

"Why don't you just open it?" Ava said. "It won't bite."

I glanced at the faces watching me and smirked nervously. "You sure about that?"

With trembling fingers, I reached for the top of the box. Melanie's hand shot out to stop me. "Wait. Maybe you should take a calming breath first? The initial connection might be a little overwhelming. But it will pass."

Greer nodded when I glanced at him, reassuring me that everything would be fine. Then I mustered the confidence to face my destiny. Still trembling, I carefully removed the lid and allowed the walls to fall away from the life force. I gasped as my lungs vacuumed from the air rushing out, and a bright light radiated from my navel, straight through my shirt and into the center of the rings. The light that had once alternated between blue and white grew into a sphere of brilliant sapphire, barely subdued enough to be gazed at. For a moment, I feared the light connecting me to the rings would suck me into the center and trap me inside.

All three of them leaned closer, and I could see the growing concern in Greer's eyes. "It's okay," I said, shaking my head as he reached for me. "It feels good."

The gold rings circled faster around the dazzling ball of light. Now I could see the fourth one—the silver siphon that fed from the coven's power. It wobbled from the momentum of the others, unable to keep up the pace, growing thinner by the second until it looked tarnished and dull.

Melanie's eyes flew wide. "I think it's going to disintegrate!"

"Damn right it is," I said.

The four of us watched as Alasdair Templeton's siphon weakened and slowed, growing brittle and dissolving before our eyes.

The power of the Queen had strengthened the life force and easily destroyed the intruder, as if it were a gnat buzzing around her cheek. It was over. The coven was free. *I* was free.

CHAPTER THIRTY-ONE

"Stop doing that!" I cried. "We'll never get out of this bed if you keep that up."

Greer fell back against the pillows and ran his fingers lazily across my stomach. "Do we need to?"

I turned to face him, taking in his beautiful face and wondering how I'd gotten so lucky. Lying next to him, knowing that I'd do the same tomorrow and every day after that, was more than I thought possible just forty-eight hours earlier. The gods had been kind to me, and I would spend the rest of eternity repaying that kindness, gladly and without a drop of regret.

"Ava is expecting me this morning. I told her I'd be down at the shop around ten."

He brushed a stray tangle of hair from my face. "And what do you two have planned? Shopping? Tea and crumpets?"

"No, silly. Tea and labels." I sat up and sighed at the thought of swinging my legs over the edge of the mattress. "We're resurrecting the great wall of herbs. Ava said it was time to get Den of Oddities and Antiquities back to its roots. Get rid of some of the "oddities" and put a little more mojo back into the place." Hundreds of drawers meant hundreds of labels. My fingers were about to take a beating typing all those names into the database, just so our legs and knees could take a beating climbing the ladder to apply them.

"Okay. I'm up." I swung the comforter back and started to exit the bed.

"Hold it," he said, pulling me back against him. "What good is being the Queen if you can't enjoy a little luxury now and then? I think you've earned breakfast in bed."

I thought about it for a second. "Why, I think that's a fine idea." I reached for my phone on the nightstand and dialed Sophia's number. Her unamused voice answered on the other end, in the kitchen. "Good morning, Sophia. We've decided to dine in bed. We'll have the usual, please."

I hung up the phone and settled back against the comfort of the pillows. There was a brief tap at the door. Before either of us could acknowledge it, Leda came bursting into the room.

"You're still in bed?" She seemed completely unaffected by the fact that we were both naked five feet away. "Get dressed, Alex. You know I hate tardiness." She grabbed the folded sundress from the chair and tossed it to me, now averting her eyes from Greer.

I glanced at his arousal. "It's not like you haven't seen it before," I muttered, pulling the dress over my shoulders and climbing back onto the bed.

"Not quite like *that*," she said.

She was supposed to be joining Ava and me for lunch that afternoon. "I thought you were planning to meet us at the shop around noon?"

"I was in the mood for one of Sophia's omelets, so I thought I'd stop by for breakfast and then join in on all this *labelling* fun. Besides, I could use a little exercise."

"By the way," I said, "what's this I hear about you and Constantine hitting the town?"

She stilled for a moment, suppressing a brief smile. "Well, you know what they say about old habits." She turned back toward the door. "I believe your breakfast has arrived. I'll be downstairs."

I motioned to the dresser against the far wall. "You can put it down over there." He started across the room. "Wait. Bring it over here." As the tray descended onto the bedside table, I glanced at Greer and then back at our "waiter" with a firm gaze. He straightened back up and turned to leave.

"Wait," I said. I felt the outside of the coffee mug to gauge the heat. "Not very hot, is it?" I took a sip and pondered the temperature. "I guess it will have to do." Then I lifted the cover off of each plate to make sure the order was right.

"Is it to your satisfaction, milady?" Greer asked with serious regard.

"Yes, I believe it is." My fingers fluttered dismissively toward the door. "You can go now."

Sullen and grumbling, Alasdair Templeton lowered his head in submission and left the room.

THE END

Want more? Turn the page.

Curious about what happens in the future?

ONE YEAR LATER is a short story epilogue that picks up fourteen months after Alex discovers her true destiny.

Get it today. It's **FREE!**

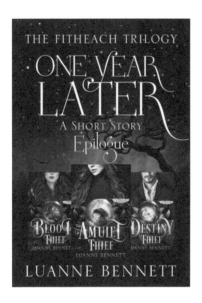

GET THE FREE SHORT STORY EBOOK
https://mailchi.mp/c3810f43e04d/insider-signup

Or visit my website for the link.
luannebennett.com

FOLLOW KATIE BISHOP TO SAVANNAH, GEORGIA!

THE KATIE BISHOP SERIES

ALSO BY LUANNE BENNETT

THE FITHEACH TRILOGY

The Amulet Thief (Book 1)

The Blood Thief (Book 2)

The Destiny Thief (Book 3)

THE KATIE BISHOP SERIES

Crossroads of Bones (Book 1)

Blackthorn Grove (Book 2)

Shifter's Moon (Book 3)

Dark Nightingale (Book 4)

Bayou Kings (Book 5)

HOUSE OF WINTERBORNE SERIES

Dark Legacy (Book 1)

Savage Sons (Book 2)

King's Reckoning (Book 3)

Sign up for news and updates about future releases!

LuanneBennett.com

ABOUT THE AUTHOR

LUANNE BENNETT is an author of fantasy and the supernatural. Born in Chicago, she lives in Georgia these days where she writes full time and doesn't miss a thing about the cubicles and conference rooms of her old life. When she isn't writing or dreaming up new stories, she's usually cooking or tending a herd of felines.

I love to hear from readers. Contact me at:
www.luannebennett.com
books@luannebennett.com
facebook.com/LuanneBennettBooks

Made in United States
Troutdale, OR
06/01/2023